Praise for *Now I Know*:

'I commend it to all adventurous readers ... journey with many surprises, into themselves' *Margaret Meek, School Librarian*

'It is a remarkably perceptive, compassionate novel about adolescent search for inner certainty in a shifting, shifty world' *The Canberra Times*

'Not a word wasted in the hands of this master craftsman. Strongly recommended' *Magpies*

Praise for *The Toll Bridge*:

'Surely one of the most original and rewarding teenage novels of the year – not to be missed' *Books for Keeps*

'This work is informed by a sophisticated literary sensibility that will keep mature readers on their toes ... [it] suggests even more than its intricate plot spells out, leaving readers with much for pleasurable contemplation' *Publishers Weekly*

now i know
Aidan Chambers
the toll bridge

Definitions

NOW I KNOW & THE TOLL BRIDGE
A DEFINITIONS BOOK 978 1 862 30287 7

This collection with Afterword first published in Great Britain by Definitions,
an imprint of Random House Children's Books

Collection copyright © Aidan Chambers, 2007

1 3 5 7 9 10 8 6 4 2

NOW I KNOW
First published in Great Britain by The Bodley Head Children's Books, 1987
Red Fox edition published 1995
Red Fox edition reissued 2000
Copyright © Aidan Chambers, 1987

THE TOLL BRIDGE
First published in Great Britain by The Bodley Head Children's Books, 1992
Red Fox edition published 1995
Red Fox edition reissued 2000
Copyright © Aidan Chambers, 1992

Definitions are published by Random House Children's Books,
61–63 Uxbridge Road, London W5 5SA,
a division of The Random House Group Ltd,
in Australia by Random House Australia (Pty) Ltd,
20 Alfred Street, Milsons Point, Sydney, NSW 2061, Australia,
in New Zealand by Random House New Zealand Ltd,
18 Poland Road, Glenfield, Auckland 10, New Zealand,
in South Africa by Random House (Pty) Ltd,
Isle of Houghton, Corner Boundary Road & Carse O'Gowrie,
Houghton 2198, South Africa,
and in India by Random House India Pvt Ltd,
301 World Trade Tower, Hotel Intercontinental Grand Complex,
Barakhamba Lane, New Delhi 110001, India

THE RANDOM HOUSE GROUP Limited Reg. No. 954009
www.kidsatrandomhouse.co.uk

A CIP catalogue record for this book is available from the British Library.

Printed and bound in Great Britain by
Cox & Wyman Ltd, Reading, Berkshire

now i know

PREVIEWS

Stars spinning
he points the compass.
His hands bear the universe.

A man jogs round the curve of earth,
white shorts and sweating white sweater.
He breathes cloud embryos into the dawn,
seeing only the narrow path.

Again Nik sees her
striding behind her antinuke banner,
grinning, drenched.
(But not marching, not her, ever.
Process, yes; belong, protest, yes.
But never march against marching.)
No matter all those other hundreds
Loved on sight
Of all her.

The explosion lifts him up
hurls him down
a crotch-hold and body-slam.
Out.
Conditioning him for death.

Tom said to the duty officer, 'I'm on the crucifiction, sarge.'

'Super's off his head,' the sergeant said. 'Set a kid to catch a kid.'

'That your guess?'

'Kids anyway. Take more than one to do a thing like that.'

'What about the one they strung up?'

The sergeant consulted a report. 'According to the only witness, he's about seventeen.'

'Where's he now?'

'Gone.'

'Gone!'

'Vamoosed.'

'How come?'

'You're the one playing detective.'

STOCKSHOT: *The best in this kind are but shadows; and the worst are no worse, if imagination amend them.*

NIK'S NOTEBOOK: This by Simone Weil:
Hitler could die and return to life again fifty times, but I should still not look upon him as the Son of God.

Good that. Ms Weil quite someone. Also says we must get rid of our superstition about clock time if we are to find eternity. What does she mean? ETERNITY? Time no more?

Things happen one after the other, yes? Or do they? But that's not how we remember them, is it? I don't. I asked Julie. She doesn't either. Who does? Life only makes sense when it's out of order. Ha!

Also: Things happen simultaneously. Julie says everything is now. Making the connections is what matters.

Selah.

To
Margaret Clark

ALL WRITING IS DRAWING

IN THE BEGINNING
THERE WAS A YOUTH GROUP
who decided to make a film about
GOD
AFTERWORDS
no one could remember
how they came to make such a decision.
None of them could remember being concerned about
God at the time.
But for one of them
what happened is here
NOW

BEGINNINGS

There were three beginnings.
From the beginning, you see,
we are to be given our words' worth.

The beginning of the beginning

One evening, Nicholas Christopher Frome was lying idly in his bath when the thought struck him that eventually he would die.

He had of course thought this before. He is no fool.

But that evening it penetrated his consciousness with a terrible clarity. A clarity so pure, so undeniable that, despite the pleasant heat of the water, he turned cold inside.

What made the thought so terrible was not the knowledge of his eventual death, but the realization of the separateness of his being.

He was not, he understood completely for the first time, merely his parents' son, nor just any seventeen-and-one-month year old youth, nor simply another member of the multitudinous human race.

He was *him self*. A separate, individual, unique and self-knowing person who would one day snuff it.

I am not, he thought, anyone else. Only me.

The cold inside froze his body. He stared, amazed, at the bathroom's perspiring ceiling.

I am me, he thought, and one day this Me will come to an end. I shall not be.

His stomach curdled.

He sat up and spewed into his bathwater.

There is never one particular moment, one small event, whether in life or in a novel, that is the only beginning. There are always as many beginnings as anyone cares to look for. Or

I

none at all of course. But when Nik was thinking afterwards about what happened, he decided that the moment when he sat up in his bath and spewed his guts out came as near to being the beginning of his story as any.

The beginning of the end

Thomas Thrupp. Keen, ambitious, a would-be chief constable and yet only nineteen. Naturally suspicious, he trusts nobody, not even his granny, possesses a certain dangerous charm, and is said to be at his best in tight corners. Tom would never throw up at the thought of his own death.

One morning Tom was summoned to his superintendent's office. Earlier that day a young man had been found crucified on a rusty metal cross. The cross was not stuck in the ground, after the manner of ancient custom, but was dangling from a crane in a scrap yard across the railway tracks from the centre of town.

The super believed a gang of yobs had perpetrated the crime and that a young copper might sus them out more quickly than an older man. So despite Tom's lack of qualifications he ordered him to investigate. Besides, the super reckoned him a likely lad, attractively hungry for success. What Tom lacked in experience he'd make up for in ruthlessness. The super admired ruthlessness as much as he admired desk-top efficiency. (There were no papers cluttering his desk, just a closed file, a calendar and a photo of his wife.) He had Tom marked out as good at both. Tom also reminded him of himself when he was a young plod. (The super could be very sentimental on occasion. Sentimentality is, of course, the flip side of ruthlessness.)

Afterwards, in the briefing room, Tom said to the duty officer, a man of years, 'I'm on the crucifiction, sarge.'

'Super's off his head,' the sergeant said, entering up the duty book.

'Thanks for the vote of confidence.'

'Got all the confidence you need.' The sergeant sniffed. 'Set a kid to catch a kid.'

'That your guess?'

'Kids anyway. Take more than one, a thing like that.'

'What about the one they strung up?'

The sergeant consulted a report. 'According to the only witness, he's about seventeen. Five-eightish. Short brown hair. Thin face. Pale, but who wouldn't be under the circs. Slim build. Bony. Attired only in his underpants. Dark blue y-fronts with white edging. Very natty.'

'Marks and Sparks,' Tom said, scrupulously jotting the details into his notebook. 'Could be anybody.'

'Not quite,' the sergeant said.

'Where's he now?'

'There you have me.'

'Sorry?'

'Gone.'

'Gone!'

'Vamoosed.'

'How come?'

'You're the one playing detective.'

'This kid was hanging there and we lost him?'

'Quick on the uptake, I'll grant you that.'

'Jeez!'

'Could be him you're after.'

'Very funny, sarge. What else is news?'

'Wouldn't hang about if I was you.'

'Another good one. On form today.'

'Crack this, could make a name for yourself.'

'That's what the super said.'

The sergeant grinned. 'No slouch, our super. You fail though, and it'll be all your fault. Know that, don't you? Incompetent trainee officer ballses up, etcetera. You win, and the super takes the prize for daring use of bright young man. 'Course, he'll let you bask in the reflected. Get your pic in the *Police Gazette*.'

'You're a real encouragement, sarge.'

'As I say, I don't think you need any. So long, lad. Givem hell.'

The end of the beginning

JULIE: Hello . . . hello? . . . one two three . . . Is it working?
[*Pause.*]
Dear Nik, this is a Julie tape-letter. It's all Nurse Simpson's idea. Blame her. She's hung a microphone from my bedhead. She says all I have to do is talk quietly and the microphone will hear me. Which is just as well because I can't do much else but talk quietly.

So now, though I can't write to you, Nik, I can talk to you. And if you want to reply in the same way, Simmo says she'll put headphones on me so that only I can hear what you say. But it'll be a slow-motion conversation because of the post. And you won't be able to interrupt and answer back.
[*Pause. Tape surf.*]
I still can't see. My eyes are still bandaged. Most of me is still bandaged. I feel like a shrink-wrapped jelly-baby. The consultant says I'll be like this for a few days yet. In doctor's language I think 'a few days yet' means 'for a long time yet'. But she sounds nice. She has a gentle middle-aged voice and is sometimes with a squad of young students who go very quiet when they reach me. Simmo says that's because I'm such a knockout, but I know the sort of knockout I must be, and so must you.

Which reminds me: thanks for coming to see me. All that way! Why couldn't it have happened nearer home? There can't be much to see of me either, wrapped up the way I am. And wires and tubes and gear hanging off me as if I were one of Frankenstein's monsters in the making.

In fact, I don't feel I have a body any more. I feel more like a mind inside a carcass. Just now, all I am is a mouth saying words because I've just guzzled the dope they give me to kill the pain and keep me docile. I can't even feel my body. It might as well not exist. So I'm having an identity crisis. How do you know who you are if you've no body to speak of? I'm working on the answer. I'm nothing but words in my head all day. And dreams all night. Sometimes harsh words and usually horrible dreams. They say the dreams will go away, but what about the words?
[*Long pause.*]

Other people are only voices too of course. You can tell a lot from people's voices when that's all you've got to go on. Their voices give them away and they don't know it. You can hear when they're being genuine and when they aren't, and whether they're naturally kind or cruel, or thoughtless or strong or weak, and if they're being brave. And if they're hiding something. If you listen very carefully, you can hear the lies hiding behind the words.

That's how I know I'm not the knockout that Simmo pretends. And that the consultant doesn't mean a few days when she says about the bandages coming off my eyes. I can hear the lie in their voices.

I don't ask whether I'll be able to see again when the bandages do come off. I couldn't bear it if they lied about that. And they would lie, wouldn't they, if the answer was no?

[*Long pause. Sound of deep breaths being taken in and slowly exhaled.*]

Sorry. Didn't mean to say any of that. Promised myself I wouldn't. Doesn't mean anything. Just came tumbling out. Haven't talked to you for so long. Seems years. Lost track of time and days. Seems like I've been here for ever and won't ever leave.

So nice to talk to you . . . Nice . . . Silly word. I mean . . . such a relief . . . to be able to talk to you and say some of the things churning in my head, even if they have to be recorded and take two days to reach you, knowing the post, even if sent first class, and that'll cost the earth.

Sorry . . . there I go again . . . I've tried talking this letter twice today already but made Simmo wipe the tape. Neither time was right, because I went off all over the place, saying things I didn't mean . . . The drugs, I expect . . . And not actually having you here . . . Seems ridiculous, talking blind into thin air. Well, this time I'm making myself see your face, as though you really were here, and not letting myself think of anything but your face and what I want to say. But even so I . . .

[*Pause.*]

Where was I? . . . Oh, yes—your visit. I knew you were here. I felt the touch of your hand. But I couldn't say anything. I tried very hard but nothing happened. Like one of those dreams when you strain to move but your body won't budge.

Well, what I want to tell you is this. Your touch, the touch of your hand, made me believe I could live again. Till then I hadn't believed and was praying for the end to come quickly. But your touch, and knowing it was you, made me believe I could make it. And made me want to. Thank you for that gift, dear Nik.

[*Pause.*]

Being ill, I mean being very ill, makes you feel useless. Makes you feel you're a burden to everyone. You feel all of life is passing you by. Your own life becomes meaningless. There's no sense in it any more.

[*Pause.*]

What you believe matters. I'm learning that the hard way. I believe everybody matters. Being ill or being well shouldn't have anything to do with it. Everybody has a part to play in building the world God has given us. I'm a Christian because I believe that, and I believe it because I'm a Christian. But how do you play your part when you're trapped by illness?

If you were here, Nik, you'd be interrupting like mad by now!

What I'm trying to say is that I've decided that perhaps it's my job while I'm like this to work out what illness . . . means. And why not? There's nothing else I can do.

[*Pause.*]

I can't talk for long at a time because even talking tires me. I must stop soon. But I wanted to ask if you'd do something for me. Simmo has brought me some Talking Book tapes of the Bible. She says there are other books—novels and poetry—she can get for me but she doesn't know what I'd like. If she sends you the list, would you choose something? I'd like you to because then it will be like you giving me a book you want me to read, the way you've done before, and I can imagine you're listening with me. Then we can talk about it in our tape-letters. If you'd like to, I mean. Only if you'd like to.

[*Pause. Deep breaths, in and out.*]

I know that must sound pretty silly. Such a little thing. But you've no idea how such pitiful little things mean most when you're in my predicament.

6

Something else, while I'm on silly things. I quite often burst into tears. Into sobs, I mean, because my eyes can't cry. Reaction, I suppose. 'Just your nerves, love,' Mum says. She says it so dolefully that I can't help laughing. Between crying and laughing for no reason, I'm sure Mum thinks I've gone off my head.

Anyway, I'm making such a big production out of it because if I start howling when I'm recording you'll hear. And it'll sound ghastly. I hate the idea of you hearing it. I don't mean to cry. I'm not looking for sympathy. There's just nothing I can do about it. Simmo says, 'Forget it, he'll understand.' And I know you will. But I wanted you to be prepared. I can't edit out or press the pause button or anything like that. A case of 'look, no hands'. It's just that suddenly everything comes over me in a great overwhelming wave . . . and the wave breaks . . . and . . . *nurse! . . . quick! . . .*

†

The day after Nik threw up into his bath he was asked by his history teacher, Leonard Stanley, if he would like to help a youth group who were making a film. The group needed a researcher.

They were making a film about what would happen if Jesus Christ returned today. They weren't a church group—far from it. But one evening they had had a long discussion about the politics of the Middle East and the arguments for and against the state of Israel, and they had arrived at the conclusion that the world was no better now than it was at the time of Christ's first visitation in Palestine two thousand years ago. They had agreed that if Christ returned today, and lived in their own West of England town, never mind in Palestine, he would be treated no better, and possibly even worse, than he was treated then.

The group's idea was to use their film of Christ's second coming to make strong criticisms of life today. They supposed that staid old fogies could hardly get upset if Christ was the person who showed up the bad things that go on and the old fogies responsible for them. (They considered anyone over the

7

age of thirty to be an old fogey. One of them wore a sweatshirt that said so.)

Truth to tell, though, only a small minority of the group were in the slightest interested either in the life of Christ (now or two thousand years ago) or in politics. They would have been hard put to say which they found more boring. What interested the majority was being together and having some fun. Within the group there was another minority who were not interested in politics but were interested in film-making, and wanted to use cameras and sound equipment and create spectacular special effects, and generally wanted to carry on as if they were big names in Hollywood. So as usual in human affairs, as well as in youth groups, the decisions were thrashed out between the few vocal members of each minority while the rest waited with as much patience and as little attention as necessary till the most determined ones got their way.

In all this the group was led and encouraged by their organizer, a man of twenty-seven called Frank Randwick, a motor-mechanic by trade and a youth leader by desire. He it was who first suggested the idea of making the film, and he immediately appointed himself its Director.

Of course the political hotshots gave themselves the job of writing the script. And early in the discussions they realized that none of them knew very much about the life of Christ or about Palestine in his day. The script-writers did not want to be bothered about such insignificant details. But they found themselves opposed by three of the so-far silent girls.

As it happened (and rather appropriately, you might think) the girls were cast to play the three Marys: Mary the mother of Christ; Mary Magdalene, who legend has it was a converted prostitute; and Mary of Bethany, the sister of Martha and of raised-from-the-dead Lazarus, who is celebrated in the Bible for anointing Christ's feet with balmy oil and afterwards wiping them clean with her presumably long and luxuriant hair.

These three suddenly vocal girls declared that if the group was going to film Christ's story they should at least get the facts right. The script-writers said to hell with facts, what mattered was the message. It wasn't the facts of Christ's life that interested them, they said, but telling people about life now.

The girls were determined, however. Check the facts or they wouldn't take part. And as it seemed a very neat way of getting their own back at the script-writers for being so boring about politics, a number of the rest of the group supported the girls.

In the face of this opposition and with the astuteness of born politicians, the script-writers said okay, the facts would be verified. But later, in secret, they agreed with each other that they'd do what they liked anyway, whatever the facts were, just as soon as shooting started and everyone's attention was occupied by the excitements of filming.

They demanded, however, that a researcher be appointed to help them. As no one in the group wanted such a thankless and unglamorous job, the Director approached the Head of Nik's school, who passed the buck to the head of the history department, Leonard Stanley, who nobbled Nik, because Nik was one of his better history students.

But Nik was not keen.

He said, 'I'm not bothered about religion and I don't believe in God.'

Leonard Stanley said, 'But think what a marvellous project it will make. History in action. You can submit your notes and an essay about the whole experience as part of your exam assessment work. No one else is doing anything like it.'

Nik said, 'I'd prefer black holes. I'm interested in black holes. They're more important than God nowadays.'

'Black holes,' Leonard Stanley said, 'don't have a history.'

'Everything has a history,' Nik said. 'At least, that's what you tell us.'

The teacher shrugged. 'Nobody knows much about black holes yet. That's what I mean.'

What he really meant was that he didn't know much about black holes himself and didn't want the bother of finding out in order to grade Nik's work.

'Now God,' he went on quickly, 'God has been around a long time. We know quite a bit about him. About religion, anyway.'

Nik smirked. 'God has never been around at all. He's an

9

invention. God's a fiction, sir. Just a story. In the past people needed some all-powerful being to explain things they couldn't understand, and to calm their fears. Or to blame for the awful things that happened to them, like illnesses and earthquakes. And sometimes they used God to scare other people they didn't like. But it's no good any more. It doesn't work. We know better now. God is dead. If he was ever alive, that is. That's what I think, anyway.'

Leonard Stanley snatched a winning point, poking a finger at Nik's chest. 'In that case,' he laughed, 'God's all history. Isn't that right?'

Nik couldn't help nodding an unwilling agreement.

Leonard seized his advantage. 'And you can't have a better subject for a history project than a subject that is nothing but history, can you?'

Nik said, 'I still prefer the history of living things, if you don't mind, sir.'

'Look,' the teacher said, turning on his serious manner. 'People are living. People have histories. People have a long history of believing in God. A history that goes back to the beginning of people. And a lot of people, probably the majority of people in the world, still do believe in a God of some kind.'

'And look where they've got us,' Nik said. 'They fall for this God stuff and before you know it they're fighting each other about whose God is the real one. Then they start torturing their enemies to try and convert them. And they end up fighting holy wars and killing each other, and anyone else who doesn't agree with them. All in the name of this God they think they own and who gives them the right to murder in his name. It's not on, sir. I don't want anything to do with it.'

Leonard Stanley liked nothing better than this kind of heated argument from his students. He believed it helped them discover how exciting history is. Not that he expected anyone actually to do anything as a result of the arguments. Talk was one thing, action another. But this time he had quite mistaken the character of the student he was arguing with.

Leonard rubbed his hands and said, 'Listen, Nik. People do all those things for other reasons as well as religion. For politics, for example, and family feuds, for money, or food, or to gain territory, or because of jealousy, or even for love. All you're saying is that religion includes the whole of the human race, the good and the bad. Which makes it a perfect subject for a historian to study.'

'But,' Nik said, 'the Christians say God made people in his own image, don't they? So if there's a God, and if he made people in his own image, and they go round murdering each other and doing horrible things, then it's all God's fault that the human race is like it is, and the sooner we ditch him the better. But if there isn't a God, then there's no point in doing history about him because it's a waste of time.'

Leonard said, 'I'm not saying whether there's a God or not. Historians don't answer questions like that. What they do is tell the story of people and how they got to be the way they are. It's people who interest historians. All I'm saying is that religion is one of the most powerful forces—maybe *the* most powerful—in the history of people everywhere. So we should study it.'

Now it was Nik's turn to shrug. 'Maybe.'

The teacher took a step closer, a sign the argument was over. 'Don't give me any maybes, Nik. You know I'm right. This project is a perfect opportunity to investigate first hand one of the most potent forces in human life. And you can do it by researching its effects on real, ordinary people of your own age. Anyway, it'll be fun. And it'll get you in amongst others. You spend too much time on your own.'

'I'll think about it,' Nik said, not happy at the turn the conversation had taken.

'Don't think about it. Do it. Okay?'

Nik knew he'd be badgered till he agreed. 'I'll give it a go, sir. But under protest.'

'Protests I can live with,' Leonard said, and stalked off, thinking force of argument had won the day.

He was wrong. Nik knew, without admitting it to himself just then, that throwing up in his bath at the knowledge of his own separateness had much more to do with it than argument.

EYE DEES

Nik's first few meetings with the group were interesting enough. The historical information they needed was easy to find; and he mildly enjoyed the joshing and jokes which seemed to be what most of the group came for.

He quickly fell into the habit of arriving just in time for the film-making part of the proceedings, and of avoiding the whoopee afterwards by saying he had school work to do and dodging away. A few people teased him for this, hinting at darker, sensational reasons for his leaving. 'We've heard that before,' they'd say with winks and nudges and obscene fists. 'Who is it? Come on, tell us.'

Some, he knew, thought he didn't hang around like the rest because he was snobby and standoffish. But Nik was used to this. From infancy he had never felt comfortable with large groups, worst of all when everyone was his own age. One of his earliest memories was of standing in the middle of a swarm of babies at nursery school and screaming till his mother took him away. Later he always kept clear of gangs and parties. And these days he felt particularly suspicious of what he called 'teenage playgroups', unable to imagine why anyone needed them or why any sane adult wanted to run them.

A teacher once accused him of being 'chronically unclubbable', as if this were a dire ailment. Others often called him a loner, their tone of voice leaving no doubt that loners were never approved of. He both resented this and was proud of it.

In self-protection, and out of cussed principle, he had encouraged this view of himself as an oddity, making an aggressive virtue of being an outsider. He even acquired a kind of following of boys, and of girls too, who admired his remoteness and tried to imitate his slightly aloof manner, his wary look through his glasses, the bite in his talk, and his disdain for any physical activity.

Recently, this body of admirers had become vocal. Someone

had given them what was intended to be a scornful name, the Nikelodeons. Others, both for and against, took it up and with startling speed Nik found himself the unwilling focus of a fashion which people took sides about. Even second- and third-years were soon calling themselves Nikies. They could hardly be called a club as the whole point of Nikishness was to be unclubbable and fiercely individual. But they took to standing about together and off-handedly acknowledging each other when they crossed paths in corridors.

Then one day NIKS SCORE ALONE was found scrawled across the team lists on the soccer notice-board. And the next day N = 1 was sprayed on the maths room wall. After that Nik-graffiti appeared everywhere. The best of it was collected and printed in the school newspaper.

THE NIKELODEONS OF LIFE PLAY THEIR OWN TUNES

BETTER A NIKEL THAN A KNUCKLE

NOW I KNOW I WON

Secretly, of course, Nik enjoyed his temporary notoriety. Everybody likes to be noticed. But he never openly confessed it, nor that being a loner had one enormous disadvantage. It literally meant that he was frequently alone, when the truth was he would have liked companionship now and then.

This partly explains why he stayed with the film group. His project gave him an excuse for being there without his having to acknowledge any other reason. He thought of himself as an outsider, an observer, one of the group without belonging to it. So he didn't feel he was giving in to any of those human weaknesses he scorned.

In his role as observer, and on Leonard Stanley's instructions, he kept a notebook in which he recorded the events of each session, wrote up the information needed for the film and for his essay on religion. But very soon he began to use it as a kind of journal of his secret thoughts and comments on what happened to himself. (Though it must also be admitted that his notes became as long as they did because he had just been given a word processor and using it was a novelty.)

But there was another reason why Nik stayed with the group. This is how it came about.

At Nik's sixth meeting the Director settled the casting of the film. There was plenty of crude joking, about, for example, the appropriateness of the boy who was Judas, and whether the girl who was Mary Magdalene was experienced at certain aspects of life that would fit her for the part of a reformed prostitute.

Towards the end of the evening the Director said, 'Agreed, then. That's the cast.'

Mary Magdalene said, 'Except for Jesus.'

'Yeah, what about him?' Saint Peter said. 'We can't make a film about Jesus turning up again if we haven't got anybody to act him.'

The Director said, 'Why not? He could always be just out of shot. Or the camera could be him. Everything seen from his point of view. I've considered it.'

General uproar.

'Arty-farty,' John the Beloved shouted.

'Gimmicky,' Doubting Thomas yelled.

'You have to see him,' John the Beloved went on. 'I can't eat the last supper with a camera for Christ.'

'All you ever think about is your stomach,' Mary of Bethany said.

'That's all you know!' Jason the clapperboy said with a mock simper.

'Trouble is,' the Director said, 'we don't know what he looked like.'

'Handsome,' Mary the Mother said. 'He'd have to be, wouldn't he? He'd not be ugly, not the son of God.'

'Why not?' Lazarus said.

'Like you!' Doubting Thomas mocked. 'Type cast, you are. Won't need no make-up. Like death warmed up without any.'

'You leave my brother alone,' Mary of Bethany said.

'What I mean,' Lazarus said, ever undaunted, 'is that God might of let Jesus be ugly to show that ugly people matter as much as handsome people.'

Groans.

'Depends what you're after,' Brian the camera boy said.

'We all know what you're after,' Sally the continuity girl said, grinning, and not at all resisting the yoke of Brian's arm.

The Director said, 'What's ugly and what's handsome anyway?'

Doubting Thomas said, 'Can't say I have much trouble deciding,' and looked lasciviously at Mary of Bethany, whose luxuriant black hair had landed her the part and Thomas's obvious admiration.

'All I'm pointing out,' the Director said, 'is that everybody has their own idea. And then there's fashion. Ideas about what's ugly and what's beautiful change from time to time.'

'Yeah,' Rachel the sound recordist said. 'In the eighteenth century they liked fat women and men dressed in long curly wigs and lacy clothes.'

'Dishy,' Jason the clapperboy said, only, as usual, to be ignored.

'We ought to have some idea of what Christ looked like though, oughtn't we?' Judas said. 'We've got to cast somebody.'

'I think he'd have nice eyes,' the Magdalene said.

King Herod yawned, never one for discussion, and said, hoping to put an end to this one, 'Nik ought to know. He's the researcher.'

Nik said, 'That's the trouble. We don't know much about him at all.'

'Tell us anyway,' the Director ordered.

Nik flipped pages in his file. 'It'll be easiest if I read you a summary.'

Mary Magdalene said, 'Not long, is it? Want to be home early tonight to wash my hair.'

This was taken as an incredibly funny joke. The Magdalene frequently had this effect, though she never quite understood why. (The Director had cast her as the Magdalene expecting she'd have this effect on audiences too, for his secret intention was to direct the film as a send-up of religion, he being a rabid atheist himself.)

When everyone had quietened, Nik said, 'Only a page. You can survive that.'

'If it isn't boring,' Doubting Thomas said.

'Can you tell the difference?' Nik said, and went on, 'Extract from—'

'Never mind the frills,' script-writer Tony muttered.

Mary the Mother said, 'He's only trying to be accurate.'

Nik read.

STOCKSHOT: *Jesus of Nazareth has been the central figure of the most widespread religion of the past two thousand years, yet almost nothing is known of his earthly life. We can confidently state that he lived in Palestine in the time of Herod Antipas, tetrarch of Galilee, and that he was crucified under Pontius Pilate. Beyond that, we have only the devout literature of his disciples and followers, and we see and hear Jesus only through their record. Our lack of historical information is due in part to the fact that to his disciples Jesus was not a memory but a living Lord, and when they came to set down his story they presented him not as the Jesus of past history but as the Christ of their living faith.*

'That'll do,' Thomas said.

Nik said, 'There's more.'

'Not about how he looked?' the Magdalene asked.

'No.'

'Then we might as well make him look any way we want. And I don't care, as long as he isn't one of them wallies they put in pictures in churches.'

'How would you know?' script-writer Harriet said. 'You never go into a church.'

'I do! I was in one when our Jim got married four years ago.'

Laughter.

Mary of Bethany said, 'I don't want no creeping Jesus neither. I'm not wiping his feet with my hair if he's one of them. I'd get the giggles anyway. If I'm going to act the part I have to believe in the characters. I couldn't believe in no weeping-willy.'

'No weeping-willies,' the Director said. 'Promise.'

Nathaniel, quiet as ever, said, 'Ought to look ordinary. He must have looked like the people where he was born, mustn't he? So he should look like the people round here if he's born here. He'd look like everybody else till God called him, then he'd look special.'

Brian, sneering, said, 'You make him sound like a religious Clark Kent.'

'Who's Clark Kent?' Nathaniel asked, and was bewildered by the cries of mockery.

'You laugh,' the Director said, 'but there's a lot in what he says. In any case, I think I know who I'd like to play the part.'

†

NIK'S NOTEBOOK: ME play JESUS. Five thousand exclamation marks.

He said he didn't want anybody to play the part who also wants to be an actor. He wants a non-actor. Someone, he said, who can just BE. Someone who can just be an idiot, Judas said, as he would, he having wished to play Jesus himself.

Our Beloved Director is out of his leptonic mind.

Selah, as they say in the Godbook.

All this Bible-reading research is going to my head. I just looked up *selah* in the dictionary. A Hebrew word of unknown meaning, it says, which is a lot of help. Except I do like words of unknown meaning, because then they can mean anything you want them to mean. The dic. does say, though, that *selah* probably had something to do with an instruction in music. Like saying: Pause here. Which makes it very suitable for this songandance.

Also: Suppose Our Beloved Director has more than a lepton for a mind after all. Suppose the only leptonic thing about him is his leptosomatic body. He is all of 1.46 m. in his legwarmers, and is about as thick as a leptocephalus when last seen in a suitable state to be measured for swimming trunks—a service I observed the costume person of female gender performing for him last week behind the counter in the nosh bar when OBD thought we were all doing relaxation exercises in the drama hall. No wonder they call him Randy Franky, as he is so frankly randy. (I was hunting for a packet of Smarties at the time, finding the consumption of Smarties more relaxing than re-laxation exercises with a bunch of sweating would-be super-

17

stars. Also: what the ding do women see in him, when there's not much to see of him at all? I still have not understood about sexual attraction and must make a special study of it soon.)

OBD is leptocephalic in other ways as well: like slippery and wriggly. He also looks slimy to the touch. I have no intention of finding out if he really is. But withal he is fascinating in a primitive kind of way. The gang say he is okay when you're in the bad and that persons of youthful age who find themselves in trouble flock to him for advice and assistance. Being sheep, they would. All I can say is I hope I'm never in trouble with no one else to bleat to.

Selah.

I am without any doubt whatever a NON-actor. For a start, the gushing pretension of would-be actors puts me off. Ergo ego. I watch them preening in front of the rehearsal mirrors in the drama hall. Just waiting for applause. All they want is to be liked. Plus admired, adored, idolized, flattered, etc. And they're more groupy than glue. If they're on their own for more than five minutes they get withdrawal symptoms and go walkabout, looking for kindred lost souls to coagulate with.

Why me? I asked OBD.

His reply: Many are called but you is chosen.

Very convulsing. I told him he himself should play a small but perfectly formed Almighty, as he already seemed to ALMOST know the lines.

Reply: All right, you big Dick—I mean, Nik!—get on with it because you're cast.

Much laughter from the groupies.

Me: I have been told my natural curiosity is one day likely to land me in hot water. Despite this warning, I joined your crazy filmthing because you wanted a researcher to save you the trouble of doing the work yourself. This I don't mind. I enjoy researching, and God turns out to be quite interesting in an uninteresting sort of way. But me play Jesus! Pick on someone your own size!

OBD, riled by this second reference to his diminutive stature: Look, Lord Bighead, you joined this project because your history teacher told you your work on the film could be submitted for exam assessment, and you thought what a nice easy option it would be. So just do your researching and quietly think of playing Jesus Christ, okay? There's weeks yet before shooting starts so you'll have plenty of time to turn us down if you don't want to do it. In which case, your researching will be finished and you can seek pastures new among people of a better class who are more worthy of your superior talents than this our humble company.

Etc. yammer yammer yak yak. Quite took off with the putdowns.

I said I'd think about it, just to shut him up.

Well, he does kind of breathe at you. He wriggles close and exhales up at you from beneath your nostrils, he being minuter than everyone else in the movie except that pricky clapperboy. And his breath stinks of mints. He chainsucks those nasty little mints with the hole in the middle. This habit he makes even more attractive by spearing the mint through its hole with the sharp point of his pink little lizard-like tongue and then sticking his tongueyed mint out at you while he listens to what you're saying. Distracting. He was doing it during our heated exchange, which is why I couldn't think of any speedo-witty retorts to his insults.

The rest of Our Gang enjoyed this no end, naturally, and orchestrated it with much hooted laughter in the manner of a Greek chorus gone off their heads. Especially when OBD said that I was exactly his idea of the sort of anybody person who can't act and wouldn't be noticed in a crowd even if everybody else left.

A sort of renta-nobody, John the Baptist quipped.

Mintbreath breathed: A nobody would suit my idea of Jesus Christ exactly. And you, he said to me, will make a very successful nobody.

Selah.

If he was trying to rile me in revenge for being turdy with him, he succeeded. But:

I AM NO NOBODY

And I have a passport to prove it. Required last year when Grandad took me to northern Sweden to meet some old buddies from his days at sea.

There is a terrible picture of me staring at the Qwik Foto camera on Paddington station. Even my own mother wouldn't recognize me. And my passport says in official government printing that I am Nicholas Christopher FROME, British Citizen and Student, 1.75 m. taille, with no distinguishing marks.

When I come to think about it, this just shows how useless a passport is at telling who you are. For example: 'No distinguishing marks'. Ridiculous. I'm covered in distinguishing marks! Not that I'd want other people to know about most of them.

Like the brown mole, 1 cm. diameter, just below the hip bone on my right thigh. And the scar, 3.4 cm. long on my left kneecap, where I fell on a jagged stone at age nine yrs four mths while being chased by cruds in the playground at school, their intention being to tie my arms and legs into reef knots, they being good little boy scouts busy learning their tenderfoot and desirous of practising brotherly love and scouts' law on me. This experience has left me with serious reservations about boy scouts and brotherly love. As churches of all kinds often run scout troops and talk a lot about brotherly love, this also makes me suspicious of churches, apart from my difficulties with God.

Circumcised. 9.6 cm. limp, a slim 13.3 cm. when roused. (Last checked two nights ago, when I was disappointed to find no further development since the previous measurement a month ago. There's more hair though—and about time.) My mother was fanatical about cleanliness and thought my father a dirty old man, even at thirty, which is old, I know, but not old enough, surely, to class him as a DOM. Anyhow, my fifth member was given the chop shortly after my second birthday (or so I've been told; I've no memory of this presumably painful occasion) to make sure I could be kept germ free and could be thoroughly inspected for any signs of DOMishness by Mummy in the bath at night, which she insisted on right up to the time when she . . .

I prefer not to remember that distinguishing mark. Forget it.

Why am I spewing all this out here? It has nothing to do with God and Our Gang. Must be this word processor. You just keep writing like you were talking to someone, when really it's

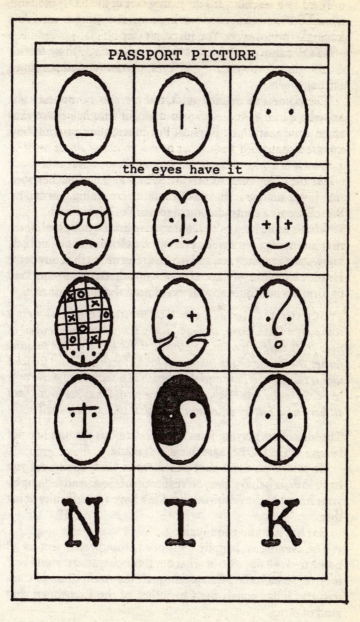

only a dumb machine. It's the gazing face of the VDU that does it, and the green fingertip moving across, writing words. And having writ moves on. You just can't stop.

STOP damn it. Where was I? Oh yes: Distinguishing marks.

Also: light brown hair, grey eyes, glasses (not all the time), etc., all 'visible'.

The point I'm making is that there can be nobody else anywhere in the whole spacedout world who has *exactly* the same combination of physical attributes, thus proving how unique a somebody I am.

Which is a nice thought till you remember that everybody else is just as unique a somebody. Which also means, therefore, that being unique is the most commonplace thing you can be. Which seems a contradiction in terms. But never mind.

What's more I haven't even started to list the things *inside* me that are never ever visible, even to myself, and which nobody knows about except me, and which are more me than any of the visible bits. None of these ever gets on a passport, or any kind of form, so how does anyone ever know about anyone else?

STOCKSHOT: *And as the mole on my [right thigh] is where it was when I was born, though all my body has been woven of new stuff time after time, so through the ghost of the unquiet father the image of the living son looks forth . . . That which I was is that which I am and that which in possibility I may come to be. So in the future, the sister of the past, I may see myself as I sit here now but by reflection from that which then shall be.*

The idea of me playing Jesus is also ridiculous because I do not believe in God. OBD said this didn't matter.

He said: You don't have to believe in God, ducky. All you have to do is behave like you're the son of God. And judging by your normal behaviour you shouldn't have any difficulty doing that.

Har har har and good-night.

The evening so happily concluded, Mintbreath sent us all home to work out who or what our Bible characters would be if they returned today. Caiaphas equals the Archbishop of Canterbury, Judas equals the Chancellor of the Exchequer: that kind of thing.

Not me. He wants a nobody for Jesus, he can have a nobody. A nobody who refuses to be anybody who is not the somebody he already is. If I'm going to play Jesus (which I'm not) then Jesus Christ is going to be me.

Selah.

Who cares anyway? As far as I can tell from my researches, the only thing you can say about Christ is that he never turns out to fit anybody's idea of how he ought to be. Everybody tries to make him into what they want him to be. In my opinion, nobody wants to know what he was REALLY like, because they all know instinctively that they wouldn't like what they found if they did.

I'd cop out of this movie right now, but I keep wondering WHY. Why do people believe all this guff about God? And what does it feel like to believe it? What does it DO to you? I mean, even *intelligent* people fall for it! It must DO something. Mustn't it?

That's the trouble with being too curious. Once you're hooked you can't give up. I keep churning it over in my mind and I know I might as well get it out of my system right now. I mean, it would be such an indignity to get old, like in your twenties, and still be interested in God. You'd never live it down. It's so juvenile. So I'll tackle God and Jesus Christ now and then get on with black holes, which is at least something worth looking forward to. (Question: Is God the Father a black hole? Is God the Son a white hole? Is God the Holy Ghost a quasar? Explore and discuss.)

Selah.

Anyway, I told Mintbreath I'll play Jesus if I can convince myself Jesus is important enough to bother about, but that I'd only be doing it under protest.

To which OBD replied: You think Christ was willing? So who wants to be crucified?

Har har har and a second good-night.

ACTION: Fixed interview with Revd Philip Ruscombe BA, Vicar of St James, tomorrow, 7 p.m., at the vicarage, to ask Important Questions About God.

Start with the priests. If they don't know about God, who does? How does anybody know?

Not that Christ had much luck with the priests, come to think of it. They were the ones who wanted him dead.

†

Only one witness, an insurance agent, Brian Standish, reported finding a young man hanging from a cross. Later that same morning Tom sought him out in his office.

'Don't look much like a policeman,' the insurance agent said. 'And I went through all I know half a dozen times at the station.'

'Helps to hear it first hand, sir.'

'Have to make it quick. Up to the eyeballs. Coffee?'

'No, sir, thanks.'

'Well, let's see. As I told the sergeant, I was jogging. Morning stagger, do it every day. Same route: along London Road, left past the council depot, under the railway viaduct to the canal, along the towpath, up into Cheapside, along Rowcroft, up into town and back home along London Road. Some days do it twice, if I'm feeling strong, which isn't often. Today I did it twice, though I'm beginning to regret it. Didn't see him first time so don't know whether he was there or not. I'm not one for the scenic beauties. Anyway, it was a bit foggy this morning and parky. But the second time round, the fog had cleared and the sun was bright. That's why I spotted him. The sun caught him. He was swinging, you see, turning slowly like a life-size crucifix on the end of a wire. The sun flashed on his face, I think. At any rate, it was his face I saw first, hanging up there, right above me, over the hedge along the towpath. Stopped me dead in my tracks. But I mean dead. Took my breath away for a second. The look on his face. The pain. But smiling. Grinning more like. Mad almost. Weird anyway. I thought he was a gonner. But then I heard him say something. Saliva slavering from his mouth. His body was shining with sweat, ribs sticking out, belly sucked in. Like a chicken carcass hanging in a butcher's shop. And his legs! Bent, very awkward. And those underpants! Not a pretty sight!'

'Blue with white trimmings?'

'Shouldn't laugh, but the underpants were comic somehow. Not that I laughed then. Too stunned.'

'And he said something?'

'Blabbering. Couldn't make head or tail.'

'Important, sir.'

'Sorry, not a word. Delirious, I suppose. Not that I stood there listening. As soon as I realized what I was looking at, I scrambled up the bank, pushed through the hedge into that dump—which, by the by, it's time the council made them clear, junked cars piled all over the place, rusty scrap everywhere, a bloody eyesore, a blot on the town, the sooner the bypass goes through the better ... Where was I?'

'Pushing through the hedge, sir.'

'Right. Wasn't till I was in the dump I realized he was dangling from a crane. Couldn't believe it! Fifteen feet off the ground on a cross made of rusty metal hooked onto the end of a crane! He was strapped on with strips of polythene round his arms and legs. Looked at first like there was nothing holding him at all. It was only then I realized I'd expected nails and blood streaming out. When I saw there wasn't, it was almost as big a shock as seeing him first. And I panicked a bit, I suppose. Funny thing, you expect the worst and when you don't find it, you go to pieces. Usually a calm person myself. Have to be in my line of business. But you don't find people on crosses every day, even in insurance. And we don't do a policy covering crucifiction.'

'So you did what, sir?'

'Ran about like a spooked rabbit. I was going to try and get him down. But then I thought, what happens if I push the wrong levers and he goes twanging up into the pulley or crashing to the ground? Pole-axed or pile-driven, that's what. Either way, a big claim against yours truly. So I started thinking whether to fetch the fire brigade, the ambulance, or the police. Or all three. But I couldn't believe what I was seeing, and I thought, if I don't believe it myself, who's going to believe it when I tell them over the phone? So there I was dodging about and getting nowhere while the kid was babbling on like he was in Parliament, spouting a lot of hot air that didn't make any sense.'

'But you finally went for the police.'

'Daft, I know, running all that way. Could have dialled the three nines. But somehow I just had to *see* somebody to tell.'

'You arrived at the station at six thirty-three, according to the report sheet. Told the duty officer what you'd found. He sent you in a car with two officers back to the scene.'

'And he'd gone.'

'But the officers believed your story?'

'The driver knew me. Stan Fields. Belong to the same bowling club. He could tell I wasn't joking. And of course there were the footprints. The cross was lying on the ground directly under the crane and strips of polythene were scattered all round. They'd been cut. But that wouldn't have made a case, would it? The footprints did though. Very fresh, and all round the cross. I knew mine because of the pattern of the soles. I was wearing new running shoes, expensive, with an unusual pattern on the instep. We could see the print of them all right. But the other prints crisscrossed over mine, so they must have been made after I'd been there.'

'You were at the station by six thirty-three. How long to run there from the scene?'

'Oh, eight minutes. Ten at most.'

'You were back at the scene by six fifty according to PC Fields' report. So there was a maximum twenty-seven minutes for whoever it was to get the boy down and away. And you didn't see anybody anywhere near the scene all the time you were there?'

'Nobody.'

'And you can't identify the boy?'

'Sorry. Never seen him before, as far as I know. Not that I go round looking at kids his age. See enough of my own two, thanks.'

'They about his age?'

'Fifteen and sixteen. He might have been seventeen. Hard to tell under the circs. Certainly not younger than sixteen, I'd guess. Too well hung—if you'll pardon the pun.'

'I've the other details you gave the sergeant, sir. But perhaps you've thought of something else since then?'

'Sorry. Would help if I could.'

'Then I'll not hold you up any longer, sir. Thanks for your time.'

'Best of luck. Hope you catch them. Need to crack down on this sort of thing. Too much violence everywhere these days.'

†

JULIE: Dear Nik. Can't start without saying a name, as if I'm talking to thin air and not to another person. When I pray I start Dear God. Same thing. Somebody . . . *other* . . . has to be there. So: Dear Nik.

[*Pause.*]

Funny about names. At the beginning, when I thought I was dying, names suddenly seemed very important. I used to say my own over and over to myself. Julie . . . Julie . . . Julie. JulieJulie-Julie. And Sarah . . . Sarah, because that was the name my father called me when I was little. I was christened Sarah Julia, did I ever tell you? But when I was twelve I took against Sarah because I read in the Bible about Sarah being childless till she was very old. I thought, I want children when I'm young, so I won't let anyone call me by a name that might put a hex on me. As if names could work bad magic. I told everybody they had to call me Julie, and everyone did, except my father, who said I'd always be Sarah to him. Sarah my solace, he'd say.

When I thought I was dying I thought: There you are, you're going to die without any children after all. Dad was right to call you Sarah. SarahSarahSarah, I said. And saying it over and over made me feel like I used to feel when I was little, as if all my childhood was inside that name, and saying it made me into a child again.

[*Chuckles.*]

SarahSarahSarah I said in my head until it stopped making any sense at all but was just a sound that didn't mean anything. As if I'd worn it out. And then my childhood faded away too and I was in hospital again, thinking I was dying and feeling the pain.

I thought I was only saying those names in my head but Simmo told me I was saying them out loud some of the time. She told me this last week when we were talking about you. She said yours was one of the names I kept repeating. Nik . . . Nik . . . Nik. I shouted it sometimes, as if I was calling to you. That's why they sent for you to come quickly. But most of the time, Simmo says, I just said Nik . . . Nik. Quietly, like it was a magic spell that would make something good happen.

And names do, don't they? Even babies know that. They soon learn if they say Mummy they get fed or hugged or looked at. If you speak a person's name they come to you or look at you. And when someone else speaks your name you feel pleased. You feel wanted. You feel *there*. Alive. Even if they're saying your name with dislike, at least you know you're you, that you exist.

Once, when I was little, about eight, I asked my dad, 'Is there a God, Daddy?' Dad said, 'I'm not sure. I think so.' And I said, 'But there must be, mustn't there, because he has a name.'

Anyway, that's why I kept saying your name and my own name when I thought I was done for.

Does this mean anything? Am I just rambling? The drugs make me ramble sometimes.

[*Pause.*]

I'm only trying to explain that names make sense of the nothing you feel you're going into when you think you're dying. At least they did for me. Thinking you're going to die is like setting out on a long journey that frightens you to a place you know nothing about. And saying the names of the people you love seems to bring them to you, to be with you. And your own name is like a space suit you live inside. While you've got it on you're all right. You live inside it. Without it you'd melt into the nothingness and be nothing yourself and never reach your unknown destination.

[*Sounds of Julie drawing in and exhaling deep breaths.*]

Sorry! Simmo says if I breathe in deeply when the pain comes and let it out slowly I'll feel better. As if the big breath comes inside, wraps up all the pain and fear and sadness like broken glass in cotton wool, and carries it away when you breathe out. Sometimes it works. This time it left some glass behind.

[*Breathing in. Breathing out.*]

I never knew pain is so . . . consuming. I mean *real* pain, not just hurt. Real pain sort of eats you. Gnaws you all over like a thousand rats chewing at your bones. And it burns you with sharp flames.

Now I know why people in the old days talked about hell being a place of fire and torture. Real pain is a kind of hell.

I've been trying to think about what pain *means*. Why do we have to have it? Why do people suffer?

I haven't got far yet. Except to hate it with a deep deep loathing. I've never felt such hate for anything before. Perhaps I have to get rid of the hate before I'll be able to think about what pain means? Just as I had to stop thinking I was dying before I could begin to get better. I managed to take that step thanks to you, Nik. Perhaps I have to do this thing about pain on my own? Perhaps that's what it means – what it's for. For learning to be on your own. Do you think it could be?

Doesn't sound right somehow. If only you were here we could talk about it, like we talked from the first time we met. I remember our first time together, every moment. Frame by frame, you might say—or your leptonic Director might!

[*Quiet chuckles.*]

That's another thing I'm discovering about illness. And about not being able to see anything, or move, or do anything at all. You remember a lot. Memories come flooding back—like remembering myself so vividly as a child when I say Sarah-Sarah. In the last few days I've remembered things I haven't thought of since they happened years ago.

Which reminds me of that poem . . . how does it go? . . . I expect you think it's trite . . . but, there, you see, I've suddenly remembered it when I haven't thought of it for ages . . . I've got it:

> I remember, I remember,
> The house where I was born,
> The little window where the sun
> Came peeping in at morn;

He never came a wink too soon,
Nor brought too long a day,
But now, I often wish the night
Had borne my breath away!

[*Pause.*]

Heavens, it's much gloomier than I thought! How funny! I only remembered the sun peeping in at dawn. That's why I liked it. I learned it when I was . . . what? . . . nine, I suppose. I found it in a book, and thought it was specially for me because the sun came peeping into my room at dawn too.

But I didn't remember the night bearing my breath away. Just shows what you don't notice when you don't need to! There've been plenty of times since what Simmo calls my little mishap that I've remembered the house where I was born and wished the night would bear my breath away so there would be an end to the pain.

I don't remember the rest of the poem, and now I'd rather like to know how it goes on. Could you find it for me?

I wonder if the poet lived in her memories as much as I'm living in mine? I'm beginning to think we only know who we are, only know ourselves, through our memories. I mean, think what it would be like if we couldn't remember anything. We wouldn't be able to do most of the things we like doing, never mind the things we don't like doing. We wouldn't be able to learn anything. We wouldn't even be able to learn from the mistakes we make all the time, because we wouldn't be able to remember our mistakes no matter how painful they were.

Grief! We wouldn't know the people we loved, either! We wouldn't have any memory of them so we wouldn't be able to think about them, or what it was like to be with them. We couldn't love them because we wouldn't be able to remember what we liked about them so much.

And how could we trust anyone? We'd have nothing to go on, no past experience to tell us this person is honest and this other one tells lies. If we could remember nothing of our past could we be anything now? Except confused, I suppose. And frightened, because we wouldn't know what was safe and what was dangerous. We couldn't believe anything because we wouldn't remember anything to believe in. Not that we'd know what belief meant anyway. We wouldn't know what anything meant.

I've never thought memory was quite as important as that! But I suppose it is.

[*Deep breathing.*]

I'm tired out. Time for another drug-scoffing session. I eat more drugs than I eat meals. Till the knockout pills arrive I'll think of you, Nik, and the memory will keep the pain away. You, the first time we met. All that rain! You, the first time I took you to church. Disgracing yourself! You the night before . . .

[*Snatched-at breaths.*]

Sorry, have to stop . . . *Nurse!* . . .

[*Cries of pain. End of tape.*]

MEETINGS

NIK'S NOTEBOOK: The vicar of St James is pathetic. St James was the son of Zebedee, brother of John the Beloved, called Boanerges. Boanerges means 'son of thunder'. St James's vicar is no son of thunder. Son of silence more like.

Except when speaking of golf (said: goff). Waxes chatty then. Goff clubs are the first thing you meet inside his front door. Along with pong of mouldy wellies and decomposing dog. Dog a podgy black labrador with watery eyes, slavery mouth, and a limp in the left foreleg. Turns you off animal rights. Vic calls him Bugsy when not calling him Old Chum.

Vic is a bachelor. Tall, balding, pink-faced, smelling vaguely of Old Spice and musty incense. Also large-bellied. Rumour says he's oathed to celibacy. But what woman would have him? He came along the path from church in flapping black cassock, like a converted Dracula, Old Chum hobbling along behind.

The vicarage is occupied by neglect. Cold even with sun shining in. Took me into what he called his study, a sort of religious knocking shop. Large gooky pic of Virgin Mary in fetchingly soulful pose staring from one wall. A fairly explicit full frontal crucifix made of carved wood hanging over the fireplace. A jumble of bookshelves crammed with heavy dull tomes, mostly holy manuals, tombs for dead words, covering most of the walls. A bulky desk big as a snooker table piled with controlled disaster of paper. (He should persuade the parish to stump up for a word processor, he'd save himself a lot of garbage, but maybe God wouldn't approve? Is there a God in the machine? If there is in mine he-she-it only says what I tell him-her-it to say. That's the sort of God I like.)

He waved me into one of two exhausted armchairs beside the empty fireplace. The fplc mouth blocked by an old headstone, from the churchyard I guess, its inscription worn unreadable by weather. Made the room seem ominous. The room a tomb. Sitting with a memorial to your own death in the great reaper's waiting room.

Selah.

Vic says, suspicious: Wanted to ask about God, did you say?

Me, nervous: Wondered if you could explain belief.

Vic's left eyelid twitches: Belief! Tricky subject. What was it you wanted to know exactly?

Old Chum collapses between us like a whale expiring on the beach. The way he lies, the headstone becomes his. Maybe it is, because I'm not sure he's alive even when he's limping about.

Me: Not sure, *exactly*. What belief means, I suppose.

Vic smiles. Ah! he says with relief.

He picks up a large dog-eared vol. from a stool beside his chair. (Underneath the dog-eared vol. lies *The Times* folded at the crossword puzzle, mostly finished.)

He flips dog-eared pages and says: The dictionary tells us, let's see: *Belief. Noun. One: a principle, idea, et cetera, accepted as true or real, especially without positive proof. Two: opinion, conviction. Three: religious faith. Four: trust or confidence, as in a person or person's abilities,* et cetera. There you are.

Thumps book shut, replaces on top of *The Times*.

Silence except for heavy breathing from Old Chum. Vic bends forward and pats him. Decomposing doggy pong rises like a gag.

I gag. Cough. Try not to breathe. Fail. Say: Might need a bit more, if you wouldn't mind. I mean, how does belief feel?

Vic, looking startled, sits back in chair and says: Feel! Good lord! Can't say one honestly *feels* anything. Rather . . . that is . . . one does not *feel* belief . . . one . . . *accepts* it.

I stare at him. He toys with a pen lying on the stool at his side and stares at Old Chum. Old Chum pluffles in sleep.

Selah.

Vic is not a man in a hurry. Eventually looks up, smiles, says: Warned you it was a tricky subject. I don't mean one doesn't feel anything about one's beliefs, only that one doesn't feel belief.

Silence. Stares at pen as he toys with it.

Then goes on: One decides that God is, by and large, bad

33

days taken with good, more likely *to be* than not. This . . . one believes.

Pause.

STOCKSHOT: *Canst thou* [Vic says] *by searching find out God? Canst thou find out the Almighty unto perfection? It is as high as heaven; what canst thou do? deeper than hell; what canst thou know?*

He looks up at me. Says: If you understand me.

Pause. I stare at him.

Not quite, I say.

Vic says: No, thought you mightn't. He sighs (sounding so like Old Chum I wonder if Vic ventriloquizes the dog, or maybe even vice versa. Then also realize they look pretty much alike as well, except Vic doesn't have the watery eyes yet). He slumps further into his puffy chair and his own bulgy waist.

Silence again. Vic stares between his hillocky knees at Old Chum's hillocky body for so long I think he's forgotten me or eternity has begun without me noticing.

But then he stirs himself, glances up, says: Look, er . . . Nik? What's all this about? Thinking of asking for confirmation?

I explain. He laughs. Quite revived, he seems for a minute. (Old Chum lifts his head at the sound of Vic's laughter, takes a bleary glim, and flops, comatose again. The millennium is not yet.)

Vic: How splendid! A reluctant Jesus in search of belief in himself! That does appeal, I must say!

I'm laughing too, because it is pretty funny.

Don't be upset, says he, I'm not laughing at you, dear boy.

(I love the dear boy bit.)

I say: It's okay. I think it's a pretty stupid idea myself.

Not at all, no no, says he. Then, perking up even more: You don't happen to play goff, do you?

Sorry? say I.

Pity, says he. You know . . . Nik? . . . what I'd do if Our Lord walked through that door this minute? After the required pleasantries, of course.

I shake my head.

Vic says: I'd say, My Lord, will you honour me with a round? And, you know, Nik, it has always seemed to me that He would reply, My dear vicar, I'd be delighted. Or words to that effect.

I say: Maybe we can make that a scene in our film. (I'm only half joking, I realize as I say it.)

You could, Vic says in all seriousness, do worse. Better than pretending to perform miracles. More likely. More real. More to do with belief, in fact.

But, I say, how would you know he was Christ?

Ah! says he, now there you have it, you see. That's what belief *is*. I'd know because of believing. It doesn't feel like anything. It's just *there*, a fact of one's life.

Now it's my turn to stare at Old Chum while trying to sort out this nugget. Then: Sorry, vicar, but I don't find that very clear.

Vic slumps even further into his own and his chair's upholstery and looks deeply disappointed.

He says: Convincing is what you mean.

I do? say I.

He nods, sighs: I'm not very good at this, I'm afraid . . .

I didn't mean . . . , I say, feeling embarrassed.

Vic, flapping a hand: I know, I know. But I'm not. One must have the courage to acknowledge one's limitations. And I have to admit that I'm not too good at talking about God. Never really have been. Every week I hold confirmation classes. Mostly young people of thirteen or fourteen, and mostly attending because their parents want them to. Rather like baptism, you know. Parents want their children done just to make sure. Hedging their bets. If God exists, having it done might get him on your side. If he doesn't, who cares?

He chuckles. Chummy fluffles and slobbers.

Well, Vic says, I talk to them. Tell them as best I can about church and prayer, and about God. They listen – rather dutifully, I have to admit, and politely. Too politely, I sometimes think. Might be better all round if they argued. They do ask the odd question now and then, but just to show willing and to be kind, I'm sure.

He smiles, but sadly, and goes on:

Some drop out. But mostly they stay the course and go before the bishop in their best new clothes for the laying on of hands. All very pretty and pious and their mums and dads looking proud. But as I stand at the bishop's side and witness the performance of this holy rite I know that six months later they'll mostly have given up any pretence of being in the slightest interested in God or church or anything religious. And I wonder how much their falling off is a failure of mine.

He pushes himself up in his chair, not looking at me. I sit stone still. I'm not sure he's talking to me now. He might not even remember I'm in the room. Is he just talking aloud to himself? I feel a bit guilty, like I'm eavesdropping on a private confession.

He speaks so quietly I strain to hear: Of course, if you suggest to them that they aren't Christian any more, they're most indignant, quite insulted in fact, and tell one sharply, and not so politely any more, how Christianity isn't the same as being a church-goer, and how, if it comes to that, the church has betrayed Christ because it's more interested in old buildings and out-of-date customs than in people and their needs, and how the church supports evil rulers and amasses wealth while people die in oppression and hunger and terrible poverty. And frankly, Nik . . .

He does remember I'm here after all!

. . . I have no answer to such accusations. I'm quite inadequate to the task of explaining that what we're really talking about is the Being who, by definition, is so all-containing of ourselves and the world and the entire universe, as well as whatever unimaginable wonders lie beyond, that it is impossible to say anything meaningful at all. God is a being who is beyond being. How can one speak of such a . . .

He raises his hands, shakes his head, shrugs.

I nod, meaning: I understand the difficulty.

He sighs again. Says: And now you come, asking me to tell you what belief is. What am I to say?

Now I have to shrug.

And it's his turn to nod and smile sympathetically: You're quite right to ask, I don't mean you aren't, dear boy. But I find myself in a quandary. I'm like a man who's found a sack of gold but can't tell anyone where he found it because, if he ever knew, he's forgotten now. And whenever he tries to share his gold with others, it turns to sand even as he pours it into their hands. You can imagine how embarrassing that is! For a vicar especially.

He laughs, but for some reason I can't join in.

One even gets to the point, he says, of hiding the fact that one possesses gold oneself so as to avoid the embarrassment of people asking for some. One even sometimes tries to pretend that not having is the same as having. That the gold is an illusion. Which is a painful kind of betrayal. Of those people, like you, who ask, and of one's faith. Worst of all, it is a betrayal of God.

He mutters the last sentence so quietly, so shamefaced, that, though I sit forward to hear, I look away from him at once.

Silence. Long, long silence.

Broken at last by Old Chum. He wakes like a canine Lazarus, staggers to his doddering paws, shakes decomposition into the airless air, and hobbles to the door.

Vic comes to and says with bluster: Sorry, dear boy, not much help to you, I'm afraid.

It's okay, I say. And it's time I went. Things at home . . .

Of course, yes, Vic says. I'll see you out.

At the door he slips a goff club from its bag and putts a pebble from the step. Old Chum lumbers after it like a geriatric caddy and disappears among the overgrown garden bushes.

Pity you don't play, Vic says. Easier to talk on the fairway. Fresh air. Exercise. Should try it. Strongly recommended. Give you a lesson, if you like.

He is a different man from the one I've just been talking to. More lively but less likeable. The real Vic is hiding behind a shield of hearty gamesmanship.

Thanks. Sometime, I say, and retreat towards the gate.

You've only to ask, he calls, waving his club in farewell.

I wave a non-committal hand and escape through the gate, thankful that a high wall makes it unnecessary for me to look back.

†

37

Nik—Sorry to have been so little use last evening. After you left, a thought occurred that might be helpful. I suggest you see some friends of mine. They are a kind of monk. Don't let this put you off. They're quite sane. They're called The Community of the Holy Innocents. CHI for short. (We do have monks and nuns in the Church of England, though most people don't seem to know!) I think they might be able to answer some of your questions better than I.

If you can stay a day or two you might even discover some of the answers for yourself. Seek and ye shall find, as the saying is.

Whether you do or not, I think you'd have an interesting time. The brothers will put you up free of charge. (Though you may be expected to help with a few small chores.) And without any religious obligation of course. I mean you don't have to promise to let them convert you in order to qualify for free bed and board!

Do try. You won't regret it. I spend a spell there every year and always return refreshed. Write to Brother Kit CHI, at the address overleaf. Say I suggested the idea.

God bless.

Philip Ruscombe

†

Lacking clues, Tom visited the scene-of-crime.

No one was there when he arrived. The cross lay in between a battered mobile crane and a pyramid of old tyres. He poked about, finding nothing except a confusion of footprints drying in the mud. Whatever else there might have been would, he supposed, have been carted off for lab treatment.

An old man, hands in pockets, came wandering up.

'After something?' he said, unwelcoming.

Tom flipped his identity wallet.

The old man was small and stocky with high, hunched shoulders. He wore a grubby cap and a torn old pullover that might once have been green and was covered with flecks of wood shavings and a powdering of sawdust. His trousers were baggy, tired grey, probably part of an old suit. His face was clean shaven, though spiky bristles grew in the creases of rugged lines. A prominent nose—almost a beak, Tom thought—and pale sharp eyes. He looked about sixty but could have been older. A hawk-like man.

'Thought your lot had finished here,' the old man said.

'You know what all this is about then?' Tom said.

'Roughly.'

'Work here?'

'Now and then.'

'Meaning?'

'Now and then. Supposed to be retired. Bloody fool idea. Retirement is for the dead. I keep a workshop. Do a few odd jobs. Nothing regular.'

'Here early this morning?'

'How early?'

'Six o'clock?'

'Too early for me, that is. These days any road. One benefit of being retired, you see. Can please yourself.' The old man laughed.

'But you know what happened?'

'There's plenty of gossip.'

'And what does the gossip say?'

'That some kid was strung up on a cross during the night but disappeared after he was found this morning. Something like that.'

'Does the gossip say who did it?'

'Hooligans, likely.'

'And who the kid was?'

'No. Nothing about him.'

Tom nodded. He felt he was being stonewalled.

'And what do you think, sir?' he said with too careful politeness.

The old man sniffed and grinned. 'Nothing much.'

'You don't seem very bothered.'

'Why should I be bothered?' the old man said, looking away. 'Anything can happen these days, and mostly does, if you wait long enough.'

'Could I have your name, sir?' Tom said, taking out his notebook.

'Is it that bad!' The old man chuckled.

'Might need to talk to you again, that's all.'

The old man, shrugging, said, 'Arthur Green.'

Tom said, 'You don't own this dump?'

'No!'

'Who does?'

'Wouldn't know. Fred Callowell runs it.'

'Is he around?'

The old man nodded towards a hut where the access road ended. 'That's his office. But he's often out, buying and selling.'

'Was he here earlier, would you know?'

'Better ask him.'

Tom looked round at the wilderness of scrap metal and pyramids of corpsed motor cars.

'You'll be here all day?'

'Can't think there's anything more I can tell you.'

'All the same, you never know.'

Tom walked away, past the closed hut, along the access road to his unmarked car parked out of sight by the railway bridge.

Arthur Green watched him go, then hurried to his workshop, two buildings along from Fred Callowell's hut.

†

The day after Nik visited the vicar of St James's, he read a notice in the local rag, headlined:

CHRISTIAN CND
PEACE RALLY

Demonstrators were invited to form up in Field Road, near the maternity hospital (how the new mums would love that), at three o'clock on Saturday afternoon, before marching through town (how the shopkeepers would love that) to Stratford Park (how the bowls players would love that) for the inevitable speeches from local and (minor) national notables.

A good chance for Christian-watching. Besides, he approved of the cause if not the method. Crowds and slogans never succeeded in convincing him of anything except that they were likely to be wrong.

Nik stationed himself in the park well before time on high ground in front of a large lean-comfortable tree, from where he would have a good view of the proceedings. When he arrived few other people were there. Six or seven young men and women wearing armbands printed with M (for Marshal) were busy being important around a scaffold platform draped with Christian and CND posters. An older man in a baggy suit was giving them orders from the platform, calling everyone 'Brother' or 'Sister' in a way that, Nik thought, gave Christianity a bad name and mixed it up with loony trade unionists. A knot of policemen and one policewoman stood to one side, trying to look dispassionate, and muttering jokes to each other, which, from their side-glances, Nik could tell were about Baggy-suit.

Five minutes before the demonstration arrived, a blaring out-of-tune brass band heralding its coming, the already grey and overcast sky started pouring rain as if to douse a fire. This settled, after its first enthusiasm, into a steady, drizzling fret. Under his tree, and dressed in his usual, though dishevelled, ex-army combat jacket, Nik was bearably protected. The police, ever prepared for the worst, donned waterproofs snatched from their van. The marshals, exercising Christian fortitude, made no concessions but laughed a lot and moved about even more busily.

Baggy-suit tested the microphone, tapping and blowing on it, saying, 'One, two, three . . .' and then intoning, 'He maketh his sun to rise on the evil and on the good, and sendeth rain on the just and on the unjust.'

'Matthew five, forty-five,' shouted one of the marshals from the ground and the others cheered.

He at the microphone said, 'Hallelujah, brother. The Lord reigneth; let the people tremble.'

His acolytes groaned, mocking his pun.

'Psalm ninety-nine,' yelled back he of the memory.

'Brother,' Baggy-suit called, waving at Nik, 'can you hear me up there?'

Cupping his hands to his mouth, Nik shouted, 'Mark four,

nine,' this happening to be one of the few quotations that had stuck in his memory from all his recent reading.

'What did he say?' he at the microphone asked aside of a marshal.

Marshal of the memory shouted, 'He that hath ears to hear, let him hear.'

Baggy-suit coughed. 'Thank you, brother,' he said and climbed down.

JULIE: All that rain! And me holding up that silly poster someone had pushed into my hands while we were forming up. Rain was running off the handle straight down my arm. My hair was soaked and streaked in rat tails all over my face so that I could hardly see, and water was streaming down my neck. I remember you telling me afterwards that I was beaming great smiles and you thought I must be alight with the vision of God or something. But really it was only the rain trickling between my boobs and making me nearly giggle. Nothing holy.

NIK'S NOTEBOOK: Carrying a poster

Made me laugh. Saw her straight off, even before she was near enough to see her face or even tell that she was a girl. A kind of energy or something. Don't know. Also, most of the others were playing at being demonstrators, looking around with a kind of pretend humility, but at the same time saying: Look at me, I'm protesting. As if protesting made them better than the people who weren't.

Note for history essay: If you're protesting something – a belief or an opinion or an injustice, or anything – does your protest only 'work' if there are a lot of other non-protesting people to see you? Suppose it depends a bit on this, or who's to know? But it oughtn't to. And if protesting only depends on the publicity value, and isn't worth anything *in itself*, is it worth anything at all?

But this girl wasn't being anything but herself. You could tell she *meant* it. Felt it. Her thoughts were her own. I mean were part of her.

Seems to me most people don't/can't think. They only think other people's thoughts. People who enjoy being in crowds are mostly like that. They like speeches and demos because they are told what to think. And because they are with a lot of other people the same as themselves, which makes them think they're thinking for themselves and doing something about what they think. But they aren't. It's all a trick, a con. What they're really doing is giving themselves up to somebody else who is just using them.

Selah.

This girl. Couldn't take my eyes off her. She was so *her*. But she was taking part in this demo. How could she? She wasn't just a goggle to look at. There was more to her than that. Why was she there at all?

She was dressed in a floppy blue sweater that was too big and jeans you could see, even from the odd glimpse of them I got, had been worn by a male (or else she was hermaphrodite). As the sweater got wetter and wetter it hung heavier and heavier on her, and clung to her, showing her top half was indisputably female. She kept brushing the hair out of her face, and looking round with this slightly silly grin, as if she was observing what was happening as much as she was taking part. And what she saw was amusing her.

Even before the trouble started I was thinking maybe I'd try and talk to her afterwards.

STOCKSHOT: *Who is there?*
I.
Who is I?
Thou.
And that is the awakening—
the Thou and the I.

The trouble Nik mentions started five minutes into the first speech. A couple of hundred demonstrators were crammed

43

together in front of the platform. On the platform nine or ten people were trying to look godly and peaceful. Two press photographers were darting about like sheepdogs herding a flock. The police, about twenty by now, were scattered around the edge of the crowd like blue fence posts, listening and watching with professional poker faces. Nik, under his tree uphill from them all, had a view of the whole scene and, by panning right, of the road from the park entrance.

He was paying little heed to the speech, being too busy watching the girl. She stood in the middle of the crowd, her back to him. But even this hedged back view fascinated him. He willed her to move just for the pleasure of seeing it. Most of all, he willed her to turn and see him, and be as eager for him as he was for her. He wondered about tracking through the crush till, standing beside her, he could see her close up and be ready to speak.

And would have done had he not been distracted by the sudden appearance along the road from the entrance of an open truck driving fast and festooned with Union flags and flapping posters bearing such messages as:

NF
KEEP BRITAIN SAFE
BRITAIN FOR THE BRITISH

and biggest of all:

NF v COMMIE NUKE DEMOS

Paraded on the back was a rampant squad of jeering, stamping men, late teens and early twenties, geared in bovver boots and black leathers, bullet heads shaven close, fist-pumping arms tattooed and harnessed in studded bands. The rain gave them an armoured glaze and spumed in their wake.

What happened next happened very fast, of course, and took everyone by surprise, as it was meant to, which also added to the confusion, causing people to behave irrationally, against their convictions and even against their natures.

Some of the nearest police and demonstrators, hearing the

truck's approach, turned to look. One policeman walked towards it, his arms spread wide, flagging it down. The truck skidded to a halt in front of him at the edge of the crowd. As it stopped five or six of its squad jumped down from the side nearest the crowd and advanced, jeering, towards the approaching policeman.

This, however, was a blind. From his vantage, Nik observed six or seven more squaddies jump down from the other side, split into two groups, and sprint round the crowd, one group heading one way and one the other.

Before anybody had quite grasped what was going on, the leading squaddy had reached the platform, leapt onto it, snatched the microphone from the speaker, and was shouting into it himself:

'This demonstration is another communist-inspired attempt to undermine the will of the British people to protect itself against foreign aggressors and against those who have no right to live here . . .' Et cetera, ad lib.

Julie at first thought this was part of the demo, some kind of stunt arranged by the organizers to help liven up the meeting and make their point in a dramatically ironic way. So she laughed and booed and mocked, thinking she was joining in the fun. Others around her must have thought so too because they reacted with similar amusement. But very soon, several events happening at the same time forced everyone to realize this was no stunt but was brutally real.

Before the invader had said much more than is quoted above some of the platform party surrounded him, shouting objections, and trying to wrest the microphone from his grasp. This brought two more squaddies leaping up in support of their man. Their intervention turned the disagreement into a scuffle and finally into a brawl with fists as well as words being thrown. (Thus in minutes providing a graphic demo of how wars begin: provocation; angry objection; resort to physical violence; and so to battle.)

Just as soon as his leader was interfered with, a squaddy stationed at the side of the platform for this very purpose grabbed the wires trailing from the mike and cut them with clippers.

Meantime (mean time indeed) the gang of squaddies who had jumped down on the side of the truck facing the crowd were approached by three or four of the nearest police, coming to the aid of their mate who had flagged the truck down. The squaddies let the police reach them then dodged away in all directions, bulldozing through the crowd and snatching at banners, which they flailed above their heads, thus turning posters for peace into weapons of war (and demonstrating the neutrality of matter). As they bludgeoned swathes through the protesters, people scattered, shouting, stumbling, falling, ducking away, the squaddies yelling and whooping, and raising Cain by way of yet another demonstration that all men are not brothers.

During this riving diversion the oldest (he was forty if he was a day), biggest, most fiercely and expensively leathered squaddy of all, who had so far sat watching from the truck's cab, climbed onto the back, and from there, using a bull-horn, continued the speech begun by his platform henchman.

A couple of police, hearing this, detached themselves from the keystone kops pursuit now in progress against the crowd busters, and turned their attention instead to the silencing of the truculent orator. Only to find, as they ran towards it, that the truck moved off just fast enough to prevent them reaching it, circling skilfully, zigging, zagging, curling along the edge of the disintegrating crowd, thereby leaving the bill behind, sloshing about in the mud churned up by its wheels, and causing further mayhem among the protesters now fleeing outwards from the mêlée.

NIK'S NOTEBOOK: Planned. All of it worked out beforehand and executed like a military op.

She was trapped. And stood her ground, still holding up that gormless banner. Others near her scattered. But not her.

One of the black leather boys came right at her, shoulder charging. She went flying, arms spread-eagled, legs kicking. Her banner rocketed out of her hands. He caught it in mid air, swung it, and batted her across the buttocks like she was a shuttlecock, sending her pancaking flat-faced into the mud.

That did it. Observer turned activist. Pacifist turned belligerent.

I've never felt anything like it. Me, I'm a watcher, not a doer. The world is splitting at the seams with doers. People who think they know best, who want to be in charge, want to be the ones who make the running for the rest of us. Mighty Mice dressed up as Supermen.

One of the reasons I like history is that it tells about the doers. And it seems to me the bigger the doer becomes the more he/she turns into a murderous, power-hungry, hypocritical, self-righteous, arrogant prig. While ordinary non-big-doers like me and Grandad and all the tellywatchers of the world, who want only to live our lives unmolested, are supposed to be thankful, and admire these Big-Doer creeps, who always pretend they're doing what they're doing for the sake of the rest of us, when they're really only doing it for themselves. And they pay ad-people (who are no better) to make ads and TV programmes presenting them as heroes.

I HATE HEROES.

Selah.

But when I saw her splattered into the mud by a turd in black leather, something happened I'd never felt before. A Doer made me so angry I did something about it. Without thinking. That split-second. Even as his body hit hers. It was a violation against me as much as against her. Just because there was something ... I don't know ... different ... intense ... separate about her. Something I wanted. Wanted to ... *know* I suppose is the word.

Right now, just an hour after leaving her, I don't understand. But anyway, I piled in.

Geronimo!

JULIE [*Singing*]:   Mud, mud, glorious mud,
                        There's nothing quite like it
                        for cooling the blood.

[*She laughs.*]

Mum has an old record of that. I think it's called 'The Hippopotamus Song'. When I was little I used to play it over and over and end up hysterical.

When I hit the mud and felt the mess on my face and hands and the stickiness squeezing through my clothes that song flashed into my head. They'd frightened me when they started running through us, yelling and thrashing about. But the mud and the hippo song cooled my blood and I thought, 'Let them come after me again and it'll be the hippo song for them this time.'

Well, you know what happened then! [*Laughs.*] If my face hadn't been covered in mud so that I couldn't see, I would have known at once whose side you were on, because they were all in leathers and you were in your usual sloppy outfit. But I couldn't see and you were yelling, 'Get up! Come on, get up!' One thing I can't stand is people yelling at me. It infuriates me. I was trying to get up anyway. But you grabbed my arms and pulled at me, and that angered me even more because I don't like people grabbing me either, so I struggled. And what with you pulling and me tugging to get loose we both went off balance and then I slipped in the mud and we both went flopping down, me onto my face again and you onto your bum.

[*She laughs so much she starts coughing, and breathing heavily, and has to pause to recover.*]

'Excrement!' you said, using the crude word.

'Don't you swear at me, you barbarian!' I said, or spluttered rather, because I got a mouth full of mud, and that made me furious with myself as well as with you, which, of course, only made things worse.

And I know what you're thinking right this minute, Nicholas Frome, as you listen. You're thinking how prudish I still am about ruderies, despite all your efforts to corrupt me. But I don't care. I don't like them, and that's that. I don't see any need for them. In fact, I think they're a kind of violence. You say rude words are just explosions that relieve tension. Well, I've some experience with explosions remember. And I don't think any kind of explosion is meaningless, or is just a relief of tension, not even if they are only explosions of words.

Words can't ever be just explosions anyway. They're always words. They all mean something. They all affect people somehow. The people who use them and the people who hear them. And I don't just mean their dictionary meanings.

Saying that makes me think words are like people. They have bodies. You can see them, and you can like the look of them or not, just as I like the look of Nik. It's as interesting back to front as it is front to back. Kin as well as Nik. And the two tall letters protect the little eye. Like a spine. You. Always there. The core. The DNA of Nik. And you, the eye, the ee-why-ee. Watching. A lovely, neat, playful word. And just like you!

And words have intellects as well as bodies. Their dictionary meanings, and their meanings when they're put into sentences. Like these sentences I'm saying to you now. They make some sort of sense, I hope!

And words have emotions just like people do. The things they make you feel when you hear them or read them. Like the words in the sentence 'I love you' which you have to admit no one can ever quite explain just from dictionary meanings, but which get you pretty stirred up if they're said to you.

And sometimes their emotional meanings don't have much to do with their dictionary meanings. Just as sometimes what people think about something is quite different to what they feel about it. They aren't thinking words, they're feeling words. Isn't that right?

So I don't know how you can say that any word can ever be just an explosion that relieves tension. Though I expect, as usual, you'll find some argument to use, because you just love arguing for arguing's sake. But really, in your heart you know I'm right. The truth is you like using ruderies for their shock effect.

Hey, I'm starting to argue with you again! That's a good sign, isn't it? I must be getting better!

[*Pause.*]

Now I've forgotten what I was talking about before I started rambling on about words! None of which I'd thought before now, by the way. So that's one good thing about being ill—it gives you time to think.

INTERCUT: *Crowd scattering in every direction. Police chasing squaddies. Platform party in disarray, scuffling among themselves while squaddies vandalize the scaffolding under their feet. Vocal truck continues its erratic course, ranting still.*

Arrests being made of belligerent members of both parties, who are frogmarched to a police van and bundled inside.

JULIE: Oh yes! Us in the mud.

'I've had enough of this stupid game,' I thought, and my anger turned red. I've a dreadful temper, if I give in to it, as you've good reason to know.

Then you started pulling at my arms and yelling at me again, and I thought, 'This barbarian won't give up!' So I grabbed a nice pat of mud in each hand and plopped them in the general direction of your face. You let out a terrible squawk so I knew I'd hit the spot. [*Laughs.*] I ought to feel sorry for doing such a thing. After all, I might have blinded you—she says with feeling! But I don't so I'll have to work at it. Please God, I'll be sorry, honest—but not yet, because it's still funny to remember, and I need all the laughs I can get.

Whoops! Gloom and doom showing again.

[*Deep breaths.*]

'Hell!' Nik said, letting Julie go, he recoiling bottom down as before, and she, released, slithering onto her front again.

'I'm trying to help you, goddammit!' he cried, wiping gritty mud from his face so he could see again.

'Don't you swear by God to me, you pagan!' Julie spluttered, biting on mud and wiping her eyes.

Nik spat. 'I'm only trying to get you away from this.'

'I can look after myself, thank you!'

She could see him now and sat back on her haunches. 'I thought you were one of those barbarians,' she said, grudgingly.

Nik, outraged, said, 'One of that mob!'

'Well, I couldn't see!'

'Excuses, excuses!'

The rain began falling in torrents again.

'Go and boil your head,' Julie said, slithering to her feet.

'A good Christian thought,' Nik said, pushing himself up too.

'I don't feel very Christian,' Julie said. 'Not after being attacked by people like that and being soaked in mud and being pulled about by—' She slipped again, and sat with a bump on her behind. 'Dear God, give me strength!' she shouted in anger, striking the ground with her hands.

Nik broke up.

'Thank *you*!' Julie said, glaring at him, but then could not help herself smiling.

'Here,' Nik said, 'give us a hand.'

She did, pretending reluctance. He helped her, slitherily, to her feet. But at once she took her hand back; and without difficulty, for the mud greased their palms.

Nik regretted this loss.

'Come on,' he said. 'Let's go.'

'Go!' Julie said, a fierceness returning. 'Go! You mean run away from . . . [*nearly speechless*] . . . *them!*' She looked Nik accusingly in the eyes. 'Run away yourself. I won't.'

Nik stared back. Then held out his lonely hands, cruciform, and asked, smiling, 'Run from what?'

By now they were an island in a lake of mud. What action there was scuttled about on the shore. No one marauded near them. The platform was a shambles of collapsed metal and torn posters, the party gone. The demo demolished, ended.

Nik could watch Julie close up at last. She was smaller than he, and smaller than he expected. Slight even. Her clothes clung, soaked, to her frame, modelling her small breasts, and bulgy, too thick buttocks, and fleshy thighs. Her triangular face, and cap of bobbed black hair, close-gripping from wetness, set off her round strong skull, which shone, for him, as if in a halo, out of which her blue-grey eyes stared fiercely at him.

She was to Nik, quite simply, beautiful. A being he wanted to take hold of and fit to him.

His limbs began to tremble. He hoped that if she noticed she would only think he was cold from the wet.

'We might as well,' he said. 'Go, I mean.'

Julie did not move, except to turn her head and look disgustedly at the scene around them, her dripping hands held comically out from her sides, as a penguin holds its flippers.

'There's nothing to stay for,' Nik said, unable to think of anything brighter. His intelligence wasn't working, or rather had slipped from his mind to his body. All he could think of was wanting to touch her. She had pale skin, almost bleached in this rain-cloud light. His eyes fixed on a small round scar indented into her left cheek near the corner of her mouth. Shaped like an O, it made him think that the blunt end of a pencil had been jabbed there. But the blemish only made her more attractive. He wanted to finger the mark and ask how she got it.

As he drank her in she blinked and sniffed and sucked at her lips. She might almost have been cosseting tears, but he knew she was only placating the rain coursing her eyes.

He was so engrossed he did not notice a young policeman running towards them.

(Tom coming between them.)

'Are you okay, miss?' he asked, but he was sussing Nik.

'We're all right. I was knocked down. He came to help.' Julie smiled, showing her teeth. One of the two front ones was chipped to a guillotine angle. She tongued it as she smiled, a habit of hers, Nik soon learned. He longed to kiss her mouth, tongue and all.

The policeman waited a moment, summing them up before saying, 'If you're sure you're okay?' He turned to run back to the van waiting for him. 'You'd best be getting home;' he said, and trotted off.

Nik resented him. Not so much for giving orders as for his intrusion.

Tom gone, Nik and Julie, statuesque in the rain, looked at one another, aware now of how wet and cold they felt, how clarted in mud. But neither moved.

Julie ended their silence. 'He's right. I ought to go home.'

'I'll take you,' Nik said. 'If you like.'

'Don't put yourself out. Only if you're going my way.'

'I'm going your way.'

'But you don't know which way is mine.'

'Yes I do. Whichever way you go is your way. And I'll be with you, so I'm going your way.'

Julie laughed at last, indulging him.

NIK'S NOTEBOOK: I mean—it's grotesque. All that puppy-dog stuff. Can't believe I behaved like that. As if I'd lost control of my mind, as well as of my body. All a-tremble and saying pukey things. She must have thought I was some kind of schoolboy idiot, drooling over her like that. Not drooling exactly. Blethering.

I daren't think about the things I said on the way to her place. And I'm certainly not tapping them into this wp. The VDU would turn red from embarrassment (instead of staying green from envy of my brilliant mind, fantastic good looks, etc.).

Naturally, I just *had* to tell her about this batty film, didn't I! And she laughed, as any intelligent person would because it is unquestionably one big joke. So I came on all ho-ho-ho and smart-assed about it, which can't have been any more winning. I can't stand supercilious creeps, even when I myself am the supercilious creep I can't stand. She must have noticed. But she took it well.

I hope.

Selah.

I parted with the immortal words: Can I see you again sometime?

Gawd!

Yes, she said, and I nearly piddled myself. (Nearly relieved myself from relief!) Sunday morning, she said.

I knew from the way she said it what the catch was.

So long as I go to church with you?

Why not? she said. It'll be good for your research if not for your soul.

At least I didn't tell her, thank heaven, that I couldn't care less if it wasn't good for anything because I'd do anything for her right now.

But why would I?

It's not that she makes me randy. She does make me randy, no question. But her body wouldn't make me randy on its own. She isn't like the girl playing the Magdalene. Her body does the trick all on its own. What does it with Julie is something . . . *inside* . . . her body. Something I want to reach in and take hold of. The sex would be a way in. A pleasant way in, sure. But it wouldn't be for itself, like it would be with Mary M. Not just for the sensation, I mean.

I think I mean.

53

But what's the 'something' inside her that I want to get hold of? And how do I know it's there if I don't know what it is?

Come to think of it, it's like a black hole in space. We know it's there but we don't know what it is, and we don't really know yet what happens if you go into it. Maybe if you go into that dark magnetic space you suffer a total change. Become the opposite from everything you are now. Male to female. Weak to strong. White to black. Human to—what? Inhuman? Superhuman? Maybe you pop out through the binary white hole into a whole new universe? A bit risky. Or, of course, none of those things might happen. You might just vamoose. But fantastic. Worth the risk.

†

JULIE: I lie here now remembering that day. After you'd gone, looking so pleased with yourself, I got straight into a hot bath and soaked away the mud and soothed my bruises and thought, 'Oh dear, what now! Have I done the right thing?'

You see, even after just that first sopping hour together I knew you'd get serious about me, and that I'd have a job keeping myself from getting serious about you. And the trouble was—the trouble is—I hadn't planned on boyfriends. Not serious ones, anyway.

You weren't part of my scheme of things, dear Nik. Not at all.

INTERCUT: *Julie's room. An upstairs bedroom in a small terraced house. The walls are painted brilliant white, and are bare of all decoration except for a slender cross made from two pieces of sea-scoured driftwood which hangs in the middle of one wall. Beneath the cross stands a prayer desk of plain oak on which lies a Bible and a loose-leaf file containing passages from books, poems, and other writing Julie has copied out for use during meditation.*

Against the opposite wall is a single bed with a white-painted tubular frame. The bed is covered with a light blue counterpane that matches the curtains hanging at the only window. In the corner between the window and the prayer desk is a small armchair. Against the fourth wall, by the door, is a light wood bookcase full of mostly paperbacks. One shelf contains religious books; the other three hold novels, poetry, some biography. After that is a door to a wall cupboard where Julie keeps her clothes.

The bare deal floorboards are stained a shining dark oak colour. A strip of cheap, dark blue carpet lies by the side of the bed. The window looks out onto a small back garden—a garden shed, square of lawn, carefully tended vegetable patch chock-a-block with plants—and beyond, over the roofs of terrace houses stepping downwards, to the other side of the valley where some fields, then streets of houses, rise up to the skyline.

The window is open and sun is streaming in, but the curtains are not blowing in a breeze, summertime sounds cannot be heard. Only now do we realize that we are looking at stills. But the noise of a football match being shown on television seeps into the room from next door.

JULIE: I haven't told you this before. Didn't want to. Couldn't bring myself to, if I'm honest. But now I have to tell you, I think. It's time. Because whatever happens when they take off the bandages—whether I can see again or not—nothing will be the same as before, will it? Can't be.

[*Deep breaths in and out.*]

I think about it a lot. About when the bandages come off. And about the future after that. When we know for sure what's left of me. [*Chuckles.*] Not that I'm any the wiser for thinking about it so much. More confused, if anything. Except, I know some things that weren't decided before will be then. What you are to me, and what I am to you. That'll be the important thing the great unwrapping will make me—us—sure about.

You see, dear Nik, what I haven't told you is that for years I've thought that I want my life to be all for God.

[*Laughs.*]

I know, I know! But don't give yourself a hernia from hilarity. Lots of girls go through a nunnery phase just the same as they go through having crushes on hockey sticks and horses and pop stars and even on yummy teachers. I know that. But I

55

got over those things before I was fourteen. This is different. The same way it's different when people decide they'd like to become doctors or computer programmers or scientists. I want to be a God something. I don't know exactly what kind of something, but something for God.

I was trying to work out what that something would be when you came along. I was looking for the best way. A way that would be right for now, for today, and not a way that used to be right years ago but isn't any longer.

Not that I've said anything about it to anyone else. Mum knows, of course, and Dad, and my brother. Oh yes, and Philip Ruscombe. But no one else. I like to be sure of myself before I say anything to other people. And being a God-something isn't the sort of subject people talk about very easily without . . . well, without laughing, I suppose. They find it hard to believe you mean what you say, or that anyone could seriously want to do anything like that these days. So I was quietly sorting it out for myself. Till you came along.

Suddenly there you were, and I couldn't think why I cared. Not at the time. I remember lying in my bath that Saturday afternoon, half of me still smouldering with anger at the pagans, and the other half wondering what on earth it was about you that disturbed me so much. I mean, you aren't especially good looking. Sorry about that! You're fairly clever, I suppose, but you aren't a genius. And you're younger than I am. I don't mean only in years, but in yourself. You're still a schoolboy.

So I'm no fashion plate, and I'm not even as clever as you, but I do have a job, however lowly, and have had for two years. I feel like a grown-up woman, not a schoolgirl any more. [*Laughs.*] Yes, I know. But everyone can be wrong!

Apart from those things, you were big-headed. All the way home you made fun of everybody else. The leptonic OBD, the kids in the film group, Leonard Stanley, the CND organizers, the NF mob, the police. You were quite funny, I admit, but you were unkind too. So when you asked if you could see me again I only said yes because I thought you'd give up when you knew going to church was part of the bargain.

It wasn't until I was in the bath that I realized I wanted to see

56

you again, and wanted to see you in more than an ordinary way. I worried about that for a while, feeling as if I were betraying God or myself in some way. But then I thought, 'That's ridiculous. God will just have to take her chance.' And so will I. Because if I can't survive a crush on a bigheaded schoolboy, then I'm not likely to survive all the difficulties that'll be thrown at me if I work for God. So, I thought, 'Perhaps this quirky schoolboy is a sort of test, perhaps he's a temptation I can use to find out how determined I am. In which case, I might just as well relax about him and get on and see what happens.'

If I'm honest, though, I have to admit I didn't think you were much of a challenge. Didn't think you'd last long after church, even if you actually turned up. But here I am weeks later, still battling! And I've enjoyed every minute. Truly.

[*Pause.*]

What I'm trying to tell you is that I've got the same sort of feeling now that I had about you in my bath. And just like then, I don't know why. But this time the feeling says the test is near its crisis. That there'll be an end . . . No, that's wrong. Not an end but another beginning . . . Very soon. Which is why I want you to know, before it happens, the way things are. So that whatever happens there's no deception, and no pretence. Only honesty and truth. Or the truth as near as I can get to it.

Does this make sense? Do you understand?

I'll worry till I know.

REVELATIONS

That first Sunday morning, when Nik met Julie at her front door, she said, 'I don't mean to be rude, but would you mind if we didn't talk at all till after church? I'll explain later.'

'If that's what you want,' Nik said.

So they walked side by side, unspeaking, along empty streets, up through town to St James's, set on a hill above the hospital and below the cemetery.

Nik smiled to himself as they approached, thinking, 'On the trip from sickness to death stands the church of God, and it's uphill all the way.'

Julie plodded along with such abstracted concentration that she might have been by herself. Her gait was urgently mechanical, her eyes fixed on the ground ahead, unseeing.

What was going on? Nik wondered. What was she thinking about? Was she worried? Or feeling ill and forcing herself to church? Or fed up? She certainly didn't look pleased or happy.

No, she looked more like someone utterly absorbed in a book. Consumed. That was the word.

Julie yomping to church puzzled him. Which made him all the more curious.

NIK'S NOTEBOOK: Must the insides of churches be like deep-freeze warehouses? St James's is a late-Victorian stone pile with walls painted white to try and brighten the place up. But all this does is make it look cold as well as feel cold. Is this what Jesus Christ intended for his fans?

'Thou shalt build in my name large, cold mausoleums that shalt cost thee a bomb to keep up. These thou shalt perfume with the odour of damp dust, dirty underwear and dry rot. There shalt thou gather with glum faces, sit near the back, utter long prayers in mournful voices, sing tedious songs out of tune and very slowly, and generally give thyselves a thoroughly bad time.'

Not that I've been in many churches. None at all for ages, in fact. Maybe they've changed. Maybe they're terrific fun places now. But not St James's, that's for sure. I think the people who go there must be masochists. Or else they all have terrible guilt complexes and think going to church is a penance that they suffer for their sins in order to keep in with God.

One of the troubles I have with Christianity is that I don't feel guilty about anything. Maybe I'm a religious defective?

Selah.

There were sixteen people. I counted while Julie was kneeling down, doing her kick-start prayers after we got settled in a pew near the back. She wanted to take me nearer the front but I wouldn't let her. Who might be there and see me? I'd never live it down.

Early morning communion. You'd never get me up before ten on a Sunday morning for anything normally, and sitting there with the shivers waiting for the performance to start while Julie did her hands-together act beside me, I began to wonder why ever I'd got up so early this morning. Is Julie worth such sacrifice?

Mostly the sixteen were old women on their own. One young couple carrying a nearly new baby. Nobody paid any attention to anybody else. I thought Christianity was supposed to be about brotherly and sisterly love and doing unto others etc. Going by this morning's evidence, what Christians want others to do to them is pretend they aren't there. Not that I was there long enough to find out if things warmed up because I disgraced myself soon after the service started.

The trouble was caused by an old nun kneeling in the pew in front of me. Julie said afterwards that she was on holiday from her convent. I knew she was a nun because she was dressed in a dowdy grey frock and thick wool stockings and black clodhopper shoes. Her head was covered in a blue scarf-thing with a white face band. Nothing like the old-fashioned nuns in books, who always look weirdly fetching to me. I mean the ones in flowing robes tied with rope and with crucifixes and beads and holy baubles dangling all over them. And their faces peeking out from their fly-away wimples. The climb-every-mountain sort of nuns.

Well this modern C. of E. nun wasn't anything like that. She wasn't just dull, she was actively unattractive. I expect they think they should look as unfetching as possible so as to avoid dreadful temptations of the FLESH. The sins of the flesh always sound so cannibalistic. Not that you'd want a nibble at this old dame or make a pass at her of any kind unless you were ninety and feeling pretty desperate.

I wouldn't have paid her much attention except she was right in front of me and her insides kept gurgling like a water system with dicky plumbing. After a while, the eruptions went into another phase. She'd rumble, then there'd be a short pause. Then she'd let off a string of three or four very lady-like little farts. Nothing gross. And very quietly. So quiet in fact that I don't think she could hear them herself. But I could, being in direct line of fire. Maybe she was gunning for the heathen spy behind her.

At first I just smiled. Things got started. Old Vic came in dressed in a white nightgown with a piece of green curtain like a poncho over his shoulders and pottered about at the altar. He looked a lot better doing that than he looked when I talked to him. More at home, really. I could see he believed it all, just the same way you can tell when a good actor likes his part and is really into it. Completely absorbed. So I was getting interested in what was happening, and forgetting about the cold and how early it was. Meanwhile, old rumble-tum was bubbling and popping off in front of me.

But then the prayers started. I managed the Lord's Prayer all right. It's a great piece of writing when you come to think of it because it's so easy to remember and always seems okay to say even when you're not in the mood and don't actually believe all the other religious stuff. Like a great poem, I suppose.

At any rate, we got through that without any trouble. But then Old Vic launched into: 'Almighty God, unto whom all hearts be open [*rumble, gurgle*], all desires known [*glug*] and from whom no secrets are hid [*pause*]: Cleanse the thoughts of our hearts . . .'

And she pooped.

That did it. I started to get the giggles. Julie gave me the kind of sideways glare your mum does when you're little and being naughty, which didn't help. So I buried my face in my hands like a humble sinner having the thoughts of his heart cleansed, and hoped the noise of my half-stifled guffaws would be taken for the sound of a holy purgative at work.

Which I'm sure would have done the trick. Unfortunately, just as I was composing myself again, there came an ominously prolonged growl from the old girl's innards, followed by a cliff-hanger of a pause. Then she let loose a very unlady-like raspberry.

This Julie also heard. She gave the old girl a startled look, then glanced at me, who was watching events through my fingers. We eyed each other for a second. And then she broke up. She stuffed the knuckle of her thumb in her mouth and hung on to the prayer position, eyes front.

This sight did nothing for my equilibrium. Which was not at all helped, either, by my memory recalling at this inopportune moment that hymn they make you sing at infant school: 'God be in my head, / and in my understanding; / God be in my eyes, / and in my looking; / God be in my mouth, / and in my speaking; / God be in my heart and . . .' *Poop-poop.*

At which I really collapsed. I flung myself down behind the pew and rammed as much of my sweater into my mouth as it could take without suffocating myself. Here I slunk while the bout of laughter wracked my tortured frame.

O God, I thought, don't let me . . . don't let me . . .

(I've just realized this was the first time I've prayed since I was ten and asked for Mum back. When she didn't come, I decided God wasn't there after all or he'd have done something about it. As if God was nothing more than a megastar Santa Claus.)

So there I am, doubled up in this prayer box with a mouth full of sodden sweater, shaking with frustrated giggles, while Julie kneels beside me as rigid as a memorial, and the old nun goes on happily rumbling and pooping, and at the altar Old Vic tells the lord we're humbly sorry for all our sins, when this wizzened old guy appears in the aisle bending towards me with a worried look on his face and a glass of water in his hand and hissing: All right? . . . Like a drink?

Had to leave, nothing else for it. I'd have died if I hadn't or had hysterics. Death or cachinnation. Neither quite the thing in church. Not that church anyway. And I didn't want to make life worse for Julie, did I. A knave in the nave.

'I'm not sure you're fit to be let out in public,' Julie said afterwards.

'Why?' Nik said. 'Doesn't God have a sense of humour?'

'As she made you, I suppose she must have.'

'She?'

'Why not? If God is everything, that must mean God is a she as well as a he, mustn't it? So if you call God he, I don't see why I shouldn't call her she.'

'Or it, as he/she is everything and must therefore be stones and stars as well as male and female?'

'Why not?'

Nik shrugged. 'It's your God. But I didn't know you lot went in for such explosive worship.'

'She's a very old nun and a bit deaf.'

'And full of the power of the lord.'

'See what you're like at her age. If you live that long.'

'The trouble was, I thought maybe you'd want us all to join in with a rousing chorus of—'

'You're not going to turn crude, are you?'

'Is it a sin on Sundays?'

'No. Just tedious.'

'You weren't exactly the soul of solemnity yourself.'

'D'you always talk like that or only on your off days?'

'Depends on the company I keep. But it was funny, though. Admit it.'

'It was funny. But she's a dear old woman, and a friend of mine, and very devout. She'd be horrified if she knew.'

'Won't say a word, honest.'

They were walking back to Julie's house.

'Tell you what,' Nik said. 'You've taken me to your church. Now I'll take you to mine.'

'Surprise, surprise! Where?'

'Selsley Common.'

Julie laughed. 'With the kite flyers and the babies being aired and the dogs out for walkies.'

'And the cows. Don't forget the cows. Free range cows as

well. None of your battery farm religion up there. Not like your place, with everybody stuck in a pew being fattened up for heaven.'

'So you're a closet pantheist really. That explains your mucky mind.'

'No, no. You've got me all wrong. I'm not a pantheist. I'm a *pen*theist.'

'Oh dear!'

'Well, actually, if you must know, I just like a good view. Besides, when we get back to your place you might not invite me in, whereas, if we go up on the common—'

'It'll take the rest of this morning and half this afternoon, and I've promised to help with the cooking. So we'll go in my car, if you don't mind, and be back by eleven. Will that do?'

'You've got a car?'

'Don't get excited, it's not a Porsche.'

'I don't care if it's a motorized orange box, it's better than my leg-powered bike.'

'Never mind. When you're grown up you can put an engine in your pram and be just like all the other big boys.'

'Wow, thanks! Will I have to wait long?'

'About another twenty years at your present rate of progress.'

'That long!'

'Be glad. Most of your sex never grow out of being little boys.'

'Don't you like men?'

'When I can find any. There aren't that many around.'

NIK'S NOTEBOOK: She's not butch, I don't mean that. Just tough-minded. You wouldn't think so to look at her. And she's poker-voiced but not poker-faced. So just to hear her, you'd think she was as hard as nails. When you look at her, you know she's a kidder.

Her car is a prehistoric Mini she claims she maintains herself with a little help from her brother who just happens to be a motor mechanic. She treats it like she was ignoring it. Drives like that too. Functional precision.

I said: She goes well.

63

She, she said, refers to human beings. This is a machine and hasn't a soul.

I said: You don't like machines?

She said: They're all right. Very useful. But machines are machines. If you treat them like people you end up treating people like machines. Which I'm against.

I didn't argue about that because I don't know if she's right, but I shall have a think about it and when I've decided it'll make a nice subject for another day. And that's something else I like about her. Two things in fact. She makes me think. And she likes a good argument.

Selah.

Being such a Christian nation, the great British public was still fervently worshipping the lord between the sheets so, of course, the common was the way I like it. I.e.: Empty of the human animal. Except inevitably for one or two compulsive underwear flashers. It's amazing. It doesn't matter where you go or what time it is there's always at least one panting and puffing middle-aged duffer lolloping across the landscape like a lost soul everlastingly on the hunt for the way out.

Note for film: If Christ came back today, he'd have to turn up as a body-building health-freak jogging fanatic with a regular programme on TV. Otherwise, none of the great proletarian masses would pay him any attention at all. So I suggest we start the film with a TV ad in which our recycled Christ performs his first miracle: turning a titchy chickenwhite wimp of a man into a bronzed Tarzan by one application of New Messiah suntan oil and then telling him to take up his metal and pump. That done, he says, Follow me, and they go off together, jogging into an explosive sunrise, as the title CHRIST COMES AGAIN appears on the screen.

Selah.

We parked at the far end, near the cattle grid, and walked to the edge. The usual great view, clear enough today to see Wales and the Black Mountains. In the valley, the glint of the Severn snaking; the twin towers of Berkeley nuke power station, square tombs picked out by the sun; the bluff of the scarp fluffed with trees gloomy in shadow close by on the bend, hiding Bristol; in the other direction Haresfield Beacon blocking the view to Gloucester. And through the upriver gap, the Malvern hills breasting up from the plain. A sharp blue sky edging on the horizon to pale grey.

We were standing side by side taking it all in when a strange thing happened.

In a field steeply below us was a man. He was bending over, his hands in the grass. As we watched, he suddenly sprang up, a rabbit grasped in one hand by its back legs. As he rose, he swung the rabbit up into the air, caught its head in his other hand and brought it down, across his raised leg, snapping its neck sharply across his knee. Then he held the rabbit out at arm's length by the back legs.

The animal gave a number of convulsive kicks that made its body jerk and its loose head flop about. And the man, waiting for the death to end, looked up the hillside, where he saw us watching. He grinned, and raised his empty hand and waved, and when we didn't wave or move at all, he held the dying rabbit high above his head and shook it at us in triumph, making its head flip-flap again. Then he turned and set off down the field in a bounding kind of run, the rabbit jigging about in his hand, till he reached a gate in the hedge, vaulted over, and disappeared from sight.

For a while neither of us, so stunned, even blinked. Then Julie let out a painful, bitten cry and slumped to the ground, where she sat cross-legged, staring across the valley, stonefaced, but her eyes pleading.

I waited, not knowing what to do or to say. What I wanted, just like yesterday, was to touch her, take hold of her. Yesterday I didn't. Couldn't. Today, seeing the bleakness of her, frozen there, a kind of grieving, I couldn't not. So I crouched down and put my arms round her.

STOCKSHOT: . . . *by history and parables we are nourished; by allegory we grow; by morality we are perfected . . .*

†

Something niggled at the back of Tom's mind. A hunch.

His sense of smell was as acute as Nik's sense of touch. And the old man at the scene-of-crime had smoked roll-your-owns. Had reeked of it, even in the open air, a musky-sweet acidy stench coming off his mucky sweater. Tom had disliked him at once, and not only because of the stink of tobacco. More because of the cheery pretence of being co-operative that didn't hide well enough a suspicious attitude.

One of the first things Tom had learned to recognize after joining the force was the prejudice, the mistrust, the dislike, that many people harboured against the police. For a while this had upset him; after all, he only wanted to uphold the law; and people were pretty quick to call the police when they were in trouble. But soon he had grown a skin thick enough to protect himself. 'As a copper,' the sarge had told him one day when Tom was beefing about the way someone had treated him, 'you're on your own. Don't ever expect anybody to help you. Then all you'll get are nice surprises.'

Besides, in criminal investigation the first rule is that nobody's above suspicion; not even yourself. So why care what people think? Mugs or villains, they're all the same because anybody can break the law. Some do more often than others, and some worse than others, that's all. Nobody's honest, everybody's a villain, and his job was to stop them if he could and catch them if he couldn't. As he enjoyed the excitement of running a villain to earth more than the steady plod of prevention, he'd always wanted to be a detective. Now he had an unexpected early chance to prove he was up to the job. And he was damned if he was going to balls it up.

What he needed was to know the chat. That was what all the CID bods started with. Straight on the blower to their snouts, thus saving themselves time and leg work. But not being a CID man yet, Tom didn't have any snouts to bell. Never mind, everybody had to begin sometime, and there was no time like the present.

At this present time of day there was only one place where the juvenile scum would be. Though eleven-thirty was early for the best mouths. They'd still be festering in their pits, giving themselves hand jobs over page three while waiting for their mums to nag them downstairs for mid-day fish and chips. But you never knew your luck.

Tom parked in the multi-storey and walked through the shopping precinct to the snooker hall.

†

'My arm's going to sleep,' Julie said, easing away.

'Pity,' Nik said, 'I was enjoying that.'

'Let's walk a bit. The breeze is cool.'

They got up and sauntered. A few more people were about by now. A pair of early teenage girls on podgy ponies cantered by. Further along, two young men, all togged up, eye-catching, prepared a hang-glider for flight, fitting together the jigsaw of the glider's bits and pieces.

'This job you do,' Nik said. 'What is it?'

'Nothing special. I'm a dogsbody in reception at a health centre in Gloucester. I see the patients in, type letters, keep records, run errands for the doctors—that kind of thing.'

'You're going to be a doctor?'

Julie laughed. 'No no! I'm not clever enough for that. It's just a job. Not that I'd want to be a doctor, even if I could. Too squeamish. As you saw just now.'

Nik, not smiling, said, 'Was that really squeamishness?'

Julie, glancing at him, shook her head. 'Not just.' Her mouth was drawn tight. 'Can't bear wanton cruelty.'

They walked a few paces in silence, letting the after-image fade. The cantering girls went galloping heavily by close enough to smell the animals' body heat and feel the earth shudder beneath their feet.

'Do you ride?' Nik asked.

'No. I did go through the phase of wanting to, though. Desperately. But the nearest I got was riding a bike, which I gather,' laughing, 'doesn't provide quite the same thrill.'

Nik, laughing too, said, 'They say it's all sex really.'

'Some people say everything is all sex really.'

'Do you?'

'Do you?'

'Well—'

'Come on, be honest.'

'Can't say. Haven't enough experience to know.'

Julie snorted. 'Ha! There's a cop-out for you.'

'But it's true! I don't have enough experience to know.'

'Will you ever?'

'What's this—sixth-form phil. and psych.?'

Julie, mocking, said, 'Fill and sike!'

'Philosophy and psychology,' Nik said, not taking the bait.

'Nothing so grand,' Julie said. 'Only just managed fifth-form English and maths. Didn't even get as far as the sixth form, never mind fill and sike.'

'You don't seem to do badly without.'

'Common sense, that's all.'

'So do you think it's all sex really?'

'I'm not quite that out of date.' There was self-defensive sharpness in her voice.

'And,' Nik said, enjoying this sign of weakness, 'you've enough experience to know?'

'No one can ever have enough experience to know. I mean, to know the answer to a question like that. Though some people pretend to.'

'So?'

'You're teasing.'

'No, I'm not.'

'But it's obvious.'

Nik shrugged. 'Then tell me.'

'Some things you know from your own experience, yes? Some you know because other people you trust tell you about them from their experience, yes?'

'Okay so far.'

'But no matter how much you set out to experience, you can't ever experience everything. Not in one lifetime.'

Nik thought a moment before saying, 'Agreed.'

'And no matter how much you trust other people, you can't know for certain they're telling the truth about the things you can't experience for yourself.'

'True.'

'But you *believe* them because you trust them. So some things you only know because of belief. Because of faith. Yes?'

Nik pretended to puke at having fallen into Julie's trap. 'Okay, yes, put like that.'

Julie pulled a face at his vulgarity. 'How else can you put it?'

Their path was taking them close by the hang-glider. It was fitted together now, a large, neat, kite-like toy, hard to imagine carrying anyone safely into the air. A challenge to courage. The pilot, however, was preparing to take off. Nik and Julie stopped to watch as he harnessed himself to the frame, helped by his friend, gathered himself, ran, and launched into the air.

'Would you like to do that?' Julie asked.

'Not a lot,' Nik said, shading his eyes from the glare of the sky with a hand the better to see the pilot's progress. 'Would you?'

'Yes. Must be fun. Think he'll make it?'

'Probably. There's a good breeze now, and he looks as if he knows what he's doing.'

'But you don't know he will.'

' 'Course not. Do you?'

'No. But I believe he will. So do you.'

Nik grinned, eyes still on the glider fluttering a few metres above the scarp. 'Does it matter whether I do or not? It's his funeral.'

Julie gave him a doubting glance. 'You say that, but you don't really mean it.'

'I don't?'

'You're not that callous. Least, I hope you aren't, or I've misread you. You're just avoiding the argument.'

Nik grinned at her. 'Sure? How do you know?'

Julie shrugged. 'What would you do if you knew he couldn't manage, and would fall and kill himself?'

'But I don't know that.'

'But if you did? Really *knew*.'

'All right, what you want me to say is that I'd try and stop him.'

'Yes. But *would you*?'

They were eye to eye now.

'You're being serious,' Nik said.

'I'm being serious.'

'Okay, yes, I'd try and stop him.'

The glider, sails smacking, wobbled, dipped, slewed, steadied, hung for a moment between up and down, and at last soared, slipping and pawing, out and up and away over the valley, rising into the absorbing sky.

'You believed he could,' Julie said, sitting on a bench, 'or you wouldn't have stood by watching him try.'

INTERCUT: *Long shot of a lake in northern Sweden. Late summer. Evening. The sun has just set. The lake, shaped like a Y, is surrounded by undulating low hills, some covered in fir and birch, a few with fields of grass and ripe corn. The water is mirror flat, reflecting in its darkness a cloud-cushioned sky.*

A small rowing boat sits in the middle of the lake, at the elbow of the Y. A figure in the boat rests on oars, very still. The only movement comes from a dabble of ducks feeding and larking along the edge of the water nearest our view, and from a finger of white smoke rising unruffled from the chimney of a wooden cabin painted rust-red which is set on the brow of a hill at the edge of a wheat-blond cornfield that runs down to the lake near the foot of the Y. The only sounds are from the cackling ducks and the occasional echoing calls of a searching water bird.

Nik and Julie sat for a moment taking in the view.

'Why didn't you want to talk on the way to the church?' Nik asked when they had looked their fill. 'You said you'd explain.'

'Do I have to?'

'Yes. Research: Believers, behaviour of.'

'In that case, did you make a note of your own behaviour just now?'

'I'm not a trustworthy specimen.'

'Can't say I like being thought of as a specimen.'

'That's what we all are, us animals, didn't you know?' Nik said. 'We're all each other's specimens. We're all observed and we're all observers of everybody else. You even believe Big Brother God—sorry, Big Sister God—is watching us all, all the time. The spy in the sky.'

'Do I?'

'What then?'

'Another day perhaps.'

'I've annoyed you.'

'No.'

'Irritated you.'

'You're a smarty-pants sometimes.'

'Only meant in fun. Self-protection even, if I'm honest. I want to know. Really.'

'If you're that keen.'

'I'm that keen. Cross my heart and hope to die.'

A young mother with a toddler hooked by its podgy hand to one of her fingers went strolling by at baby pace, mother-and-child a confession of pride.

When they'd passed out of earshot Julie said, 'I was concentrating, that's all.'

'What on?'

'The service.' She looked at him, testing his seriousness. 'On God.'

'You mean you were praying,' Nik said.

To their left the second hang-glider took off, a more confident launch than the first, and laddered its way into the sky.

'The thing is,' Nik said, 'I'm not sure exactly what you were concentrating on.'

'The Gospel for the day.'

'What does that mean?'

'If you'd kept your mind on the service,' Julie said, smiling at him, 'instead of making fun of poor old Sister Ann, you wouldn't have had to leave in disgrace, and would know what the Gospel for the day was.'

'But I didn't, I did, and I don't.'

'Every time the Eucharist—the Holy Communion, the mass, whatever you want to call it—is celebrated, a passage from one of the Gospels is read out. I was thinking about the one set for today.'

'Which was?'

'The Feeding of the Four Thousand.'

'You mean the Five Thousand.'

'No, I mean the Four Thousand. If you'd done your research better you'd know there are two stories.'

'It happened twice?'

'According to Mark and Matthew. Luke and John

only mention the Five Thousand. That story comes up in November. On the twenty-fifth Sunday after Trinity to be exact.'

'It all seems pretty unlikely to me. But what were you thinking about?'

'Not about whether it happened, anyway. I'm not very bothered whether it did or didn't. Seems to me the literal truth about most things is never very interesting. What I was thinking about was what the story means. That's the important thing. Jesus gave the four thousand food and after they'd shared it there were seven basketsful left over.'

'Twelve after the Five Thousand.'

'You've done some research!'

'And what were you thinking?'

'I was thinking how odd it is that supposedly Christian countries like ours and the USA and France and Germany and Italy have so much food we let it go to waste or hoard it, while non-Christian countries like India and most African nations are starving. And how both the story of the four thousand and the one about the five thousand are about sharing. They're about Christ giving everybody who was there enough to eat so that they could stay and hear what she wanted to tell them.'

'She!' Nik laughed.

'Leave that for now, till we've done with the loaves and fishes. It's pretty shaming when you think of it like that. We hang on to the spare food we've got, while other people starve. No wonder they don't want to listen to us. Never mind that it's a sin, a real disgrace, that we behave so selfishly. So murderously, in fact. Because keeping food from a starving person, when you've got enough food to keep her alive, really is murder, isn't it? There's no other word you can honestly use for it, and nothing can excuse it, either.'

Julie drew breath.

Nik said, 'But if you think that, why do you stay a Christian?'

'Because I am a Christian. I believe in Christ. It isn't Christ's fault that we murder other people. It's ours.'

'Okay, I suppose what I mean is, why do you stay a member of the church?'

'I didn't say it was the church's fault, either. I said it was what the so-called Christian countries did. That's different.'

'You mean most of the people in the Christian countries aren't really Christians?'

'Isn't that obvious? But even if it were all the church's fault—and, sure, the church is partly to blame—I'd still remain a member for all sorts of reasons.'

'Like?'

'One of them is that Christ is the image of God getting her hands dirty and I'm one of God's people. You can't put anything right by abandoning it. You only abandon something if you think it's finished, or so far gone it's beyond redemption. Sometimes, I'll be honest, I do feel as if the world, or people anyway, have had it and might as well be dumped. But then I remember I'm a person myself, no better than anybody else, and that I'd rather not be dumped, if you don't mind. Besides, God didn't think we were beyond redemption so she got stuck in and dirtied her hands in order to help put things right. That's what the story of Christ is about. And so that's the least I can do.'

She paused.

'Anyway, that's what I was thinking on the way to church. Since you asked!'

Nik said, 'You should be a priest.'

Julie laughed. 'The thought had occurred!'

'Your sermons would be a lot better than most, that's for sure.'

NIK'S NOTEBOOK: She wasn't preachy, though. I mean, she wasn't trying to make me accept what she was saying. Wasn't trying to convince me or convert me. More like she was thinking aloud. Trying to sort something out for herself. The kind of thinking aloud that makes you interested, even if before that you were bored stiff with the subject.

It's strange. She's convinced, but unsure. I can't think how to express it. It isn't that she doubts, but that she isn't satisfied that she's got it right yet. She's a believer who you feel won't be happy—no, that's wrong . . . Who won't be *content* till she's solved a vast, complicated mystery. And she's working at it all the time.

Selah.

So she made me think about the Feeding of the Four/Five Thousand. Afterwards, I tried doing what she said she'd been doing. Concentrating on the story. Just to see what doing that felt like. And to see if the same sort of things came into my mind as came into hers.

They didn't. What struck me wasn't that there turned out to be enough food for everybody to eat all they wanted and leave great basketsful behind (so litterbugs are biblical as well). That's fairly predictable when you think about it. I mean, if everybody shared what they had with them, because this guy they admired started them off by sharing the loaves and fishes he and his mates had brought with them, then naturally there'd be more than enough. That's what happens at bring-your-own parties. They always end up drowned in drink and buried in food.

No, the really interesting thing, I think, is that four and/or five thousand people came all that way to be with him. (*They've been with me three days now . . . some of them have come from a distance.*: Mark 8, vv. 2,3.) Nobody yomps across miles of rugged country in scorching hot weather just to be with a schlunk. And in those days in that area there can't have been a big population. So a high percentage of the locals must have turned out for the jaunt. Which means there must have been quite a lot of something about him.

If it happened at all, of course. The whole thing might be just a fiction. I.e.: all cod.

Is God a cod?

Were the loaves fishy?

Have we used our loaves about the five thousand?

Were the five thousand only bait on a hook in a crook's book?

If so, who was shooting the line? Jesus of Nazareth?

Didn't he have better fish to fry than a few thousand poverty-stricken peasants from an outback area of one of the third-world outposts of the Roman Empire?

In brief: Was Jesus a con-man?

74

Seems to me a good con has to be (1) easy to set up, (2) simple in design so that there's as little as possible that can go wrong and give the game away, (3) that it's quick in yielding results, and (4) that it's hard to detect.

If the Loaves and Fishes a con:

+ It didn't yield anything except twelve and/or seven basketsful of leftovers that must have already started ponging badly in the hot sun, and that the conman and his gang had to pick up off the ground after the punters had gone home.

Whoever heard of a conman who stayed around to pick up rotting litter after the show?

+ It was far from simple in design or organization. For example, where would you hide the loaves and fishes to feed five thousand hungry people when you were stuck in the middle of nowhere? How would you cart all the stuff there unnoticed, when transport was by man or donkey power? How would you keep all that fish from going off without freezers to keep it in? And how could you know beforehand how many people would turn up and so be sure you had enough for all?

Anybody who tried a dodge like that in the middle of nowhere would have to be an idiot. And anybody taken in by it would have to be a jerk. Was Jesus an idiot? Were all his fans jerks?

Or is the story a fraud? And does it matter? Julie doesn't think it does. So how can she believe in something that's supposed to be historically true while thinking that it probably never happened?

Selah.

That's as far as I got before I gave up. More questions at the end than when I started. I quite enjoyed it, but I'm not sure it did anything for me.

†

The local snooker hall was no prettier than an old lag at the best of times. That morning, a couple of blacked-out windows had been opened, allowing in thin daylight that made the neons above the tables look like they couldn't get it on for yawning,

75

and letting out too little of the stale stink of cold fag. Tom's nose twitched.

Burleigh the bouncer was there, as usual, banging away as if a snooker table was a pinball machine. At another table, In-off Jones was playing a spotty-faced youth. Tom didn't know the name. Thirteen? World champion before fourteen. Didn't anyone ever ask why he wasn't in school? He was already three up and it looked like In-off wouldn't visit the table.

None of these any use. But lounging against the wall as far from the grey stream of daylight as he could get, a sour smirk on his designer-stubble face, was Tom's lucky strike.

He sidled up with suitably nonchalant deference so as not to spook his quarry.

'Morning, Sharkey,' he muttered in the required bored and offhand manner.

'It is?' Sharkey said, flat as last week's beer.

'Early for you.'

'Late, more like.'

'All-night job, was it?'

Sharkey sniffed. 'Job? Don't know about no job.'

Tom chuckled. 'Bird, I mean, Sharkey. Nothing nasty.'

Sharkey gave Tom an appraising glance. 'Never talk sex before the pubs open. Bad for the heart.'

'First I knew you had one.'

Sharkey spat at his feet. 'Jokes is even worse. Give me violent headaches. Specially bad ones.'

'No sex, no jokes! What's left to talk about?'

Sharkey's body showed signs of coming alive. 'Honest, Tommy, I wish you wouldn't. Does terrible things to my reputation just bein seen with you.'

'In here! Come on, Sharkey! Bouncer can't remember where his backside is when he wants to wipe it, never mind who he's seen together. In-off is one of your own. That spotty kid has cue balls for eyes. Why be anti-social?'

'Pimpin for the super is it?'

'You're not to his taste, Sharkey, you'll be happy to know. Anyway, I'm not on duty, am I?'

'Not on duty! When are you lot ever off? Listen, Tommy, I'll tell you. It give me a horrible shock when I see you geared in blue. You was always all right at school. A bit on the swatty side, I admit, but a knockout at the footer and generally speakin on the right side. I quite liked you then. But when you come out in blue I thought, my God, you can't trust nobody no more if a nice straight guy like Tommy goes and does the dirty. So do us a favour, eh?'

'Just what I am doing.' Tom turned his back to the room and spoke with befitting secrecy. 'There's some damage on hand.'

'Oh, yes? Your bike had its tyres let down?'

Tom waited a tolerant pause. 'Listen, Sharkey, I'm putting myself on the line to help you a bit. Okay?'

Sharkey stuck a greasy-nailed finger into his ear and wobbled it about. 'Am I hearin right? You're helpin me?'

'This is very nasty damage I'm talking about, Sharkey. And the super has you down for the villain. He's thinking of having a fatherly chat.'

'Need to send more than you to bring me in.'

'I told you, I'm off duty. Here to help. In my own time. Don't know where you are, do I? Haven't seen you for days.'

'Your boss wants me, and you come warnin me off. What do you want, Tommy?'

'Last night a young bloke was hung on a cross by person or persons unknown.'

Sharkey gave a noiseless whistle. 'Very nasty!'

Tom nodded. 'As I said. He was found this morning but disappeared before we got to him.'

'I can see why your boss might be a touch off colour.'

'And why he's acting supersonic.'

Sharkey tutted. 'A supersonic super! Very good, Tommy. You're comin on.'

'And you'll be coming in, Sharkey, unless a few answers are found smartish. Like who did it.'

'Not me, that's for sure. I'm a Catholic. I wouldn't go round crucifying people, for God's sake!'

'Didn't know you were religious.'

'I'm not.'

'You just said you're Catholic.'

'That don't mean I'm religious, though, do it? I mean, I'm

not one of them fanatics, always prayin and goin on about God and bein saved. That's obscene.'

'But you go to mass and make your confession and get forgiven and all that caper?'

'Now and then. Not a lot, but enough.'

'Well, how much is enough?'

Sharkey shifted uneasily. 'Enough, that's all! How the hell do I know, I'm not a priest. And I'm no saint, neither, I know that. I go when I feel like it and that's enough for me.'

'But you believe in it, all that about God and Christ?'

'You have to believe in somethin, don't you? Any idiot knows that. Anyway, I was brought up that way. All my family goes. Even my old man goes a couple of times a year so there must be somethin in it cos he don't believe nothin till it stands up and hits him.'

'Pity he doesn't go a bit more often. Might have kept him out of the nick.'

'Yeah, well, him bein in the nick doesn't have nothin to do with God. That was your lot did that.'

'What, putting him away because he couldn't resist climbing through other people's windows and carting off a few items of their property? Thou shalt not steal. Isn't that what it says?'

'He was out of a job and doin the best he could for the family. Not that a rozzer like you would understand family loyalty. You'd shop your own grandmother if it helped your record.'

'That's a bit unfair, Sharkey, seeing I'm standing here trying to help you so you don't get any aggro for something you didn't do.'

'Sure you are, Tommy, and I'm still waitin to hear what you're gettin out of it.'

'Enlightened self-interest, Sharkey. That's what keeps the world turning, didn't your dad tell you? You scratch my back and I'll scratch yours. I'm tipping you the wink about my super having the hots for you. If I can tell him some interesting news, like I've got a lead on the villains, I reckon I can hold him off for today while he checks it out. That'll give you time to use your considerable powers of persuasion among your friends and come up with a whisper. Somebody has to know something.

Shouldn't be too hard for you to give us a pointer that I can pass on to my guv. The culprit or culprits get collared and you get left alone. I get in good with the super, and that'll do me for now.'

'Very neat,' Sharkey said with undisguised distaste. 'You'll make nice pork.'

'Thanks for the compliment.'

'Any time.'

Tom sighed. 'So don't bother. Let the super talk to you himself. I don't care. You're clean, you know that. You can prove you were somewhere else at the time in question. Why should you worry?'

Sharkey took a deep breath. 'Yeah, yeah.'

''Course, you'll be held on suspicion for a day or two. Till we check out your alibi. And while the super is concentrating on you and your mates, whoever strung the kid up will be spoiling the scent.'

Sharkey pushed himself from the wall and took an agitated couple of steps away and back again. 'All right, all right!' he said. 'I don't like what happened no more than you. But I don't like bein fitted up neither. Which is what this is. I know what you're up to, Tommy, and I tell you, it's worse than anythin I ever do. Next thing, if I don't do what you want, you'll plant something evil as evidence against me.'

Tom looked suitably aggrieved. 'Come on, Sharkey, you've got me all wrong! I'd never do a thing like that!'

'Not right this minute, you wouldn't. Not this time. But you will, one day when you want a villain bad enough you'll do it. And you'll tell yourself, what the hell, he's a villain anyway; if he didn't do this he did some other job we didn't catch him for, so what's the odds. That's your sort of thinkin, Tommy. You always did act innocent, even at school, but underneath you're as evil-minded as all your mob.'

Tom looked Sharkey eye to eye, heated himself now. 'It won't happen, I tell you!' he said through his anger.

Sharkey grinned his bright teeth.

Tom looked away first. The room was unchanged from a few moments ago, the click of colliding balls echoing as in a dismal cave. He hitched his jeans and composed himself.

'Up to you,' he said, his voice still not relaxed, and shrugged, thinking he had lost.

But Sharkey spat and moved towards an empty table. He picked up a white ball from the baize and bowled it with a twist of his wrist that sent it bouncing off the opposite cushion, another and another, before returning precisely to his waiting fist.

'The car park behind Hill Pauls at half-one,' he said.

Tom couldn't help smiling. 'I knew you'd see sense.'

Sharkey sent the ball careering round the table again.

'Piss off,' he said. 'You bog the place up.'

INTERCUT: *The Swedish lake in longshot, as before. Hold the scene: the dying sun's rays glancing on hilltops, the hut in dusk-time shadow with the white ribbon of smoke rising, the little boat utterly still on the water. Five seconds. Then pull a steady, unhurried, soft-focus zoom towards the boat and its occupant.*

'Now it's my turn,' Julie said as they walked back to her car.

'For what?'

'Research. You've been investigating me. Now it's my turn to investigate you.'

The hang-glider came swooping to earth a hundred metres ahead of them, the pilot planting his feet neatly on the ground in a fine judgement of speed and height and moment of stall.

'It's all very well,' Julie said, 'being superior and snooty about religion and other people's beliefs—'

'I'm not!'

'Yes, you are. But are you really telling me you've never wondered about God?'

'Naturally. Doesn't everybody?'

'All right then, not just wondered but—I don't know—experienced anything?'

Nik gave her an uneasy side-glance. 'What sort of thing?'

They strolled past the hang-glider, now again a lifeless kit of spars and stretched sailcloth which the pilot was dismantling for transport in a bag you'd have thought far too small to hold a flying machine that could carry a man into the air.

'I don't know,' Julie said. 'Something that made you sure, even for just a minute, that there's more to all this—' she waved a hand at the view—'than some sort of meaningless accident with meaningless ingredients inside the meaningless stewpot of a meaningless universe.'

Nik smiled at her. 'Do you always talk like that or only on Sundays?'

Julie grinned back. 'Depends on the company I keep.'

They walked a few paces in silence.

'Yes,' Nik said, forcing himself. 'Something happened once.'

When he didn't go on, Julie said, 'Are you going to tell me or leave me in suspense?'

'I haven't told anybody before.'

'If you don't want to—'

'No, it's not that. Not with you, anyway.'

'Was it embarrassing?'

Nik laughed. 'Not embarrassing. A bit silly maybe.'

It was last summer. Grandad took me to Sweden. I live with my grandad, did I tell you? He was in the merchant navy for a long time and made friends with some Swedes then. That was quite a long time ago but they've kept in touch. Christmas cards, a letter now and then.

When he retired last year he decided he'd have a holiday, go to Sweden, and look up his old mates. He took me with him for company, and because he thought it would do me good. He's always going on about me seeing more of life instead of getting it out of books. He's not a big reader, isn't Grandad. Not a reader at all, as a matter of fact. For him, books are a last resort.

Anyway, he took me with him and I enjoyed myself most of the time. We ended up in northern Sweden, not far from the Arctic Circle, and Grandad met his old mates, three of them, and they all got high on the excitement of being together again.

'Come to the forest,' they said, which apparently is the big thing with Swedes when they want to let their hair down and have a good time and be specially friendly. So they bought a car-load of food and booze and drove us off for miles into the country to a little wooden house, more a hut really, all by itself in a field beside a lake surrounded by hills.

That was quite interesting because the cottage had been the farmhouse where one of the men had been born and where his father had been born and where his parents had lived all their lives. The place was pretty well unchanged. There were only two rooms. The biggest had an open fire with a huge brick oven behind that you could sleep on top of in winter to keep warm. There was no electricity and no running water. And an outside dry lav that stank. We had to use Gaz lamps and carry water in plastic containers from a modern house a quarter of an hour's walk away.

We camped there for four days. Most of the time the men spent sitting around remembering the old days, telling stories about life on the rolling road in tramp steamers and grumbling about how dreadful it all is now with modern tankers and ships that just about sail themselves automatically and crews that are pampered and don't know anything about real seamanship.

I got fed up with that fairly soon. There was a small rowing boat belonging to the house so I started going off in that and exploring the lake and the shore around it. And I would land somewhere and walk through the forest. The Swedes have a law that allows you to go where you like because the land is supposed to be for everybody. So you don't have to worry about trespassing or tetchy farmers like you have to here. There was masses of wildlife to see as well.

Well, one evening I was walking through a wood when I saw a bull elk. It came looming out of the trees into a clearing. I nearly panicked. I'd no idea they're so big. So strong and bulky. They've huge flattened antlers, really amazing in size, that grow out of their heads like the branches of a tree and make them look top heavy. And they've overpowering hind quarters that squash the breath out of you just to look at. Fearsome. But magnificent. Lordly. They really are. Proud. Regal. I could see why people use words like that.

He mesmerized me. I couldn't move, just stood there staring at him and feeling like an idiot. He looked me up and down and sniffed and then stalked off quite slowly as if I was beneath contempt.

When he was gone I felt so weak I had to sit down till I was calm and got my strength back again. I felt like I'd had a shock. I was shaking all over, my heart was beating fast, I was panting, the bones had gone out of my legs, and I couldn't think at all, never mind think straight. And all the time I was grinning inanely. If anybody had seen me they'd have thought I was mad.

As soon as I recovered, all I wanted to do was get back to the cottage and tell Grandad what I'd seen. But when I arrived they were already three sheets to the wind, as Grandad says, and at the stage of laughing loudly and singing bawdy seamen's songs in raucous voices. That made me spitting angry. I was desperate to tell Grandad about the elk and there he was, that stupid with booze he couldn't have understood even if he'd have listened.

There was nowhere I could get away from them in the cottage. And nobody else for miles, except the local farmer and his family where we got the water, but they hardly spoke any English even if I'd felt like going to them, which I didn't. I didn't fancy wandering about in the forest again either. I did think of sitting like a spare part in the car listening to music on the radio till they were all so blotto they collapsed. But they might have taken it into their heads to drive off somewhere, and I'd have been trapped with them, which didn't appeal at all. The only thing left was to take the boat out on the lake. At least I'd be well away from them, and I thought a good stiff row might do me good.

So I ran down the field and pushed off in the boat and rowed like crazy up and down the lake till I was drenched in sweat and was choking for breath and could hardly see for blood pumping in my eyes and my arms couldn't pull another stroke. I felt like those guys look at the end of the boat race every year, the ones who lose. You know—the way their bodies slump over their oars and their faces are twisted in agony and they're gasping. And somehow I felt I'd failed too.

I sat like that, letting the boat drift in the middle of the lake till I got my breath back and my muscles stopped snapping like overstretched elastic, and my mind settled down to being as normal as it ever is, and my ears stopped popping, and my eyes were seeing properly again.

INTERCUT: *The shot of the lake. Zoom in to a close-up of the figure in the boat till he fills the screen, head to middle: Nik. We watch as he does what he describes in a voice-over:*

And it was then the thing I'm trying to tell you about happened.

As I came to my senses, everything suddenly seemed clearer. There were some birds, some ducks, dabbling about on the edge of the lake and their calls seemed sharper than I could ever remember hearing any noise before. They were all I could hear. Everywhere else was complete silence which the noise of the ducks seemed to make intense, so that the silence was like a noise itself.

My hands were resting on the oars and I could feel the grain of the wood, though up till then they'd seemed smooth. The sun had set, there wasn't a breath of wind. It was the time when you can almost see the dusk creeping in. But that evening everything stood out sharply as I looked, and the colours, though they weren't bright like in sunlight, seemed to glow with a sort of purity I'd never seen before.

And as I looked a deep sense of peace came over me, a calmness that wasn't at all like feeling relaxed, but made me feel full of energy while being quite still inside. And it was as if time was . . . not stopped . . . but waiting. Hanging in the air. I felt I was looking into eternity and that nothing mattered any more because everything was in harmony, like a marvellous tune. Nothing mattered and yet everything mattered, every smallest detail, and all was well at last.

I sat there in the middle of the lake expecting that this strange sensation would pass. But it didn't. I didn't move, just stared and stared in a sort of happiness I didn't want to break. I watched the sky slowly change as dusk turned to night and stars came out, needle-sharp points of light in a darkening, deepening blueblack vastness that made me feel I was shrinking smaller and smaller till a sort of pain came over me, a mixture of joy because of the beauty of it all and sadness because of my insignificance compared with all that unendingness. But I was part of it, however unimportant I was. And I wanted to be totally in it. Absorbed into it, not separate.

And then, when the stars were fully out and it was night, even though there was still light on the horizon because of how far north we were, the strangest thing of all happened.

I started getting a hard-on. Honest! I'm not just being rude. I had an erection! And I wanted it—all that out there, I mean. I wanted all that—I don't know . . . nature. Peace. Eternity. Whatever it was. Like wanting a girl. I wanted to be in it and to possess it. Wanted to belong to it and wanted it to belong to me. And I wanted to hold it in my hands and feel it with my body. And . . . honest . . . I wanted to come in it!

I know this must sound mad. But it didn't seem like that at the time. It seemed natural. I wasn't surprised or ashamed or anything like that. I just felt this overpowering desire. Stronger than anything I've ever felt before.

I didn't think about it. I just stood up in the boat, and quite deliberately, as if I was performing a sacred act, a ritual ceremony, I took off my clothes, one thing after another, folded them up neatly, which I never do usually, and laid them in the stern.

Then, when I was completely naked, I stood erect, everything erect!, and looked around, all around, part of me still expecting this strange mood to pass, but it didn't. The air was cold by then, northern cold, the cold that comes off snow. And the cold of the air felt as sharp and alive to my skin as the colours and shapes of everything were to my eyes and the sounds and silence, the silence most of all, were to my ears.

And I loved it. Desired it. Was randy for it. Wanted to be in it. And there was only one way. I put a foot on the gunwale, pushed up, and jumped.

I went in feet first, straight down into the dark water. The air felt cold, but the water was freezing. God, it was cold! Knocked the breath out of me like a punch. And knocked down what was standing up as well. Like a fist of ice grabbing the goolies!

As soon as I surfaced I started laughing. And the air felt warm so I splashed about a bit just for the fun of it. Then hauled myself into the boat, shivering, all passion spent!

And I tell you, I shall never forget that evening. Never. It's as clear to me now as it was then. And I know it will be all my life.

'That must sound pretty ridiculous,' Nik said.

'No, it doesn't,' Julie said.

'Every detail,' Nik said, 'still sharp. Especially the feeling of happiness and peace and wanting to be part of the vastness. Whatever the vastness was . . . Is.'

'God,' Julie said.

Nik snorted. 'I knew you'd say that.'

'Sorry I'm so predictable.'

They had arrived at Julie's car. She unlocked the passenger door. As Nik stooped to climb in, she kissed him lightly on his passing cheek. Nik checked himself and turned his head, hoping for more. But Julie was already on her way to the driver's seat.

†

Tom waited. After his talk with Sharkey he'd felt pleased, spending the time since then running and rerunning his performance, rewriting the script where he felt he had done badly, storing away the better moments for use again in future. What excited him most was the prospect of hooking Sharkey as a regular snout. His first, and quite a catch. As ageing leader of the town's least prissy teen squad, Sharkey knew everybody that mattered among the juves, and was well placed with the grown-up pros. He'd be a prime source of hot gossip.

A wary predator, was Sharkey, and, true to his name, always on the move. But, thought Tom, predators can be preyed on. Kept alive, given enough time, enough rope, they led you to more tasty fish. Already there were the makings of a useful relationship. Act the clever weakling, Tom told himself. Let Sharkey snap and bite and play the big man all he wants. Make him believe he can break free whenever he likes, and flatter him. But every now and then give the line a jerk. Then he would spit out the juicy gobbets he'd swallowed, no trouble at all.

There was one thing all sharks and all pack leaders feared: that the rest of the pack would find out their weakness and turn on them. Back-bite time.

As he stared at the view from the Hill Pauls car park, Tom decided that Sharkey's weakness was that he was a romantic.

For people like Sharkey, being a leader, and believing they were champion of a cause, mattered almost more than anything. They didn't really care who they led, or what the cause. Those things were often as much a matter of accident as of choice. Sharkey led the Sharks because that was the best of the gangs that played around the streets where he lived. And he was a villain who thought he was Robin Hood because he'd been born into villainy and taught the Robin Hood garbage by his petty criminal dad. If he'd been born in the plusher parts of town he'd maybe have organized the lads into a computer club and been a gospel Tory. It wouldn't have mattered so long as he was the leader and believed himself in the right, fighting against the odds.

Take away their self-righteous confidence and people like Sharkey were lost. Undermine their position as a leader, or better still, disillusion them about their cause, and they were finished. Not just in the eyes of their pathetic followers, but in their own eyes. Take away their belief in themselves and their destiny and they self-destructed. Romantics love failure as much as—even sometimes more than—success, so long as they fail as martyrs.

Take Sharkey in, send him down for his petty crimes as martyr to the cause of the ordinary bloke against an oppressive system, and he'd survive his porridge proudly, come out a bigger hero than he went in, and be all the better prepared for villainy because of what he'd learned inside. But show him how you can leave him on the streets a reject with no following and he would do anything you want to prevent it. Sure, he would twist and turn and snap a lot, and you would have to slip him some nicely laundered reasons why he should do the dirty on himself and his kind, but in the end he'd give.

And you know what the really chuffing thing is, Tom thought, smiling to himself as the game became clear. The really chuffing thing is you get him anyway. Because in the end he gives himself up. Play him long enough, make him do the dirty often enough, and finally he goes to pieces because the disillusionment about himself gradually corrodes his self-respect. And his romantic soul can't stand that! Then there's nothing left except the humdrum boredom of self-disgust, or the romantic's last resort: a nasty little romantic death. Suicide. The Roman way of getting your own back—on a world entirely against you, and on yourself for being a weak twittish human being like everybody else.

I don't like romantics, Tom thought. Don't just dislike them, I despise them. They're just as dangerous as psychos and worse than straightforward, out-and-out villains whose only motives are excitement and greed.

At which moment Sharkey appeared, his heavy frame hunched, his pasty face puckered, reminding Tom of a nocturnal animal, used to the cover of darkness and tangled undergrowth, that's been flushed out into open country in bright sunlight. Though in fact this was one of those moist grey days that make slugs happy. So, thought Tom, why not Sharkey?

'Good news?' Tom asked.

'Sommat funny goin on,' Sharkey said, eyes busy for overseers.

'Don't look like you're dying of laughter.'

'Everybody's heard but nobody knows nothin.'

'Come on, Sharkey, you can do better than that.'

'No, honest. Nothin. Can't understand it myself.'

Tom said with deliberate whining scorn, 'All your connections and you can't come up with *anything*?'

Irritation flickered round Sharkey's eyes. For a moment Tom was sure he was going to hit him. But instead he slouched against the wall and said, 'You're full of shit, Tommy.'

Tom grinned. 'And you'll be full of porridge before long.'

Sharkey sniffed. 'Yeah, well, I need more time. Nobody who'd really know is around yet. Too early.'

They stood side by side in silence, Sharkey waiting for Tom, Tom turning over his next move. Was Sharkey testing him? Trying him out for size? Or maybe he'd heard something and was holding back till he was certain he really did need to give it away? Should he push him hard now, or play him along?

While they stood there the sun found a break in the cloud and, like a theatre spot, cast a beam that fell on a window in a house across the valley, which reflected a brief flash of light at

Tom's thought-glazed eyes, making him blink and attracting his attention.

As if the sunflash was a heliographed message, the event perked up his senses, sharpening his mind. Not that he knew at once what the message was. But he knew something important had come to him. A clue to the answer he wanted, if not the answer itself.

Natural instinct—the instinct that would make him a talented cop—as well as his yet unfinished training told him to stay silent for a minute till he could act without betraying any of this to Sharkey.

Then he said, 'Look, suppose I can keep the super happy, how long do you want?'

Sharkey shrugged. 'Dunno, do I? Till tonight when there's more of the lads around. Half-seven? How about then?'

Tom pretended doubt. 'Risky. Not sure I can hold him off that long. I'm putting myself on the line for you, Sharkey, if I do this. You'll have to turn up something. Okay?'

'Yeah, yeah, sure, you're a big mate, Tommy. All ready to go down with me, aren't you.'

'Best I can do.'

'Best I can do as well. And I don't like meetin like this neither. Can't you think of nowhere better?'

'How about the nick?'

'Very comic!'

'Seven-thirty sharp, bottom end of the railway car park, back of the old goods shed. Nobody'll spot you there. Okay?'

'I must be a proper mug,' Sharkey said, and slouched off, leaving Tom to nod at his back unseen, and grin to himself with satisfaction. Hooked or not as a regular, Sharkey was damn good practice, a useful rehearsal for bigger shows.

ADVANCES

JULIE: Dear Nik: Today they took the bandages off my chest. Not the ones round my eyes or hands, though. So I still can't see or do anything for myself. But isn't this good news?

They drugged me beforehand, of course, and clucked and cooed, trying to reassure me, like midwives at a rebirth. And it did feel like a kind of resurrection.

Afterwards, I asked Simmo to tell me honestly how I look. She said the wounds are healing very well but that it's too early to tell how bad the scars will be.

At first I was so glad to be rid of the bandages I wanted to shout for joy. I can't tell you how good it was to feel air on my skin again, and to move my arms and legs without being fettered by those suffocating wrappings.

But this afternoon I slept for a while and woke up feeling very low. Depressed about everything again. A kind of emotional relapse, I suppose, or perhaps just a hangover from the drugs. Whatever it was, I began to loathe myself. I kept imagining my body covered in repulsive scars and gashes, and my face disfigured, and my hands paralysed like claws, and my skin all scaly like a reptile's. I was sure I'd turned into a freak, something hideous that people wouldn't be able to look at without feeling ill. It seemed as if I'd been bandaged up a reasonably normal human being, and had somehow changed, like a caterpillar in its chrysalis, but instead of coming out a beautiful butterfly, I'd come out a monster.

After going on like that for a while, I began to hate myself all the more for being so defeatist.

Mother arrived just then. She'd come over because she knew about the unveiling. They'd told her yesterday, apparently, when she rang as usual to ask about me. They didn't tell me they were going to do it until they were ready to start this morning. Mum had thought they might take the bandages off my eyes as well and wanted to be here so I could see her if they did. That's what she said. But I know that really she was worried I might be blind, and wanted to help me through the ordeal.

[*Pause.*]

Well, I still don't know. And I can't use my hands because they're covered in what feel like boxing gloves. Now I know what it's like to be incapable, and totally dependent on other people for even the simplest things. Worst of all is that they have to do all your most private things for you. Everything from wiping your bum to picking your nose.

Don't laugh!

[*Chuckles.*]

You'll think it a bigger joke than Sister Ann in church, but they do! Even pick your nose, I mean. They use those little sticks with cotton wool on the ends. Though, to be honest, they aren't entirely successful. When Simmo does it, she gets on with it, using her own finger! 'Let's see what we can find up here,' she says, matter-of-fact as always, just as if she were clearing out a cupboard. But I can't tell you what a relief it is. I never thought picking your nose is so important. But if you don't do it . . . well, I suppose you'd clog up and always have to breathe through your mouth, which would be awful.

At school there was a girl who always seemed to breathe through her mouth. We used to hate her sitting beside us. Though, I have to say it was more usually boys than girls who did it. And then we made fun of them. Used to call them Gobgasper. How rotten we were! Perhaps they'd never discovered about picking your nose. Because it's one of those silly things that everybody must do but nobody talks about.

Well . . . I'm talking to you about it now, I know. But that's different somehow. I'm allowed to because of the state I'm in. Sick people—or very sick people anyway—are allowed to break the rules a bit, aren't they? They are in here. You can tell how sick people really are, no matter what the doctors tell them, by how much they're allowed to get away with, like being rude to nurses or messing the bed or shouting all night long and keeping everybody awake. If you aren't very sick, you're soon told off.

Just as dying people can tell the truth about themselves no matter how bad they've been, and everybody thinks they're wonderful for confessing, and forgive them at once. Whereas if they'd stood up in a crowded room and confessed when they were healthy and strong they'd have been arrested. Or else become one of those sordid people who appear on TV talk shows and tell about their criminal or wicked private lives while the audience ogles and gasps and thinks how daring they are.

[*Pause.*]

I've lost myself, as usual. Where was I . . . ? Oh yes—picking my nose, and what an affliction it is not to be able to do it.

I keep thinking about affliction. Only natural I suppose. And I did say I'd try and make it into my God-work, because I couldn't do anything much else.

Actually, I said I'd think about pain. And affliction isn't the same thing. One of my discoveries. I might as well tell you about it because talking to you is raising my spirits again, and talking about what I've been thinking might help me sort it out better than just keeping it in my head. I've found I can only get so far thinking to myself. The thoughts start going round and round, getting nowhere and confusing me more than I was before I started.

As a matter of fact, I found that out before. And I used to write my thoughts down, which helped make me sort them out so that I could think clearly in my head again. But as I can't write in my present blind and boxing-gloved state, perhaps saying what I've been thinking will have the same effect. If you don't want to be bothered with it, just switch off. I'll never know if you do, so you won't upset me.

Usually I give my written thoughts a title in the book I use to write them in. I'd better do the same now. So let's see . . .

[*Pause. Then in a more formal, thoughtful voice:*]

Meditation on the Nature of Affliction

The best example of affliction I know of is Christ nailed to the cross.

She wasn't ill. She hadn't committed any crime. She didn't nail herself up. She was put there by other people. Not because

92

of anything dreadful that she'd done, but because of what she was.

She was Christ, just as a man is a man, a woman is a woman, a black person has black skin. These are not choices people make for themselves. They are accidents of birth. Inescapable facts.

You can rejoice in being what you are. But you can suffer for it too. So what you are can be an affliction. An affliction is not something you bring upon yourself. It's something visited upon you over which you have no control. As being black can be an affliction in a country of white, prejudiced people. And being a woman can be an affliction in a society ruled by men.

That's why Christ can be for everyone, because she came to earth as a man and was herself afflicted by the men who ruled at that time. So she is an ally of all the afflicted, who are the touchstone of human frailty. Not because of themselves, but because of what they reveal about everyone else. As a black person walking into a room full of whites very quickly reveals the real attitudes of the majority.

My suffering here is an affliction. I know now it's the first real affliction that's come upon me in my life. And like all the afflicted, I'm a victim of the actions of others. Actions of which I was innocent. I mean, I lacked knowledge of them, and was given no choice about them. Being afflicted is therefore like being a slave. You have no choice about what happens to you.

When affliction comes upon you, it always brings with it two consequences. The first is physical pain. The second is an uprooting change in your life.

Physical pain can often be lessened or even ended by someone taking action—yourself perhaps or a doctor, for example. Just as Simmo gave me drugs this morning to dull the pain of my unveiling, or the pain of hunger can be ended by eating a meal. Then happiness returns. The pain is forgotten. So physical pain is not the same thing as affliction. I used to think toothache was an affliction. But now I know it isn't. It's simply a pain. I can do something about it.

[*Pause.*]

The real pain of affliction isn't physical. It's the pain of knowing you can't escape the disaster that's befallen you. This pain isn't physical, and it isn't emotional, though both can be part of it. No. It's a spiritual pain. It's like sorrow, which is the pain of separation. The affliction separates you from the life around you—the life you would prefer. It separates you from other people. But worst of all it separates you from the fulfilment of your self. Of your *being*.

I'd prefer to be walking, seeing, doing things with my hands. This affliction that's come upon me has changed my life. Stretched out on this bed, shut up in this room where others are not allowed unless they're tending me, I'm separated from people. From everyday, ordinary life. Often, I feel I'm not even a member of the human race any more. And it prevents me from fulfilling myself in the work I chose.

So my body, my mind, my life with others are all nailed to a cross of affliction that removes me from my true self.

No wonder Christ, nailed to her cross, cried out against God. Now I know what 'My God, my God, why have you forsaken me?' really means. For I have heard myself cry out those same words in the most painful time of my affliction when there seemed to be no one out there. Not even God. But only an absence. A hell made of nothing. A place alone, for myself alone.

Then I felt accursed. Marked for ever as a reject. Abandoned. Prevented by the evil of my affliction from helping myself.

And no one else can help. Not even the afflicted can help each other. Their afflictions prevent it. Christ, nailed to her cross, couldn't climb down and help those hanging on either side of her. And I can't get up and go next door when I hear my neighbour's alarm call sounding in the night.

And people who are not afflicted can't help—can't remove the affliction—because they don't, they can't, *know* what it is like. For affliction can't be described. Other people might be able to relieve the physical pain but they can't remove the deep soul-strangling knowledge of separation that an affliction gives you.

[*Pause.*]

Affliction makes you into a thing. An object. Something like a machine that needs attention now and then to keep it going, and makes noises, and sometimes causes trouble. An object that can be kept ticking over if it's given the right fuel and maintenance. And that can be switched off and even dumped if you get fed up with it.

Affliction makes you anonymous. It takes away your personality. Just as happens when one person thinks of another as only an object for sex, or as a slave. Or as a racist will say of those he dislikes, 'They all look the same to me'. Or as a pagan will say, 'The trouble with Christians is . . .', as if all Christians were one kind, one thing that lacks any individuality.

[*Pause.*]

Looking on the bright side, not all afflictions are for ever, thank goodness. Christ came down from the cross. But the wounds were still there, of the nails and the spear, and the crown of thorns. Even in her glorified body, when she wasn't flesh and blood any more. So, though affliction may not be for ever, it leaves its mark on you for ever. Its name is engraved on your soul if not on your body.

I don't know yet if my affliction will pass. I don't know what scars it will leave on my soul. I don't even know yet what good I can make of this evil.

[*Pause.*]

That's the hardest part. Something I can't think out yet. How to turn such crushing evil into something good.

[*Pause.*]

Except . . .

[*Pause.*]

I don't know . . .

Even while I'm saying these thoughts to you, Nik, something keeps coming back into my mind. Your hand. Remember? That awful time when they were sure I would die and they brought you here because I was calling your name?

Your hand was like a thought . . .

Like a message.

[*Pause.*]

Didn't I tell you the touch of your hand made it possible for me to believe I could live again? I can't remember exactly because I was still in a bad way and heavily drugged when I recorded the first tape.

Whatever I said, what I *meant*, I know now, was . . . What? . . . Well, here I am trapped in this bed like a creature in a zoo, having to live quite unnaturally, not at all the way I used to or want to, living a kind of horror, struggling against it, and I keep remembering the touch of your hand . . . And what it did . . . what it *does* . . . is make me want to love.

[*Pause.*]

The words fail. I'm tiring I expect. No wonder!

But that's the nearest I can get just now to what I mean. Your hand . . . *you* . . . made me want to love. And there is nothing my affliction can do to stop that. It can't kill that part of me. The part that can love.

[*Pause.*]

Which means something very very important. I think. Or is it just sentimental rubbish? You'll tell me. But I can't say any more now. I've worn my thoughts out. The tape must be nearly full anyway. So I'll rest and think about what it means later and tell you about it another time.

†

Tom waited till Sharkey was well clear before leaving the car park. While he waited he considered the sun's heliographed message. Why should that bright flash of reflected light have so caught his mind as well as his eye?

He studied the houses across the valley, searching for the one with the swinging window. It wasn't easy for him to find at that distance because now they were all bathed in sunlight, anonymous boxes with few distinguishing marks. But then he saw it, an upstairs window swinging on its hinges like a lazy weather vane. And as he watched, a woman appeared and pulled it closed. As the window turned, it flashed another brief message from the sun.

At once Tom realized what it was telling him. Standish, the insurance agent, had said that his attention had been attracted by the early morning sun flashing on the boy's face. But does the sun *flash* on faces? It hadn't flashed on the face of the woman at the window. Light only flashes from hard shiny surfaces. Like glass.

He needed to make a phone call.

The nearest box was outside the railway station. He couldn't prevent himself sprinting across the car park into the back of the station, had to restrain himself from getting to the front by crossing the line instead of using the pedestrian bridge, and felt the omens were good when he found the phone box empty and in working order.

Stay cool, he told himself while he dialled. Don't let on.

The secretary connected him to Standish as soon as he said who he was.

'Just another question, if you don't mind, sir. I wonder, can you remember, was the boy wearing glasses?'

'Spectacles, you mean?'

'Yes, sir. Specs.'

'Wait a minute . . . Goodness! . . . Yes, I think he was. Fancy not remembering a thing like that.'

'No matter, sir. But you're sure?'

'Positive, now you mention it. How do you know? Found him, have you?'

'Not yet. Just an idea, that's all. We'll let you know when there's any news, sir.'

Tom's next call was to the duty sergeant.

'Sherlock Holmes is it?'

'Maigret, sarge, no less.'

'Margaret who? Is there something you haven't told me, laddie?'

'Very witty, sarge. Listen, would you have a squint at the scene-of-crime report for the crucifiction and see if a pair of specs is listed.'

'Wait.'

Tom heard pages being riffled. Then silence except for the sarge's habitual clicking of his tongue in a tuneless tattoo.

'No, lad, no specs.'

'Sure, sarge?'

'Looked through twice.'

'Damn.'

'Onto something, are we?'

'No. A dead end.'

'Pity. But never mind, Margaret old girl. Even real detectives have their off days.'

'Sarge, you're always so supportive. Like an old truss.'

'You mind your manners, boy, or you'll be back in the blue and on the plod double quick instead of poncing about on the loose.'

'How could you, sarge! That's professionally insulting as well as sexist!'

He put down the phone before there was time for reply.

†

Dear Nik: Thursday is my birthday. I'm taking the day off so that I can go to Norwich, as a treat, and visit the place where someone used to live who I admire. A kind of pilgrimage. Her name was Dame Julian. She had visions on the day of my birthday, 8th May, but a few years before I was born. In 1373 to be exact. Afterwards she wrote a book about them. She called it *Revelations of Divine Love*. You should read it. Good for your research. Might get a surprise as well. She called Christ Mother Jesus. 'Jesus Christ, who sets good against evil, is our real Mother,' is what she actually wrote. Here's some more:

> *I came to know there are three ways of looking at God's motherhood. The first is that our human nature is made. The second is that God took our nature, which is the beginning of the grace of motherhood. The third is the work of motherhood which God spreads out over everyone—the length and breadth and height of it is without end. And all this is one Love . . . In essence, motherhood means kindness, wisdom, knowledge, goodness, love . . . By the skill and wisdom of Jesus Christ we are sustained, restored, and saved with regard to our sensual nature, for he is our Mother, Brother, and Saviour.*

Interesting? Interested? There's lots more.

I thought I'd drive over after work on Wednesday evening, slum it overnight somewhere nearby, leaving all Thursday for sight-seeing. Drive back Thursday evening. Late back but worth it. For me anyway. How about you? Would you like to come? Would they let you off school? Be good for your education.

Let me know. *Julie*

Dear Julie: I can resist everything except temptation. Sure I'd like to come.

But I thought I'd better check up about Thursday before saying yes. Especially as I'll be mucking about with dames who have visions. Dead and alive. Dangerous stuff that.

So I've been doing some runic arithmetic. The results:

This old dame had her 'visions' (really?) on the eighth day of the fifth month of the year one thousand three hundred and seventy-three. That is:

8   5   1373

Reduced to their fundamental number (because I know you like getting down to fundamentals) this becomes:

$8 + 5 + 1 + 3 + 7 + 3 = 27 = 9$

Let's do the same with your birth date, which, if you are nineteen this year, must be:

8   5 $1967 = 36 = 9$

Each of you reduce to nine!

The figure nine is a cardinal number composed of the prime number three, three times repeated:

$3 + 3 + 3 = 9$

I don't need tell you that three is a mystical number, and so is nine. According to your lot, God is 3-in-1. In your birthday and the date of the old girl's visions the three-in-one is three times repeated, making the religious magic even stronger because that makes nine.

Now take your age and reduce it to a single number as before:

$19 = 10 = 1$

Similarly, your birthday this year:

8　5　1986 = 37 = 10 = 1

Also, find the difference between the year of the old dame's 'visions' and your birthday year:

1986 − 1373 = 613 = 10 = 1

Three ones! And:

1 + 1 + 1 = 3

How about the difference between the old dame's vision year and your birth year?

1967 − 1373 = 594 = 18 = 9

Glory! Now we have three nines. 999. The emergency number.

And the three-in-one thrice repeated and thrice repeated. Strong magic this!

Let's get a grand total. Add up all the reduced figures and reduce them to one final all-inclusive Big Deal number.

Old dame's 'vision' year:	9
Your birth year:	9
Diff bn old dame's vision yr & yr b. yr:	9
Yr age:	1
Yr birthday this yr:	1
Diff bn OD's vision yr & yr birthday this yr:	1
TOTAL:	30
REDUCTION (3 + 0):	3

BINGO!!! The mystic trinity: three-in-one!

Your God is in all the figures. How can I not go with you? Something stupendous is bound to happen.

But what about the day?

This year 8th May is a Thursday.

What do we know about Thursday?

1) Thursday's child has far to go.

This sounds okay. You plan a journey that day. (Well, you

start on Wednesday, but after six, because you have to work till about then, don't you? And in ye olden tymes, the day always began the evening before, right?)

2) Thursday is the fifth day of the week, as defined in Collins English Dictionary.

What happened on the fifth day? Quote:

And God said, 'Let the waters bring forth swarms of living creatures, and let birds fly above the earth across the firmament of the heavens.' So God created the great sea monsters and every living creature that moves, with which the waters swam, according to their kinds, and every winged bird according to its kind. And God saw that it was good. And God said, 'Be fruitful and multiply and fill the waters in the seas, and let birds multiply on the earth.' And there was evening and morning, a fifth day.

[First Book of Moses, commonly called Genesis,
Chap. 1, vv. 20–3, Revised Standard Version.]

So on Thursday life got started. A bit of the old how's your father sounds all right to me. Can't miss out on that.

Trouble is, there's all that stuff about how Thursday got its name. You know: Thor's Day. Quote (Collins E.D. again):

Thor: Norse myth: the God of thunder, depicted as wielding a hammer, emblematic of the thunder bolt.

Wowee: Thunderbolt Day. Could be exciting.

Further: Funk and Wagnall (don't you just love the name?) tell much more about old Thor in their *Standard Dictionary of Folklore, Mythology and Myth*, which your 'umble researcher naturally consulted:

Such as Thor being *one of the greatest of the Gods; God of yeomen and peasants and opposed to Odin, God of the nobility*. Which makes him a hammer of the people and an okay guy as far as I'm concerned.

Added to which, he was *large, strong* and *capable of epic rages* so bad even his own mother, bless her, couldn't stand them, so she gave him away to foster parents, motivated of course by that caring, supportive concern for their offspring's welfare we all expect from doting, selfless progenitors.

He was such a Jack-the-Lad among ye gods that, Fun-Wag report, *In many localities no work was done on this day*. Great. I'll tell them at school that I've joined the Thorians and can't come Thursday because it's our day off. Thursday's Thor's day, folks. Lay-about day. Bring your own hammers and rages and lay about all you want. Epic eppies are all the rage. Rage, rage against the dying of the light, etc.

STOCKSHOT: *There is only one definition of God: the freedom that allows other freedoms to exist.*

More about Thursday, because there's more to Thursday than Thor, would you believe:

Apart from saying it is the fifth day of creation, your lot add:

a) *Maundy Thursday*: Christ washed the feet of his disciples the day before he died, right? The day before he died is supposed to be Thursday. So Thursday is the day your lot remember this.

I got all confused by the 'maundy' bit. So I looked it up. Derivation: 13th century Old French: *mande*, meaning 'commandment', which you'll know but I didn't came from JC's words: *Mandatum novem do vobis*: i.e., 'A new commandment I give unto you'. The new one being, I guess, that they must love one another. (You see, I really was paying attention during RE, after all.)

b) Thursday is also supposed to be the day JC ascended into heaven. My grandad says they used to have Ascension Day off when he was a kid. They all did something together, as a school, like a seaside outing to Weston or a walk from Berkeley Castle to Quedgeley, all along the Severn, with picnics on the way and a bonfire and bangers and a singsong at the end, then buses home dead tired and filthy but happy. He says they were the nicest days he can remember, and they sound pretty good to me too. We don't do things like that now because Ascension Day isn't a holiday any more. Nobody thinks of celebrating somebody rising up into the sky by having a jolly jaunt. Not even astronauts any more.

Maybe there's some use in religion after all, even if it's just that you get a good time once a year as a kid. Well, and Christmas Day as well. And Easter, come to think of it—they used to have nice times then too, like rolling hard-boiled eggs down hillsides, which sounds wild. And, my grandad says, they always had off the patron saint's day of their local church, and Whit week. I'll make sure us Thorians have lots of pi-holidays. (Hey, I've just realized that 'holiday' comes from 'holy-day': a day off for a religious reason. Yes, I know, I'm thick.)

My last bit of research:

8th May: you were born under the sign of Taurus, the bull. You are therefore supposed to be EARTHY, MELAN-CHOLY, and STRONG-WILLED. I should have known after the CND demo. That day you were certainly earthy (covered in it, in fact), melancholy (very fed up, if you ask me), and strong-willed (stubborn is the word I'd use). But you don't look like a bull, I'll grant you that. Quite nice, actually, in an un-bullish way. Just shows how appearances can deceive.

Taurus and *Thor, the thunderbolt* and threes and nines and footwashings and ascensions into the sky!

When added up, what does this mean?

Answer: I am invited to accompany a wilful, moody, sensual but religious female, whose life is dominated that day by the power of one (the self: one is one and ever more shall be so), three times repeated (a triangle, strongest of all shapes and signs), adding up to 999 (an alarm call with spiritual/magical properties), on a birthday pilgrimage (something I don't be-lieve in) to a place where an old woman who died over six hundred years ago (a herstory) saw what *she* thought were visions of God (but which I think must have been hallucina-tions because I don't believe in visions).

This trip is to be made in an ancient chariot, and we are to spend a night together in uncertain circumstances, before a day when the female's God ordered that we love one another and on which s/he/it rose up into Paradise, but which is also the day of the hammering thunderbolt wielded by a rival God, champion of the peasants, he of the epi-temper.

If I had any sense I'd stay at home. There's bound to be trouble.

You might say all this is just superstition. I might say all religion is just superstition.

I'll bring my sleeping bag, I mean the inanimate one, and some guzzle and some grub. Where and when do we meet? *Nik.*

Dear Nik: What rubbish. I've never had such a long ridiculous answer to a simple invitation. Have you noticed that it is always the atheists, doubters, disparagers, and faithless who are the ones who are most superstitious and put their trust in silly omens?

I'll pick you up at your house, 9.00 p.m., Wednesday. Can't manage before because I'm on late surgery that day. *Julie.*

PS: Here's my own precious copy of Dame Julian for you to read. Homework for our trip. You'll learn more from it than from all that so-called research. I'd like it back, please, on Wed. *J.*

†

Disgruntled that his hunch hadn't paid off, Tom left the telephone box, crossed the station car park and went into the Imperial Hotel. He reappeared a few minutes later, half a pint of bitter in his hand, selected an empty one from among the clutter of white-metal, umbrella-shaded tables squashed between the front of the pub and the station car park, and sat down to ruminate in the sun.

He recognized none of the few people sitting around him, mostly junior office types having their lunch, and they paid his scruffy presence no heed. Just as well; he was not in the mood for company.

Nor for patience. He'd never been one for letting events take their course. He liked to be in with a chance, busy with the action. Even when he was little his mother used to complain that he was never still, would never give up. 'There's something wrong with you,' she'd say, 'you're not normal, you've got St Vitus's dance or a hyperactive thyroid or something worse, you always have had, even before you were born you started wriggling about, kicking the life out of me weeks before you were due, and you've been kicking somebody ever since, I don't know where you get it from because your dad's not like that and I'm certainly not.'

Which was right enough, Tom thought, smiling into his beer; she was thirteen stone if she was an ounce and never got out of her chair till she was forced to.

On, on, don't hang about. The ideal detective, according to the super, should be well nigh invisible till the time came for making an impression—as when bagging a villain. Then he should act with memorably forceful visibility. 'Memorably forceful visibility' was the super's own memorable phrase. Tom was eager for his first forcefully visible moment. Impatient for it, in fact, as he was impatient for everything he wanted. Bagging the crucifiers could provide the chance.

He swilled the last of his beer, took possession of himself, and made an exit with professional unobtrusiveness.

Unthinking of why, he allowed his instinct to lead him, like a sniffer dog, back to the scene-of-crime, this time walking there by way of the canal towpath, which, hedge-lined, hid him from the workshops he'd have to pass if he used the road to the dump. He wanted not to be spied by curious eyes.

As it was he was overtaken by a party of three flab-jigging middle-aged joggers, puffing heavily and grinning a lot at each other to prove they were enjoying themselves. Sauntering the other way was a teenage girl in gripping top and jeans who was shapely enough to make him turn as she passed so that he could assess her bum, a sight that reminded him he had not had it up for a week, a deprivation he must do something about soonest.

Are you still alive down there? he silently asked. As the sight of the girl's backside made it necessary for him to adjust himself, he had no doubt of the reply.

At the dump he poked about among the garbage, beginning where the cross lay and working round in widening circles, unhurried. The cross, he noted, was hardly a cross at all but more a T shape. As he went, he pushed and delved with his toes, flipped and lifted and nudged with his hands. But wary of disturbing anything in case he spoiled evidence. Now and then he paused, straightened up, glanced at the manager's hut and the adjacent workshops for sign of life. But nothing showed, and no one came to inquire. Which struck him as odd even then. Surely there was someone around in the middle of a working day?

Thirty-five minutes passed. Tom had spread the circle as wide as he felt was worth it so he started back towards the middle, but tracking counter, viewing things contrarily.

A pyramid of used tyres lay on the edge of his circle. First time, he had skirted it, paying only a cursory glance, not fancying a climb on its treacherous rubbery mess. This time, he gave it more attention, decided a close inspection was necessary, and began goat-stepping his way up, prying only with his eyes into the jumbled cavities.

As he climbed he felt himself tensing with excitement. He was warmer, he was sure, as in a game of hide-and-seek. His blood pulsed. There *was* something here, he knew it.

But he reached the top without success. Began to doubt himself, his hunches, his rozzer's instincts.

Then saw.

A glint, a miniature of the flashing window.

On a side of the pyramid from that facing the scene-of-crime, two steps below him, clinging to the rim of a tyre by a bent arm, its one remaining but cracked lens catching the light, hung a pair of granny specs.

He almost let out a whoop.

ASSAULT

NIK'S NOTEBOOK: Four days after.

They say I'm still shocked. Shouldn't I be?

They say I should rest. Not think about it.

How can I not think about it, with the press and photographers still sniffing round all the time and interviewers trying to talk to me, and people pretending to be friendly when all they really are is curious, and the police asking questions?

Anyway, I WANT to think about it, damn them. But my own way. Not their way. And how can I with them all rabbiting on and confusing me?

Treat it as research. Hold it away so I can look at it, get it in focus, think about it.

It might be the most important thing of all.

IS.

But couldn't hold it away from me without my wp. Hands keep having spasms when they shake uncontrollably. And my legs, when I stand, will suddenly give way, as if all the bones had melted. But can prop myself up in my chair and tap away without too much trouble, watching the green fingertip write words, words that glow like green jewels quarried from the depths of the VDU.

Words on the VDU are different from words you write on paper. Not so much your own. Not anyone's. Removed. So less dangerous, less upsetting.

Anyway, whatever they say, I'm going to think about it, and the only way I can think about it without breaking into a sweat and having my hands shake or my legs melt, or even, dammit, bursting into tears, is to record it, look at it in words held away from me, not mine, but themselves—OTHER.

Words words words. I like words. Begin to like words more than people. Not like: LOVE.

LOVE: that which cannot be done without; wish always to

be with, be part of, belong to, know intimately inside and out, entirely, WHOLE-LY, for ever and ever amen.

Shining bright words in amazing patterns of endless variety. Drawings of the inside of my head.

Selah bloody selah.

STOCKSHOT: *People like you must* look *at everything and* think *about it and communicate with the heaven that dwells deep within them and listen for a word to come.*

Chapter One   THE JOURNEY

We drove via Cirencester ring road, through Bibury to Burford, on along the Witney bypass, left at north Oxford for Bicester and Buckingham, then Stoney Stratford and the Newport Pagnell bypass to slow and awkward, in-the-way Bedford. After that St Neot's and the flat, straight A45 towards Cambridge. Outside of which she stopped just off the main road on the edge of a parcel of trees.

Driving the way she drove in her ancient car and mostly in the dark with me navigating, using a flashlight to see her AA map and never having been further east than Witney and nearly losing us in rotten Bedford because I missed one of the signs, took three hours and ten minutes.

She said: We can make Norwich in an hour or so tomorrow and here's as good a place as any to bed down.

I said: Why not push on?

Because I'm too tired, she said. I've been working since seven this morning, unlike you coddled school kids. Besides, I thought you might like to see a bit of Cambridge tomorrow. It's supposed to be beautiful, and you ought to give it the once over as you're the sort who'll end up at university there.

She laughed. Me too, but from surprise, not humour. Never considered it. Would I want to?

And what sort end up there? I asked.

The clever, curious and uncommitted, she said, and laughed again.

Chapter Two SURPRISE

Julie said: There's a small tent. One of us can use that, the other can sleep in the car. I don't mind.

I said: You choose.

She said: You take the tent. You'll be able to stretch out. I've dossed down in the car before and it doesn't bother me.

When we'd prepared for the night, we sat outside the tent drinking coffee from a flask I'd brought. Half eleven by then. A still night. I remember: An owl hooting over the fields. The warm air. A clear sky like a vast VDU with bright full stops scattered over it—the hundreds of trillions of millions of stars and galaxies, sucking black holes and popping white holes, and quasars with their red shifts and pulsars bleeping their radio call signs, and how many other unknown universes beyond? And smaller than all, bigger than all, a beaming moon. And us here on earth, a speck of sand floating in the unthinkable ocean of endless space.

This seemed the right romantic moment to spring her birthday surprise. I reached into the tent and produced the parcel like a magician from under my sleeping bag, and laid it in her lap.

What's this? she said, lighting the Gaz lamp to see.

I said happy birthday.

A present! she said. And reached over and kissed me. On the lips. Not passionately. But not just sisterly either. Which I misread.

Selah.

She delicately undressed the parcel.

A book, she said, fingering the cover. You shouldn't have!

People always say that, I said, full of witlessness at the sight of her glowing.

Well you shouldn't, she said. *A Humourment*, she said, misreading the title the same as I did when I first saw it.

A Hum-U-*ment*, I said.

By Tom Phillips, she said. Never heard of him before.

She began flipping pages, making surprised noises of pleasure at what she found.

Strange, she said. Unusual. Pictures with words in them. What's it about? How's it done?

I said: He explains at the end. One of my favourite books. A sort of vision but a bit different from old Dame Juliana's.

Thanks, Nik, she said. I'll read it properly when I get back home. It's a lovely gift.

And she reached over and gave me another unsisterly kiss and a hug as well this time. Which I misread even worse than before.

Chapter Three   COUNTRY MATTERS

I said: If you want, we could, I mean . . . if you like, we could . . . you could sleep with . . . in the tent . . .

She smiled and at once looked down to hide her face.

I laughed, not exactly voluntarily. More a spasm of nerves.

She said: Another birthday present?

I said: Well, no, well I mean, if you like . . . well yes, I wouldn't mind . . . Or put that another way—I would mind, I'd like it a lot, to be honest.

Pause.

Are you, she said, making a pass at me?

Pause for controlling of breath.

Yes.

Silence, her head up, eye-balling.

Julie: Did you think I expected something like this?

I shrugged, not knowing then what I'd expected, but knowing now that I'd hoped for it.

She looked down, hiding her face again.

The longest pause so far.

Then, almost whispered: I'm sorry.

I spluttered: Hey, look, it's okay, it's all right, I . . .

No no!, she cut in. I don't mean, I'm sorry I don't want to sleep with you. I mean, I'm sorry, I should have known, I should have thought . . . inviting you, you know, like this, you'd expect . . . it's only natural . . .

She looked up, her expression pained. The first time I'd seen her unsure of herself in the face of me. Vulnerable is the word.

She had seemed so utterly strong till then, so unshakeable and knowing.

I couldn't speak. Didn't know what to say. Confused about myself and her and what I'd just done, which already, then, seemed twittish, and now seems worse than grubby and makes me cringe. How could I be so crass?

But instead of letting it go, trying to apologize and forget, I sat there, staring at her, even letting myself feel angry, as if she had done something wrong to me.

She said, shaking her head: I'm stupid, I'm really stupid!

I shook my head, meaning: No you're not.

I don't know, she said, perhaps . . .

What? I said, wanting to know, but the word came out like a rebuke.

Just . . . !

Her turn to stammer and fluff. She looked away, a blank stare into the night blackened by the glare of the fizzing lamp.

. . . Perhaps I wanted you to try.

I said, cloddishly puzzled: Wanted me to try?

A sort of test, she said.

A test, I said, and now the anger took hold: Great! Well, I failed. Asked too soon, did I?

She laughed, which didn't help, misreading her again.

Just like a man! she said.

Not surprisingly, I said.

Thinking you're the only one who can fail. I can fail too, you know.

You're the one who set the test, I said.

Look, she said, you've got it wrong. What I mean is, I think perhaps . . . She sighed . . . Perhaps I asked you to come with me hoping you'd try something, but not admitting it to myself.

Why would you do that?

So as to test myself. To find out if I'd let you . . . If I'd sleep with you.

But you haven't. Not yet!

No.

So you haven't failed yet.

Not with *you*, she said, glaring at me. But with *myself*.

Selah.

Moths were buffeting the lamp, burning themselves, fluttering away in maddened circles, but coming back for more. Julie turned it off, plunging us into star-pricked night again.

What she was telling me didn't sink in. I still felt I'd been rejected, and was at fault for even trying. But I was thinking, why shouldn't I? I was only letting her know what I wanted, how I felt about her. What was wrong with that? And I really did think she had given me a hint, that her birthday-present kisses were more than thank-yous.

I couldn't help asking: Is it that you don't fancy me?

No no! she said, sounding now as irritated as I felt. Just the opposite if you must know!

Then why? Is it religion? Sex before marriage, all that stuff?

Yes! . . . No! . . . Yes, of course it's got something to do with religion. How could it not? My religion is about all of my life, not just about the bits of it that don't matter. But no, it hasn't got anything to do with sex before marriage and what you call all that stuff. It isn't like that any more—God, I mean, religion, Christianity. Not for me. It's only like that for you because you haven't thought about it enough, haven't *lived* it, but only assumed things . . .

There was anger between us now.

Selah.

Rows are stupid. That's why they seem so funny afterwards. Not always. But often. We laughed about this one next morning, while we were driving into Cambridge.

But the real joke about rows is that they're futile. I'm no expert on girls or how to deal with them, and I'm no expert on sex. But I am expert on rows, thanks to years of training by my row-loving parents.

When I felt anger bubbling up between us I thought: This is just the way it used to be at home! The thing would boil up, like a kettle full of water, until it boiled over and we'd all get scalded.

I thought: I'm even sounding like my dad. Like I'd caught a disease from him. Verbal cancer. Why don't I just shut up!

Switch off, goon! I thought. Or make it different, make it *sane!*

Selah.

Look, she said, I'll try and explain. About the sex, I mean.

Don't bother, I said, like a sulky boy who's been refused an ice-cream.

For my own sake, as much as yours!

Pause. The night echoing its deadness.

She shuffled closer, as if crossing a boundary.

She said: It isn't that I don't fancy you. I do.

There was a change of tone in her voice, a new tune, a caressing sound.

She went on: I didn't admit it before. Not even to myself. I've been pretending, I suppose—that you were just a funny, interesting schoolboy who said he was researching for a half-baked film project but who deep down was really trying to sort out his ideas . . . his relationship . . . with God.

And me, she said, I'd help you, wouldn't I! I was older and more mature, wasn't I! I'd open you to religion, show you the way, bring you to God! I'd convert you!

She laughed, self-mocking.

Isn't that great! I hate it. That I'd even let myself think it, I mean, never mind try and do it. Wanting to make converts, wanting to persuade people to believe what I believe the way I believe it. I can't bear it when I see other people trying to do that. Like those creepy evangelists on television, with their glossy suits, and their big rallies, and their stage-managed fervour, and their packaged sincerity, and their sanctimonious humility that somehow always makes you feel they possess a God-given superiority over the rest of us.

She heaved a sigh and rubbed a hand across her eyes.

One of the reasons I like Philip Ruscombe is that he's hopeless at conversion. If you had to make converts in order to qualify for Heaven, he'd fail. Not because he doesn't know how, but because he can't bring himself to do it.

It's one of the great temptations, you see—wanting to prove the strength of your own faith by making others believe what you believe. It shows you're right.

She huffed.

But it doesn't prove anything of the sort. All it proves is that you're condescending and arrogant and good at doing what half-decent actors can do, or advertising agents, or pop stars, or politicians, or con men, or any of the professional persuaders. They sell illusions. And that's all they do. And they feel good when they succeed. That's what their lives depend on.

Which isn't true about religion. Or shouldn't be. Your belief shouldn't depend on what other people think about it. And it certainly should not depend on whether other people believe the same as you.

She laughed.

But there I was, she said, falling into the trap. Wanting to make a convert! And the funny thing is that I was only *pretending* I was trying to do that. What I was really doing was falling into a different trap—fancying you and not admitting it to myself.

I said: Sounds as if wanting to convert me was a substitute for having it off with me.

Could be.

So you admit you fancy me?

Yes.

And you don't have any worries about sex?

Not the way you mean.

And I fancy you and certainly don't have any hang-ups about sex, so why don't we—

Because, she said firmly, for me there's a bit more to it than that!

Selah.

Can't remember word-for-word what she said then, but do remember her reasons. They went something like this:

Sex is a maker of life, as food is a sustainer of life.

Sex can also be an appetite, as eating is an appetite.

Just as you can eat for the sake of eating, so you can enjoy sex for the sake of it.

There is necessity in sex for making life. There is no necessity in sex for the sake of it.

One of the illusions that the Big Persuaders have sold us is that sex for the sake of it is necessary—that we've failed or lost out or somehow actually damaged ourselves if we don't have sex for the sake of it.

Julie doesn't want to make a new life, just for the sake of becoming a mother. And her appetites are all for God. She wanted to know more about God—wherever that took her, whatever it demanded, whatever God meant. She wanted to know more about herself as she looked through God's eyes, as she put it. She wasn't denying herself anything so that she could have something else. She was using all she had for one main purpose that meant more to her than all the other things on offer in life.

She laughed a lot about all this. She knew, she said, that most other people would think her weird, which is why she didn't talk about it. She also knew what she said sounded old-fashioned, just about extinct in fact. But it was the way she was and she just accepted it.

She wasn't saying everybody should be like her, or that she even thought she was right. She knew most people thought that sex was there to be enjoyed any time you liked, so long as you didn't force yourself on anyone and didn't do anything that hurt the other person. And she didn't disagree. But for her, she said, her sex, having sex, was such an important part of *her*, of her*self*, that she couldn't treat it as if she was just having an enjoyable meal with a friend.

Anyway, she said, it was wrong to compare sex and food. They weren't the same. When you share food, you share something from outside both of you. Each person takes part of the whole and enjoys it in the company of the other. When you consume food you consume something of the world about you and so you make yourself part of that world. But when you have sex you give part of yourself, part of your own interior being, and take a part of the other person, part of their inner being.

Something more is involved than simply keeping yourself physically alive, or enjoying yourself with someone you like. Food keeps you alive and binds you to the world we live in. But sex has to do with making life itself, and binds you to the life that's greater than any of us, and greater than the world we live in—the life that Julie calls God.

Sex has something directly to do with God. And as God fascinates her, is the most exciting, most important Event (her word, her capital E), she wanted to use her sex (her sexuality, her womanhood) to help her get to know God. Even though she doesn't understand yet how to use it that way, and fails sometimes to resist the temptations that confuse her.

But no giving in to temptation tonight? I said.

Not tonight!

We both laughed.

I told her I thought I understood but that I'd never be able to do it myself, even if I thought it was right.

She said: Because you don't believe yet. You want to know what belief feels like, don't you? Well, I'm telling you what it feels like. Belief makes it possible for you to do crazy things other people who don't believe can't do.

Not even if they want to?

Not even then.

So you could sleep in the tent and you'd be okay after all?

Now I can.

Now but not before?

Because, she said, now I know that I was unconsciously testing myself I'll be okay. Knowing that, I can resist temptation.

I said, laughing: But what about me? I'm just a weak unbeliever! Maybe I won't be able to keep myself under control.

Then you'll get a good strong believing tweak where the temptation hurts most, and I'll evacuate to the sanctuary of the car.

Selah.

We spent the rest of the night talking. Or most of it.

And it was the happiest night of my life.

I'm wondering why.

Because we shared without demanding?

Because we gave without taking?

Because we received without expecting?

That's what Julie would say, I think.

But then the next day happened.

Dear God, if you are there, WHY?

Chapter Four   THOR'S DAY

When we finally went to bed I lay awake, mind frying fat after our talk.

116

Whenever Julie turned over I felt the shifting shape of her against me, but muffled through two layers of cloth, an echo of a body.

Mind frying fat, body hungry.

I sweated.

My bare arm outside to cool me, my hand on bare ground. Soil like flesh. Stones beneath my fingers like bones. Naked earth.

Remembering Sweden. The huge magnificent elk, the lake, the boat, myself starkers in the sky, in the water, knowing as never before never since how everything is part of the same beyond-everything life. Remembering the timelessness of it, how I seemed to see into the heart of things and understand the mystery of the universe. Remembering the randy longing to be absorbed into it, to come into it, to lose myself in it.

All that feeling swept over me again as I lay there, and is so impossible to put into words. The words contradict each other:

a joy that hurts with sadness
a sadness that is pleasurable
a pleasure full of terror
a terror that excites
an excitement that calms
a calmness that frightens.

And I feel I am just about to make sense of it when it fades away and is gone, leaving behind a longing for it to come again, to feel the power of it, the awe.

Now in the tent my nakedness was wrapped in an imprisoning envelope, like the body of a maggot imprisoned in its cocoon while it is changed into a butterfly. Was I being changed like a maggot? And if so, into what? Does the maggot know what it will be when the time comes to break out? And who is performing the trick? Or am I my own magician and don't know it?

The fat sizzled, burning thoughts to a frazzle.

And then the birds burst into their dawn chorus and blazed away, obliterating my thoughts and making me feel so exhausted at the sound of such wide-awake energy that I fell asleep at last.

But not for long.

Julie's morning cold hand woke me, searching out my face hidden in the warm depths of my cocoon. She was dressed, her stuff cleared away, all ready for off.

We'll stop, she said, somewhere along the road to wash and eat. Have this to get you going.

She stuck a slice of apple in my mouth.

Eve! I tried to say through her juicy gag.

If you're playing that game, she said laughing, just remember that the nasty little serpent who caused the trouble by lying to Eve about the apple was a he.

Pax, I said, holding up crossed fingers, pax!

How about unpaxing yourself so we can get moving?

Groan groan.

Best I can do this early, she said, and left me to slough my cocoon.

Selah.

Forget the damp morning, the grey clouds, the soggy grass, the geriatric car coughing and wheezing before it would start. Forget the shivery trip down the road to the nearest caff. Forget the caff's tired washroom and the pongy loo. Forget the half-asleep waitress and the spongy toast. Forget our silence because I still hadn't come to and Julie was miles away like Sunday mornings and for the same reason. Forget the drive into Cambridge, both of us perked up now and warm and the grey clouds letting through shafts of sunlight, brightening our spirits. Forget our chatter and jokes about last night.

Forget parking the car. Forget the explosion we heard as we walked away, heading for the centre of town, where the noise came from. Forget the worn-out joke I made, that the revolution had started at last. Forget the screaming sirens we heard soon afterwards, and the crowd we saw as we turned a corner, and more people running to join it. Forget us wondering what was going on, and edging our way to the front. Forget the policemen holding the crowd back.

Forget the scene down the empty street. Forget the blackened, crumpled, smoking remains of the exploded car. Forget the shattered windows of the buildings all around, the junkyard rubbish littering the road.

Forget the man lying splattered in the road. Forget his ripped clothes, his blackened body. Forget the draining blood. Forget his tortured, torturing cries.

Forget Julie asking the policeman what was happening. Forget her distress, her outrage, that nothing was being done to help the wounded man. Forget the policeman saying they were afraid the man might be the bomber himself, that he might be boobytrapped. Forget the bullhorn announcement that we should all clear the district in case of a second explosion.

Forget Julie flaring into anger. Forget her suddenly slipping past the policeman and sprinting towards the stricken man. Forget the policeman yelling after her. Forget my own shouts, screaming her name: Julie, Julie, come back, come back! Forget the awful gut-sick sense of doom. Forget my own desperate unthinking wild dash after her, the policeman beside me springing off at the same second.

Forget, as I pounded with leaden feet, seeing her reach the splattered man. Forget, forget seeing her bend over him. Forget her hands outstretched as if towards a lover. Forget, forget.

And then there is nothing to forget because my mind was blown and there is nothing to remember.

Only the breathtaking shock of Thor's thunderbolt.

The explosion lifts him up,
hurls him down,
a crotch-hold and body-slam.
Out.
Conditioning him for death.

RETREAT

NIK'S NOTEBOOK: Now I know I must be calm.

Now I know I must write clearly.

Now I know my life has taken a new direction, and I must map it.

I know this because I've just got back from the hospital. What I saw there taught me.

They sent Old Vic for me. Julie's mother phoned him. Julie was asking for me, calling for me from her deep unconscious. They asked Old Vic to take me to her, hoping my presence would help somehow.

We drove there in his down-at-wheel Volvo, big enough for his bigness, big enough for Old Chum collapsed on the grubby crumpled rugs in the back. Not big enough though to lose Old Chum's decaying pong. But I hardly noticed after the first few throat-grabbing minutes.

We followed the same route we drove five days ago. Then in the dark, now in the light. Stared at the things I hadn't seen then but couldn't *see* now. Couldn't think about them. My brain was stalled. Couldn't move it from Julie.

I'm trying hard to write this the best I can. For Julie.

Because of her, the sight of her, a different voice speaks in my head now. But finding the right words, putting them in their best order, is taking ages. The green fingertip deletes and inserts and repositions time and again, and with long pauses, while I listen in the silence for the new voice, which comes like a faint radio signal from far away.

But writing—doing the writing—also soothes me.

Going through Banbury we passed a funeral.

I thought: I am seventeen and have not yet died.

A mother with a baby in her arms stood watching the coffin being loaded into the hearse.

I thought: I am seventeen and I am still being born.

Writing this now I think: The green fingertip writes my birth.

I have not had such thoughts before. Where do they come from?

This is also how I know that I have changed direction. Have changed.

I do not like hospitals. I do not like their barracked look, their clean metalled clatter, their disinfected smell, their contained air of calamity, of pain bravely concealed behind forced smiles. I do not like the way they make illness and suffering a public spectacle.

For years and years you can be healthy and live your life in private. But when you get ill, seriously ill, you are put into a public room with strangers and there must perform the most intimate details of your life in full view of everyone. And this happens at a time when, because you are so ill, you need privacy the most. A double suffering. Organized torture.

But I feel uneasy writing this. Because another thing I do not like about hospitals is that they always make me feel I should be eternally grateful for them. The slightest criticism seems like a blasphemy, a sin, for which I might be struck down by some ugly and revengeful disease. But this is superstition.

INTERCUT: *Julie in her hospital bed in an intensive care ward. Her eyes are bandaged but the rest of her face shows, scorched. Her hair burned away from the forehead, she is grotesquely bald. Her arms lie by her sides, covered in bandages encased in transparent polythene and ending in what look like swollen stumps. The rest of her body is covered by a single sheet and looks barrel-shaped because a wire cage over it keeps the sheet from touching. Nik stands at the side of the bed between a nurse, Simmo, and Old Vic, with a middle-aged woman, Julie's mother, behind them.*

Nik is staring at Julie, appalled. Her head twists slowly, side to side. She tries to raise a hand but it flops back onto the bed heavily, as if weighted. She moans, an agonized, anguishing sound only just decipherable as Nik's name.

Nik's face buckles. Instinctively, he stretches out a hand towards Julie's, but hesitates when hers falls back. Then, slowly, he gently places his hand against her cheek.

Julie's moaning stops. And the twisting of her head.

For a moment the whole room is tense, waiting.

Slowly pull focus into a big close-up of Julie's face. Nik's hand on her cheek.

Silence, except for the sound of clinical machines and of Julie's breathing, which gradually settles into a calm, quiet rhythm.

Then, with a just discernible movement, Julie's head presses against Nik's hand, snuggling.

Julie sighs.

In the car, coming back, the world was torn.

I have never seen anything that shattered me as much as the sight of Julie.

Yes, I have seen worse things, more terrible. TV pictures of thousands of people starving to death in the African drought. Old film clips from the second world war of the Nazis' death camps with heaps of naked and emaciated bodies rotting outside the gas chambers round which the survivors shuffled like ghosts. Those are two of the very worst. They stick in the gullet of my memory. Just thinking of them upsets me. But not in the same way, not as crushingly somehow, as the sight of Julie and thinking of her now.

For I have felt her charred flesh on my hand and heard her pain through my bones.

Those other, greater horrors someone else saw for me. Camera men, reporters. Professional peeping Toms. Their pictures come between me and those famished Africans dying now, those humiliated men and women and children herded to their deaths before I was born.

Knowing about famished Africans and murdered Jews sickens me, angers me, saddens me, but does not change me.

Knowing about Julie has already changed me only hours after seeing her. Even though I am not yet sure exactly how.

But being there, putting my hand on her suffering, is what caused this.

These are two different ways of knowing. Now I know this too. Two different kinds of knowledge. One is the knowledge of history. The other is the knowledge of my own life, my own being.

And now I also know why the man they called Doubting Thomas insisted that, until he placed his finger into the holes made by the nails in Christ's hands, he would not believe. They should not have called him Doubting Thomas but Knowing Thomas.

Every I is a You; every you is an I.

We were through Bedford before either of us said anything. I couldn't have done before then. Too screwed up. Too near to tears. I think Old Vic was too.

How do you speak about such things? How do you write about them, come to that? Without diminishing them, I mean. Without *insulting* them.

How do you tell such truths?

I don't know.

Why do I try?

I don't know.

I only know that I want to try. Must try.

Not speak about them. Write about them.

So I must try and find out how to write the truth.

Not for Len Stanley. Not for the stupid film.

For Julie. For me.

Vic broke the silence after Bedford's bottleneck, which seemed to put a wedge between me and Julie.

It wasn't up to him to advise me, he said, but didn't I think it would be a good idea if I went away for a while, had a change, did something different away from news reporters and over-kind friends? There was nothing more I could do to help Julie just now, he said, and I would be better able to help her later on, when she was on the mend, if I was fit and well myself.

I said I didn't know where I could go or what I could do, and didn't have any cash anyway.

Vic said he didn't want to press me on the point but I might consider going to stay with the monks he mentioned before. He'd be happy to take me there and fetch me back and the monks didn't charge anything for staying with them so I wouldn't need any money for travel or accommodation. And there was always plenty to do around their house or in their garden if I wanted to repay them and keep busy. Besides, he said, trying to make light of it, I'd get some more material for my research.

I said I'd think about it, talk it over with Grandad, and let him know. Vic said: I've come across people before who say they'll let me know. They often don't. So, if you don't mind, I'll call in now and hear what your grandfather thinks.

And he did. Grandad was keen, surprise, surprise. I thought he'd pooh-pooh the idea. He can't stand anything to do with the church usually. But he said: Go, get out from under my feet, better than drooling round here all day.

I'm not sure. Going there seems a betrayal of Julie. Like going on holiday while she is sweating it out. I want to be here, ready, in case. But Grandad says there's no point. They can fetch me from the monastery as easily as they can from home.

They both went on at me. I argued, but then Vic said we should take the doctor's advice, and he phoned him. Much matey chat; they obviously know each other. The doc said if I felt up to it, it was a good idea.

So in the end I said yes, and Old Vic phoned his monk pal and arranged to take me.

†

'Could be anybody's,' the sergeant said.

'But might be his,' Tom said.

'Could have been there for months.'

'Don't look it. Forensic will tell.'

'Up to their eyes. Take a day or two.'

Tom thought, then said, 'Suppose our chappie lives round here. And suppose he gets his specs from a local optician. And suppose the optician can fit specs to customer. We'd have a trace, wouldn't we, sarge?'

'That's a lot of supposes.'

'Can't be many opticians in town,' Tom said, reaching for the yellow pages. 'Worth asking. If nothing comes up, the specs can still go to forensic today.'

He found the place, ran a finger down the list.

'Four. One optician—dispensing. Three opticians—ophthalmic, whatever the difference. All in the centre. No sweat.'

He scribbled names and addresses into his notebook, carefully replaced the specs into their protective bag, winked at the sergeant, said, 'Worth a try,' and made for the door.

†

NIK'S LETTERS:

Dear Julie:

I'm in the monastery Old Vic wanted me to visit. He brought me here today. They think I should have a change after what's happened.

At least you've come out of the coma. That's great.

I know you won't be able to read this yourself. Maybe one of the nurses will read it to you. Anyway, I wanted you to know where I am. They've said I can telephone every day for news of how you are, and I'll smuggle out these messages from a spy in a foreign land every day too.

This place isn't anything like I thought it would be. And as I know you're a fan of monasteries, I'll describe it for you, so you've another—and a male one!—to add to your collection.

The house is largish, a square stone building in a public park on the edge of town. Downstairs there are four big rooms and a big central hall with three tall windows, Regency style, looking out over the park, and a wide stone staircase with an ironwork banister curling up from it. Quite grand really. The house dates from the sixteenth century, but what you see now is early nineteenth, when some rich exploiter thought it would be nice to have as a country cottage. Some cottage! He also landscaped the grounds. Now the whole thing belongs to the local council, who rent the house to the monks because nobody else wants it, apparently. The public use the park for walking their dogs, jogging, etc., and of course for nefarious activities that must be educative for monks!

One of the rooms is a dining room. The monks call it the refectory. One is a sitting room, with squashy second-hand

125

chairs and tatty scatter rugs on a polished wood floor. They call this the visitors' room. It's where they see people who have just dropped in for a short visit. One is the kitchen. Big enough for all the usual mod cons plus a table that will seat eight. And one room, near the front door, is the chapel. Everywhere, except the visitors' room, is sparely furnished. White walls. Bare polished wood floors.

The chapel is panelled in dark oak from the days of the rich gent. A modern altar made of a square slab of light oak supported by a single up-swelling pedestal, so the whole thing is like a fountain of wood. Grandad would like it: good craftsmanship. More like a piece of sculpture in wood than an ordinary altar. It's set in the middle of the room, diagonally, so it's like a diamond in the cube of the room. A lamp made of stainless steel shaped like a crown hangs above it. Round three walls are long prayer benches, also light oak, and standing on stainless steel legs, with bench seats behind for about six people each. Above the three-quarter panelling, the walls and ceiling are painted white. White-globed lights hang down above the prayer benches, three lights to each bench. The windows are casements and look out over the park. Polished floor. No religious images except for a plain wooden cross, light oak again, set on the wall without prayer bench. Under it there's a lectern made of slatted strips of light oak, holding a Bible for readings during the services (which the monks call 'offices' —but I suppose you know that). It's quite an austere place, but feels very peaceful and smells of incense, which I liked, a kind of sweet, woody smell that reminded me a bit of Grandad's workshop when he's cutting certain kinds of pine.

I like the chapel very much. Not all the usual churchy clutter or fusty atmosphere. It's odd in an interesting way as well. The combination of old and new, dark and light, clean lines and uncluttered space. I feel I want to stay in it you'll be surprised to know!

Upstairs, there are ten or maybe twelve small bedrooms. Some of them have been made by partitioning rooms as big as the ones below. The monks call them cells. Each has a single bed (I guess they'd have to be single, come to think of it!), a chest of drawers, a desk or table, and a sit-up chair. Bare polished floors again. Almost everything white, except for the desk and chair. A wooden cross on one wall.

There are two bathrooms. There's a larger room packed to bursting with bookshelves—they call it the library. And there's another larger room with some easy chairs in it, a table with magazines and newspapers on it, a couple of small desks, a record player, a bookcase in a corner, and a TV set. And a carpet, but an old threadbare thing. The monks call this the common room.

The upstairs is called Enclosure, because only the monks and male guests (ahem!) who are staying in the house are allowed there. Something to do with the monks' vow of celibacy and keeping silence.

Behind the house there's an area that used to be a tennis court. The monks have fenced it off so they can't be seen by people in the park, and have converted it into a vegetable garden, with a small greenhouse and a bit of lawn where they can sit. They hang out their laundry there too. (I don't know why, but I was surprised by the washing. Somehow, I never thought of monks having washing. As if they were permanently clean! But I suppose they get their underpants dirty, like everybody else.)

We arrived about an hour and a half ago, at 3.30. The only person here was a man I thought must be an odd job labourer. He was dressed in mucky old shirt and jeans and a pair of battered trainers. He was scrubbing the kitchen floor. Old Vic didn't bother to ring the door bell or anything. Just walked in, went straight into the chapel, did a quick prayer, then led me into the kitchen, where this bloke was on the floor, scrubbing the boards. As soon as he saw us, he jumped up, all smiles and hello-o-o-s. Brother Kit.

Didn't know what to make of him at first. He's very small. Not stunted or anything grotesque, but nearly a miniature person. His head is quite big, though, with sticking-up brown hair cut short, almost a crew, which makes him look top-heavy, and he wears glasses with thick frames. But he is quite different from the leptonic OBD. He and Vic were a sight: Laurel and Hardy. Old Vic loomed and boomed, Bro. K. squeaked and chuckled.

Couldn't believe this funny little bloke in mucky gear was a monk. Not just a monk but a priest as well. He put a kettle on a vast Aga stove, shifted us into the visitors' room, said, I'll be back in a jiff, disappeared for five minutes, then returned carrying a tray with mugs of tea and a plate of cake on it. But now he was dressed in a very light grey, very loose and floppy sort of down-to-the-ground frock with a hood on the back, and a black leather belt buckled round his middle with a plain wooden cross hanging from it at the side. His habit of course.

He said: Thought I'd better look the part, and grinned.

I felt peculiar, the way you feel when you're fully clothed in a sitting room with someone dressed only in their undies. One of you is out of place. And you never know what to do with your eyes because you can't help staring at the other person, especially at the private parts. Only, in Bro. K.'s case, the private parts were his chunky wooden cross and his mucky cuffs sticking out from his habit's big-mouthed sleeves, and his trainers poking from under his skirt.

All a bit comic, like he was an actor dressed for a play who had strayed among the audience instead of waiting back stage. But somehow fascinating as well.

While we were drinking our tea and eating the cake (Old Vic put it away like he hadn't eaten for months) Bro. K. chatted ten to the dozen with Vic about things I could only half understand, and made jokes they laughed at like naughty schoolkids. Very unholy, both of them. Didn't think Old Vic could be so lively. He really enjoyed himself.

All sorts of questions kept coming into my head I could hardly stop myself asking. Like how Bro. K. got to be here, and what he did about sex and not having any money, and where were the other monks? And ridiculous things like did he lift his skirts when he went for a pee or was there a secret opening?

After tea he showed me round, then took me to my cell. I felt like a condemned sinner being locked up. He left me to get settled in while he has a private session with Old Vic. I expect Vic is telling him about you and me.

Soon as I unpacked (not that I brought much, just a change of clothes and toilet stuff and a book), I sat at my desk by the window, which looks out across the park that slopes down to a small lake (a large pond really, with a few ducks on it) and across to some trees that mask the main road. And suddenly I felt very lonely, even a bit panicked, knowing I'm to be left here on my own.

I expect you think this is pretty much a laugh, considering what you're putting up with. But it just occurred to me that I've never ever been anywhere on my own before. I've always been with someone I knew—my mum or dad when I was little, Grandad since the breakup, teachers and friends on trips from school—and you to Cambridge.

Makes me feel scared, would you believe! Like I was when I was still a kid, and even a little like I felt at the worst time during the breakup, not knowing what's going to happen next.

And I'm nervous about whether I'll do the right thing, or make an idiot of myself. I mean, how *should* you behave in a monastery?

Why did I agree to come? What am I doing here? It was a goofy idea. And why should I have a 'rest' while you . . .

Footsteps along the landing. Bro. K., I expect, coming for the condemned man.

Love, *Nik*.

✝

JULIE: Dear Nik: I got your tape. Thanks for visiting Mum. I know she likes to see you. She can talk to you about it in a way she can't to anybody else, because you were there, and that helps.

Yesterday, they said they were so pleased with my progress that they're hoping to take the bandages off in about two weeks. Then they'll know whether my sight is okay or not.

Today's Thursday. Thor's day! Every Thursday I spend some time praying about what happened, and for all the times when bombs are set off and hurt people. I heard on the radio there was another today, in Beirut again.

I was thinking this morning about my bomber. He must have known he'd die. Probably thought of his death as a martyrdom. Dying for his cause. But they never found out who he was, or what his cause was. The police told me nobody claimed responsibility. They thought he was probably acting alone.

They said there is more and more danger from individuals or very small groups who nobody knows anything about but who are determined to use violence, and use it without warning, unpredictably, and don't mind if they die, in fact they want to die, as if their own death were part of their protest.

Perhaps my bomber was like that. And when I think about him, I wonder if he was trying to say something about the way we live, the sort of society we live in. That's what most terrorists seem to be doing. They want us to change, and live differently—in some way they believe would be better for most people. And I want that too, so why wouldn't I ever let off bombs?

People who set bombs off must have a very strong belief that they're right and they want to change things as quickly as possible, even if achieving it means they die doing it. I can understand that. I can even understand why they're often admired and made into heroes. Everybody with any goodness in them wants to change our way of life for the better of poor people, and the sick, and the oppressed, and are against those who keep all the power and wealth to themselves. And it seems so hard to make things change that I can understand why some people get frustrated and go to extremes to try and bring about even a small difference. And letting off bombs is dramatic and satisfying, I imagine, like making big banging noises when you're little, and startling the grown-ups so that they pay attention to you.

Perhaps one of the reasons I'm not keen on that sort of protest is that it always does seem to me a bit childish.

But that's not the main reason I don't go along with it.

People who bomb and shoot want change now, this minute. They want the world of our lives—the world they can see and touch—to be different at once. And they believe this is possible. All their belief is concentrated on their lives—their physical, bodily lives—here and now. Even if they believe in God and a life beyond what we can see and touch, they want Heaven on earth, and they want it immediately. And if they can't have it, they prefer to die. So they're ready to suffer and sacrifice themselves, and other people too, in order to bring it about.

Perhaps they're right and it is possible. To make changes

quickly, I mean. I suppose in theory it is. I just don't agree with them. I love the world I can see and touch. I long to see and touch it again. Not being able to has taught me just how much I love it. But it's also made me realize something else I was only half aware of before. Which is that, however much I love the life I know, I've never really felt that I belong here. I mean, I've never felt that the world is my home. To me, it's like a waiting room at a railway station or the departure lounge at an airport. I'm on the way from somewhere I can't now remember to a destination I know very little about yet.

This particular waiting room, our world, is quite nice to be in. Most of the people are considerate and thoughtful. But some, it's true, aren't too pleasant, and have bagged the best seats and behave a bit as if they owned the place and push their way to the head of the queue for the food and drink. Quite a lot of people have even forgotten they're on a journey at all, and have started settling in as if they expect to stay here for ever. And they cause quarrels and even fights, because they're afraid of losing their place, or they want more space, or more than their fair share of what's on offer.

So what do I do? Make a bomb and blow the nasty people up? One bomb in a Cambridge street isn't world-shattering. But to my mind, one bomb in a Cambridge street means just the same as letting off all the nuclear bombs in the world and blowing us all to bits.

I don't just want to ban The Bomb. I want to ban all bombs, whatever, and all bombers, whoever, and all bombings, whyever. There have to be better ways of saying no and making changes.

Anyway, being a stranger away from home my mind is more fixed on my journey and on my destination than it is on this waiting room, even though the place is very beautiful and full of interesting things that help me pass the time without getting bored.

But for the bombers, I think, all there is is the waiting room. And if they can't run it the way they want to, they'd rather destroy it and themselves too. The only future they've got is here. And if they can't have it the way they want then nothing else matters.

For me, because I believe my future lies somewhere else, somewhere beyond the waiting room, I'm not so keen to cause chaos now or to blow myself up. Getting on with my journey, reaching my destination, depends on staying alive now and keeping myself fit for the rest of the journey. So I concentrate on that. I'd like to be comfortable, of course, and have a pleasant time, and get along with the other travellers. But I don't put all my store on that.

Death doesn't worry me. Not death itself. But suffering does, my own or anybody else's. Because suffering is an impediment. It gets in the way. All that stuff about it strengthening our character and refining our will, and teaching us that we're only human and must put our faith in God. No. Suffering is bad for us because it makes pain a substitute for thought. The way religious fanatics talk about suffering is the way people used to talk about bringing up children. Spare the rod and spoil the child. Beat the evil out of them. Make them fear punishment and then they'll learn to do good.

I don't believe in a God of fear. And I don't believe that we only learn that we're human by being made to suffer. If we can't think out for ourselves what we are, and if we can't make decisions about ourselves and the way we want to live and the way we want to die without being tortured into them, then we aren't worth anything. The people who put their faith in bombs, in killing and in violence, all belong to those inadequate people all down the ages who believed in fear and torture. They may not have begun that way, they may have begun by acting from the best of motives. But in the end, the only cause they truly believe in and live for is torture itself.

I expect that seems pretty simple-minded to you. Full of holes! But it helps me, because it tells me that whenever I'm faced with doing something, there'll probably be two ways of going about it. One that'll make things worse for somebody else and one that might help make them at least no worse off.

[*Pause. Clatter of metal utensils and indecipherable chatter.*]

Got to stop. Simmo's just come to change the bandages on my eyes. My daily squirm when I'm supposed to have my character refined and realize just how human I am.

Isn't it funny how pain is easier to bear if you can grip

something with your hands. Because I can't I groan and moan instead, and feel foolish and ashamed afterwards for giving in like that. But Simmo is terrific. All the time I'm moaning she says, 'Go on, let it out, have a good yell!' And that helps.

†

NIK'S LETTERS:

Dear Julie: 9.50 p.m. The end of my first day as a Spy in a Foreign Land.

I'm in my cell. I'm bushed. What a day! But don't want to go to bed yet. Brain too busy sawing wood. Writing to you might calm me down.

I hate not being able to see you. Couldn't, I guess, even if I was at home because of the distance. Damn distance. Damn money that makes distance no problem. And, also, I feel a bit locked up here. Not that I am. Just the way I feel.

When I phoned the hospital this evening, they said you're improving. You had a comfortable night last night, and are 'as comfortable as can be expected'. Did you know that? I hate the coolspeak of hospital people. They wouldn't let me talk to the ward. Too busy, they said. Huh!

I think of you all the time. You'll laugh when I tell you I even prayed for you tonight. Must be the religious atmosphere. Well, not prayed exactly. The monks included your name in the list of people they prayed for after Compline. (I always thought Compline was that milk powder stuff they give geriatrics who can't eat proper food. Maybe it's spelt differently?) Anyway, the last office of the day. (I'm picking up the jargon, you see.)

I admit I asked them to add your name to the prayer list, and I did say it to myself when they read it out, and willed you to get well. That's nearly praying, isn't it? But not quite. My idea about prayers is that they have to be addressed to someone—to a God—before they're really prayers. And I wasn't addressing anybody. No, that's wrong. I was speaking to you.

But I'd better start from where I left off yesterday.

Old Vic stayed for Evensong and for supper afterwards, which we have at 7.00 p.m. I was glad he did because he

133

showed me the ropes in chapel and during the meal. (Meals are strange. There's a funny routine about passing things, for instance. At the start of the meal everything goes round the table, passed to the left from one to the next. It's bad manners not to pass things. And you're supposed to keep an eye on the blokes next to you to see if they need anything and pass it before they have to ask for it. This doesn't matter so much at talking meals, like supper. But at silent meals, like breakfast, it matters a lot, otherwise you might never get the marmalade.)

Old Vic also explained about Silence. Silence is when the monks (and their visitors!) are not allowed to talk AT ALL, except in the visitors' room on special business. Silence happens from 8.30 p.m. till 9.30 a.m. the next day (the Greater Silence) and from 12.00 till 1.00 mid-day, and from 5.00 till 6.30 in the evening (the Lesser Silences). During those times you're supposed to pray and concentrate your mind on God, etc. Reminded me of you and your Sunday morning silences on the way to church. When it's time for Silence a little bell is rung in the hall by the monk whose turn it is, and all the talking stops. It's peculiar at first, everybody suddenly going dumb on you, like they've suddenly taken agin you. They even go distant; their eyes don't see you any more, as though you didn't exist for them. Least, that's how it is with Bro. K. I haven't had much chance to talk to any of the others yet.

But I already like Silence. Whatever is happening you know there's soon going to be this pool of quietness. Bro. K. says they all look forward to it. All the real monks, anyway. He says Silence is a true monk's natural state, part of what he is born for. When someone comes to try the life, the others watch to see if he takes to Silence, because it's a good sign of whether or not he's suitable. Apparently, some people can't stand it and go to pieces and have to get out quick.

By the time Vic left it was Greater Silence. Bro. K. had already asked me if I wanted to live the kind of day the monks do or just please myself. Out of curiosity, and because I thought he would like it (creep creep), I said I'd follow their day. Little did I know! This place is a slave camp.

He gave me a folder and said everything I needed to know to start with was in there and we'd talk tomorrow. Tinkle-tinkle little bell and Bob's your uncle: no more chat. I went to my cell and did my homework. Here is my timetable:

5.30 a.m.: Get up. (Couldn't believe my eyes!)
6.00—8.00 a.m. Chapel:

Matins (i.e. Morning service. 20 mins)	Whatever am I
Eucharist (20 mins)	going to do in
Silent Bible reading (20 mins)	chapel for all
Meditation (60 mins)	this time?!

8.00 Breakfast (Usually cornflakes, egg, toast, honey or marm., tea. But today is Friday, a 'fast' day, so tea and toast only!)

8.30—9.00 Housework (This morning I had to clean my room, one of the bathrooms, and dust and tidy the visitors' room. I didn't get properly finished, which for some reason amused the others.)

9.00 Work starts. (Wasn't all this other stuff work? Today I weeded the garden. By now I was beginning to think this was getting too much like home.)

10.30 Coffee break. (Thank goodness! Coffee and biscuits.)

10.45 Work again. (I peeled spuds & prepared peas & salad stuff for lunch & supper, and washed up the breakfast things, etc., in the kitchen.)

12.00—1.00 Silence. (Hurray! Private prayer & meditation. I sat in the chapel because I like it there, and nearly fell asleep.)

12.45 Mid-day office. (Some prayers said aloud together, a psalm, a bit from the Bible.)

1.00 Lunch. (Bread, fruit, tea, because it's a fast day. I'll starve at this rate. At least Grandad doesn't stint on the food. Usually there's cheese as well.)

1.30—2.00 Rest. (Lay on my bed and wondered what I was doing here.)

2.00—4.00 Work. (Given a book to read about the monastery. Then sent for a walk round the park, which is just as well because I was nodding off again.)

4.00—4.30 Tea. (Tea. Usually cake as well but not on fast days.)

4.30—5.30 Reading Time. (But for me today a session with Bro. K. until Silence put a stop to the chat. See below.)

5.00—6.30 Silence. Private prayer. Did mine in chapel.

6.00 Evensong.

7.00—7.45 Supper. (Cauliflower cheese, pots, peas, salad. Rice pud. Coffee. Fast over because it is officially tomorrow after 6.00 p.m.)

7.45—8.30 Recreation. (All the monks and live-in visitors meet in the common room and talk about their day's work, etc., plus gossip and jokes. A kind of family get-together. I was nervous at first but am getting used to it. It's meant to be a relaxing social time. On special days they have treats —drinks and sweets or whatever they've been given. Vic had left them a bottle of whisky so they opened that to celebrate me staying with them, which I thought was a pretty lame excuse to have a booze-up, especially as I wasn't given any and had to have Bro. K.'s home-brew beer instead.)

8.30 Silence.

9.30 Compline.

12 midnight. Lights out, except with special permission from Kit.

See why I'm bushed? Haven't worked as hard in my life, not even when Grandad is in one of his slave-driver moods.

The hardest work of all is in chapel. At first, I thought that would be the easiest—a doddle just sitting there in that nice room watching the monks do their stuff. But to start with, it's very hard to concentrate at six o'clock in the morning, and when the offices are happening you have to bob up and down, kneeling and sitting and standing, and find the right place in the office books. You feel an idiot if you don't join in or do the wrong thing—kneel when you should stand, etc. So you have to keep your wits about you. And unless you're just going to slump like a pudding in your seat during the private patches you have to decide how to spend the time 'meditating'.

In fact Meditation is the most difficult of all. I've heard people talking about it like it's a spiritual happy hour when you float inside your head in a kind of cosy limbo. Well, it wasn't anything like that for me. I hadn't a clue what to do, so I tried thinking about what monasteries are supposed to stand for and why people want to be monks and nuns and whether Jesus

Christ would be a monk if he came back. But I hadn't been at it long before my mind started wandering all over the place, thinking about anything but what I wanted to think about. The harder I tried to keep it on the subject, the more it wanted to think about something else. Like an itch: the more you try to ignore it the itchier it gets. I got to wondering, for example, how Grandad was doing on his own, and how you were feeling and if you were awake at this unGodly (?) hour. (I guessed you would be, knowing how keen hospitals are to wake everybody up before anybody in his right mind would want to wake up. Hospitals and monasteries are alike in this respect, I guess. Which isn't surprising when I come to think about it, as hospitals were first started by monasteries! Maybe that's why nurses still look a bit like super-efficient nuns.) After that I started thinking about breakfast. I was famished and kept having visions of luscious bacon and fried bread sandwiches and lashings of marmalade and toast.

This had a dramatic effect on my innards. They started rumbling and gurgling, and generally making a lot of lavatory noise. I was certain everybody in the room could hear. Could feel myself blushing. I had a quick glance at my watch because I was sure it must be nearly eight. It was nine minutes past seven. I'd been meditating for eight minutes. Couldn't believe it! Looked up, and caught Bro. K. watching me, a grin all over his face. He looked away as soon as our eyes met, which is just as well because I'm sure I'd have had the giggles if he hadn't. It all reminded me of Sister Ann at St James's. Remember? How could you forget! Luckily, the others kept their eyes to themselves. But they've been calling me Rumbletum ever since.

I'd better tell you about the others. There are six of them. Kit, David, Mark, Dominic, John and William. I'm the only visitor. A novice, Adam, is expected tomorrow. He's been with them eight months and is coming here from their main house to stay for three months to experience life in a 'working' house.

Kit is in charge. Which he says means being the dogsbody who does what they all decide should be done when they meet at their weekly 'chapter'. They vote for their 'prior' every two years and nobody can be prior more than twice. Kit's on his second jag. He looks after the house, sees to visitors, and because he's a priest, celebrates the Eucharist every morning.

The others have ordinary jobs outside, except for William, who is the youngest, twenty-four, and only recently made a full member. He came to the house two months ago and is still looking for a job, so at present he helps Kit when he isn't job-hunting. David is an electrician working with a building firm in the town. Mark is a teacher in a local primary school. Dominic I'm not sure about yet but he seems to have something to do with social work among unemployed teenagers. John is a gardener with the council and works in the park and local cemetery.

What happens is that they all go off to their jobs like ordinary people at whatever times they have to. Dominic, for instance, has irregular hours sometimes. At home, they do their monk work and keep the daily timetable as best they can. They don't put themselves out to convert people. They think of themselves as representing Christ in ordinary life, and they only talk about their faith if someone asks them about it. They believe what they are and the way they live is what matters, not how many converts they make or whether people even know they are monks. When they're outside they wear ordinary clothes exactly like the people they work with. In the house, during Silence and for chapel, and when they are being monkish, they put on habits like the one I described Kit wearing.

Whatever they earn they pool. And they allow themselves a certain amount of pocket money each week so that they don't have to cadge from their workmates. They don't believe in begging or living off other people's charity. They think that working for their living is part of being like other people and not becoming somehow special. At the end of the year, what's left over from their earnings, if anything, they give away so that they never have anything to rely on or ever get cosy and lazy and right-wing.

There's a lot more to tell, but later . . .

Anyway, they aren't a bit like I expected. Not pompous or devout in a stuffy way. You don't feel they're going to pin you in a corner and give you the holy third degree. Which somehow only makes you keen to talk to them about what they believe.

I'm quite impressed in fact. When they're together during Recreation and meals, they're lively and quite funny—they're always making ghastly jokes. So I'm beginning to enjoy myself, if I'm honest.

The way they behave in chapel is the most interesting of all. They do everything in a kind of routine way, but somehow they make it seem special as well. Can't explain it yet. But I quite look forward to the offices already, just to watch them and be part of the ritual. It's like a play or a very serious game, yet it's also private and—I don't know—*essential*. If they didn't do their chapel work, they wouldn't be anything, just a bunch of reasonably nice blokes living in the same house and pooling their pay. What they do in the chapel seems to make them into what they are outside chapel. As individuals as well as a group, I mean.

This is all confused. I'm too tired to explain properly.

I'll just tell you about what Bro. K. said to me this afternoon, then I'm off to bed. He explained about the community, then asked me how I'd like to spend my time here. All depends on how long I'm staying. Said I could just treat it like a holiday. Or I could go on like today, helping out and joining in with as much of their life as I like. (You needn't suffer all of Meditation! he said, laughing.) Or I could do a proper Retreat, which he would 'direct'—i.e. guide me about what to do. This is a kind of organized three or four days when I try and think seriously about myself and what I believe and my attitude to religion, etc.

I didn't know what to decide so Bro. K. suggested I think about it over night and tell him tomorrow. I made this the thing I concentrated on during the Silence this evening. I've almost decided I'd like to do the Retreat. Might as well, as I'm here, and it's something I've never done before. And you've made me think about spiritual things. Though, the only result so far is that I don't know where I stand at all now, whereas I was quite sure before.

I told Bro. K. that I think I'm an atheist.

He said: At least we can try and help you to be a good one.

I said: What's a good atheist?

He said: The same as a good Christian—one who doubts.

I said: Do you doubt?

Sure, he said, thank God!

I said: Why thank God? Don't you want to be sure?

He said: There's a line in a book by Graham Greene: 'The believer will fight another believer over a shade of difference. The doubter fights only with himself.'

I quite like that line, too.

Love, *Nik*.

†

The first three opticians on Tom's list were of little help. There was no quick way, they said, to trace the owner of the specs, even if he did happen to be a customer. With enough time and trouble they would be able to work out from the remaining, cracked lens what the prescription was; then, if they searched their records, they might be able to match prescription to customer. But only *might*. Besides, it would all take days not hours, and was a long shot because the likelihood was that the owner wasn't a customer.

The fourth optician wasn't at first any more keen to get involved.

'We do traces for the police sometimes,' he said, 'but frankly, it costs so much time and effort I'd only be willing if the case is really serious.'

'Serious?' Tom asked.

'Murder, rape, something of that order.'

Tom smiled. 'Would crucifiction count?'

The optician cocked his head. 'You're kidding.'

'Confidential info, sir.'

'Grief!'

The optician bent his head to inspect the twisted spectacles lying on his desk where Tom had delicately placed them.

'All right to touch?'

'Carefully, sir.'

The optician shifted them with the end of his pen, bent closer, and used a small magnifying glass to inspect the inside edge of one of the arms near where it hinged to the frame.

'Could be in luck,' he said, straightening. He was a tall man, thin, grey-haired with a bald patch on the crown that Tom thought looked like a monk's tonsure. Grey-suited, rugby club tie, rotary club badge in his lapel, flushed complexion, very precise manner. Probably near retirement. One of the town's pillars. Would know everybody. Worth keeping on his right side; never know when he'd come in useful. Like now, maybe.

Tom gave the optician his best schoolboy grin of excitement.

'For a time,' the optician said, warming to the work, 'we stamped a small mark on our frames. Thought it might prove useful, save time in other ways. Turned out not to be the case, so we gave up the practice about a year ago.'

'And there's a mark on these?'

'Must have been among the last pairs we did.'

'So you know who the owner is?'

'When we gave it up, the records were stored in the basement. Almost threw them away, but somehow, records being records—'

'When do you think you might know?'

'Let's see . . .' The optician consulted his appointment diary. 'Busy the rest of the day. Won't be free till after we close. Then time for the search. Say seven. How will that do?'

Tom, champing at the bit of his impatience, said, 'Okay, sir, if that's the soonest you can manage. I'll call back then.'

'I'll do my best.'

The optician inspected the frames with his magnifying glass again, jotted down the mark. Tom carefully retrieved the evidence.

'Seven o'clock, then,' he said and left, feeling at once excited by his success and irritated by the enforced delay before he could get his hands on the reward for playing his hunch.

†

NIK'S LETTERS:

Dear Julie: Meditation this morning was no better than yesterday. Is my mind always this slapdash and all over the place? After Silence, when I had to polish the upstairs landing (hands and knees and old fashioned gluey wax you have to buff up, which takes ages if you put too much on—sweat, sweat), I had a session with Bro. K. I told him I thought I'd like to do a Retreat but that I didn't think I'd manage.

Bro. K.: Why?

Me: Because I've discovered I can't concentrate for more than two minutes, never mind for three days.

Bro. K.: We all have trouble with distractions. It's normal. Most people never notice how much their minds jump from one thing to another. They can't concentrate for long on one thing. One of the things Meditation teaches you is how to focus your attention, all your being, on one thing, one idea.

I said: But apart from that, I don't see how I can spend three days meditating and what you call praying when I don't believe.

He said: I thought you didn't know what you believe?

I said: I don't.

He said: Then this is as good a time as any to start finding out. Use your Retreat for that. You've got to start somewhere. Start there.

I said: But how?

Bro. K.: How does anybody do anything? Take something obvious. For example, how does somebody who wants to be a football player become a football player?

Me: Practice?

Before that. How does he know he wants to be a football player?

Probably because he saw football being played and thought he'd like to do it.

Right. Then what?

Gets a ball and kicks it about?

And?

Gradually learns to control it.

Watches good players playing?

And learns from them. And joins a team. He'd have to do that because football is something you have to be in a team to play.

Bro. K.: So he slowly gets better and better and if he really likes the game and is good enough at it, he might end up playing with a major side.

Me: Yes. But belief isn't a game, is it?

Bro. K. laughed. No, he said, but it's something you have to decide you want. Like you begin by deciding you want to be a footballer. At first you don't know anything about it. But you find a ball and play with it. And—this is the important thing—you copy what real footballers do—the people who already know how to play well. The same with belief. You learn about it by doing it. And you learn what to do by copying what believers do. You want to know about belief? Behave like a believer. But the first thing is deciding you want to believe. Deciding to play football is an act of will, isn't it? So is belief.

Me: Julie—the girl we're praying for—says that belief is a gift. She means a gift from God.

Bro. K.: Doesn't she ever doubt?

Never asked her.

Ask her then. I think what she might really be talking about is conviction—a kind of *knowing*—rather than about belief. Most people who believe in God have times when they doubt. When they lose their sense of conviction. But they go on believing. They make a decision to accept the idea of God, even though they're doubtful, rather than the idea that there's nothing. In other words, they make a conscious act of will to believe. There's no other way.

But that seems hypocritical to me.

It's only hypocritical if you pass yourself off as someone who *knows*. You only have to say you *believe* but don't *know*. A true believer is someone who's searching for knowledge. That must be true, mustn't it? Because as soon as you *know* something, you're not a believer any more. You're a *knower*. You've found out the truth and can prove it. But first you have to be a believer. So a believer is simply someone who's decided what kind of knowledge he's searching for. Not just any knowledge, but knowledge of what he calls God. Just like a biologist searches for knowledge about animals and how they live, and a medical doctor searches for knowledge about human sickness and how to cure it. They can be those things—biologist or medical doctor—and be a believer as well—a searcher after knowledge of the ultimate, the above all, the source of all knowledge. See?

I see what you mean. Don't know if I accept it!

Sounds to me like what you want to be is an academic, God help you!

It's just that I don't have any strong feeling I want to believe. All I think I want is to know about belief.

Bro. K. sucked in his breath. Then you're on dangerous ground, he said. Because where belief is concerned, you can't find out about it without taking the risk of accepting it—of becoming a believer. So watch out!

Why?

Look, Nik, the problem is that you're trying to behave like a biologist studying the behaviour of an animal, when the subject you're studying isn't an animal and can't be investigated like that. You've made the classic mistake of using the wrong tools for the job. Like wanting to know what the air around you is made of and trying to cut it open with a hammer and chisel to find out.

With belief, he said, you have to live it if you want to know about it. You have to be your own laboratory, your own set of tools, your own specimen. You have to observe belief at work in yourself, if you really want to understand it. That's why some people say belief is a mystery. You can't take it out and examine it. You can't cut it open on a dissecting table. You can't even describe it very successfully. And you can't explain it to someone else. Plenty of people have tried, and they've all failed. You can only experience it and know what it is by living it.

I said: But you have to will yourself to believe first?

No other way, I'm afraid, Bro. K. said.

By the time we'd got this far, it was coffee break.

After coffee I told Bro. K. I'd stay till the end of the week, and do a Retreat, and that during the Retreat I'd think about what he'd said about belief and try and behave as if I believed. I mean, what had I to lose?

He said that was okay so long as I agreed to follow his guidance. I said I would, unless he asked me to do anything I thought was wrong.

He said: Right, you start now. Between now and lunchtime I want you to write your Confession.

I said: What! My confession! I don't have anything to confess! I don't feel guilty about anything.

He laughed his funny squeaky chuckle and said he was very glad I was already fit for Heaven. But guilty or not, he wanted me to write whatever came into my head under the title *The Confession of Nik Frome*.

I said I didn't know where to start.

He said: Start at the beginning, with your birth.

But why? I said.

Explanation later, he said.

I said: This is too much like school.

He said: So why are you complaining? School is where you should be right this minute!

So I said I would try but he wasn't to be surprised if all I had by lunchtime was a blank page.

He said: If your life has been nothing more than a blank page so far then at least there's nothing you want to cross out, lucky chap!

Anyway, I did it. You won't believe what came out! And because you won't believe it, I'm sending you a photocopy. I had it done when I was sent for my afternoon exercise in the park. Walked into town instead and had the copy made at a quick-print shop. (I'm not supposed to go into the town. Too much of a distraction! But as far as I can see the place is a dump with about as much to distract you as there is in a morgue. I.e.: only dead bodies.)

I'm not really telling the truth. The real reason I'm sending you what I wrote is that it tells you about something I want you to know about but never told you.

The Confession of Nik Frome

(or as much as he could manage in an hour-and-a-half)

I was born seventeen years and four months ago. This is not really a confession, as it is not a secret and I do not feel guilty about it. The guilt belongs to my parents. I did not ask to be born. They caused it to happen. I do not know if they decided to create me or if I was an accident. I never asked them. All I know is that, judging by what happened afterwards, I feel like an accident.

I can't ask them now because my parents aren't around to ask. They were divorced seven years ago, when I was ten. Since then I have lived with my grandfather (my mother's father). He was a ship's carpenter who set up his own woodwork business when he gave up the sea because he wanted to spend more time with my grandmother. She died the year before I came to live with Grandad. He is now officially retired, but he still has a workshop which he goes to every day as if he were still working. He does odd jobs for people. He says a person is the size of his work. I think he means that people need their work to give their lives a purpose and to make them feel useful. He can be cantankerous sometimes and difficult to live with. Everything has to be just right and ship-shape, and he hates clutter. But he is mostly fun and I love living with him. He has been very good to me, and has taught me many things. One of the things he has taught me is to be sceptical.

My parents divorced after many rows. And now I come to think of it, I do feel guilty because of something I *didn't* do during the last and worst row. I will confess this.

The problem was that my father couldn't, as my mother put it, 'keep his hands off other women'. And my mother's problem was that she was nearly insane with jealousy. (This may explain why, ever since that time, I have disliked people who sleep around, especially when they boast a lot about it. And I have disliked even more people who are possessive. So I guess I think jealousy is a worse sin/crime than lust. Another thing I like about Grandad is that he doesn't try to own me, or coddle me, but wants me to be my own independent self.)

On the night when the last great row happened, my father arrived home late from work. My mother had already hyped herself into a state, convinced he was with 'one of his whores'. She was stomping around the house, banging things, tidying and dusting, as if making the house ultra-clean would somehow show my father up, be an affront to him—his uncleanness against her cleanliness, like it was a competition.

This is what usually happened, and was one of the signs that told me there would be a mighty row soon. During the rows she often shouted at him that he was 'a filthy beast'. At the time I didn't realize exactly what she meant. I was only eight, remember. I used to think she meant Dad didn't wash himself enough, because Mum had a thing about being properly washed and used to say my hands were filthy if I came in with them even slightly grubby from playing in the garden.

Mum had laid the table ready for supper and the food was overcooking in the oven. I was hungry but didn't dare ask for anything. When Mum was in a pre-row mood she made a big production of getting anything for me and I had learned that it was best at these times to keep out of the way. That night I sat in a chair in the corner pretending to read a comic.

Dad arrived two hours late. By then Mum was going at full throttle. She let him have it as soon as he got inside the back door. (I should mention that Dad was a big man. He worked as a fitter in a local factory and used to do body-building. Mum was thin and not very tall. When Dad had had a couple of pints of beer and was feeling in a good mood he used to call her his little sparrow.)

Whenever Dad could get a word in he kept repeating that he'd only been kept on at work for an emergency job. But Mum wouldn't listen. She rampaged on. Usually, Dad rode out these storms by letting Mum shout herself to a standstill and then wheedling himself into her good books again during the next day or two. But he didn't do that this time. Mum started listing off his previous misdemeanours. Dad said what a good memory she had. Mum opened a drawer, took out a pocket diary, and said she didn't need a good memory because she'd been keeping track of his 'filthy habits' for two years.

This sent Dad into orbit. Now he started ranting and raving and stomping round the room, accusing Mum of spying and having a cesspit for a mind, and all sorts of stuff I couldn't understand the meaning of and can only half remember now. I got so scared I hid behind the armchair I'd been sitting in. I could feel that the row was turning into a fight.

They were standing either side of the table, yelling across it at each other. Mum shouted at Dad that he was a coward. This made him speechless with rage. His face turned red, his eyes almost popped out. I was sure he would burst. Instead, he grabbed the tablecloth and gave it an almighty heave that sent everything on the table flying off in all directions.

There was a terrible clatter. Crockery smashed onto the floor. Cutlery flew into pictures that fell off the wall and shattered. A knife stabbed the chair I was hiding behind as if it had been thrown at my head. Salt and sugar and mustard and milk sprayed everywhere. A bottle of tomato ketchup burst against a wall, spreading a splat like blood across it. The room was a mess.

After the crash there was a tense silence. I think we were all stunned by what had happened, even Dad. Then Mum let out a piercing scream, and the next thing I knew they were almost locked together. Mum was banging away at Dad's face and body with her hands, and kicking his legs with her feet. Dad was trying to smother Mum's attack while keeping his legs out of range. And they were bellowing and cursing at each other enough to bring the ceiling down. They looked like they were doing a very violent (and when I think about it now, comic) dance.

At this sight I broke into terrified tears. I thought Dad was going to smash up the entire house, including Mum and myself, and that Mum was aiming to murder Dad. Such a prospect crossed all my wires and I became hysterical. I ran from my hiding place and tried to hurl myself between them. Dad tried to push me away, but succeeded only in punching me in the face. Mum, aiming a foot at Dad's shin, hit my knee instead. That made me scream and claw at them all the harder. Dad yelled at me to get away. Mum yelled at Dad that hitting children was all he was good for. In the ensuing struggle, with me less than half Dad's height, the only result was that my head finally rammed into Dad's groin.

Dad doubled up, his hands grabbing his crotch. At that same instant, Mum's feet got tangled in my legs. She tripped and went sprawling among the broken dishes on the floor. As for me, suddenly left flailing at empty air, I slipped and fell on top of Mum.

Then began the worst part of all. Mum struggled upright and hugged me to her. Seeing what had happened, Dad came for me and tried to pull me to my feet with one of his hands while the other held his still no doubt painful goolies. Each of them tried to grab me from the other. So a furious tug of war got going. Accompanied by me screaming blue murder and them shouting at each other again. The frightening thing to me was that I felt like I was a parcel that two people wanted only because they hated each other. After that, even if they had patched it up and stayed together, I don't think I would have trusted either of them ever again.

As it turned out, Mum won the parcel. She was always more determined and stubborn than Dad. When he gave up, she clutched me to her till her grip was so tight it hurt. Dad stood, snorting and cursing, and glaring thunderously at Mum.

Get out! she hissed at him. Get out and never come back!

He stood his ground for what seemed to me like hours. Then, without a word, he turned and went out through the front door, which he rarely used. He shut the door behind him very quietly, I remember that clearly. It seemed somehow more frightening, more ominous than the noise there'd been. Right now, as I think of it, it echoes in my memory like an unfinished sound.

I've only seen my father four times since then. Our meetings have always been awkward and have left me feeling unhappy. I haven't seen him for two years now, and I don't want to.

I stayed with Mum for six months after Dad left. Then she made friends with an Australian working near where we lived. Soon he came to stay with us. I was nearly ten by that time and reacted badly. I went through a patch of throwing tantrums and stealing things—money from Mum's purse, even shoplifting in the end. I was never caught, but Mum found out and we had a row of our own that was a mini-version of her rows with Dad.

After that I deliberately made myself as unpleasant as I could, finding ways to annoy them both and smashing things accidentally on purpose, and especially spoiling any occasion when they were enjoying themselves. I won't go into details. Maybe I do feel a bit guilty and ashamed of this.

It was during one of these upsets that Grandad suggested I go and live with him for a while to give us all a chance to sort ourselves out. Three months later, Mum announced she was going to Australia with Bill, her friend, to live, and said I could go with them if I wanted. I said no, and she didn't try to persuade me. I still think she was pleased and didn't want to change my mind. Grandad said he was happy to have me go on living with him. And that was that. Mum went and I haven't seen her since. For a time, she wrote every month. Now less and less often. I stopped writing to her ages ago.

End of story. Except that I haven't said what it is I feel guilty about *not* doing. I feel guilty that I didn't ask for my supper before Dad got in on the night of the Big Row. If I had, I would have been sitting at the table when he came in. They would have had their row, but he would never have pulled the cloth off the table with me sitting there. And if he hadn't done that, they would never have fought as they did, between themselves and over me, which is the most demeaning, painful thing that has ever happened to me in my life. And if they hadn't fought like that, they would probably have stayed together.

What I mean, I suppose, is that somehow I feel responsible for their breakup. That's ridiculous, I know. But, it seems to me, that's the truth about guilt. It's irrational, ridiculous, a terrible waste of yourself, like a kind of sickness. It's a contamination. We should discover how to get rid of it, as we would if it were an evil disease.

I've only a few minutes of my hour-and-a-half left. I didn't intend going on so long about this one event in my life. Usually, I try not to tell people what happened. It embarrasses me. And compared with what some kids have had to put up with it isn't anything, so who cares?

I guess I should also confess that I've done pretty much the sort of things everybody else seems to do. I've told lies, all of them pathetic. I've hated people and wished that ghastly things would happen to them. I've felt superior to some people and secretly envied others. I had a sexy pash on a friend when I was about fourteen, then decided I preferred girls, lusted after various ones, who just thinking about would make me masturbate in desperation at not being able to have them, till a girl called Melissa did a sort of routine job on me one evening when I think she couldn't find anybody better to make out with.

But I don't feel any guilt about these things. They seem so

pitifully ordinary. I think what a lot of people call guilt is just fear of the consequences when they've done something they shouldn't. They're guilty in the sense that they did it. But they don't feel remorse. Which is what I think guilt really means: remorse that you've done something, whether it's 'officially' wrong or not. Remorse means regret for doing it and being determined not to do it again. Not because of what other people might think, but because you feel what you've done has diminished you in your own eyes, made you feel less and worse than you want to be.

So I guess my worst confession—my *only* confession really —is that I feel less than I *want* to be. Not some of the time, but most of the time. And I regret that. Want to do something about it.

End of time.

✝

Notes on the crucifixion

Background

1) There was nothing unusual about crucifiction. It was used for almost a thousand years, first by the Phoenicians, then by the Romans. It was abolished by the Emperor Constantine, first 'Christian' emperor of Rome (there's a laugh!) in AD 337.

2) The Romans were the real experts. They improved the method until they could cause the maximum of pain, and could regulate the time it took for the victim to die—shorter or longer.

3) After the defeat of the Spartacus rebellion in 71 BC, six and a half thousand crosses lined the Appian Way from Cappadocia to Rome, each bearing a rebel.

4) So wearing a cross round your neck to show you are a Christian, or just as a nice piece of jewellery, is like wearing a gallows or a guillotine or an electric chair or, more likely these

days, a hypodermic needle. You're wearing an instrument of torture and death.

How was it done?

5) Christ's cross was T shaped (called *crux commissa*), not like the one usually shown in churches and paintings.

6) After his interrogation he did not carry all the cross to the rubbish tip of Golgotha, but only the cross-piece (*patibulum*) made of cypress wood, weighing 75–125 lb. Carrying this for approx. 750 m. through narrow, crowded streets from Pontius Pilate's praetorium, where he was tried, to the execution site on Golgotha was torture. He was also flogged at the same time, just to make life more fun for him.

7) The nails used to pin him to the cross were not driven through his palms, but through his wrists. The palms would not have supported the weight of the body. The nails would have torn the hands in two down through the fingers. 20 cm. nails with blunt ends were hammered into the wrist through the gap between the wrist-bones. This was extremely painful. When going through, the nails impaled the median nerve. This caused the thumb to bend across the hand so strongly that it cut into the flesh of the palm, causing worse pain still.

8) The cross-piece, with the victim's hands nailed to it, was then hoisted up and attached to the upright (*stipes*), which was already waiting, planted in the ground.

9) The victim's knees were then bent upwards. The sole of one foot was pressed flat against the upright. A 20 cm. blunt-ended nail was hammered through the foot, between the second and third toe-bones (*metatarsals*). When the nail came out, the other leg was bent until the nail could be hammered through the second foot and on into the wood.

10) The victim was left to hang from the three nails. There was very little loss of blood, but the pain was unendurable.

11) To prolong the death struggle, the executioners could:
   a) tie the arms with ropes, thus easing the weight on the wrists and reducing the pain;

b) a 'saddle' or seat could be fixed to the upright where the victim could rest on it, thus easing the strain on the feet, allowing the death to take up to three days.

12) To shorten the struggle they smashed the victim's legs so that he could not push up on his feet and ease the strain on the wrists and arms.

13) The downward strain on the arms and shoulders and chest prevented the victim from breathing properly. He began to stifle, and the muscles therefore suffered agonizing cramp from lack of oxygen. If this was unrelieved, the victim suffocated in less than an hour.

14) But with his legs bent and his feet nailed, he could push up and relieve the pain in his chest. For a while he could breathe more easily. But the pain of his full weight resting on the nails in his feet was so fierce that he soon slumped down again.

15) The victim's temperature rose rapidly and very high because of the pain and exertion. Sweat poured from his body. This caused excruciating thirst.

16) The victim went on alternately hanging down from his wrists and pushing up on his feet until he could take no more, gave up and died. In Christ's case this took six hours.

17) Crucifiction is thought to be the cruellest form of torture and death known to the human race.

†

NIK'S LETTERS:

Dear Julie: It's afternoon Reading Time. I'm supposed to be reading a book by Simone Weil that Bro. K. gave me. She's good. You ought to try her when you're fit again. But I'm breaking the rules—sin, sin!—in order to write this because I want to post it when I go out later on.

I'm in my cell, looking over the park. It's a lovely sunny evening. There's a weird old woman standing on the other side of the pond feeding the ducks. She's dressed in layers and layers of clothes that are all too big for her, and wrinkled woollen stockings and old football boots. And she's singing. My window's half open and I can just hear her. I think she's singing *Over the Rainbow*.

My job this morning was helping Bro. K. paint the woodwork at the back of the house—kitchen window frames, back door, etc. While we worked, he talked to me about my Confession. I've noticed he usually tries to find a manual job to do while we talk. He says it makes it easier for people to say things that might be embarrassing if you're sitting in chairs with nothing else to do but look at each other. I guess this is the monastic equivalent of the psychiatrist's couch. Maybe shrinks ought to take their patients gardening while they bare their psyches. Weeding the garden while weeding their minds.

Anyway, Bro. K.'s technique helps me. Not that either of us did any psyche or soul-baring. I'm beginning to see that what matters is not *how much* is said, but *what* is said.

Kit quizzed me about my parents, and told me a bit about his own. (His dad was a shop assistant all his life and lived for his family—two sons and a daughter—and for his fishing— fanatical, apparently. His mum was a home help. Used to take Kit with her sometimes when he was little. He told some creasingly funny stories of things that had happened on these visits. His mum was also devoted to the church in what Kit called an 'Oh my God!' sort of way. He said it was from his mum that he caught the religious bug and learned not to take it too seriously.)

But what he really wanted to say to me was that he thinks that what happened with my parents caused me to lose my trust in people, especially people who get close to me. And not just my trust in other people, but in myself as well. Belief, he said, is partly to do with trust. For a start, you have to trust your inner instincts, your 'inner faith', that there's more to life than meets the eye, if you're going to decide *for* belief rather than *against* it. If you don't even trust yourself, never mind others, you find it hard to 'put your faith in' anyone or anything. You tend to believe only in what you can know through your senses—what you can see, touch, taste, smell, hear. And even then you doubt, because so often your senses mislead you. Poison fruit can look beautiful and taste sweet but . . .

He didn't make a song and dance out of saying this, just said it and then chatted on about something else. But I knew he was right. I didn't realize till I wrote about it yesterday how hurt I still feel about the breakup. And that hurt does invade my life still. I guess everybody has a deep hurt inside them. Most people probably have much worse hurts than mine. But I guess, whatever your hurt is, you have to heal it somehow.

Kit has been giving me passages from the Gospels about the crucifixion to meditate on. I objected at first, but he told me to think of them simply as a story of what happened to an ordinary man, and to try and sort out what it meant and how it had happened and why, and what he did about his hurt. Simone Weil is interesting about this, though not easy. So my Silence times today have been spent trying to concentrate on that.

Which reminds me to tell you that I'm really hooked on Silence. Can't wait for the bell! And I'm gradually learning how to control my mind then. If I start by going straight to chapel and spend the first half hour there, working myself in, then I can go to my cell or the library or even into the park and keep myself concentrated. Like I was enclosed in a Silence capsule. A Silence Support Vessel—an SSV! I still get plenty of distractions, of course. In fact, I'm more often distracted than concentrated. But I'm slowly getting my mind organized *towards* concentration, rather than *away* from it.

Does this make sense? Which is another thing I'm discovering, by the way. That the usual way of explaining things doesn't seem to work when you're talking about what goes on in your mind when you're in the SSV. The words don't seem right. Inadequate, ridiculous. Banal was Kit's word, when I tried to explain this to him. They don't have enough meaning. Enough *go*. Enough energy.

During Silence, especially in chapel in the early morning, when it's very beautiful with the rising sun streaming into the room from the end window, I don't find myself thinking in words like these I'm writing now. I'd think of them as a distraction. They'd irritate me and I'd try and shut them up.

The words I think in when I'm in Silence come—I'm not sure how to put this—in 'clusters'. More like they were objects than individual words. Or, maybe it's better to say the words in the clusters seem to make an object, something three-dimensional, and mobile. They come out of the Silence and go into the Silence and are made of the Silence.

Does that make sense? I think it might to you because I think you must have experienced it. I'd not dare say it to anyone else because they'd think I was crackers. I did say it to Kit, though. As my Retreat director, I have to describe to him what I think is happening to me. He says what I'm describing is what he calls prayer. I haven't agreed to this yet because I still think of prayer as being addressed to another person like myself only more powerful—a God. Kit says I've got to grow out of being crude.

After telling him this, Kit set me another writing job. He asked me to try and write down a 'cluster' so we could look at it and discuss it together. I didn't think I could do this, because words on paper aren't three-dimensional and don't 'make' an object, do they? And apart from this, the clusters slip away as soon as my mind is distracted. Trying to write them down would certainly be a distraction. It's almost as if Silence Thoughts are so elusive that they vanish the split second I take the eyes of my mind off them. Just a slight movement of my body, a blink even, and they're gone.

Which is something else Kit is helping me think about: how I use my body during Meditation. He's making me attend to my posture and position and the effect these have on my concentration and the thoughts that happen.

I start by sitting relaxed but squarely and upright. Not rigid or uncomfortable, but not slumped. When I've got myself settled and going—quiet inside and ready—I kneel, supporting myself with my forearms on the prayer bench in front of me. Upright but relaxed again. I keep my eyes closed, or look at the words of the text I'm meditating on. But I'm finding that when you're concentrated, your eyes go blind even though you're looking at something or even someone, which I now realize explains that funny absent stare I noticed when I first came here and Silence was rung. People who've learned the trick, like Kit, can kind of switch off from seeing what's around them and switch on to seeing their interior Silence Thoughts in one go.

When my knees tire of kneeling, which is fairly soon compared with the experts, I either sit back on my haunches for a while or sit up in my seat again.

It's when I'm kneeling upright that I'm finding the clusters appear. One came this evening so I made an effort to remember it so I could write it down later. It didn't quite work. I lost the 'essence' of it—the *energy* of it. But maybe it's a start, like learning how to make a photograph with a poor camera and doing your own processing when you've never done any before and don't really know how. You're bound to get a hopeless picture. And it *is* only a picture, not the real thing.

So here's my badly shot, badly processed picture of today's Cluster smuggled from the S S V!

This is how it happened. I was feeling tired by the time the 5.30 Silence started. I sat in chapel, not able to concentrate very well, my mind drifting. I tried kneeling, but wasn't getting far, mostly just enjoying the quiet and the calm and the view of the park through the window. After a while I looked at my watch, because I was feeling hungry and hoping that Evensong and supper weren't too far off. But not as much time had passed as I expected, so I held my watch to my ear to make sure it was still going. It was. I tried giving myself up to Silence again, and after a minute or so, the Cluster came.

Tick-Tock

(or: Death as a Way of Life)

Clocks tick
regularly turning   time is intensity
Earth time   of experience
                          short or long   in density
How time seems   I am
for me
now fast
now slow
is not clock-
time never changes   I am that
                          I have been
For me
yesterday is sometimes

further off than
last year
and sometimes
ten years ago
is more present
than last week

          Time is what I am

Yet there is death
death in time
conspires
but death
is not me

That which I
have been most
not
that which clocks
regularly ticking
tell
I must be

          What God is

Hell is time
unending endings
everlasting deaths

waits in time
for an end
in eternity

Time is all
Now
where else
can I live

          God is
heaven
being timeless

in these words

†

Notes on the crucifiction

On Good Friday 1983 three people were nailed to wooden crosses in Manila as their way of celebrating the Crucifiction.

Manio Castro, aged 31, and Bob Velez, aged 41, remained on their crosses for five minutes after the nails had been hammered through their hands.

Luciana Reyes, aged 24, was nailed to her cross for the eighth year running in Bulcana province. 10,000 pilgrims and tourists watched.

These events were reported, with pictures, to newspapers world-wide by the Philippine News Agency.

On Good Friday 1985 in the Manila suburb of Manaluyong, Donald Rexford, aged 38, was crucified for the fifth year running with four-inch stainless steel nails driven through his palms. He was hoisted up for seven seconds, and turned round twice so that one thousand onlookers could view him. Rexford was celebrating his reunion with his American father. When asked how he felt he said: 'It's okay. It's my way of giving thanks.' The event was reported, with pictures, world-wide by the Associated Press.

✝

NIK'S LETTERS:

Dear Julie: Just phoned the hospital. They let me talk to Simmo. She said you're on the mend, doing really well, surprising everybody. Hurray! *And* that you've been tape-recording letters to me. Terrific! Can't wait to get home to hear them.

She also told me the first of my letters had arrived and that she read it to you and that you laughed and said it made you feel better. Great! Helping you feel better makes me feel better.

This morning Kit read 'Tick-Tock'. He said it was a poem. I said it wasn't. I don't know how to write poetry. Don't even read it much. He asked if he could use it during his meditation tomorrow. Said I should write some more.

I'd better explain, because you can't see it yet, that it can't be read like prose. You have to read it across as well as down. A bit like a crossword puzzle, Kit said. A Cluster isn't just vertical or horizontal. It's three-dimensional. And the phrases, the lines, are like mobile sculpture: they move around one another, making different patterns and shapes—different meanings but all linked. Or they would if I could write them really well. To write them really well, though, I'd have to make them into a hologram! Can you imagine, words weaving in and out of each other and criss-crossing, moving all the time, always combining and recombining to make new sentences, new meanings. Wouldn't that be great.

That's the way I think of the world. And not just the world but the entire universe. And, if I was forced to say what I think God is, then that is what I think he/she/it is: the whole convoluted, ever-changing, unthinkable cluster of Whatisthere.

We only ever know little bits of it.

159

But today I have to tell you about how I was a naughty boy.

Yesterday evening, Adam, the newly arrived novice, asked me to play tennis with him. I'm not sure I like him. He's a big lumpy bloke, twenty, with a loud confident voice. A rugger-playing type—thick arms, muscly chest, very thick hairy thighs that strain the seams of his shorts. Gross really. Apish but not very monkish. Plays tennis as if he's fighting the third world war.

I lost. Hardly even scored, in fact. Afterwards he said: Well, at least we had a bit of fun! And he patted my bum with his racquet. Have you noticed how sporty types are always patting each other's bums while making hearty remarks?

Let's take the long way back, he said. Don't want to go in till we have to, do we?

He was like a conscript in the army on a night out instead of a volunteer monk. As we were walking along, he asked me if I had any money on me. I had, so he said: Let's have a drink. And he took me into a pub near the park gate. He asked for a pint of beer. He downed his in one go like he hadn't drunk anything in months, banged his glass down, did a lot of lip-smacking and said: Any chance of another? So he had a second pint. Living it up! I have to confess, I did feel at the time a bit like a kid playing truant.

He drank his second pint more slowly and we started talking. I asked him why he joined. You can do a lot worse, he said.

I said: Sure, but being a monk isn't like being other things.

Right, he said. One of the things I like is that it's a bit special. And that it's a good laugh.

I said: A laugh?

Right, he said. (He says Right a lot.)

I said: What's funny about it?

He said: Everything. The way we go on, the things we do, the way other people—lay people like you—treat us. And the brothers, of course. They're the biggest laugh. Take Kit. He's a laugh just to look at.

So he had a good loud laugh to prove it.

I said: What about you? You're one of the brothers. Are you a good laugh?

Right, he said, 'course I am.

I said: I don't know what's so funny.

He said: Grown men wandering around in floppy dresses with solemn faces and making a fuss about not talking to each other for hours on end. Doesn't that strike you as funny?

I said: But what about God?

Adam said: What about him?

I said: You do believe?

He laughed like I was some kind of idiot. Naturally, he said.

I said: I don't see what's natural about it.

Right, he said. (I thought: If he says Right once more, I'll throttle him!) Right, that's your problem, but it isn't mine. I've never had any problem about God. Always seemed obvious to me, ever since I was little. That he's there, I mean. Can't say I spend much time thinking about him.

I said: So what do you do during Meditation?

He said: Pray, of course.

I said: What about?

He said: Kit must have explained what monks do, he likes explaining what monks do. (I thought: I'll bet you and Kit don't get on.) I said he had.

Adam said: Well then, you'll know we divide our time between worship, study and work, right? All a monk's life is a kind of prayer. But during meditation I pray for people who need it, and about things going on in the world and stuff like that. Doing that is part of a monk's job. What we're here for. I don't mean just praying for what people need. I mean praying *for* them because they can't pray for themselves. Or won't more likely. I mean, we have people whose job is to generate electricity and people who grow food for us, and suchlike. Well, a monk's job is to generate prayers that help keep the human spirit alive. And the price of that sermon is another pint. The labourer is worthy of his hire.

And he patted my bum again with his racquet.

When he had his third pint, I said: You mean you believe your prayers make a sort of energy that keeps the entire human race going?

Sure, he said.

I said: And if all the praying stopped, we'd all go phutt?

Right, he said. Not straight off, of course. Not like us all being shot at the same second. But gradually, like slow poison. I mean, he said, it has to be obvious even to a non-believer that people aren't only bodies and minds. Well, a monk's job is to help keep the other part fit, right? And it's worth doing because most people don't bother. In a way I'm a sort of life saver. So I'm doing a job that's a bit special and is useful and I get plenty of fun out of it. Nobody can ask for more than that. Does that answer your question?

Before I could stop myself, I said: But what about girls? (I'd been dying to ask since I came here, but it isn't the sort of question I could ask Kit.)

Adam laughed extra hard and said: I thought you'd never ask! Look, he said, I can take them or leave them, right? Like God, no problem. Before I joined I had a few hot pashes, naturally. Who doesn't? And I've been a bit hot under the habit a few times since. But you're not really talking about girls, are you? You're really talking about sex. And when it comes down to basics, sex is nothing more than a steamy cuddle that ends in a mucky dribble. To be honest, I'd rather have a good game of tennis myself.

There didn't seem to be any answer to that and anyhow it was time we got back for Compline.

As we approached the house Adam said: You're not thinking of joining us, are you?

I said I wasn't.

He said: Just as well. You'd have a bad time.

I said: Why?

He said: Because you think too much. You'd get hung up on wanting to know the reason for doing everything instead of just getting on with it. You take yourself too seriously. You should relax and enjoy yourself more.

This got up my nose. I said: What do you know? You've only been a novice for a few months. You're not even a proper monk yet. You can't possibly know all about it.

Right, he said laughing and patting my bum again, but anyway, thanks for the game.

And we went inside. The bell was ringing for Silence.

I don't know why he annoyed me so much. Maybe he just

wasn't what I thought a monk (even a trainee monk) should be like. Anyway, I couldn't concentrate at all during Compline and didn't stay in chapel afterwards.

Kit followed me out, waved me into the visitors' room, and gave me a right going over, very coldly polite, for playing tennis with Adam and going to the pub. First off, because, being in Retreat, I should have asked Kit for permission, and then because Adam, being a novice, ought to have asked permission as well but hadn't, and then making it worse by going drinking. Kit made it sound like we had both been very naughty boys and that it was all my fault.

I said I didn't see what all the fuss was about.

Kit said: Didn't you agree to go into Retreat? I'm simply pointing out that you've broken your own agreement. Not a crime, but a neglect of a willingly accepted responsibility. As for Adam, he knows well enough that the hardest part of a monk's life is his vow of obedience. This evening he kicked over the traces and it's my job to help him back into harness. You said you wanted to share our life. This is part of it.

I said I didn't see that any harm had been done.

Kit said he didn't want to argue tonight, but would talk about it tomorrow.

I went to my cell feeling pretty cheesed, had a bath, which calmed me down a bit, and lay on my bed thinking about you.

How do I think of you? As someone I want to be with. As someone as young as me, but 'older', if that makes sense. As someone I like to look at, not just because you're good to look at, but because just looking at you makes me smile and feel happier. As someone who I want to know all about and yet who seems more and more secret the more I get to know her. As someone who knows her mind and who I envy for that. As someone who is strong in herself without seeming to need anyone else to help her. As someone who makes me think and *unsettles* me in a way that makes me feel more alive.

I'd better stop before this list gets too long.

Anyway, it's almost midnight and I'm ready for bed. Tomorrow is the last day of my Retreat.

Love, *Nik*.

✝

At seven o'clock prompt, Tom was back at the optician's.

'Any luck, sir?' he asked as he was led inside.

The optician was flushed. 'The owner of these glasses was crucified, did you say?'

'It's possible. We aren't sure yet.'

With a touch of melodrama, the optician placed a piece of paper on the desk between them. On it was a name. Nicholas Christopher Frome.

'Mean anything to you?'

Tom thought. 'Rings a bell but I don't know why.'

'The car bombing a few weeks ago?'

Tom looked at him.

'"Pilgrim lovers victims of terror bomb"?'

'Christ!' Tom said.

The optician smiled. 'Glad those old records came in useful after all.'

'You're sure, sir?'

'Most of my patients are as old as I am. I get very few youngsters these days. No trendy frames and no young staff. I remember him. He came to me because I treated his grandfather. Nice boy. Mild myopia. Slight astigmatism in the left eye. I've written his address on the other side.'

Tom's first instinct was to race off. But the optician said: 'Bit of a facer, eh? If he is the chap you're looking for, the press will have a field day.'

The optician was right. Which made Tom think again. One false step now, and goodbye plain clothes.

'Could I use your phone, sir?'

'Help yourself.'

Tom dialled the station. The super was still in his office but not at all pleased to be held up.

'I've an official dinner in half an hour, Tom. This had better be good.'

'I think I've traced the crucified man, sir.'

'Why bother me with what you think? I want certainties.'

'There could be bad publicity. I thought I should check.'

'Who is he?'

'Name of Frome. The boy involved in the car bombing a few weeks ago.'

'Jesus!'

'Yes, sir.'

'Who else knows?'

'Only the optician who helped us trace him. I'm with him now.'

'Right. Listen carefully. Have you any other leads?'

'Might have, sir, in about half an hour.'

'Splendid. Follow that up. We'll check on your info from this end. You've done well. Now, give me the boy's address and then put your optician on so I can gag him. If this gets out, all hell will break loose.'

†

NIK'S LETTERS:

Dear Julie: I'm back home. Old Vic fetched me last night. There's a lot to tell. In future I'll send tapes so you can listen instead of someone having to read my letters to you. But I've just discovered that my Walkman is on the blink and I can't get it fixed till tomorrow, so I'll send this as a stop-gap. The last Epistle of Nik the Spy in a Foreign Land. At least I can use my wp again, which is a relief. All that writing made my hand ache and took ages.

Kit kept me at it right to the end. He might be little and funny-looking but he's no slouch.

Yesterday, he made me scrub the kitchen floor as my house-work. It's H U G E, that floor. Big as a football field is how it felt after about five minutes. And the floorboards are old and splintery and full of ridges. All the time I was scrubbing the others kept tramping in and out, messing up the parts I'd done, because they wanted hot water or cleaning equipment for their own jobs. Adam was the worst. He was in and out half-a-dozen times. I'm sure he was doing it deliberately. And grinned down at me every time with a superior smirk. Could have sloshed him with my floorcloth. I felt humiliated, down there on my knees, bum in the air, scrubbing like a skivvy.

By the time I was finished I was really in a bad mood. And sure Kit had done it to punish me for going out with Adam. I was also moaning to myself about being exploited by a bunch of self-righteous hypocrites, etc. etc. Am I an unpaid char? I was thinking. Did I come here to be treated like a servant while they swan about pretending to be holy? What's scrubbing this floor got to do with me getting well again and finding out about belief?

When I finally got back to my cell, long after the others had finished their jobs, I found an envelope from Kit lying on my bed. Enclosed, a copy of what was inside.

When you've read it, you'll be able to imagine how I felt! I spent the rest of the day thinking about what it says.

I'm beginning to understand what he's driving at.

When the time came to leave I was sorry. Part of me wanted to stay. But another part wanted to be back home. So much has happened in the last few days. I need to sort it out. And I ought to get back to school. I'm missing stacks of work.

This morning I woke very early and felt odd not going down to chapel. How quickly a habit like that gets a hold. I tried meditating in my room but it didn't work. So after a while I gave up and cycled to St James's for Old Vic's early service to see if that helped. The usual six people there, plus the man who always looks nervous when he sees me because he thinks I'm going to have a hissy fit again.

I told Old Vic I'd be writing to you. He said to give you his love and prayers and tell you he plans a visit next week. If I can, I'll come with him. There's so much to talk about.

Love, *Nik*.

Dear Nik: The job I gave you this morning is the one we all dislike doing the most. Unless you are already a saint, you will have grumbled to yourself about it, just as we do. However, I hope you will understand, when I explain, that in an odd way I was paying you the best compliment I could. For we would never usually subject our guests to such a task. We keep its pleasures for ourselves!

But we have enjoyed having you with us. We have admired the courage with which you have thrown yourself into our unnatural life. For unnatural it is, and hard enough for anyone to enter into, even more so when recovering from such a terrible experience as the one you suffered recently. We have all been praying for you and Julie with extra concern, and will go on doing so until we know you are both fully recovered.

When you arrived, I talked to Philip Ruscombe about you. We agreed that offering you the challenge of our life, and all of it, not just the easy parts, would be the best way to help. In your position, some people need rest and comfort. For others, cosseting is a mistake. They become depressed from dwelling too much on their misfortune. Both Philip and I strongly felt that you would thrive best on re-engagement in the business of life. And that this is what you would want. So we weren't surprised when you accepted our offer.

In these few days I think you have discovered at least a hint of what it is that breeds our belief and sustains our faith. Including the surprise of our doubt. I have witnessed with great satisfaction how you have come to understand the place of Silence in our life; and how the *Opus Dei*—the Work of God—which we perform in chapel (the monk's true workshop) is our power base.

Besides this, you have wholeheartedly shared yourself with us in community. I hope what you found helped restore your wounded faith in the ultimate goodness of working people when they live in trust together.

But when I was thinking all this about you last night, I wondered if you had also understood about our holy serfdom! I mean the grinding, tedious aspects of our life—of all working people's lives. Our visitors often miss it, because they are not with us long enough or only have eyes for our obviously religious activities. You have been so inquiring about us that I decided you might even welcome a practical insight into this side of us. And so I gave you the kitchen floor.

Our belief is lived out, is *known* to us through images of action. We pray, we worship, we work manually, we study. We do not live out our belief only in words written down. Indeed, I find it much easier to scrub the kitchen floor than to write this. So when you read it, remember that while you were groaning and grumbling on your knees in the kitchen I was groaning and yes, even grumbling a little, at my desk, writing to you.

I know I shall fail to explain what I mean. But I have learned that in such failure there is a kind of success. For my failure announces the infinity that I call God. It demonstrates God's *unwritableness* (if there is such a word, which I doubt!).

Your 'cluster' seems to me to be the evidence of your own struggle with that truth. God is not to be captured in anyone's prose. Others discovered this before you. The Psalmist, for example, whose words we repeat at every office in chapel, knew that God can only be celebrated, but never captured, in words of *special* worth. So you too were led to speak, to write, in other shapes—in words of special worth to you. You will not allow me to call them poetry. All right! But the Psalms are poetry, and the Sermon on the Mount and much else in the Bible. Poetry seems to me much closer to *writing God* than is any prose. So will you allow me to make one last Retreat leader's plea and ask you to read more of it? I have attached a poem I have long loved and often found useful during meditation, just in case. It may not be to your taste, but I hope you will give it a chance.

Now about the kitchen floor. Let me try saying it this way:

The young men who come here to try their vocations are of two kinds. The first kind are those who are attracted by the trappings. They love the *idea* of being a monk. They like wearing the habit, like feeling special, enjoy the ritual of chapel, and make a great fuss of their vows. Their attention is on themselves and on the drama, the romance, of being a monk. They are like actors playing monks in a never-ending play. They often do not stay long. They get tired of playing the part.

The other kind are in love with the *work*. With the business of our life. They sometimes find the trappings irksome, and ask awkward questions of us older brothers about why we do some things which to them seem out of date or which make us different from other people. Why we wear the habit, for example. This can make them at first more difficult to live with than the other kind. But their attention, their *energy* is given to the slog of prayer, the discipline of worship, the hidden grind of our labour.

The first kind are here to fulfil their fantasies about themselves. Scrubbing the kitchen floor doesn't usually feature in their desires. At first, they may think of it as romantic—an act of humility in the style of St Francis. But they like everybody to know how humble they have been! And after a few months of such drudgery, they begin asking if they have not done it for long enough. They think scrubbing the floor is only for beginners. A job for those on the lowest rung of the ladder. For them, monastic life is like an ordinary profession, with a system of promotion, and a hierarchy of seniority. You start at the bottom doing the worst jobs and work your way up to ease and comfort and power over others. They often have a vocation to be Superiors, in charge of monasteries!

The other kind are here to search for God in the work of God in community. These are the people (and they are the fewest of all) who have a true vocation. Scrubbing the kitchen floor may make them grumble, but in their heart of hearts they know it must be done. It must be done for the practical reason that there is no one else to do it. But more importantly, it must be done for the spiritual reason that in the meanest work, in manual labour, in necessary drudgery, we encounter the disgust of monotony.

Those who give their lives to God, rather than to the elevation of themselves, soon learn that scrubbing the kitchen floor is forever the test of the strength of their givenness to God. They know that their life as a monk is not about climbing ladders of professional success, but about lifelong acceptance of their commonplace equality with their brothers, and, through the community, with men and women living and departed all over the world.

This is what I wanted you to glimpse today, on your last day with us. It offers you another clue, another piece of evidence, about what belief is—what belief 'feels like'.

Belief not only begins as an act of will, but it is sustained by the drudgery of everyday work. My belief is kept alive by the monotony of everyday prayer—which is the same for a monk as daily training sessions are for an athlete, or daily practice is for a musician. It is nothing elevated, you see. It is not usually accompanied by beautiful feelings or holy thoughts. It is not a kind of trip into a spiritual wonderland of pleasure. It is like scrubbing the kitchen floor—a routine necessary chore that helps keep the place clean and in good repair.

When you feel confident in your faith, such work is not difficult. It is even enjoyable. But when you lose your confidence, when you are off form, when the dark night of the soul besets you, and faith seems hollow and ridiculous, such drudgery, though tedious, even disgusting, anchors you to reality. It is all that is left to keep your belief alive. And then, when faith returns, it finds a home fit and ready to inhabit.

In this a monastery is no different from anywhere else. Everywhere in the world there are people who seek only their own elevation—comfort for themselves and power over others. And there are people who give themselves to *the work*.

If you remember us at all when you return home, I hope, Nik, that you will think of us scrubbing the kitchen floor.

I pray for you. *Kit.*

P.S. Here is the poem I promised. It is by George Herbert.

Love

Love bade me welcome; yet my soul drew back,
　Guilty of dust and sin.
But quick-eyed Love, observing me grow slack
　From my first entrance in,
Drew nearer to me, sweetly questioning,
　If I lacked anything.

'A guest,' I answered, 'worthy to be here.'
　Love said, 'You shall be he.'
'I, the unkind, ungrateful? Ah, my dear,
　I cannot look on thee.'
Love took my hand, and smiling did reply,
　'Who made the eyes but I?'

'Truth, Lord, but I have marred them; let my shame
　Go where it doth deserve.'
'And know you not,' says Love, 'who bore the blame?'
　'My dear, then I will serve.'
'You must sit down,' says Love, 'and taste my meat.'
　So I did sit and eat.

ENGAGEMENTS

JULIE:

Dear Nik: I can see! I CAN SEE!
[*Laughs.*]
Isn't that great!
[*More laughter.*]
I expect Mum has let you know.
But I want to tell you about it myself.
[*Heavy breaths.*]
I'll be calm now.
[*Pause.*]
They took the bandages off yesterday. Oh, Nik, I've been sitting up in bed just staring at everything, and grinning like an idiot! Everything looks so new, so . . . *fresh*.

Some things *are* new, of course. I mean, I'm seeing them for the first time. Simmo, for example. Not that she's a *thing*. But, after all this time talking to her and being looked after by her, being dependent on her more than on anyone else, I'd never seen her till yesterday. And there she was! And the other nurses. And the doctors. And this room I'm in.

I'm having to readjust myself. Almost as if I'm a new patient, just arrived.

But the amazing thing was the view out of my window. I still can't get over it. And I just have to tell you about it.

But I've jumped ahead of myself. I should tell you about everything in the right order, the order things happened.

[*Pause.*]

I knew ahead of time when they were going to take the bandages off. They told me a few days ago they thought my eyes were about ready. So I asked them not to tell anybody —Mum or Philip Ruscombe or you or anybody who would worry and want to be here. I wanted to be sure about the result myself first, and have time to cope, whether I was blind or not.

I don't mind telling you now, I was pretty worked up. I prayed about it a lot, and Simmo had talked to me, buoying me up and preparing me for the worst, just in case. She's been really terrific all along.

But even so, I didn't know how I'd take it if the news was bad. And, to be honest, I didn't think I could cope with people who are close to me standing around and being sympathetic at the same time as I found out the truth myself.

Besides, I knew it would be a strange kind of experience. Having taken my sight for granted for nineteen years and then suddenly to be blind, which is something you can never take for granted, not for a single moment, and then after worrying about it for weeks, to face the unveiling, when I'd discover if the gift I'd always taken for granted had been given back to me . . . Well, I wanted that occasion to be as unfussy, as clear and simple as possible. I wanted to give it all my attention.

Anyway, the doctor agreed. No one to know. And just her and Simmo with me.

Before the doctor arrived Simmo prepared me. An extra careful clean-up of my room. Fresh sheets on the bed. A new nightie she'd brought me specially. And the blind on my windows pulled down because my eyes might be damaged by strong light after being covered up for so long.

Humankind cannot bear very much reality. Who said that? It's a line of poetry I read somewhere. Remembered it when Simmo pulled the blinds. My eyes couldn't bear the reality of unshaded sunlight.

What Simmo does, it seems to me, Nik, is exactly what you've been asking about. What she does is what belief *is*. Simmo being faithful day after day to people like me is belief. Nobody proved anything to her that persuaded her to do it. No one promised her much of anything, as a matter of fact. She just decided for herself that she would spend her life this way. I suppose what Brother Kit told you is right after all. Belief is an act of will, as much as it is anything. It's given you, true. But you have to decide to accept it.

[*Pause.*]

There I go again! Another sermon. But you did ask, even if it does seem centuries ago. And you keep on telling me no one knows the answer, and I keep on trying to tell you that they do. It's just that you're blind to it! You don't want to see it yet. You're like someone closing his eyes when he thinks he is going to be hit in the face. You're doing it so as to protect yourself. You know that if you accept the answer you'll have to do something about it. Because belief is about deciding what you mean to yourself. And once you know that, you have to do something about it, and you don't want the trouble this might cause. Not that I blame you. I'm only pointing out what's so.

[*Pause.*]

If you haven't switched off, I'll tell you the rest of the story of my seeing again. And no more sermons today, promise!

[*Pause.*]

Simmo got everything ready, then propped me up in bed in all my laundered glory, and I waited and waited for the doctor, but she didn't come and didn't come. Some emergency. She was two hours late! I was exhausted from keeping myself poised for the big moment. Even Simmo was sounding frayed.

Naturally, as soon as she arrived I felt guilty about grumbling to myself when she'd been attending a patient who really needed her, and so I came on too cheery and offhand, overcompensating like mad. The funny thing is, I've seen this kind of thing happen time and again in the surgery at work, and yet when it happened to me I behaved just like everybody else. But doctors get used to people acting like clowns, and she chatted to me for a few minutes to settle me down before she started the unveiling.

Which didn't take long. I deliberately kept my eyes shut till the bandages were off and the pads were removed and Simmo had cleaned the skin and rubbed in some sort of salve. Then the doctor said that was it, everything was ready and I could look.

I opened my eyes and blinked a few times, like you do after a long sleep, to get them working again, and there in front of me was the room I've been in all these weeks. Smaller than I'd expected, and even the gloom with the blinds down seeming too bright. And there was the doctor standing on one side of my bed and Simmo on the other. And my hands like stumps because of being wrapped up, lying on the bedclothes.

At first all I could do was stare at everything. I don't remember what I felt. Except astonishment and relief. But then I started laughing, giggling really, and the doctor and Simmo started laughing too, and Simmo gave me a hug and a kiss, and the doctor kept saying, 'Well done, well done!' as if I'd just won an Olympic medal, and before any of us knew it we were all streaming with tears, even me, which was somehow marvellous too, because I thought if my eyes could cry they must really be okay. So for a while it was blubbing day in Side Ward Two, and before long Chrissy and Jean, the nurses on duty in the main ward, and all the walking wounded who've been visiting and reading and chatting to me lately, came in to join in the celebration, till Simmo had to put a stop to it in case I got over-excited and tired my eyes their first time out, so to speak. She sent everybody packing, and insisted I wear a blindfold for an hour to rest my eyes before giving them some more exercise.

[*Laughter*.]

Simmo is almost exactly like I imagined her, by the way, only prettier. You've seen her so you know. But the doctor is quite different. From her voice and her manner, I'd thought she must be tall and heavily built, one of those strong older women who are a bit tough from fighting their way up in a male-dominated profession. But in fact she looks like a kindly granny, thin as a fork, not very tall, with bobbed grey hair and a nice face with such amazing skin she doesn't need to wear make-up, and with gold-rimmed half-glasses stuck permanently on her nose. Just to look at her you'd think she wouldn't dare say boo to any kind of goose, never mind the geese she must have to put up with among her colleagues not to mention patients. Some people must get an awful shock if they take advantage of her, thinking she looks a push-over. Which just goes to show how deceptive appearances can be and how you can't always trust your eyes. So after all, seeing isn't enough for believing! [*She chuckles*.] I knew you'd want to know that, Nik!

[*Pause*.]

They wouldn't let me read or watch television, nor put up my window blinds. By night-time I'd got quite used to seeing again. Even the excitement was wearing off. But then this morning . . .

Phew!

It still takes my breath away.

[*Pause.*]

When I'd woken and settled myself for the day, Simmo came in and raised the blind. And that was the moment when I *saw*—really saw again. Simmo raising the blind was like opening my eyes for the first time, and there, through the window, was the scene I've been gazing at all day, and still am as I talk to you now.

Probably, if you were here to see it, you'd wonder what all the fuss is about. Because it's quite ordinary. Nothing to write home about in the normal way of things. Just a field of grass rather roughly cut to keep it trim. And a pond in the middle, not much bigger than a large pool. And a tree, a huge chestnut, to one side of the pool. And beyond a high old mellow brick wall hiding the main road. And above all that the sky. Nothing else. At least, nothing I can see from my bed. And framed by my window, it's like a picture. And I've watched it hour by hour all day, as the light has changed from early morning brightness to the evening glow I'm looking at now. And it's been like taking a long long drink when you're so dry you can't get enough to slake your thirst.

I looked and looked and thought: That was there all the time and I didn't know. I couldn't see it, and no one told me, so I couldn't even believe it was there and hope to see it one day. But it was there, all the time—like a ghost just waiting to show itself.

Which reminded me of a kind of poem, or maybe it's a prayer, I copied into my meditation book ages ago. It's by a Tibetan Buddhist monk from years back, fourteenth century, I think. His name was something like Longchamps—no, Long-chenpa, that's it. I remember it word for word because I've always liked it a lot.

> Since everything is but an apparition
> Perfect in being what it is,
> Having nothing to do with good or bad,
> Acceptance or rejection,
> One may as well burst out in laughter.

And I did—burst out in laughter, I mean—because those words suddenly seemed exactly right in a way I'd not understood before. Partly, I laughed because it is so odd how you can read some words time and again, liking them, and thinking you understand them, but then one day you read them again for the umpteenth time and they suddenly make sense in a way you've never understood before, a way that you know properly and deeply for the very first time is what they really wanted to say to you all along.

You see, as I lay here looking so hard and so long, I began to see everything was perfectly itself. The grass was perfectly grass, and the pond perfectly a pond, and the water in it perfectly water, and the tree so perfectly a tree. And the light! Oh, the light! It was so perfectly itself too, perfectly *light*, and yet also perfectly everything else. Because without the light I couldn't have seen anything. It illuminated everything. Made everything visible. Made everything *there*.

And I thought: Yes, the light made everything visible that is *there*. But it also *made* everything. Without the light nothing would exist. The grass, the pond, the water, the tree are all light, only light. Their perfection is made by the light.

For hours I had the amazing impression that time had stood still—that all the world around had ceased to move. I waited for the sensation to pass, for time to begin again, but the strange feeling persisted. Time seemed suspended. And I cannot forget one detail of the time I lay here watching it all.

As I watched, the sunlight played on the ripples of the water and flickered on the leaves of the tree as they moved in the breeze. And the light broke up into thousands of individual flecks. But I knew they all came from the same source. They were all, each fleck, perfect sunlight, and were also all the same thing, the Sun. They came from the sun and go back to the sun and are the sun now while they are flecks of light on the water.

The light reveals the water so we can see it, and the ripples of water reveal the flecks of sunlight so that we can see in them perfect individual particles of the sun. They don't blind us if we look at them, though we would be blinded if we looked at them all together in the perfect Sun.

And I knew that is how it is with us and how it is with God.

We are perfectly what we are, as the flecks of sunlight are perfectly flecks of sun. And we are individual particles of God who we come from and are already all the time, now, here, every day. The flecks of light don't go looking for the sun. They are the sun. In themselves and all together. And we don't need to go looking for God. We are God, in ourselves and all together.

Perhaps that's why I've always loved St John's Gospel more than all the other books in the Bible—because it starts off by saying just that, and goes on to tell us how it is that we are God.

[*Pause.*]

'In the beginning was the word and the word was with God, and the word was God . . . In him was life; and the life was the light of men.'

[*Pause.*]

As I looked and looked, it was all there, written in front of me, in the grass and the pond and the tree. Like a message written in the earth and left for me to find. Just like it was all there for you, Nik, that evening in Sweden. Only you felt apart from it, shut out from it, and wanted to plunge into it so you could belong to it. Whereas for me, as I lie here in the fading light still looking and still knowing, I feel already part of it. One of it. One with it. Me . . . perfectly me . . . confined to bed and not happy like this, but perfectly unhappily me. And happy at the same time to be me because I know I am part of that which always Is—capital I—all the time for ever. And after today, the great gift of today, I can remember and tell myself about it and try and understand more deeply still. But in my own time and at my own pace. It's all there waiting, simply *being*, like the grass and the pond and the tree were there and waiting when I opened my eyes and the blinds were raised. It won't run away.

Perhaps this is one of the good things to come out of my bomb. And maybe what was being given me in the terrible second of the explosion was time. Time to think at my own speed, I mean, and to see what I saw today.

[*Long pause.*]

It's dark now and I'm tired. I've done nothing today, nothing at all, except look at a pool of water and a tree and the light playing on them. And, dear Nik, dear God, I've been for the first time in weeks perfectly myself and perfectly happy.

†

NIK'S NOTEBOOK: The nightmares have been terrifying. Every night I was away. Julie running. The explosion. Julie in flames, screaming. The fire, like fingers reaching out for me. Then I black out.

Twice I woke up, shouting, with Dominic, whose cell was next door, holding me so that I wouldn't throw myself out of bed, which I did the first night.

Since coming home I haven't been able to sleep much. Maybe I'm afraid of the dreams? But also, a couple of press people are still sniffing around, wanting to talk to me. And that makes me furious. Grandad curses at them now, which only makes things worse. So I have to watch it when I go out. If Grandad is here, he performs diversionary tactics at the front while I skip off at the back. But I'm fed up of this.

The leptonic OBD turned up yesterday, all gush and smarm. The group send their best, etc., *ad nauseam*. Don't know whether he meant it, but he never sounds sincere, just creepy. And he's still sticking it to the holey mints with his reptilian tongue. Asked about the explosion. Everybody asks about that, everybody, and what they really want to hear are the gory details, the blood and guts and mayhem. He even suggested it would be 'a smashing idea' if we included a reconstruction of the bombing in the film.

That'd grab em, says he, rubbing his little hands together like an excited lizard. Really contemporary, that would be, really relevant. Maybe Christ could be the bomber? That's it, he says, getting quite beside himself with excitement, Christ the urban revolutionary. And the bomb he's placing has been tampered with by the CIA so that it blows him up when he's setting it. Instead of being crucified, he'd be blown to kingdom come by the fascist functionaries of the state. He lies in the road, squirming and black and bleeding, and muttering my God, my God, why have you not stood by me, and around him, peering down at him are a soldier, a policeman, a man in a dark suit with

178

a briefcase—representatives of the earthly powers that be —while he dies in agony as a church clock strikes three. I can see it all. Terrif, eh? So the political establishment wins again, just like it did the first time. And with you playing Christ, Nik, there'll be the extra human interest of knowing you went through that, well nearly that, you're still with us, thank goodness. But what a great scene, eh?

Note for school essay: It may be true that the human race is basically religious, but it is also true that it is basically brutal, bloodthirsty, and cruel. Therefore, either religion is to blame for encouraging this or one of its main aims must be to change human nature. When you think of things like burning people at the stake, holy wars, and human sacrifices made to keep in good with some God or other, it doesn't seem like most religions want to do much about changing human nature.

Not to mention the crucifiction. That's a pretty good example of blood and guts and mayhem.

Julie would say I'm being cynical. She'd pray about it. So would Kit. Even Adam. Wish I could. Last week, I might have done. Why can't I now? I feel a bit like when I was a little kid and Mum wanted me to do something, and I knew I should, even wanted to, but wouldn't, so as to assert myself, I suppose. To be me, and *not* do what someone who mattered to me wanted me to do. Is that it? Maybe, as well, if I'm honest, I have to have help. Last week, there were other people who made it seem—not exactly natural, but *possible*.

Thinking about last week, one of the things I now know I learned was how a group of people can live together, even under quite a strict set of rules, and yet not be a crowd. Not a bunch of follow-my-leader robots. I liked that. I felt I was myself, independent, private. But also felt I was one of a group who worked together and made things happen.

Been thinking about these things during the sleepless nights. And when I'm tired of thinking, and feel lonely, I put on Julie's two tapes that were waiting when I got home, and listen with the cans so as not to wake Grandad. Her voice fills my head. Trouble is, I hear her pain. She tries to sound cheerful, but the pain breaks through. Expect she's also not telling me the worst, just as I'm not telling her.

There she is lying in her bed, remembering. Here am I in mine, trying not to remember, and listening to an electronic memory of her. I know she's right, we can't do without memory. But she doesn't say that some memories hurt.

Looked up the poem she couldn't finish. Just as well she couldn't. The last lines wouldn't exactly cheer her up.

> I remember, I remember,
> The fir trees dark and high;
> I used to think their slender tops
> Were close against the sky;
> It was a childish ignorance,
> But now 'tis little joy
> To know I'm further off from Heaven
> Than when I was a boy.

Thomas Hood, b. 1799 d. 1845. He didn't last long, poor bloke. Probably died of depression, judging from his poem.

I'll not read it to her till she's better. Is religion only for kids? Or is he saying life makes you sour? He doesn't say there's no Heaven (and therefore no God). He only says he's further off from Heaven now he's a man than he was when he was a kid. Anyway, it's a bit sad, and Julie doesn't seem to remember it that way. She also seems to think it's about a little girl and by a woman. Wonder what she'll say about that.

Remembering last week is good. I've tried to live the same at home. It doesn't work. I've tried St James's. But it seems—I don't know . . . Optional. Outmoded. A hangover from something finished, done. An antique shop full of wornout nicknacks.

Note for film: If Christ returned today, he'd bulldoze most of the churches. That would make quite a scene too! He hijacks a huge 'dozer and rubbles a church. A crowd gathers. He says: My house shall be called the house of prayer and you have made it a mausoleum.

Nowadays church buildings get in the way. Millstones round the neck of belief. They stand for the wrong things. Heavy, cold, empty, geriatric, cavernous, immovable, inflexible, museum-like, bossy. They're about property not prayer.

Christ said: When two or three are gathered together in my name, there I shall be among them. *Two or three*, not twenty or five hundred or thousands. And nothing about meeting in a draughty old-fashioned barn of a place designer-built for the purpose. Or in expensive posh modern buildings, come to that.

Fact: he used to pray in the open air, or wherever he happened to be. And he held the Last Supper in the upstairs room of an ordinary house. He'd do that again. Why not? Those are the places where ordinary people are and live.

The first time round, he was arrested for claiming to be the messiah and therefore a threat to the establishment. Not this time. This is where the OBD is wrong. Nowadays, nobody would care less if he claimed to be the son of God. People would just laugh and say he was another nutter, and ignore him.

But 'dozing a building would really stir them up. Not because it's a church, but because it's a building, a piece of property. For that, they'd give him the works—arrest, fine, gaol, long lectures on how outrageous, what's the world coming to, how dare he, is nothing sacred any more, etc. etc. And when he says, But those places are supposed to belong to me, they'd say that only made things worse, he ought to be ashamed of himself. After all, what would the country be like if people started taking him seriously and bulldozed any building they owned just because they didn't like it? Think what would happen to property prices. They'd collapse. And anyway, he didn't get planning permission to demolish his church. You can think what you like, they'd say, and even say what you like, it's a free country, but demolishing buildings, that's serious. Only someone absolutely mad would do such a thing. And people must be taught respect for property. Go to gaol for five years hard labour, you horrible man.

And when he answers back, and says: I'm God, I'm God, and incites people to give up all they have and follow him, the authorities get fed up, but they don't crucify him. Not these days. They're not barbarians. They're civilized. No, they'd say he's deranged, schizoid or dangerously deluded, anyway crackers, and pack him off to the bin, where they'd convulse him with electric-shock treatment till he can't remember a thing, and inject him full of tranquillizers till he doesn't know who he is or what he is or where he is, and leave him there, out of sight, out of mind, till he ceases to be a problem by snuffing it.

So the last shot in the film wouldn't be anything gory. It would be of a forlorn, drug-dosed young man staring at nothing with a blank expression on his face, shuffling slowly along a bleak, echoey corridor without any windows, accompanied by a burly warder in a clean white coat, while on the soundtrack massed football crowds sing 'You'll never walk alone'.

Joke for a Christmas cracker: If you were the son of God, would you rather be drugged for life in a mental hospital or put to death by crucifiction?

PARTING SHOTS

'Nik!'

'Surprise surprise!'

'You're on your own?'

'Got your tape. Thought I'd come over.'

'How did you get here?'

'Train. Grandad gave me the money. Good trip. Enjoyed it. Except for the underground in London. Had to play sardines with a package tour from Tokyo.'

'Lovely to see you.'

'Great that you can. You look a lot better.'

'I'm mending. Knowing my eyes are all right is a big lift. But how are you?'

'Terrific.'

'Truly?'

'Honest. So there's the famous pond and tree.'

'No sun today though. Did you get wet?'

'It's quite a nice view, but somehow I imagined it would be—I don't know—more impressive.'

'I did warn you.'

'I didn't mean—'

'Perhaps it's the grey sky and the rain. Everything looks washed out. And I was euphoric, not surprisingly. Still . . . I shan't forget . . .'

'Brought you some prezzies. Nothing amazing. A book I thought you'd like and the regulation bunch of grapes.'

'You're very kind.'

'Neither's much cop, I now realize, because you still can't use your pickers and stealers. Sorry!'

'No, they're just right. I'll share the grapes with Simmo. She'll feed them to me. And I can manage books, though they still ration the time I'm allowed to read.'

'Are your hands coming on okay?'

'Slowly. They took the worst.'

'But they'll be all right?'

'I'm doing well. Really! Don't worry so. You're as bad as Mum. But thanks all the same. Now, what's the news from the home front? You haven't written for a few days.'

'No, sorry.'

'I wasn't complaining. Only meant—'

INTERCUT: *Nik in his bedroom with his Walkman headphones on. He is sitting, crouched, gaunt, his face strained, staring out of the window. He grips a fat black Bible tightly between his hands.*

'I know. Haven't written anything lately. Can't somehow.'

'Nothing at all?'

'Nothing. School nor you.'

'Not even your project?'

'Least of all.'

[*Pause.*]

'I was only burnt outside. Maybe you were burnt inside.'

'You always know.'

'I do?'

INTERCUT: *Nik in his bedroom as before, but viewed now from outside. His face is unbearably tense. He rises and with studied violence hurls the Bible directly at us. It smashes through the window.*

[*Enter Staff Nurse Simpson, carrying a tray with two mugs of coffee on it.*]

'Thought you might like a drink after your journey.'

[*She passes a mug to Nik, who takes it with only an impatient nod of thanks, before she sits on the other side of the bed from him, where she holds Julie's mug for her to drink from.*]

'He's not over-exciting you, is he?' Simmo says.

'It's good to see him.'

'He doesn't exactly look full of beans. A bit peaky in fact. You're not coming down with something, are you? Don't want you in here if you are.'

'I'm okay.'

'He's a bit in the dumps, I think.'

'That can be catching as well. What have you got to be in the dumps about?'

'I didn't say I was.'

'You don't have to. Your face says it for you. Aren't you pleased to see Julie sitting up and taking notice?'

'Naturally.'

'And don't you think she's done well?'

''Course.'

'Then why not show it?'

'What would you like me to do, a flipflap or a pirouette?'

'I'll settle for your nicest toothy smile. Come on, live dangerously! Your face won't crack.'

'Stop teasing him, Simmo.'

'I'm not. I mean it. He's a lot livelier on paper than he is in the flesh, judging by today's performance, I must say.'

'You don't know anything about me.'

'What, after all those letters! I'll miss them now Julie can read for herself.'

'They were only meant for Julie.'

'Somebody had to read them to her.'

'Simmo did it in her own time,' Julie says.

'Fear not, Nik, your secrets are safe with me.'

'What secrets? There weren't any.'

Simmo hoots, mocking. 'There's none so blind—'

'What d'you mean?' Nik says, smarting.

'It's obvious you two shouldn't be left in the same room together,' Julie says.

'Time I went anyway. Here, make yourself useful.' Simmo hands Nik Julie's mug. 'See you both later. And cheer up, Nik, it might never happen.'

[*Simmo goes. Pause.*]

'Don't mind Simmo.'

'Do I?'

'She was on duty all weekend and now she's covering for someone off sick. She's hardly had any rest.'

'If she's that brisk when she's tired, I hate to think what she's like when she's not.'

'More patient but just as frank. Which I like. We've become good friends.'

'I thought it was only men who fell in love with their nurses.'

'Why should men have all the fun?'

'Are you being serious?'

'Are you being bitchy?'

[*Nik scowls at Julie who is grinning at him. He feeds her some coffee.*]

'Did you mean it though?'

'Why not? Don't you love your friends?'

'Not sure I have any. Not that close anyway. Except you.'

'Which I want us to talk about.'

'About me not having friends?'

'About you and me.'

'What about us?'

[*Pause.*]

'You remember the night before?'

'Am I likely to forget?'

'What I said then still goes, Nik.'

[*Nik places his and Julie's mugs on her bedside cabinet and crosses to the window, where he stands, his back to Julie, looking at the view.*]

'You're not really talking about the night before, are you?' he says. 'You're really talking about the tape.'

[*Pause.*]

'I didn't want to bring it up here,' Julie says. 'I wanted to wait till I was home again and back to normal. But—'

[*Nik turns and faces her.*]

'You've decided.'

'Yes. I know what I have to do.'

'You can't know. Not yet. You're afraid you're not going to heal properly, that's it, isn't it? You think you'll have scars and not be attractive.'

'No, that's not it!'

'I don't care, it wouldn't matter to me. I've thought about it. It won't make any difference.'

'Listen, Nik. It isn't that at all, truly. The doctor doesn't think there'll be anything bad. Nothing ugly. That's why I wanted to wait till I'm fully recovered before we talked like this. So you could see I was okay. But—'

'But what?'

'It just wouldn't be right to let you go on thinking . . . waiting
. . . I don't know . . . *hoping*. When I know now.'

'You can't possibly, Julie! You've just said, you aren't back
to normal. You can't be sure how you'll feel when you're home
again instead of stuck here. Nobody can think straight in a
place like this. Anyway, you're still recovering from the shock
of the bomb, never mind from your injuries. They're still
pumping drugs into you, aren't they? And I don't care what you
say, you must be feeling pretty crappy and worried and fed up,
even if you do put on a good face and look happy, which I'm
not knocking, just the opposite, but I'm not giving you up yet,
I'm just not.'

'I don't want you to give me up, I'm not saying that.'

[*Nik comes to the bed and sits at her side.*]

'I love you, Julie.'

[*Pause.*]

'No, Nik, you don't.'

'I do. That's what I've come to say.'

'I'm grateful. And I don't want to make you unhappy. But
you don't love me, not the way you mean it.'

'But I *do*. Believe me.'

[*Pause. Julie smiles.*]

'Believe you?'

[*Nik, realizing the incongruity, smiles too.*]

'Okay! All right.'

'Tell me what belief feels like, Nik.'

'Chuck it, will you!'

'What does it *do*, for God's sake!'

'Knock it off, will you!'

[*They are laughing now. When it is over Nik gets off the bed
and sits in the chair, leaning towards Julie, elbows on knees,
hands clasped together, and says:*]

'I love you, Julie, and I want you. Right now in your hospital
bed I want you. Even with your eyebrows burnt off and your
scorched hair like a fright wig and your face still healing and
your poor hands all trussed up. You still turn me on as hard as
you did the first time I saw you yomping through the rain in
your sloppy pullover and your brother's old jeans, looking like
a drowned bundle of castoffs on its way to Oxfam.'

'You certainly pick on a girl's strong points.'

'But I do, I want you.'

'I believe you, Nik . . . But what do you want for me?'

'How d'you mean? I don't want anything for you, I just want you.'

'Exactly.'

'Exactly what?'

[*Julie looks at him with an amused stare.*]

'Simmo says what you really want is a girl who'll treat you like a motherly older sister you can have the pleasure of screwing whenever you feel like it.'

[*Nik slumps back into the chair. A tense pause.*]

'I bet she's keen on karate as well.'

'Don't worry. You're not alone. Lots of men are the same.'

'That's a comfort! You know how much I like being one of the crowd.'

[*Brooding silence, ended by Julie.*]

'Sorry. Shouldn't have said that. I was only trying to tell you that I don't think love and wanting are the same thing.'

[*Nik shrugs.*] 'Expect you're right, as usual.'

'Right but wrong.'

'Can you be both at once about the same thing?'

'Why not? Right about something but wrong the way you say it.'

'If you say it wrong, surely you haven't got it right yet?'

'I don't know . . . Yes, I expect so . . . Don't let's argue about it.'

[*They sit in heavy silence for some time. Julie keeps her eyes on Nik, pained by her own vulgarity and his sadness. He avoids her gaze but this does not save him. Tears begin to course his cheeks. Watching his reined distress, Julie also begins to weep. At last Nik glances at her. The sight unleashes his restraint. He bursts into racking sobs. Julie holds out her clubbed hands towards him. He rushes to her. They hold each other in a clumsy embrace.*]

✝

Tom recognized the girl as soon as she came round the corner. The one who passed him on the towpath this afternoon. The

188

one with the fetching bum. His pulse quickened along with bloodshot thoughts.

Is that a truncheon in your pocket or are you pleased to see me?

Cop the braless knockers poking the clingfilm singlet. Here was evidence he'd like to get his grabbers on. No question: on a hot evening like this a forensic frig would nicely fit the bill. Business first, natch, but mix it with some pleasure, why not? All work and no foreplay makes Tom a dull John. Blow that for a nark. And anyway, who cared about slag? The only thing she was good for was banged up in the nick between her legs. As investigating officer he had right of entry. Stand astride, I've come to skin the cat.

'And what are you staring at?' Michelle said.

'Okay, Sharkey,' Tom said. 'See you later.'

'Sure you can manage on your own?' Michelle said. 'Don't want him to hold your hand—or nothing?'

Sharkey, smirking to himself, left them to it.

Michelle eyed Tom, her arms folded, cradling her breasts.

'He says you know something interesting,' Tom said.

'I know lots of things.'

'And I know you know what I'm talking about so cut the crap.'

Michelle sniffed and looked with distaste around her.

'Do we have to talk here? It's really smelly. Can't you think of nowhere better?'

'Why? Are we going to be long?'

She gave him an appraising look, up and down, with pauses on the way.

'Maybe,' she said. 'Depends.'

'On what?' Tom asked, moving closer.

'You, of course,' Michelle said, mocking him with innocence. 'Didn't ask to come here, did I? You're the one who knows what you're after. But I'm not talking here however long it takes.'

'What about in my car? It's outside the station.'

Michelle huffed. 'You're full of bright ideas. What d'you think my friends will say if they see me sitting yakking to you in a pig van?'

'They wouldn't know. It's unmarked.'

'Yes, but you're not. Anyway, I'm not sitting talking to you in a stuffy old car outside the railway station.'

Tom chuckled and, leaning a hand on the wall either side of her head, said, 'Okay, let me have a guess. You've got a better idea.'

'Might have. We could do a quick drive up to Rodborough Common. It'll be cooler up there, and there's a lovely view of the town from a shady place I know.'

'Sounds great. But I might not have the time.'

'Oh well, if you're in a tearing hurry . . .'

Michelle ducked under his arm and, brushing against him, slipped free.

Tom twisted after her, only just restraining the impulse to catch hold. 'Okay, listen,' he said. 'Come to the car. I'll make a call. If everything's all right, we'll go.'

'Please yourself,' Michelle said, shrugged, and strutted her stuff ahead of him.

At the station, while she studied travel posters on the wall, pretending to be by herself, Tom had a word with the duty officer on his car intercom.

'Any info re that Matthews Way address, over?'

'Negative. We're checking possible alternatives, over.'

'Roger. Investigating possible lead this end. Will contact if and when. Out.'

He started the car and pulled across to Michelle, who skipped into the seat beside him before he came to a stop.

The signs were good. With the blank at Matthews Way he had time to mix it with Michelle; and she seemed less unwilling than Sharkey had said. Now why was that? But the twinge of suspicion was stifled in the lust that provoked him to over-gun the revs as he swung up Rodborough hill. He hadn't had it in the open for ages and the prospect swelled his crotch.

†

Home again from hospital, brooding on the scene—their tears, her separate determination—Nik again, though weary, could not sleep. The night too was brooding, its heavy air claustrophobic, and would not let go.

At last, unable to lie still in mind or body, he rose in the dark and left the house to his grandfather's contented snores, like foghorns marking the channel to death. Dressed only in T-shirt and jeans, he wheeled his bicycle from the garden shed and, pedalling slowly, doggedly made the journey through town and up the steep winding ascent onto Selsley Common, drawn there not only because it was his favourite place but more by a wish-fulfilling memory of his first walk with Julie.

Even there, though, he found no breeze to freshen and revive him. Oiled in sweat, and panting, he bumped across the common. At the edge he dropped his bicycle to the ground, pulled off his wringing T-shirt, and spread himself on the grass, intending to remain so only until he had cooled off and caught his breath again.

Instead, he at once drifted into sleep; utter, seabed sleep, dreamless, limpid, surrendered.

Only to be jolted awake by a voice speaking his name.

He sat up abruptly, blinking in the ghostly light of pre-dawn at the face of Mary Magdalene.

'Are you okay?' she was saying. 'Didn't mean to startle you. Just, I saw you lying there like you'd fallen off your bike and thought you might be ill. Well, I mean, you looked knocked out, if not dead.'

Nik rubbed his eyes and grasped his hands round drawn-up knees. 'I'm all right,' he said, and looked, blear-eyed, beyond the girl at the wide mist-veiled fenestral of the valley, and remembered why he was here.

The Magdalene ran a warm hand over his shoulder and down his back. 'You're cold as slabfish. How long have you been lying here?'

Nik shrugged. 'No idea. It was dark.'

She picked up his T-shirt and felt it like laundry. 'This is soaking.'

'I was hot,' he said, taking the shirt from her and pulling it on, perversely glad of its clammy penance.

'You'll catch your death,' she said.

Nik stood up and flexed his stiffened joints.

'You're not exactly overdressed yourself,' he said. She was

wearing a blatant singlet and hugging lightweight jeans. 'What are you doing here anyway?'

'Three guesses,' she said flatly.

'Doesn't sound like you enjoyed it much.'

He walked the few paces to a wooden bench and sat, his legs splayed, suddenly weary again now the shock of waking had worn off.

The Magdalene got up and followed, saying, 'I'm fed up of boring boys who have a big head on their shoulders just because they've a big dick in their trousers, and think dropping their pants for a girl like me should be enough reward for doing whatever they want and listening to the endless drivel they talk when they've finished.'

'So what happened to last night's hero?' Nik asked.

'Went off him.' She laughed disdainfully. 'Never really fancied him, to be honest. But he had nice eyes and I go for nice eyes. But by the time we come up here it was too dark to see. Not that he kept them open, I expect. He's the "Look no hands, I can even do this blind" sort, if you know what I mean.'

'I can guess.'

She inspected his face closely. 'You've got nice eyes, as a matter of fact. And your glasses frame them lovely.'

'Thanks,' Nik said, ignoring the hint. 'So what happened?'

'Not a lot. He's probably quite handy with a road drill.'

'How's that?'

'Only capable of a short sharp burst, makes a lot of noise, and doesn't dig very deep.'

Nik chuckled. 'No finesse?'

'Didn't give him the chance. I'm not usually nasty, I can put up with quite a lot, but tonight, I don't know why, I just thought, "To hell with it, if I'm not enjoying myself I'm damn sure he's not going to, not at my expense, the ape," and I shoved him off before he got properly going.'

'That must have pleased him.'

'He was even more pleased when I told him his performance broke the trades description act because it wasn't nowhere near as good as advertised.'

'And?'

'Oh, he goose-stepped around a bit, doing up his flies and

giving himself a thrill by nipping his zipper on a painful place, while he gave me a few well chosen words about me morals and me parents and what he really thought about my physical appearance. I expect you can imagine the kind of thing.'

'Vaguely.'

'And then he stormed off on his motorbike, which I expect he takes to bed with him every night, he certainly smelt like he did, and left me to find my own way home, which I didn't reckon was such a good idea, wandering through town in the middle of the night, so I snuggled up to myself and waited for dawn, and was just setting off when I spotted you flat out and beautiful and catching your death from the dew.' She smiled. 'You looked that helpless I come over all motherly.'

Nik shivered and stood up.

'What you need,' she said to his back, 'is something to warm you up. Me too, come to think of it. Tell you what, just for starters, I'll race you to the hump and back, how about it?'

She was off before Nik could say no.

Instead, he picked up his bike and chased after her.

'Cheat!' she called as he came alongside.

'Can't trust any of us males!' he called back, pedalled harder, reached the hump well ahead, dismounted, and sat waiting, undeniably feeling better for the spurt of energy.

The Magdalene arrived in a glow, panting, and, slumping down at his side, leaned herself against him.

'Look, Michelle,' Nik said when she'd recovered, 'if you like, I'll give you a ride down the hill. The law shouldn't spot us at this time of day.'

'Ta very much,' she said. 'And you can give me a ride any time.'

He nudged his head against hers. 'I'll keep that in mind,' he said and laughed.

'I mean it,' she said. 'I've fancied you rotten since you joined the group. But you never stay around long enough to do anything about it.'

Nik shrugged and they were silent for a time before Michelle said, 'I've told you why I was up here tonight. Your turn now. Why were you lying there or is that where you usually doss?'

Nik sniffed. 'Fun.'

'Now pull the other one.'

'Okay . . . Research.'

'For our stupid film, you mean?'

'Why not?'

'Don't believe you.'

'It's true! . . . Well, kind of.'

She turned so she could face him. 'I saw Randy Frank yesterday.'

'Was he poking a mint?'

'Don't be disgusting! He's all right really. He said he'd been to see you and he thought you weren't very well. He said you were still shook up from that awful bomb, and were worried sick about the girl you were with.'

Nik bristled. 'I wish he'd mind his own business.'

'Well, are you?'

'Wouldn't you be?'

Michelle nodded. 'Anybody would. I just wondered if it had anything to do with you being up here, that's all.'

Nik said nothing.

'Is she . . .' Michelle hesitated. 'Is she your girl? I mean —proper girl?'

Nik rubbed a hand across his face. 'Yes and no,' he said tetchily. 'I say yes, she says no.'

'Doesn't she love you as much as you love her?'

Nik gave her a squinted look. 'You do pry.'

Michelle said, 'Sorry, I'm sure,' and turned her head away.

But suddenly, despite his anger, he wanted to tell.

He waited a moment till the anger subsided, then with a tentative hand brought her unresisting face to his again.

INTERCUT: *Julie's hospital room. She and Nik clutched in their awkward embrace, weeping.*

'This is ridiculous,' Nik says, swivelling so that he can lie on the bed propped up alongside Julie. He wipes his eyes with his free hand.

Julie is snuffling her tears back.

Realizing she can't do anything about her face, Nik reaches for some tissues on the bedside cabinet and very carefully attends to her.

'Anyway, why are you crying?' he asks.

'Why are you?' Julie says.

'For you,' Nik says. 'For myself. I don't know! . . . For the whole rotten bloody world.'

'No,' Julie says. 'Not rotten. Bloody sometimes but not rotten.'

They are calm again. Nik settles himself comfortably. They are silent for a moment, staring ahead at the view through the window.

'Nik . . .' Julie says, hardly breaking the silence.

'Uh-huh?'

'There's something I've got to tell you, but I can't now.'

'Then don't try.'

'I've made a tape.'

'Oh?'

'I want you to take it with you.'

'Can't I hear it now?'

'No. At home.'

'I've brought my Walkman. I'll listen in the train.'

'I'd rather you listened at home.'

'Okay. As soon as I get back.'

JULIE:

Dear Nik:

This is difficult. I'd rather tell you what I want to say when I'm with you, and when I'm completely recovered and back home again.

But I think it probably should be said before then. Judging by your letters and . . . Well, anyway.

[Pause.]

I suppose everybody is strong in some things and weak in others. I'm strong in faith but weak in love. I know that much about myself.

I could easily love you, Nik. Love you the way you want, I mean. I knew that the night before the bomb. I wasn't just testing myself the way I said. That was only half the truth. The other half was that I wanted you the way you wanted me. I'd even imagined it happening. Lying in bed all the week before I'd imagined it. You and me together. I'd planned it, our night together outside Cambridge. The tent. Everything! That's my confession.

[*Pause.*]

But then, as soon as I knew you really did want me, and it began to turn out just the way I'd hoped for, I drew back. Isn't that awful! The terrible desire to know you're wanted for your body as well as yourself. And then when someone offers you that, to realize it isn't enough. It isn't what you really want. And you've led them on only to reject them.

I hated myself! Dear God, how I hated myself afterwards. You thought I'd gone to sleep, but I hadn't. All the time we were lying there in the tent, I was loathing myself. Not because I'd wanted you. There's nothing wrong with that. But because of my deceit.

I'm sorry for that. For what I did and for hating myself as well. Neither did any good.

I can tell you this now because I've thought and prayed so much about it. What I did and why.

[*Pause.*]

It's all got to do with love, hasn't it?

The more I thought about it, the more it came down to one thing. 'A new commandment I give unto you, that you love one another.'

She said that at the Last Supper, the night before she died on the cross. She'd broken the bread only a few minutes before, saying, 'This is my body,' and she'd passed round the cup of wine, saying, 'This is my blood,' and she'd told the disciples, 'Do this in remembrance of me'.

You know, to me the Last Supper is the most important part of her story. And being at the Eucharist, at the Last Supper repeated day in day out all down the years since the first time, that's for me the most important part of my life as a Christian. It heals me. Brings everything into focus. Gives me new energy. Helps me view things in the right perspective.

So if she gives a new commandment then, at that moment in the Last Supper, it's just got to be important. And the more I thought about it the more I kept wondering why she calls it the *new* commandment. What's so *new* about it? How is loving one another different from loving your neighbour as yourself, which we'd already been told to do?

And, after all, Nik, she can't mean 'love' the way you meant it that night. Otherwise, she would mean a kind of everlasting gang-bang. Which you've got to admit is impractical, if not impossible.

Then I realized only St John's Gospel, my favourite, mentions the new commandment. The others don't. And in John's story, it comes after Judas has left the room to go and betray Jesus. Also, she repeats the command three times. You'll like that. And it's tangled up with her talking about friendship. 'You are my friends if you do as I command you,' she says. 'I call you servants no longer.' So this love, this *new* love, is the love of friendship.

In the love you wanted of me, Nik, two people come together and make themselves one. Whereas it seems to me the love Jesus is telling us to have for one another is the love of two friends: the love of distinctness, of separateness. Neither wants to dominate. Neither wants to be dominated. The desire in the love of friendship is the desire for the other's freedom.

In the love you want, the two people fit themselves together physically because they want to fit together in every way—in their bodies, in their minds, in their spirits. But in the love of friendship you don't want your friend to become one with you. Just the opposite. You want your friend to be as perfectly herself as she can be.

[*Pause.*]

That's what I want for you, Nik, and that's what I hope you most want for me.

That is what I want you for, and I hope that is what you want me for.

[*Pause.*]

Lying here, at first hating myself, wanting an end to my life, I have slowly learned to love myself as a friend. That has been my cure for my wounded self. Now and in future loving you as a friend is the best of me—is all of me—I can give you.

All I can give you is the love I give myself.

The love you've been wanting from me—the love that comes from the desire to be one—I've already given elsewhere, Nik.

What I need is a friend who loves me as a friend, if I am to live up to that other love. Will you be that loving friend?

'She sounds a bit of a fanatic,' Michelle said, 'if you don't mind me saying.'

'No more than you are,' Nik said.

'Me? I'm not a fanatic.'

'Yes you are. You're a fanatic about boys.'

'That's natural.'

'So? You like doing what comes naturally. Julie likes doing what comes supernaturally.'

'Clever dick!'

'Smartypants!'

She poked her tongue at him through vulvarine lips.

Nik blew a raspberry. 'I'm not saying you aren't good at it, Michelle, don't get me wrong. Just the same as Julie's good at giving her all to God.'

'Maybe that's why you like her so much.'

'Because I can't have her, you mean?'

'No. Because she's good at what she wants. That's always a bit sexy, isn't it? I mean, there's a boy in the swimming team at the Leisure Centre. He's terrific at swimming and he knows it, the bighead. He's just gorgeous to watch, I mean he just is. It's not only his smashing body. It's everything. I dunno how to say it, but it's like when he swims he's the best he ever will be in the whole of his life. If you could have him then, while he's swimming, you just feel it would be the greatest, the last word . . . Ecstacy!'

She sighed.

'But then after, when he's not swimming, even though he's got this stunning body, it's like all that—I dunno . . .'

'Concentrated energy?'

'Yes—all that lovely concentrated energy has broken up into awkward little bits all sparking off in different directions and you're left with this big-headed, ham-fisted idiot that's about as likely to give anybody ecstacy as a side of beef in a butcher's shop.'

'I suppose it might, a side of beef, some people being as weird as they are. But it sounds to me like you should choose your meat more carefully.'

'That's what I've been thinking lately. But you know what I'm trying to say.'

'Sure. Ever since I first saw Julie I've been hot for her. Not just for sex, but because of her specialness. She knows what she wants and she's going for it, all or nothing, no side-tracking.'

'Dedicated.'

Nik glanced at Michelle with surprise. 'That's right, that's what it is.'

'And you want the same. Want it with her.'

'Do I? . . . How do you know?'

Michelle laughed. 'Any girl would know that. But if you ask me, she has to be a bit of a fool to turn you down.'

'She hasn't turned me down.' Nik pushed himself to his feet and, breathing deeply, took in the sweeping view, early morning mist now shrouding the valley so that he seemed to be standing above the clouds. 'She's offered me something else, that's all.' His eyes came back to Michelle lying on her side, her head supported on her elbow. 'Something better.' He went to his bike and stood it upright. 'Only I'm not sure I can live up to it.'

He mounted and hobby-horsed himself alongside Michelle.

'I'm getting cold,' he said.

Michelle got to her feet and groomed herself with practised vanity.

Nik said, 'Would you do something for me?'

She smiled at him askance. 'Don't say this is going to be my lucky night after all!'

He grinned back. 'You never know!'

Michelle climbed onto his saddle behind him. 'So what is it?'

'Tell you when we get there.'

'Why? Where are we going?'

'To the dump by the canal.'

✝

'Isn't this nice?' Michelle said.

'Nice it is, secluded it isn't,' Tom said, coming up behind and slipping his arms round her waist.

'Who said it was?' Michelle strained against him. 'But it's a lovely view. All of the town. And especially of the dump by the canal. Isn't that where it happened?'

'That's where it happened,' Tom said, his hands now exploring under Michelle's singlet.

'I must say,' Michelle said, using her elbows to prevent Tom's hands rising higher, 'you don't waste much time.'

'Told you—' Tom's breathing was not at all calm, 'don't have any to spare.'

'Thought you was after information?'

'I am.' Thwarted in one ambition Tom's hands set off in pursuit of another.

'Well you won't find it down there!' Michelle wriggled free and faced him. 'So what d'you want to know?'

Irritation flickered in Tom's eyes and revived his suspicion. 'Look, you—what's your game?'

'Snooker,' Michelle said. 'I'm quite partial to a game of snooker.'

'Smart ass!' Tom said.

Michelle laughed. 'How funny! Somebody else called me that only last night. Well, early this morning to be exact. But he was a bit more polite.'

'Said please and thank you, did he?'

'Lots of words you don't know.'

'All talk but no action, by the sound.'

'Wouldn't say that.' Michelle turned away and looked into the valley. A black-leathered figure on a motorbike, like a beetle on a matchbox toy, was circling slowly round a pile of crushed cars in the centre of the dump. She smiled to herself at the sight. 'Nor would you,' she went on, 'if you knew who he was.'

'Why should I give a damn who you were with last night?'

Michelle shrugged and said, 'Isn't that what you want to talk about?'

The confusion on Tom's face made her tingle with

satisfaction. She had duped him, trapped him, hooked him; he knew it and was smarting.

A glance into the valley told her that the tiny motorcyclist had driven away. The dump appeared deserted.

'All right,' Tom said, 'let's cut the crap.'

'You must watch the cops on telly a lot,' Michelle said.

Tom stepped down the bank to face her, the slope so steep his head came level with hers.

'This is official, okay?' he said straining for professional neutrality. 'The guy you were with—he had something to do with the crucifiction?'

'You could say that.'

'Say what?'

'He was the one, of course.'

'The one? Which one? The one on the cross or one of those who put him there?'

'Ah!' Michelle said. 'I see what you mean. The one on the cross.'

Tom's evident disappointment took her by surprise; she was even more startled by his reply.

'You mean Nicholas Frome?'

Tom's turn for satisfaction now. He added with tart pleasure, 'Tell us something I don't know.'

Michelle preened her hair in hope of hiding her sudden panic.

'Like what?' she said.

'Like who did it.'

She turned hard eyes on him and said, 'If you know it was Nik why don't you ask him?'

'Because I'm asking you.'

'And what makes you think I know?'

Tom grinned coldly. 'You know, and you're going to tell.'

'Who says!'

'Look—you've had a nice little game.' Tom snorted. 'Snooker!' He pulled at his nose and sniffed. 'Well, I can take a joke. And I'm not mean. I'll be generous. I'll give you a choice of balls—if you'll pardon the expression. You tell me what I want to know, all friendly, like a good citizen, or I take you in on suspicion of being accessory to criminal assault and for obstructing a police officer in the course of his duty.'

'All right, all right, don't go on!' Michelle regarded him for a moment with undisguised dislike. 'But only on condition there's no come-back on Sharkey. He's got nothing to do with this.'

'Who said anything about Sharkey?'

'Just so long as you remember, that's all.'

'Sure,' Tom said, 'no danger.'

'Promises, promises!' Michelle said with scorn, and set off in the direction of Tom's car, saying, 'Let's get it over with. Drive me down to the dump.'

REPORTS

NIK'S NOTEBOOK: I can write again.

Not tears, after all.

The crucifiction was what I needed.

Who would understand? One person's need is another person's bananas. Maybe one day I won't understand myself. So, for the record:

Len S. shouldn't have told me to observe other people. He should have told me to observe myself. I don't need to look elsewhere. All humanity is in me. All its history, all its quirks, quarks, and (w)holes (black and white). Therefore all its future too.

When you think about it, this is bound to be so. With all the fathers and mothers it took to make me, going back by compound interest to whothehellever Adam and Eve were, how could it be otherwise? And not only for me but for everybody.

My life is my specimen. My body is my laboratory. Last week the cross was my test tube.

Now I know that the only faith I can believe is an experimental faith.

STOCKSHOT: *The eye by which I see God is the same eye by which God sees me.*

But I was barmy to think Michelle would help. When I told her what I was going to do she threw an eppie. I'm not going to help you do THAT! You must be MAD! You'll KILL yourself! Etc.

Wouldn't listen. Don't blame her. Not that there was time for explanations. Sunrise wasn't far off. Thought for a minute she would shop me. But she thought I couldn't do it without help. So I said no, I probably couldn't and loaned her my bike and she scooted off home.

I wasn't so barmy as to tell her I'd already worked out how to do it on my own. Though it would have been easier with somebody to lend a hand and would have saved some of the fash that happened afterwards.

Nature and conduct of experiment

Reasons 1. Believers (e.g. Old Vic, Kit, Julie) have been telling me that, if you want to know about belief, you have to behave as if you believed. You don't think it out, they say, and then believe, like solving a puzzle. You earn it and learn it by living it.

2. They have been telling me belief is a gift which you have to want. You obtain it by willing it. Ask, and it shall be given you; seek, and you shall find; knock, and it shall be opened unto you. (Matt. 7, 7.)

3. They all talk about:
   a. The Last Supper / Eucharist / Mass / Holy Communion;
   b. The Crucifiction;
   c. The Resurrection.

They perform the Last Supper, make pictures and sculptures of the Cross, and argue about what happened at the Resurrection.

I have taken part in (a), and quite enjoy arguing about (c). Sharing a meal with friends and having a jawbang about the Big Questions is understandable / fun / good / right / natural. But hanging two- and three-d pictures on the walls of your home, never mind in public places, of a man being tortured by the cruellest death known to the human race does not seem quite pukka, old boy, certainly not kosher, cobber.

Besides, the confessed believers in God's own religion also talk about the imitation of Christ, of living your belief. They act out (a), hope for (c), not being able to do much about their own resurrections as yet, but, apart from a few of their number that they tend to regard as nutters, none of them has a go at (b) crucifiction, which yet they say is so important to their belief. So what's all this about *living* your faith?

Of course, they talk a lot about the cross as a symbol, and that's okay. But I thought I'd take them at their word, why not? That's logical, after all. It's what any scientist would do experimentally, if he wanted to study a form of life closely. And as I am my own specimen, my own laboratory, and my own experiment . . . who else for the cross but me?

Not that I ever thought of doing the Real Thing. Nails through hands and feet, and a crown of thorns, and a spear up the rip cage, I mean. I'm not a suicidal sado-masochist. What I had in mind was more like a practice version. Besides:

4. Julie says we are all in everything, and everything is in us. We are the children of God, she says.

Well, children are composed of their parents. They are their parents while also being themselves. Christ, the son of God, was/is therefore God. God is therefore also in me, and I am in God. The believers tell me this as well as telling me to behave as if I believed. And the irreligious OBD tells me I must play Christ.

Okay, I shall take them all at their word. I shall act as if, and practise being Jesus Christ. I shall do some field work, some flesh-and-blood first-hand research, and find out how he-she-it felt, even if only a little bit and not the very worst. After all, I cannot perform miracles, cannot preach to great crowds, cannot invent wise sayings. But I can be crucified.

NB: This sounds pretty lame now. But at the time, that night, after seeing Julie in hospital and hearing her tape, these seemed good enough reasons. And the only ones. But they weren't the only ones. Not even the most important. I know that now but hid it from myself then. (Another conclusion from the experiment: people do things more for hidden reasons than for stated ones. Each of us is a galaxy of secret lives.)

INTERCUT: *The shot from outside Nik's bedroom, as before but this time in slow motion. His face is unbearably tense as he listens to his Walkman. He rises and with studied violence hurls the Bible directly at us. It smashes through the window.*

Shot continues: Shards of glass fly in all directions. The Bible narrowly misses us, leaving a gaping, jagged hole in the windowpane. Nik comes to the window. The hole frames his head and shoulders. He stretches out his arms, cruciform, and grasps the casement. He stares out at us, unseeing, while we hear Julie's voice-over, as from a tape heard through headphones:

(fade up): . . . *found this passage which says it for me:* 'Now I know, now I understand, my dear, that in our calling, whether we are writers or actors, what matters most is not fame, nor glory, nor any of the things I used to dream of. What matters most is knowing how to endure. Know how to bear your cross and have faith. I have faith and it doesn't hurt so much any more.'

The Place. Golgotha. The place of the skull. A burial place for rubbish. A dump outside the city wall of Jerusalem, a small town on a trade route on the outback edge of the Roman empire in the first century of the Christian era.

This was easy. The dump on the other (i.e. wrong) side of town, across the railway line and the canal, a burial ground for clapped-out motorcars. That seemed to me a pretty good twentieth-century stand-in for the original setting. Especially as the canal is dead, killed by the railway, which isn't what it used to be, having been crippled by the automobile, junked pyramids of which rise up as monuments to travel.

And Grandad's workshop being right next to it meant I could get all the gear I might need.

The Time. Sunrise. J C was nailed up at 9 a.m. I couldn't wait till then because at that time there would be people around who would stop me. Failing that, sunrise seemed appropriate. New day, new way, etc. Not that I worked it out beforehand. Only decided to do the crucifiction experiment when I was on the common with Michelle. Though—hidden lives—the idea must have been rumbling about in the back of my mind like a brainstorm on the brew all the day before, if not longer.

The Cross. Easy again. Two or three weeks ago I saw a piece of metal from the chassis of an old lorry lying on the dump. It was made of two pieces welded together in a T-shape that reminded me of the *crux commissa.* I soon found it again that morning.

The Method. In Grandad's workshop there was a big roll of heavy-duty clear polythene sheeting. He used it to cover anything he wanted to keep dust or rain off. Also for making temporary cloches and cold frames for his garden. I cut five strips off it, each a metre long by ten cm. wide. I also looked out a six-metre length of strong rope, and cut two twenty-metre lengths of window sashcord.

I took this stuff out to the dump and laid it on the ground directly under the arm of the old mobile crane Fred Bates uses to shift wrecked cars and heavier scrap. Then I dragged the chassis-cross to the same place.

I tied the rope to the cross where the metal pieces were joined and made a noose at the other end. The strips of polythene I tied round the bars, two on each arm and one on the upright, leaving them loose enough so that I'd be able to slip my hands through the ones on the crosspiece and my feet through the other. I reckoned these would secure me to the cross while leaving my hands free.

Next I had to fix the crane. I've often helped Fred use it. When I was a kid, the crane seemed like a great big toy and Fred used to let me sit in the cab with him and work the levers. When I got old enough he started paying me pocket-money for working on the dump at weekends. Fred's a kindly, bumbling old guy who has no children of his own, which is maybe why he likes having me around. Grandad often tells him off for spoiling me but I suspect he's jealous. He and Fred have known each other since their infant school days and have a mock-insulting kind of relationship, full of jokes no one else can understand and that neither of them ever do more than half-smile at. The point is, though, that I know how the crane works and I know where Fred keeps a spare ignition key hidden in case he loses the one he carries with him.

So as soon as the cross was ready I took the two lengths of sashcord, found the key, and climbed into the cab. There I attached one length of cord to the lever that raises the hook and the other cord to the lever that lowers it. Then I ran the cords through the cab window to the point on the cross where my hands would be.

That done, I hunted out a stub of heavy metal about the size of a brick and took it back to the cab.

Everything was now ready for a trial run. I started the engine and tested the arrangement of the remote control cords. This meant first finding how to jam the stub of metal against the accelerator pedal in such a position that the accelerator maintained just the right revs to raise the cross. If there aren't enough revs for the weight to be raised, the engine stalls; if there are too many, it raises the load too fast and can jam the hook at the end of the crane's arm. As I couldn't find the right revs by trial and error, I had to judge them from experience.

When I'd done that I had to make sure it was possible to work the up and down levers by pulling on the sashcords. The levers have quirks. You have to lift and shift, rather like a motorcar gear for reverse. To achieve this I had to rig the cords round struts in the cab before a pull from outside of the cab made them function properly. I'd anticipated this, and had been thinking out the solution while getting everything else ready. So I didn't take long to get it right. Except that I discovered I only had one chance with each lever. If anything went wrong once I was in the air, I'd had it: I'd be stuck.

If I'd let myself think about it, I might have given up right then. But I didn't. The grey summer dawn was lightening now every minute. The sun would be up soon and so would people. No time for pondering. If I was going to do it, it had to be done at once or I'd be too late. And I certainly wasn't going to give up.

Besides, I felt a weird kind of excitement. From the moment Michelle had left me, fleeing on my bike, I'd worked with steadily increasing speed and passion. Everything I did went perfectly, as if I knew exactly what I was doing because I'd practised many times. And by the time I'd rigged the crane I was sweating and breathing hard, almost as I had been earlier when I arrived on the common. Only, instead of feeling utterly whacked, I was elated, surging with energy. I can remember thinking, *I am as one possessed*, and laughing out loud.

Now, two days later, when in my memory I see myself scurrying about Fred's dump in the early morning light, I know something I was not aware of at the time: a sensation of being utterly absorbed, of being wholly myself and yet also more than myself, a part of something inevitable and beyond that moment. I think what I felt must have been what people mean when they talk of fate and of meeting their destiny. That is why now I feel no guilt or shame or regret, the way some people (everybody?) think I should. I know it was a ridiculous thing to

208

do, dangerous and stupid really, but when I think of it, I find myself smiling.

The cross prepared, the crane revving, its hook lowered and ready with the noosed rope attached. All that was left was for me to slip my arms and legs into their polythene bindings, take hold of the control cords, and pull the up lever.

I took my shoes off but found that my jeans were snagging on the polythene strip. So I pulled them off; decided to make a proper job of it, and pulled off my T-shirt as well, which was wet through for the second time and uncomfortable anyway. That left me in my underpants.

Without encumbrance of clothes my legs and arms fitted easily into their straps. I took hold of the ends of the cords, settled myself as best I could on the bars of my cold metal bed and, taking a deep breath, tugged the up cord.

Which is when things went slightly wrong.

†

'This better not be another stunt,' Tom said as they approached the dump. He had driven down from the common in sullen silence.

There's nothing so funny, Michelle was thinking, as a randy boy when he's thwarted. Nor so dangerous, sometimes, neither. She performed to herself her mother's frequent refrain: Men, they're all beasts!

'Pull up just there.' She pointed ahead at Arthur Green's workshop.

Before she went in she banged at the rattly door, calling: 'Mr Green, hello. It's me, Michelle.' But Tom swept her inside on the bow of his temper before there was time for reply.

The place was gloomy and cavernous, lit only from sky-lights. But everything was neatly kept and arranged. A carpenter's bench, ancient in use but as cared for as front room furniture; tools hung and laid out in meticulous order; a circular saw, a band saw, a planing machine, all giving sharp metallic winks; even the sawdust on the floor looked as if scattered by order rather than neglect.

One corner was occupied by stacked piles of wood in various cuts and sizes, a library of timber. Another, the farthest corner, half hidden by large sheets of blockboard standing on end and leaning against a main rafter, was an inner sanctum, a den where a naked light bulb dangled from the roof, shining above an old kitchen table, at which sat Arthur Green, his knotted hands curled round a large mug, his head bent over a newspaper spread in front of him.

He turned to peer at Michelle and Tom standing just inside the door but did not rise.

'Now then,' he called.

'I've brought him,' Michelle called back.

'So I see.'

Tom made his way through the workshop, Michelle following slowly like an indulgent mum behind an over-eager child. He stopped by the partitioning boards, where he could see all of the den—its chipped sink and water-blackened draining board, its long-out-of-date oven, its couple of battered armchairs angled towards a wood-burning stove, presently dead. But other than the man at the table, nobody.

Michelle arrived at his side; Tom glanced and saw her undisguised pleasure at his puzzlement.

'So where is he?' Tom said. 'I thought he was here.'

'Aye, well he's not, is he?' Arthur Green said. 'He's gone.'

'I talked to you this morning,' Tom said. 'Out there.'

'You did.'

'You said you knew nothing.'

'No, no! I said there was plenty of gossip.'

Michelle couldn't help chipping in, 'Mr Green is Nik's grandad.'

Tom's face betrayed that he felt like kicking himself.

'Where is he?' he demanded.

Arthur Green chuckled. 'He is risen, he is not here.'

Tom said, 'This is no joke, Mr Green. It's a police matter.'

'You're right, lad,' Arthur Green said. 'It's no joke, and it's nothing to do with the police neither.'

'Your grandson is crucified and you don't think it has anything to do with the police?'

'Why should it?'

'Because it's a criminal offence. GBH at least. Don't you want the people responsible to be caught?'

Arthur Green turned to Michelle. 'You didn't tell him?'

Michelle shook her head. 'Didn't think he'd believe me.'

Tom said, 'Believe what?'

Arthur Green pushed his mug away, sat back in his chair, placed his work-warped hands flat on the table in front of him and said, 'He crucified himself.'

INTERCUT: *The scene at the dump. The cross lying on the ground with Nik strapped to it. He pulls the sashcord. The crane begins to wind in. The rope connecting hook to cross takes the strain. The cross begins to rise, pivoting on its foot. At first all goes well. But then, suddenly, Nik's unevenly balanced weight causes the cross to tip to one side. It slews and turns over. The control cords are snatched from his hands. This takes Nik by surprise. He cries out. Now, instead of lying on the cross, he is hanging under it.*

The cross continues to rise up. As soon as its foot leaves the ground it begins to gyrate, swivelling as well as swinging from side to side like a pendulum. And because of the way the rope is attached, the cross does not hang upright, but tilts forward at the top, so that Nik is hanging from it, his arms pulled back by their bonds, his chest thrust out, and his legs, caught at the ankles, bending awkwardly at the knees. It looks like, and is, a painful position in which to be trapped.

Slowly, the cross rises until it is about five metres above ground, when the crane's engine coughs, splutters, stalls, and conks out.

Silence.

The cross swings and turns. At each turn we see Nik's dumbfounded face. And as he turns, his glasses catch the first rays of the rising sun and flash at us.

NIK'S NOTEBOOK: I had worked out the mechanics. But not the dynamics.

When I said that to Grandad afterwards, he said: The story of your life.

So there I was—suspended, stuck, helpless, suffering, and alone.

My God, my God, why hast thou forsaken me?

It took six hours before J C was broken enough to ask that. It took less than six minutes before I knew why he asked it and exactly what he meant.

'I don't believe you,' Tom said.

'Told you,' Michelle said, slumping into one of the armchairs.

'Tell him, girl,' Arthur Green said.

Michelle said: 'I found him on Selsley Common last night, not long before dawn actually. He was lying on the ground, flat out asleep, nothing on, only jeans and trainers. I thought he must be ill or something. But when I woke him he was okay and we talked a bit, well, quite a lot actually. But only talked, I mean, nothing else.'

She gave Tom a look that defied contradiction.

'He told me all about the bomb and the girl he was with, how he felt about her, and about him and her and religion. And about how the girl didn't love him like he loved her, and he'd just found out. He was pretty upset about that, I think. Well, I'm sure he was actually.'

She drew a deep breath, the way people do when they're talking about a hopeless situation.

'Anyway, he asked me if I'd do something to help him, and I said I would, and he brought me down here. But he didn't say till we got here that he wanted me to help him crucify himself. I couldn't believe it! I said: No way, I said. No way am I going to help you do nothing like that, I said, that's crazy, you must be off your noddle, I said, even to think such a thing. It's that girl, I said, and her religious stuff, she's a fanatic, I said, she's mangled your brains. And lying around on the common with nearly nothing on in the middle of the night, and soaking. He was wringing wet with sweat when I found him. You must have caught a fever, I said, and he did look flushed, no question.'

Michelle took another deep breath before going on.

'Well, he said, don't worry, I expect you're right. It was just a joke anyway, he said, I didn't really mean it. I'll just stay here for a bit, he said, and make myself some tea in Grandad's workshop. You take my bike, he said, and go home. I'll use an old one of Grandad's. You can fetch mine back later, he said. Though, to tell the truth, I was really glad of the excuse to see him again because—'

She glanced at Arthur Green, thought better of saying what she had been about to say, sat forward in the chair, coughed and went on: 'But when I got home I couldn't sleep for thinking about him. And the more I thought about him wanting me to help him crucify himself, the more I was sure he hadn't been joking. And I thought: What if he does do it somehow? It'll be terrible, I'd never forgive myself for not staying with him and making sure he didn't and for not helping him a bit more. I mean, he's had an awful time lately, hasn't he? He can't be very well, can he, even if he looks all right? And people can do crazy things when they're really in love, can't they? Especially if they're rejected. I mean, everybody knows that. Anyway, in the end I couldn't bear it. And I thought: It'll be my fault if anything happens.'

The abstracted glare of desperation in Michelle's eyes allowed no doubt. She swallowed hard and continued: 'I didn't know what to do. And then I thought of ringing the workshop so I could talk to him and make sure he was all right but I could only find the number for his house. So I thought of ringing Mr Green but then I thought: What if he goes racing off to the dump and nothing's the matter, he might give Nik a bad time, and Nik would hate me for telling his grandad, and—'

She glanced at Arthur Green again and shrugged, a resigned apology.

'Go on, girl,' Arthur Green said. 'Don't you mind.'

Michelle gave him a grateful nod, snuffled against imminent sobs, drew a staving breath, and managed to add: 'I got that worried I decided the only thing to do was ride back to the dump. So I did . . . and there he was . . . hanging—' before undeniable tears welled and burst, sluicing with them the trauma and distress she had hidden from view all day.

INTERCUT: *The dump. Early morning sunlight. Michelle comes cycling hectically along the road. She sees Nik before she reaches the dump and begins yelling his name in a panic-stricken voice.*

When she arrives under the cross she flings herself from the bicycle, which wobbles away on its own until it collides with a mound of scrap and entangles itself with the other discarded vehicles.

Struggling for breath, Michelle gazes up at Nik and between gulps, shouts at him: 'You—bloody—fool!—What did you —go and—do that for!'

Nik stares back at her with a pained grin, making confused, constricted noises.

'Jesus!' Michelle says, and stamps her foot. She sees the control cords snaking over the ground to the crane's cab, runs to the crane, climbs into the cab, at once realizes the problem is too complicated for her to sort out quickly, jumps down, and sprints towards the workshop, shouting as she goes: 'I'll get your grandad.'

She disappears into the workshop.

The cross turns slowly, swaying in the first breeze of the day as it does so.

After a moment Brian Standish in white running gear bursts through the hedge above the canal, his appalled face turned up towards Nik as towards a vision. Nik mutters incoherently.

'Christ Almighty!' the man gasps. He takes in the scene, dodging and skipping as if avoiding invisible assailants. He jumps, trying to reach the cross, as if he thinks by grasping it he can pull it down. He stumbles towards the crane. But stops before reaching it, turns, looks up at Nik, says, 'Dear God!', makes a dash for the access road, stops at the edge of it, turns to look at Nik again, says, 'Hell's bells!', comes to a decision and races back to the hole in the hedge, shouting at Nik as he goes, 'Hang on, I'll get help!' and disappears the way he came.

The cross slowly turns, floodlit now in bright warm sunlight. There is birdsong. And Nik's voice in an indecipherable ritual chant.

'I better be sure I've got this right, Mr Green,' Tom said. 'You drove here on your motorbike at about six fifteen this morning in response to a phone call from Michelle Ebley. You found your grandson suspended on a cross from the crane on the dump. You got him down, and with Miss Ebley's help, carried him into your workshop. Then, while Miss Ebley looked after him, you removed from the scene the cords, the metal block your grandson had used against the accelerator, and the crane's ignition key.'

'Right so far,' Arthur Green said.

'You knew someone else had found your grandson on the cross because Miss Ebley had seen him. And fearing the police would come, you locked yourself with your grandson and Miss Ebley into the workshop. The police did arrive shortly afterwards. But you all kept quiet till they left the scene.'

'Right.'

'Not long afterwards, I visited the dump. At first you thought I was just someone poking about and you came out to try and get rid of me. When you realized I was a police officer you began to fear that we hadn't given up. This was confirmed when you learned that afternoon from Miss Ebley's brother that I was making inquiries through contacts—'

'That's one way of putting it!' Michelle said.

'You then decided that your grandson's presence here might be discovered, that the police would make a fuss and so the newspapers would get on to the story and create another stir. To prevent this happening you phoned the Reverend Ruscombe of St James's, told him the whole story, and asked for his help. He suggested that he come for your grandson and take him to the vicarage where he would be more comfortable and be safe from police or press inquiries until he was recovered and able to cope.'

'That's about the size of it.'

'In order to allow time for this to happen, Miss Ebley suggested she meet me and act as a decoy—'

'I didn't say decoy!'

'No, but that's what it amounted to.'

'Well, but—'

'And she and her friends kept me away until she was sure your grandson had been removed.'

'You make him sound like a piece of furniture,' Michelle said.

Tom ignored her. 'And that's where he is now.'

'He is.'

Tom thought for a moment before asking with an attempt at off-handedness, 'What happened to his glasses, sir?'

Arthur Green smiled wryly. 'They got knocked off when we were cutting him loose. I didn't notice and stood on them. Broke the lenses. Didn't think they'd be much use after that so I chucked them over the pile of tyres to get shot of them. I was surprised when you found them. Even more surprised you traced him from them.'

'Just routine,' Tom said.

'Oh aye? Pat on the back, though, for you, eh? The lot who came first didn't find them.'

Tom shrugged. 'Lucky break.'

Michelle gave a scoffing laugh. 'My, my!' she said. 'He's never witty as well as handy!'

Arthur Green sent her a look that said: Mind yourself.

They fell silent, avoiding each other's eyes. Doubt hung between them like the fine motes of dust making smoky the light from the naked bulb above their heads.

Outside, the eight-twenty local connection from London rattled down the valley, across the viaduct on the other side of the canal, and braked to a greaseless stop at the station.

Inside, the only sound was the tattoo of Tom's fingers drumming on his thigh.

Michelle's patience snapped first. 'Is that it, then? We can go home, can we?'

Her irritation seemed to make up Tom's mind. He braced, stood up, and pushed his chair under the table, as if rising from a polite meal that's gone on too long, saying: 'Not yet. I'll have to report back.'

'Aw, come on!' Michelle sprang to her feet and confronted him across the table. 'What for? We've told you everything. Nobody else was involved. Nik's okay. What more d'you want? Nobody's done nothing illegal.'

'Oh no?' Tom's own patience was crumbling too. 'Removing evidence from the scene of a possible crime. Concealing a wanted man. Misleading and obstructing an officer in the course of his duty. Try those for starters.'

'Refusing an officer the pleasure of a bit on the side during the course of his duty. Does that count as well?'

Tom's face flushed. 'Look, I've had enough of you!' he said, pointing his finger at Michelle, who, flaunting herself, sneered: 'You haven't had me at all yet, you big dick!'

Arthur Green rose between them. 'All right, all right, that'll do, the pair of you!' he said with unbrookable firmness. He gathered himself, a tired old man giving in to consequences he has known all day must eventually be faced. 'Now, let's try again before there's more harm done. Listen, young man, I know you've got your job to do, and I'm not trying to stop you. All we've been doing is trying to keep my grandson from any more trouble. But all right, maybe I've overstepped the mark here and there and was wrong. I'm sorry about that. But nobody's been harmed. And there's nothing that can't be cleared up.'

Tom, fighting his temper still, replied with strained calm. 'I'll have to report. My governor isn't happy about this one. I reckon he'll want to see your grandson and you two and question you himself. Anyway, I can't let you go till I've new instructions.'

Arthur Green nodded. 'Can I make a suggestion?'

'What?'

'Report to your boss. If he wants to look into it personal, arrange for us all to meet at St James's vicarage. It'll be easier there. I don't think your boss'll want any more hoohah than I do, do you?'

Tom considered before reluctantly nodding agreement.

†

NIK'S NOTEBOOK: But being stranded on the cross turned out to be what Grandma Green used to call a blessing in disguise.

The blessing was that it gave me a clue for cracking the code of the indecipherable.

To start with, though, all it gave me was a nasty shock.*

---

* SHOCK: otherwise known as the Big Bang theory of the origin of the universe. This states that one day God was playing about with a lot of nothing in his-her-its laboratory in the middle of nowhere, when he-she-it had a nasty accident. *Bang!* And a few God-minutes later,

217

One thing about a nasty shock, it does bring you to your senses. Grandma Green was right about that too. What caused the shock, of course, was pain. Some people don't seem to mind pain. Athletes, for instance, are always talking about going through the pain barrier like other people talk about (or usually don't talk about) going to the lavatory: as if it is one of those normal, everyday chores you have to do if you want to stay alive. Personally, I find any kind of pain anything but normal and everyday, and always abnormal and unique. I could happily live without it.

In my opinion, anybody who says pain is a Go(o)d Thing is crazy, anybody who recommends it to others is evil, and anybody who goes looking for it is sick.

But I know I am pretty much alone in this, judging from the way most people go on.

One of the reasons why the pain of the cross was such a shock—apart from the actual, physical pain itself, I mean—was that it brought me back to my senses with a jolt and I thought:

What am I doing here?

Why did I do this to myself?

I must be sick!

---

there everything was, evolving like crazy before his-her-its very eyes. And God thought: Hello, this looks a bit dodgy, and quickly dictated a few commandments to put things back in order, but nobody would obey them. So God tried threatening horrible consequences if they didn't do as they were told but that didn't work because nobody cared less until the consequences actually happened. So God let a few really large-scale calamities occur, but that didn't put a stop to the nonsense either. So finally God decided he-she-it had better pile in as himself and do something about it before the whole business went to pot. But that didn't go too well either, as any fool would know it wouldn't, because, as any fool knows, only nothing can come of nothing, and nothing did. And that's why adherents of the Big Bang theory believe we're all nothing but a load of old rubbish floating around in the middle of nowhere with nothing to do and nowhere to go and do it. Which also explains why Big Bangers are always saying to each other: What the hell, who cares, let's have another big bang.

This is also known as the Cock-up theory of creation.

Idiot! You got yourself stuck up here, now get yourself down!

And I started wriggling about, trying to pull my arms out of their bindings. But I couldn't. The bindings were too wide to allow me to bend my arms and slip my hands out. I felt like an insect pinned to a collector's tray.

I heard myself say out loud: This is ridiculous! I can't get myself free! Somebody's got to help me!

And trying to shout: Help! ... Hello? ... Anybody ... Help!

STOCKSHOT : *The mystery of the Cross of Christ lies in a contradiction, for it is both a free will offering and a punishment which he endured in spite of himself. If we only saw in it an offering, we might wish for a like fate. But we are unable to wish for a punishment endured in spite of ourselves.*

Panic. But I remembered my research. (Facts are useful sometimes.) By tying the victim's arms to the cross the Romans could prolong his death for up to three days. And that was when his wrists and feet had been nailed as well. I was only tied, not nailed. So there was a pretty good chance of staying alive till somebody found me—three hours at most, never mind three days.

This thought calmed me down.

But then the strain on my muscles. And the sweats coming in fierce waves. And the dryness in my mouth and the taste of salt on my lips. And the strangling of my breath unless I pulled up and back with my arms. Which increased the pain in my muscles unbearably. And the sensation of my body being stretched by its own weight and tearing itself in half at the waist. And nothing to push up on with my feet. And my legs twisting at the knees, writhing against the pain.

The waves of pain.

And my eyes, as if they would pop.

Wave-pop.

Black blur and white dazzle.

And wave-pop.

And my breath breaking the sound barrier as my eyes splinter against the wall of light, the black sun blazing and flickering between here and there now and then as I turn on the axis of my heart pounding in my ears.

> The ring of singularity.
> Until I spin
> Sucking my mind
> Dazzled into another where
> And there was only now.
> And the zing of words
> In other worlds
> Stars exploding
> In clusters
>   galaxies
>   universes.
> Cross words.

STOCKSHOT: *Hold to the now, the here, through which all future plunges to the past.* (As, it might be added, all past plunges to the future through the now and here to which you hold. For everything is in the neck of the hour glass: the kiss of two cones.)

JULIE: It is the hidden that I look for.

'Where is he, vicar?' Tom demands.

NIK: Now for the life of the eyes?

'Nobody else!' Tom's superintendent says. 'Nobody at all? Are you sure? What's he think he's doing?'
   'Performing an experiment, he says, sir.'
   'Experiment? What kind of experiment?'
   'Making pictures, he says, sir.'
   'Making pictures! What does he mean?'
   'I asked him that. He said: Those who have eyes to see let them see.'
   '. . . Is that all?'
   'Refused to say anything else, sir.'
   'Is he off his head?'
   'His grandfather thinks he's still in a dodgy state after the bomb. Miss Ebley says he's in love with the girl who was involved in the explosion, and that he's upset because she's

jilted him, but I don't think she's a reliable witness, sir. The vicar believes he's suffering some kind of religious experience which has gone a little too far.'

'And you?'

'I think he's a weirdo desperate for attention. He's the sort who gives me the creeps, to be honest, sir.'

'Dangerous?'

'No no! Bit of a wimp, if you ask me. But maybe you should have a word, sir?'

'I'll have more than a word. A fine dance he's led us. And all for nothing.'

INTERCUT: *Old Vic raises up before his eyes the round ice-cream wafer and says in his vicarious voice: 'This is my body which is given for you. Do this in remembrance of me.' He breaks the wafer in half and places the two pieces as one into his mouth.*

'Get him away from here, Mr Green,' the superintendent orders, 'get him out of the road. And now. At once. I don't know which of you is right about why this has happened. And that's not my concern. But we can't have this affair getting into the media. It wouldn't just be bad for your grandson, it would be awkward for us all. Have you relatives he could stay with?'

'None he'd want to go to.'

'Well, you'd best think of somewhere, because either you get him away from here or I'll have to make some charges. Against you in particular, Mr Green.'

'What about the monastery?' Old Vic suggests. 'I'm sure they'd have him, and they'd understand.'

'He might go there. He liked it before. And they seemed to know how to handle him. He's got beyond me these days.'

'Admirable!' the superintendent says. 'If he's still shook up from the bomb, a spell of monastic quiet will do him good. If hankering after that girl is the trouble, then the best thing is for them to be kept apart till he's over it. If it's religious fever he's suffering from then a stretch in a monastery is just the place for him to sweat it out—and they ought to be professionals at that.'

'I'll go and ask him.'

'Do that, Mr Green. And let's pack him off tonight. I want

this matter cleared up. Young Thrupp will drive him so we're sure he gets there ... er ... safe and sound.'

JULIE: It's like the leaves on the branches of the tree outside my window, and the branches in the tree, and the flecks of sunlight flashing on the ripples on the pond. All around me everywhere I'm struck by how the many make one. And by the one hidden in the many. It fascinates me. Catches my attention and holds it.

Which reminds me. Philip Ruscombe visited me the other day and celebrated the Eucharist at my bedside. Afterwards I asked him what he thought prayer was. He said the best description he had ever come across was this: Prayer is complete attention.

I liked that. It sounded right. Giving your whole attention till you are part of the whole, yet are still yourself.

That decided me. I knew what I had to discover more about. How to give my whole attention. What to give it to. What to do with it. And I don't want to find that out in some special way, like the old-fashioned monks and nuns did—not by cutting myself off from other people and living in purpose-built prayer houses. I want to do it hidden among ordinary people in an ordinary everyday place while I do ordinary everyday work.

There is nothing special about me. I'm just another leaf on the branch, another branch in the tree, one of the flecks of light flickering in the ripples on the pond. One among many. Yet also myself, alone.

If God is God, then that is God and that is where God is. Ordinary people must find God among themselves or they won't find her at all. It isn't to one of the many that I want to give all my attention—you, dear Nik, or anyone. But to being one among the many.

What I'm asking is: How do I remain myself, truly and without being crushed or diminished, while being one of the many, no more special and no more privileged, no more *noticeable*, and yet be wholly of God?

That's the question I have to give all my attention to. And at first I have to try and answer it alone.

Perhaps I'll manage, with a little help from my friends.

Hello, friend!

[*Pause.*]

And you'll say: But how do you know?

And I'll say: Because I believe it.

And you'll say: But what is belief?

[*Pause. Laughs.*]

Well, I've given that question some attention lately!

And I've tried to find an answer by playing your game.

Belief. Philip Ruscombe looked the word up in a dictionary, and then both of you gave up attending to the word *itself*! So I went on playing the game.

BE . . . LIEF

Be, my dictionary says, means: *To have presence in the realm of perceived reality; exist; live*. Which being translated means, I suppose: *To live in the world you accept is truly THERE.*

Lief, my dictionary says, means: *Gladly, willingly*. And adds that the word is related to the Old English word for *love*.

So *Belief* means: that you *will* to give all your *attention* to *Living with loving gladness in the world you think really does exist.*

Perhaps what you wanted to know was all there in the word itself and you didn't need to look anywhere else. I wonder if that's why St John's Gospel begins: In the beginning was the Word!

Anyway, I do think it is true that if God is to be found by belief, she is to be found by living gladly and with attentive love in the world where we are. Because God is here and now and is all of us and everything.

I don't know how to say it simpler than that.

The kiss of two cones.

'All right, settle down,' the Director shouted. 'I can't tell you any more than that. You'll have to ask him yourselves when you see him again. His grandad says he'll be back for Christmas. Now, Michelle has a message from him. I don't know what it is, she wouldn't tell me. You'd better read it out, Michelle.'

'He sent us this letter,' Michelle said, unfolding a page of computer printout. She cleared her throat and shuffled and brushed her hair from her eyes and cleared her throat and read aloud:

To the film group. This is my last piece of research for you. It contains my conclusions.

From everything I've learned, it seems to me that if Christ returned today:

1. He would be a woman.
   Reasons:
   i. The universe is a binary system:
      Black holes / White holes;
      in / out;
      male / female; etc.
      Last time God appeared as male;
      next time as female. The system demands it.
   ii. The time of the domineering male is over;
       the time of the female has come.
   iii. Now the fish is returning to the water.
2. You wouldn't recognize her though, because she is not one but all.

Therefore, to make a film about Christ coming now you should:

1. Set up a camera on any street, in any house, and anywhere else you like, and let it film whatever people do there for as long as you can.
2. Edit the film into any sequence of shots that make a pattern you enjoy.
3. Add clips from any other films that help make your film more interesting, and which improve the pattern of your own film.
4. Print the result and show it.

One more thing:

Sack the Director. All he wants to be is God. His kind of God doesn't exist any more. You don't need him. Do it yourselves. Together. When you can, Christ has returned.

Cheers.

See you.

Nik

As soon as Michelle finished reading everybody started talking at once.

An hour later the meeting broke up in uproar.

>>> MAKING LIGHT
OF LEAFING >>>

for >>

J U L I E

from >>

N * I * K

EYE SAW

Who says we saw
What last we saw
When last we saw
  Each other?

Whose eyes we saw
No others saw
When last we saw
  Each other

Those eyes we saw
Told all we saw
When last we saw
  Each other

Our eyes we saw
Saw yes and saw
The last of
  Each other

SUN LIGHT

The sun
that flickers
the leaves
makes light
of leafing

The sun
that sunders
the waves
makes light
of weaving

The sun
that flickers
is the light
that sunders
all one
in making

The kiss of
two cones

CROSS WORDS >>>>>>>>>>>>>>>>>

water by tree
splintering sun
congregation
at the ritual
baptism of the cross

How do you say it?

    Is God is
    Is God already
    Is God always
       Always-already
     But not yet   Is
     Not-yet God   Eye es
                Why es
Yet God
  Is God
          see why I A M
God Is   M I A

      Stars spinning
      he points the compass
      His hands
      bear the universe

      He swings in the breeze
      God's weathervane

      A jogger's padding feet
      tattoo in his mind

      Where's he going
        where's he running
         and from what
      with his feet on
      the end of his legs
      and his body
      head bent
      to the ground?

Why hast thou forsaken me?

Am I forsaken?
  To be forsaken
  must have been known

Now I know
  It unknown
  knows me I ran one day Here
          Sprinted   in
Why yes   But not arrived head

      Hello J U L I E You
      With love   there
      N I K.   G O D

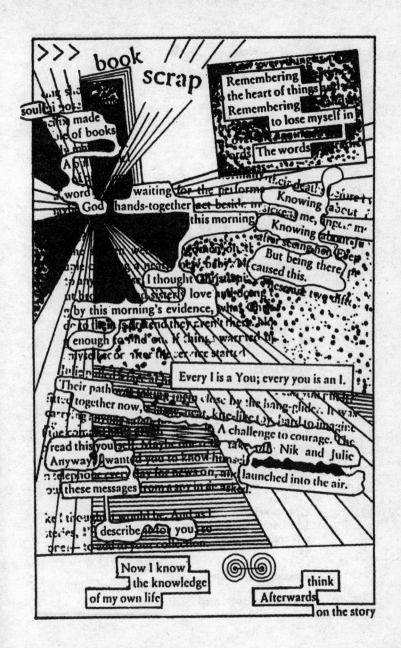

BIRTHDAY SONG

∧
∧
∧

An identity
to speak of?
I was born
a book
You should read it
Might get a surprise

Silence
my mind
my cell
myself

Silence
it's very beautiful

writing
in Silence
words
make an object
words weaving in and out
moving all the time
make new sentences, new meanings

Now I know
But
        for
the poet
living in
ourselves
we
wouldn't
learn anything

end without end

STOCKSHOT SOURCES

The Narrator gratefully acknowledges:

vii   'The best in this kind . . . imagination amend them.'
    William Shakespeare, *A Midsummer Night's Dream*,
    V i 210-211, CUP 'New Shakespeare' edition.

16   'Jesus of Nazareth . . . living in faith.'
    Donald M. McFarlan, *Bible Readers' Reference Book*, p.89,
    Blackie.

22   'And as the mole . . . I shall be.'
    James Joyce, *Ulysses*, The Corrected Text, p.159, Bodley
    Head.

34   'Canst thou . . . canst thou know?'
    The Book of Job 11 7,8.

43   'Who is there? . . . the Thou and the I.'
    Paul Valery quoted in W. H. Auden, *The Dyer's Hand*, p.109,
    Faber.

65   '. . . by history . . . are perfected . . .'
    Hugh of Rouen.

102 'There is only one definition . . . freedoms to exist.'
    John Fowles, *The French Lieutenant's Woman*, p.99, Cape.

108 'People like you . . . a word to come.'
    C. G. Jung's Letters, vol 1, Routledge & Kegan Paul, quoted in
    Michael Tippett, *Moving into Aquarius*, p.167, Paladin.

203 'The eye . . . sees me.'
    Angelus Silesius.

206 'Now I know . . . hurt so much any more.'
    Nina in Anton Chekhov's *The Seagull*, Act 4, quoted in
    Chekov The Dramatist by David Magarshack, p.191,
    Methuen.

219 'The mystery of the Cross . . . in spite of ourselves.'
    Siân Miles, Editor, *Simone Weil: An Anthology*, p.263, Virago,
    from which come the other quotations from Simone Weil, to
    whom Julie's meditation on affliction also owes a debt.

220 'Hold to the now . . . plunges to the past.'
    James Joyce, *Ulysses*, The Corrected Text, p.153, Bodley
    Head.

Mother Julian's words are quoted from *Revelations of Divine Love*
translated by Clifton Wolters, Penguin Books.

Two pages of Nik's book to Julie owe their inspiration to the work of
Tom Phillips, especially his book *A Humument,* Thames & Hudson.

the toll bridge

Acknowledgements

The publishers gratefully acknowledge permission to reprint the following:

'The Bridge' from *Franz Kafka: The Complete Stories* by Franz Kafka. Copyright © 1946, 1947, 1948, 1949, 1954, 1958, 1971 Schocken Books Inc. Reprinted by permission of Schocken Books, published by Pantheon Books, a division of Random House Inc. English translation reprinted by permission of Martin Secker and Warburg Ltd. This translation first published in England in 1973 by Martin Secker & Warburg Limited, 14 Carlisle Street, London W1V 6NN. Copyright © 1934, 1937, by Heinr. Mercy Sohn, Prague. Copyright © 1946, 1947, 1958, by Schocken Books Inc. This translation copyright © 1973 by Martin Secker and Warburg Ltd.

FOR ADAM

Take this as a gift. The only gift I can give you that might, one day, mean anything to you.

I've visited you often. You never know me, never recognize me, always treat me as someone you're meeting for the first time.

But soon I have to go away. Perhaps I shall never see you again. And who knows, one day it might all come back to you, everything that happened in the weeks we spent together. And if it does, what will you want to know? What will you ask? What will you think of me and Gill and Tess?

And what will you do? About yourself, I mean. That's the only important question. One reason why I'm writing this is to show you how you seemed to me, to us, how we thought of you.

As I write, I remember we once argued about gifts. There is no such thing as a free gift, you said. All gifts are a payment for something. I didn't agree. A gift is only a gift if it is freely given, I said. But maybe you were right. Perhaps a gift is always an exchange for something received. Or hoped for. Perhaps this gift is a kind of repayment for the life I live now. And perhaps by giving it I hope to quieten my conscience about leaving you.

Whatever the truth is, use (y)our story any way you like. Make of it what you will.

Déjà-vu

Adam comes to me like a ghost. For a moment I think he is a ghost. And as so many times afterwards he turns his appearance into a game. He pretends to be a ghost, but only when he discovers he has made a mistake.

Searching for a place to shack up for the night, he finds the little eight-sided house by the bridge, no lights, looking empty and dead, and thinks he is in luck. He does not know I am inside; and it is Hallowe'en.

He forces the door quietly. This gives him no trouble. The lock is old and weak, and he is strong. Even though he is not tall – he's thin and lithe – he sometimes seems to possess a big man's strength, which belongs to the hidden part of him, his mystery.

He forces the lock so quietly I do not wake. I have been living in the old toll house for three months and am sleeping well, which I did not while the place was strange and I was unused to being alone.

Having broken in he sees by moonlight the door he does not know leads into the only bedroom, where I lie sleeping, and decides to try this room first. Just inside is a creaky floorboard. He steps on it. The sound wakes me with a start. I sit up, see a ghostly silhouette against the moonlit window, and scream.

At which, '_Woo-whoo!_' he flutes and flaps his arms.

I really am scared, for a moment at least. And he, it is true, is an apparition, but of a kind I know nothing about. He also, he says afterwards, is scared, his _woo-whoing_ and flapping arms a reflex action. So he acts the ghost and I act spooked, each of us acting in self-defence, each having taken the other by surprise.

I fumble for the switch on my bedside lamp, a bulb stuck into an old stoneware cider bottle stood on an upturned orange box (bottle and box found in the basement that is a lavatory-cum-woodshed the day I arrived).

'Who the hell are you?' I shout, acting indignant while my fingers fail me with the switch.

'*Woo-whoo?*' he flutes again, this time more like an owl with stomach cramp than a haunting spectre.

I find the switch at last and we scrutinize each other, blinking in the raw light.

He is not exactly reassuring. Wet black hair hugging the round dome of his head. Foxy features smeared with mud, perhaps from a fall. Body draped in an ancient army combat cape, also muddy and the cause of his ghostly silhouette. Very wet and weary jeans poking beneath, and marine boots scarred from battle.

'I don't know you from Adam,' I say.

He laughs. 'Right first time.' And pulls off his cape. Beneath which he is leaner than I expect, the cape having lent a false appearance of bulk. A tatty soggy sweater, rust-red and out at his bare elbows, hangs on him like a skin ready to be shed.

And shed it he does.

'Hey, hey, hold on a sec!' I say. 'What're you doing?'

Sloughing his boots and jeans too, he says, 'How d'you mean?'

'I mean here . . . I mean stripping . . .'

Half out of bed, intending to be more forceful, I see, now he confronts me in the nude, the kind of cock boys in shower rooms honour with surreptitious glances. I stay where I am, the duvet hiding my middle.

'Frigging soaked,' he says, as if this explains everything.

'So?'

'Fell in the river.'

'What – cape and all? A wonder you didn't drown.'

'No, no. It was on the bank where I climbed out. I'm freezing.'

He turns his attention to the room, not that there's much to see. My bed – mattress on old iron bedstead. Lamp on orange box. Fireplace blocked off by sheet of cardboard. Books lining mantelpiece, river-rubbed stones for bookends. A few spare clothes hanging from a hook behind the door. Bare walls, long ago white, now a scuffed, geriatric grey.

Back to me, weighing me up, before he says, 'Any chance of a kip?'

Given the obvious idiocy of taking in, like a feral dog in the middle of the night, someone I know nothing about, except he is

3

called Adam, has an enviable cock, and has just been careless enough to fall into the river, my second surprise of the night comes when I hear myself reply, 'Sure. Expect we can fix up something.'

❖ 2 ❖

But there was more to it than cock-and-bull. For two months I'd been living like a hermit. By desire, I mean, not accident or compulsion. Wanting to be on my own, having had enough of doing what was expected of me, of being what other people wanted me to be: Dutiful only son of ambitious parents. Conscientious student swatting to be good enough for university. One of the lads, doing boring spare-time activities so as to be sociable. Faithful boyfriend of ten months' standing (and not enough laying, if anybody ever gets enough). And the rest of the ratbag people call normal.

In fact, an actor playing roles in other people's plays. And I was fed up of performing. I didn't want to play at anything. Not son, schoolboy, friend or, come to that, lover. I just wanted To Be. And To Be on my own.

Around Christmas – God, the play-acting you have to do at Christmas! – the Great Depression set in. At first my parents put it down to anxiety about the coming exams. Teachers dismissed it as a side effect of being a year ahead of other people my age, plus tiredness – the price any over-achiever working hard enough in his final year had to pay for success. 'Keep at it,' they said, 'you can relax in the summer.'

By Easter what my father called The Glums weren't any longer patches of 'being low' now and then, but were a permanent monstrous misery. Even Gill, my girlfriend, started to complain. And she, egged on by Mother, harried me into seeing our doctor. Who tested for glandular fever, coyly referred to as 'the kissing disease' (negative), diabetes (clear), anaemia (full-blooded), and finally pronounced a chronic case of old-fashioned growing pains for which he prescribed a course of vitamin pills. One more boring routine to add to all the others.

Result: The Glums worsened, dragging with them clouds of lowering headaches that broke into sudden storming rages which usually ended in rows and me smashing anything smashable, preferably items of Mother's favourite knick-knackery.

Otherwise, when not slogging through school work, I spent hours locked in my room brooding on the more satisfying aspects of being pissed off and the likely rewards of self-slaughter. Among which was the pleasure of taking others with me, especially Gill (spite: couldn't leave her behind for others to get their gropers on) and the cheerier yahoos at school (revenge, there being nothing more infuriating when you're depressed than other people's high spirits).

One of the rows finally brought everything to a head. Exams over, nobody wanted to go on coddling this whingeing creep (except Mother of course). And Gill it was who finally flashed the storm that ended with me deciding I'd had enough. People disgusted me. I disgusted myself. I wanted out.

The way out turned up in the wanted ads. (Well, when you're depressed you try anywhere.) Next after: *Condom Testers Required – help a leading rubber company design next year's chart toppers* . . . (think of all the times you'd have to do it on command, tumescent or not) was this:

Young Person temp. toll bridge keeper
pvt. est. Mod. wage, few resp., free
acc. toll house. Gd refs nec. Box 365.

'You'll starve,' joked Father, 'you can't boil an egg.'

'Who'll do your laundry?' cried Mother. 'I'll be worried sick, you living on your own, no neighbours, no phone, anything might happen.'

'You'll be three hours away even by car,' wailed Gill. 'How are we going to see each other?'

'What a mangy option,' scoffed the lads.

'Taking money from a few passing cars all day hardly sounds academically challenging,' objected teachers. 'If you want time out, go abroad, see life, gain some experience, don't stick yourself away in a dead-end job in the middle of nowhere.'

'I'll learn to cook, I'll do my own laundry, maybe it will be good for us to be apart for a while, I want a change from academic challenge, thank you – I want to be on my own and challenge myself and experience *my* life before I find out about other people's,' I said to scornful snickers, doubting glances, dour looks, exasperated eyebrows, huffings, puffings, and shoulders hucked against this perverse (Mother's version was pre-verse) teenager.

❖ 3 ❖

Tarzan's yodels woke me, followed by loud splashings from the river. My watch says six fifty, and Adam's makeshift bed – a few cushions and a blanket on the floor – is abandoned.

5

He can't be up already, can he, not after last night? And not in the river again?

I pull on my jeans and stumble to the back-door steps from where I can view the toll-house garden and the river.

Adam is clambering out of the water, glistening in the light of the morning sun filtered through a shrouding autumn mist. Shot from a TV commercial. Deodorant or Diet Pepsi.

A tree, its leaves turning paler shades of brown, droops over the water. From a riverside branch hangs a rope. I don't remember seeing it there before. Adam, unaware of me yet, runs, grabs the rope, swings wildly to and fro, flinging himself higher and higher, the motion shaking from the tree a shower of dying leaves. When he is as far out above the river as the rope can carry him, he hollers his jungle call, lets go, and plummets, neat as a needle, feet first into the water. To surface seconds later, splashing and blowing and tossing his head and swimming briskly for the bank.

This time he sees me as he climbs out, and stands beaming like a kid let loose after a bad term at school, slicking water from his face. Definitely deodorant.

I shiver and call, 'Aren't you cold?'

'It's a great game. Ever played it?'

'No,' I lie.

But why lie? I had played it – with Dad in one of his crazy moods when I was a kid.

Some memories are not for telling, I thought then, standing at the back door blearily clocking Adam and not knowing how wrong I was.

❖ 4 ❖

Adam followed me inside.

I hand him a towel while I wash. When I'm done, I go into the bedroom to finish dressing, and tidy up. I'm an obsessive tidier, inheritance from chronically tidy parents. (You can't buck all of your upbringing. Being a tidier is one of the roles I have no choice about playing because it is written in my genes. During blue periods I resent it all the more for that.)

Coming back into the living room, Adam passes me on his way to the bedroom. We avoid each other's eyes.

I set about making breakfast. Bread, honey, tea. Even now, I never bother with anything more than this, hating all the business of getting up in the morning.

6

Adam reappears, towel round his shoulders, still damp jeans and sweater in his hands. He lurks just inside the door. I can tell what he's after, and am unsettled. Having put him up for the night, do I want to encourage him by giving anything more?

All the business of giving. When we argued about it I said, as most people do, that taking from people is what makes you beholden. But Adam said, no, if people give you a present, then as far as he was concerned there were no strings. They were paying for something he'd given them, even if he didn't know what it was. But there's another side to giving that we didn't talk about because I only half sensed it then. Which is that giving to people puts you in their debt. I learned this because of Adam. Somehow, once you've given you feel obliged to give again, and to go on giving, and feel mean if you don't. A kind of reverse emotional debt.

[TESS: This is male-order talk. Women don't think about giving like that. I've noticed, as soon as you give a man something he wants to give you something back straightaway. I think it's a power thing, as if receiving a gift were some kind of threat he has to neutralize at once or else he'll be in a weak position. Seems to me that for men gifts are a kind of trade-off, which they're not for women. We give without thinking of getting anything back. We do it all the time.]

❖ 5 ❖

I begin to wonder who Adam is. And what it is about him that worries me. Nothing dangerous exactly, nothing threatening. Something betrayed by the look in his eyes and the way he stands there, silently expecting help. What unsettles me even more, I decide, is that he makes me feel violent. I want to rough him up, hit him, chuck him out, anyway be rid of him. Why, why?

'They can dry in front of the fire,' I say, 'if you get it going.'

He crosses to the hearth and dithers.

'You don't know about wood fires?'

'No.'

'I'll do it.'

Last night's ashes, under the powder of their grey deceiving surface, are still hot, quickly ignite a couple of twists of paper, the paper flames a few thin twigs which in turn soon set fire to splits of log.

Three months ago, I tell myself as the fire grows, I didn't know

7

how to do this either. And feel a kind of satisfaction I haven't felt for a year or more. A pleasure forgotten that makes me smile, and glance at Adam, who is crouching beside me now, wanting the warmth. But he gazes into the flames with a fixed unblinking stare.

'If you'd like something to eat,' I say, weakened by his lost look, 'there's bread on the table.'

He doesn't respond.

'Adam?'

Nothing. I touch him on the shoulder. He recoils. His eyes, flicking into focus, widen as though in fright at seeing me beside him. I'm sure he is going to scream, but he catches himself, and smiles, grins rather, just like last night when I switched on the light, a fox's grin, wide-mouthed, lips stretched, showing bright handsome teeth.

'There's bread on the table,' I repeat, 'if you want it.'

'Ah!' he says. 'Right.' Springs up, full of energy again, attacks the loaf and honey with a taking-it-for-granted greed that rekindles my anger, and makes me decide I don't care who he is, I don't want to know, I don't want him here disturbing my life with the switchback emotions he stirs up, I've got to get rid of him as soon as I can.

❖ 6 ❖

A car horn sounds in the road. The postman with a parcel and a letter, the parcel addressed in Mother's writing, the letter in Gill's.

As the van drives off towards the village Tess Norris comes puttering along on her Suzuki 150, L-plate flapping. Two wheels cross without paying, but she always stops for a talk. Not that she'd pay anyway. Her father is in charge of the toll bridge and of maintenance on the estate. My boss, a joiner by trade and the sort of man who can turn his hand to anything. Tess is on her way to school, her last year, English Lit., French, and Maths.

'Dad says can you manage without being relieved today? Urgent job at the hall.'

Her voice is muffled by her helmet and the putter of her engine. Her dark hazel eyes, all that's visible of her face, rouse me the more for being framed by the mask of her visor. The rest is ambiguous in old black leathers with a red flash down the sides. And biker's boots.

'I'll be OK.'

'Want anything?'

'A loaf and a jar of honey.'

8

'Already?'

I thumb at the house. 'Visitor.'

'Male or female?'

'Male.'

'Thought you were a hermit.'

'Invited himself.'

'Oh yes! I'll have a look this after.'

'Be gone by then I hope.'

She taps my parcel with a black-gloved hand. 'Weekly survival kit?'

'What else?'

'Mummy's boy!' She laughs and revs. 'See you.'

'Cheers.'

❖ 7 ❖

The hardest part, I'm finding, of telling this story – *one* of the hardest parts – is not only getting everything in, but getting everything in in the right place. Maybe this is the right place to explain about Tess.

I first met her the day after I arrived, just at the moment when I was wondering what the hell I had done. The day before, still high on adrenalin, the empty, damp bleakness of the house hadn't mattered, had even seemed just what I wanted. Satisfactory neglect. All the clutter of home left behind, all the suffocating *stuff* I'd grown up with cut away at last. Room to think. Make everything the way I wanted it, starting from scratch. From scratch with the house, from scratch with myself.

'You've not brought any bedding and such,' Bob Norris said. 'Told you at the interview that you'd need it.'

'I'll be OK for tonight.'

'I could fetch a few essentials from home to tide you over.'

'I'll be OK, thanks. You said I'd have a couple of days to settle in. I'll go out tomorrow and buy what I need.'

'Must like roughing it. But I suppose you do at your age.'

I spent a miserable night. Couldn't get the fire going, not knowing how to deal with a damp chimney or a wood fire, filled the house with choking smoke instead. Sandwiches, brought from home, tasted like cold dishcloth and gave me indigestion. An apple, to follow, only increased my hunger. All there was to drink was water because I didn't have tea or coffee or any of the everyday things you usually take for granted. By the time I hit bottom about ten o'clock, admitted defeat, and walked to the village, the shops were shut of course, and at the pub door I suddenly felt such an idiotic mess I couldn't face the questions I knew the locals would ask. (The toll bridge and its fate were headline gossip I could have guessed even if Bob Norris hadn't already told me.) So I trailed back to the bridge and curled up as best I could in the only easy chair, hoping sleep would bring tomorrow quickly.

But I had reckoned without the night noises of a lonely riverside house, and without my own nervousness. Not the nervousness of fright, I wasn't scared, but the nervousness of being on my own for the first time in my life and of not knowing. Not knowing what caused the noises or why, not knowing if the skitterings across the floor were made by mice, whether the flitterings in the roof were birds roosting there that might invade my room, whether the ceaseless slurge of water passing under the bridge, sounding so much louder, more powerful, in the night, seeming to fill the house, meant the river had broken its banks and was flooding the place.

Once my mind is fixed on something I can't bear not knowing about it. So whenever a new sound caught my attention I got up to find out what caused it, which meant any warmth I'd managed to cook up, huddled in the chair, escaped, and I came back, usually little the wiser, chilled again, wearier, and narked.

In the way it often happens after a bad night, I fell asleep at last when dawn came, a smudged grey light that morning. And was woken, the next minute it seemed, the room bright with sun, by Bob Norris rattling at the door and calling my name, my mouth like a sewage farm, my body gutsick, painfully stiff, and my mind confused, not remembering where I was.

Bob laughed and teased, not taken in by the show of cheerfulness I tried to put on, and left me to pull myself together while he stood outside taking the few early morning tolls. I washed, brushed my teeth (still didn't need to shave more than twice a week), changed into fresh underclothes and shirt. But though this helped me feel physically better, the thought that already I had laundry to do and no one to do it for me and no washing machine to throw it into, finally made me face what I had brought upon myself.

All night long I'd told myself I was bound to feel strange at first, I'd soon settle down, get used to the place, make myself comfortable. But the sight of dirty clothes lying on the crushed old armchair in that bleak slummy room zapped any remaining particles of confidence and I wondered what the hell I was doing there.

Which was the moment when Tess walked in, carrying a bulging plastic bag and a blanket. Not, this first time, on the way to school, it being a Saturday, nor dressed in her biking leathers but in a loose white shirt and baggy washworn jeans and tennis shoes, a mane of lush jet-black hair framing the firm outlines of her face.

'Is it all right to come in?' she said, dumping the blanket on top of my laundry. 'Dad asked me to bring you this stuff.' She unpacked her plastic bag onto the muck-stained once-white pine table. Half-used packet of cornflakes, quarter of home-made brown loaf, jar of marmalade, bottle of milk, three eggs in a carton, quarter pound of farm butter, knife, fork, teaspoon, plate and mug, roll of paper towel. 'Should see you through till you can shop.' She looked me over as I stood gawping across the table. 'I'll give you a hand, if you like. You won't know your way around yet.'

All I could think was: Shut up, go away, I don't want any help, I'm going home, this is all a stupid mistake. What I managed to say was, 'Thanks, sure, yes, I could do with some help.'

[– What you didn't know at the time was that I was thinking: Why can't this creep look after himself? What's wrong with him? Why didn't he sort himself out yesterday? Why should I spend my Saturday morning booby-sitting him? I'd planned to play tennis but Dad asked me to help because he was worried you might be disheartened and leave. Then he'd have trouble manning the bridge again. Did he ever tell you that you were the only applicant willing to take the job?]

So there I was that first Saturday morning, cold, hungry, aching, bog-eyed, wanting only, longing, to bolt back home at whatever cost of derision, but my way out blocked by this high-energy girl standing between me and escape like a jailer (which she was, after all, as she was only there to help keep me there).

This is how my friendship with Tess began, the first true friendship of my life. My closest friendship still.

❖ 8 ❖

I don't think I believe in fate. Not if 'fate' means your future is planned, every detail, before you're born. Nor do I feel singled out, not like some people say they do, not in any special way, not destined to be anything but ordinary, muddling through life, as most people seem to.

But that morning with Adam, three months after first meeting Tess, as she throttled away, disappearing over the bridge, I suddenly felt I'd been here and done all this before. I know what is going to happen next, but am not able to do anything to stop it – a weird sensation of having had, sometime in the past, a glimpse into this future, of having forgotten, and only remembering now in the very second when the future becomes the present.

I hadn't experienced *déjà-vu* before. I'd heard people talk about it. But no one had said that it felt like a revelation. Suddenly the day seemed more alive, the air sharper, the light brighter, colours more colourful, objects more noticeable, more solid, more *there*. To tell the truth, as well as startled by it, I was a little frightened.

I turn towards the house, knowing I will turn in just this way. And walk inside, catching my hand on the doorknob as I pass, knowing I will catch it so but unable to prevent it. And find Adam, knowing I will, standing at the sink washing up the breakfast things, dressed in my only pair of spare jeans and my only spare sweater, sleeves pushed up above his elbows.

He will look sheepishly at me, I think as he looks sheepishly at me, and say, as he says, 'Heard you talking to somebody. Thought I'd better put sommat on in case they came in.'

At which, as suddenly as it came over me, this spooky sensation, this knowledge of the future-past invading the present, leaves me. Disappearing into my unknown future again, like Tess disappearing just now over the bridge. I feel I'm tottering on the edge of the river, and must wave my arms to keep from falling. And that I've been given a glimpse of something important, something life-changing, only for it to be swept away before I can fathom what it is or what it means.

I'm trembling a little from the excitement as well as the fright.

Which Adam notices, thinks I'm angry with him, and says, 'Was it OK, borrowing your stuff?'

Half an hour ago it wouldn't have been, but after the *déjà-vu* his cheek doesn't seem to matter because in some peculiar, inexplicable way, I know he has only done what he had to do.

I go to the fireplace and finger his clothes.

'Your own things will be dry soon.'

The warmth is calming, a comforting encouragement to do what has to be done. I plant a thick unsplit log, one that will burn slowly, on the bed of glowing cinders, and add, 'You'll be wanting to get going.'

'It's all right here.'

I stand and face him. He's leaning against the sink, his ice-blue eyes watching, his arms crossed over my best blue sweater.

'Look, I'm sorry, but you'll have to go, I've work to do.'

'Work? What work? I thought this was a squat.'

'No, no, it's a toll bridge, didn't you see?'

'It was dark.'

'Well . . . I collect the money.'

He thinks for a minute before saying, 'I could help. I could spell you. You could have some time off. Many hands make light work, as the Chinaman said when the electricity failed.'

He flashes his wrinkling-eyed grin but I won't give in.

'Sorry, my boss wouldn't allow it.'

'Ask him.'

'It's not just that. I want to be on my own, that's why I took the job.'

'On your own?'

'Yes.'

He shrugs, stares at his feet.

An awkward silence. The fire crackles behind me. With relief I hear a car approaching, go out, take the toll, come back inside.

Adam has gone. The back door stands open letting in a draught that is causing the chimney to backfire and fill the room with the heady incense of slow-burning wood. 'Vanished in a puff of smoke,' I say to myself.

I shut the door, glad he's gone, and only then see his clothes still hanging by the hearth.

Letters

❖ 1 ❖

... Surely, sweetheart, you've had enough by now? Aren't you fed up of looking after yourself? And aren't you lonely? You never mention any friends. It's not good for you to be stuck away in the middle of nowhere all on your own in that awful little house, which I'm sure must be damp and giving you rheumatism. Besides, it's such a waste of your young life. Your father says I mustn't nag, but, darling, what am I to do, I'm only concerned for your welfare, and hate the thought of you not getting the best out of life.

I'm sending you one of Zissler's pies this week. I'm sure you need feeding up and Zissler's are still the best. The woollen socks are from Aunty Jenny. She knitted them for you to wear when you're standing in the road taking the money, which is something I don't care to think about.

I was talking to Mrs Fletcher the other day. Her Brian only got a B and two Cs but was accepted at college quite easily – he's going to teach – so I don't think you should feel at all upset about an A and two Bs. I know you wanted As, we all wanted that for you of course but an A and two Bs when you were a year ahead of yourself anyway is respectable enough and would get you into any reasonable university. As a matter of fact, I had a talk with Mr Colbert at school today and he says if you come home in time for next term they'll be glad to have you back to do whatever you like till summer. He thought that with a bit of extra work to make up for the lost time you're quite capable of picking up a scholarship. Now you've had a break you'll feel better about things. Won't you think about it?

Gill called in on Saturday as usual. She puts on a cheerful face, but I can tell she misses you. I made her stay for supper and got out of her that you still haven't written or even phoned. Sweetheart, that's very unkind. She's devoted to you, and you've been such good friends. I told her — you don't deserve her! You don't either. If I were her I'd have gone off with someone else by now. Won't you just drop her a line? It would make all the difference.

Dad says thumbs up, whatever he means by that, and to tell you he's planted 120 daffodil bulbs where the begonias used to be, the ones that caught the strange disease and died last year, which I still think was caused by those dreadful cats from next door. And also would you like the radio he uses in the garage? Just ask and he'll post it. He says it's better than the old thing you took with you. He sends his love, of course. He's going round sniffing on the edge of a cold because he hasn't bothered to have his anti-flu shot this year, even though it did him so much good last winter, though the winter isn't here yet, but these autumn nights are quite chilly. When you talk to him on the phone next, would you encourage him to have his jab. I'm sure he listens to you more than he ever does to me.

We'll be out at the Smithsons on Sunday — it's his fiftieth birthday — so ring before 7.0. (And that's another thing — having no phone. I hate not being able to ring you and you having to use a call box.)

All my love, darling. I long to have you home again.

❖ 2 ❖

. . . I know she'll tell you and you'll be mad at me, but I couldn't help it. These last few months have been foul. Agony. Torture. The pain, the pain! But, honestly, I never thought I could miss anybody so much. When you went I expected withdrawal symptoms for a few days, even a week or two, but didn't think they'd go on this long. Every night I go to sleep thinking of you, every morning you're still there in my mind when I wake. During the day, when I'm doing something, I'll look up, expecting to see you, and when I don't I almost burst into tears. I have a couple of times actually, once in the middle of Gerty's French. God, the embarrassment!

I feel your skin on mine, the shape of you pressed against me, your hand on my breast, as if my body has a memory. But that only makes me feel worse because it's like loving a ghost. And then I begin to wonder if you're ill or hurt or perhaps even dead, and I can't bear it.

If only I knew what you were doing, what you're thinking and feeling. If only I knew you're missing me as much as I'm missing you. Couldn't you write? Or even just phone? I wasn't going to ask, I swore to myself I wouldn't, wouldn't make any demands. But now

I've blurted it out to your mother I might as well be honest and tell you how desperate I am, even just to hear from you.

Remember how we used to say we didn't know what 'love meant'? Didn't know if we were really 'in love' or just liked being together and screwing? Well now, if I'm not in love with you, I don't know what love can be. All the time, every minute, every day, I want to be with you, want to hear your voice, see your lovely face, caress your lovely body, wrap myself around you, put my mouth on yours, spread my fingers in your hair, feel your long hard fleshy sinewy body on mine, do *everything* with you. I want to live with you, do things for you, have you do things for me, argue with you, eat with you, read with you, dance with you, screw with you, sleep with you, die with you.

You see – I need you. Desperately. Can 'love' mean anything else?

Remember the weekend your parents were away? Our first weekend on our own together all the time. We had that silly row about condoms just because I'd bought a different kind from our usual and you didn't like it and then got the giggles when you were putting one on! Well, that weekend was the happiest two days of my whole entire life. I would give anything to have more days and more nights like them. All my days, all my nights.

This is stupid. I shouldn't be writing to you like this. Letters are hopeless. They get misunderstood. Is that why you don't write? If only we could be together even for just an hour and talk. Won't you let me visit you? Just for a weekend. Just a Saturday night.

I've taken a Saturday job in the bookshop. (Let me know of any books you want, I can get them cheap. I'll send them, though I'd rather bring them.) I'm saving my wages (for Christmas, I tell Mum) so I've money for the train, which will cut travelling time and give us as long as poss together. They're good at the shop and will let me off for one Saturday. Just seeing you would be such a relief. I won't tell your mother, *honest*. Not a word. Not to *anyone*.

I love you. I love you.

❖ 3 ❖

. . . No, I don't want you here. Keep away. Beware of the dog. Trespassers will be persecuted. *I do not want you here*.

I explained the best I could before I left. I can't do any better now. Not yet. When I can you'll be the first to know.

Please do not quote memories at me. I don't care about memories. I don't want to hear about them. You say letters get misunderstood.

You're right. But memories get misunderstood even worse. People do what they like with them. They make them mean what they want them to mean. I want to live only in the present. That is where I am.

Yes, I enjoyed screwing you. If you were here I'd screw you again. But that's another reason I don't want you here. It would only confuse things. And I think that was what I wanted with you the most anyway. I'm not sure I wanted anything else. I won't pretend otherwise.

Pretending has been one of my problems. I'd got into the habit of pretending. Trying to be what everybody wanted me to be.

I've made a rule for myself here. I will only be what I feel I am. I will not pretend, even if that means being disliked and saying no when people want me to say yes. I want to be honest with myself. I don't know how else to start finding out what I really *truly* am. Who I am, I mean. There is so much old garbage inside me already, so much *clutter*, even after only seventeen years. What must it be like after thirty years or fifty? Is that why so many old people go round looking like they're weighed down by two tons of compressed crap? I don't want that to happen to me. But how do you stop it?

I don't like all this talk about love. What people call love is only things they want from someone else. Like a good screw or a nice time together or even just someone to keep them from feeling lonely. As far as I can see that's what most people mean by love anyway. It isn't what they want for anybody else, it's what they want for themselves. Eating people is wrong.

I just want to be me. I take money from people crossing the bridge, I repair the house a bit, I keep the garden tidy, I read a lot, I mess about with a rowing boat on the river now and then, I listen to music, I watch telly, I think, and I look after myself. And no one pressures me. For the first time in my life I am completely responsible for myself. And not responsible for anybody else. I like that. It's what I want.

Leave it like that for now, OK?

17

A Yard of Ale

'Don't send it,' Tess said.

'Why not?'

'It's not you. Not how you really are. It's mean.'

'It's how I feel.'

'You feel mean?'

'The way she goes on about love. I don't want her here and I'm not going to lie.'

'You don't have to. All I'm saying is you should put it better. All this about persecuting trespassers – you're talking about your girlfriend, for Christ's sake! And not wanting to be reminded of the nice times you spent together, and telling her she's asking stupid questions.'

'Depends how you read it.'

'So why show it to me? You asked what I thought. That's what I think.'

We were sitting drinking coffee at the toll-house table (which, persuaded by Tess, I'd sanded down to fresh wood during the last few days and then waxed), on the Sunday morning two days after Adam and Gill's letter arrived. Sundays were free days, no tolls, a day off. It was ten thirty, and one of those bright still quiet autumn mornings when the sun's warmth recalls high summer and the sky is a hazed blue. All the leaves die in Technicolor.

Tess's Sunday morning visits began as a duty chore, sent by her father to check I was OK, and became a regular habit we both enjoyed, looked forward to, though we didn't tell each other this at the time. She always brought fruit or veg out of their garden or a slab of home-made cake, which she said, untruthfully, came from her mother, or something from the estate farm – butter or jam or eggs or cheese. Given the 'mod wage' I was trying to exist on, I'd have been pretty pinched without this help.

I coveted her acts of friendship, they made me feel better, though I tried to hide this from her. But I did try to be ready with something for her so the gift-giving wouldn't be one-sided. As I hadn't much cash, at first the presents were usually objects I'd found and 'treated'. Once a piece of wood I pulled out of the river that happened to resemble a fish, which I cleaned and painted with an eye and a mouth, and clear-varnished to give it a wet look. Once a George the Third silver shilling I dug up in the garden while clearing an over-grown corner, and buffed up bright.

[– See what I mean about men and gifts! Not that I wasn't pleased. It's one of your nicer characteristics – you can be thoughtful when you don't need to be. But I didn't want anything back. You just didn't feel comfortable receiving presents without squaring the account!]

After a couple of weeks I started writing poems for her, comic verses to begin with, as a joke. Because of her studying English Lit. We had that in common. We talked about her exam books. One week I gave her a parody of a poem by Ted Hughes she'd found difficult, a pig of a poem about pigs. After that, without thinking about it, it seemed natural to write more serious stuff. I made up the lines while collecting tolls or working on the house or mucking about on the river, and wrote them down and polished them in the evenings. It filled the time and I enjoyed it more than I expected. Soon I was writing two, even three, a week. (When I read them now they make me cringe. How could I ever have thought them worth giving anyone! Two years is an age. But it got me started, and I haven't stopped since. I discovered then that writing feels like a natural part of me: something I was born to do.)

'So why show me her letter?' Tess said, flipping it back across the table. 'You're going to be rotten to her anyway, aren't you, whatever I say?'

'No, I'm not! When I tried before, half the trouble was I didn't know what I wanted to say. So I made up the sort of thing I thought she'd want to hear.'

'Like?'

'Oh, about this place, and what I was doing. But I hated it. It was all an act, nothing to do with what I really felt. Not that I was feeling anything much. Just getting through each day. You know how I've been. The Glums. I sure as hell didn't want to write letters about that to anybody, Gill least of all. She knows about it anyway.'

'You're not so depressed now though, not like when you first arrived. You looked pretty bombed then, I can tell you.'

'Couldn't have stuck it without you.'

'No, well –'

'I spent a lot of time on that letter.'

'Look, you really want to know what I think? Make up your mind whether you want Gill or not. If you do, write something more loving, because, honestly, if I was her, that letter would upset me a lot. But if you don't want her, break it off, don't keep her hanging on, hoping. It's not fair.'

She was right, I knew.

We sat in silence, me avoiding her eyes and feeling myself losing my grip and slithering back into that dark craggy pit I'd been clawing my way out of these last few weeks, even beginning to think I might have escaped. But no. Like the nightmare when you're fleeing from some murderous maniac, you turn to look behind, see nothing, he's gone, you breathe at last, and turn back relieved, and there he is, right in front of you, overwhelming, unavoidable, his axe coming straight at your head – and you wake up in the nick of time.

Depression, and I'm a first-hand expert, gets treated in two ways. Either you're told you're sick, and given pills to dull the effects by stupefying you into silence so that you stop getting on everyone's nerves, or you're told you're a malingerer, a wimp, who ought to pull yourself together and stop moaning, because there's a lot of people in the world who are worse off than you.

There is a lunatic fringe as well, a school of Holy Joes who tell you depression is a sin, a wilful wallow in self-pity which any decent Christian atheist ought not to indulge in – as if depression were a punishment for being a narcissistic wanker.

Having suffered from it for most of my seventeenth year I can only say it never seemed to me to fit any of these diagnoses. It always seemed more of an affliction, like having a hand go out of action for no good reason so you can't do all sorts of everyday things you usually do without thinking, and have to put up with this temporarily useless limb flailing about, knocking things over and thumping people, causing trouble and embarrassment. While at the same time you're being slowly strangled (because your throat seizes up), and your guts churn like a sewage tank in labour (because you're worried sick about all sorts of minor problems that suddenly seem like major catastrophes), and your mind endlessly turns over the evidence of your complete failure as a human being until you've not a particle of willpower left to make yourself do anything except stare into space.

In my opinion depression is a disease caused by thinking too much about all the things you can only do well if you don't think about them at all.

'Look,' Tess said, standing up, 'it's a lovely day, there won't be many more like it this year, what are we doing sitting here? Let's take the boat upriver and I'll treat you to a drink and a sandwich at the Fisherman and Pike. I'm rich, would you believe!'

❖ 2 ❖

Tess went out to prepare the boat while I tidied up. She came back chuckling.

'There's a boy on the bridge playing Pooh-sticks.'

'What?'

'You know – dropping sticks into the river, then running to the other side of the bridge to see which one comes through first. Don't you remember? *Winnie-the-Pooh*.'

'Oh, that.'

'Dad used to play it with me when I was a kid.'

'So what's funny about a kid playing it now?'

'Well, he's not exactly a kid, he's about our age and he's by himself, and –'

'Let him. It's my day off.'

'He's having fun. I felt like joining in.'

I went to the window which gave a view along the bridge.

Adam, stood precariously on the parapet, a piece of stick in each hand which he drops with exaggerated care at the same instant, jumps down, races to the other side, leaps onto the parapet with breathtaking aplomb – and in my sweater and jeans, both the worse for his wear.

'Hey!' I shout uselessly and sprint out of the house, Tess calling after me 'What's up?' and following to the door.

Adam sees me coming and waves a greeting as to a friend he's been waiting for.

'What about my clothes?' I shout as I approach.

The affable smile fades. He jumps down. 'Eh?'

21

'You're wearing them!'

He looks at himself. 'Oh, these.'

'Why didn't you change before you left?'

He frowns.

'I need that stuff. My only spares, you see.'

'Right, sure.' He smiles suddenly, his handsome cheeky grin. 'I'll change now. That's why I'm here.'

'You'd better come in.'

Tess is waiting at the door.

Wanting to head off friendly exchanges, I say, 'This is Tess. He's Adam.'

'Adam,' Adam repeats as if prompted. 'Hi.'

'Hi,' Tess says.

'The visitor on Friday,' I say with warning emphasis.

Adam goes into the living room. Tess rolls her eyes at me in a mock swoon. I poke my tongue at her. She follows Adam. I go into the bedroom for his clothes, intending to call him in to change. But before I can, I hear Tess say, 'We're rowing upriver for a drink and a sandwich. Want to come?'

Adam says, 'I'm skint.'

'My treat.'

'Well . . . sure, thanks! I'll row if you like. Pay my way.'

'Great.'

What! I think – first my clothes, now my Sunday. What's going on here, what have I done to deserve this?

I join them.

'Adam's coming with us,' Tess says with the forced cheeriness people adopt when they know they're going against what you want and are pretending it's all right.

'Your clothes are in the bedroom,' I say, ignoring her.

'He's not going to change, is he?' Tess says. 'You know what boats are like. Ours anyway. He might as well wait till we get back.'

'Why didn't I think of that!' I say and stalk out ahead of them.

❖ 3 ❖

In the leaky old clinker-built dinghy only just big enough for the three of us, Tess has the tiller, and I'm beside her in the stern facing Adam who is rowing. Our legs interleave. Adam pulls us upstream with steady effortless strokes. His body has an animal perfection in its proportions, the neat way all its parts fit together, the easy relaxed

22

way it moves, beautiful to watch, very sexy. Tess can't take her eyes off him, which hurts me with a double jealousy – of that animal body, and of its effect on Tess – so that I resent Adam's disturbing presence more than ever.

But being rowed in a boat on a calm river on a warm morning has a soothing effect. Soon I'm lulled, as I remember being lulled as a little boy, by the lazy motion of the boat, and begin to take pleasure in Tess's body squashed up against mine, and Adam's slow, rhythmic movements, and the in-out plashings of the oars, and the glazed autumn colours of the river bank.

I think: I ought to be glad of this, ought to be giving myself to it, not begrudging, not grinding my guts with jealous resentment.

After a while, curiosity getting the better of her, Tess asks, 'Where are you from, Adam? Not from round here.'

He shakes his head. 'Up north.'

'Thought so from your accent.' She looks at me, askance. 'Two of a kind.'

She waits. Adam takes two more strokes but he adds nothing. 'On holiday or something?'

'Something.'

'A job?'

'Anything.'

'How come?'

He takes another stroke, watching his right-hand oar rise, skim, plunge. 'They chucked me out.'

'Who?'

'Parents. Well – my dad.'

'Chucked you out?'

'Hasn't got a job himself. And I've two sisters still at school.'

'But chucking you out!'

'We didn't get on either. Kept having rows. I'm better off out of it.'

'When did this happen?'

'Couple of months ago.'

'Poor you!'

He shrugs. 'I get by.'

For some reason I don't believe a word of this but I can see Tess does. He gives her *that* smile, but his eyes have a wary look, observing the effect. A look that bothers me. For a moment someone else inhabits those eyes, not the boy with the foxy grin.

23

The pub is packed with a Sunday crowd of junior yuppies from the posh commuter end of the village vying with university undergrads from across the river for the quickest-wit-of-the-year award and pretending not to pose. We manage to order with difficulty, being obviously members of the shoddier classes if not definitely under-age untouchables.

While we wait for our sandwiches a cohort of noisier undergrads challenges a squad of yahooier yuppies to a yard-of-ale competition.

'What's that?' Adam asks.

Plastic aprons to protect the yuppies' designer informals and the undergrads' unwashables are handed across the bar while a barman decants two and a half pints of beer into a metre-long glass tube with a bulb at one end and a trumpet-flared opening at the other.

Tess tells Adam, 'They have to drink all the beer from that thing like a glass hunting horn, which is called a yard-of-ale. They have to drink it at one go without spilling any, which is pretty hard to do. The one who does it the quickest and spills the least is the winner.'

'Cruel!' Adam is fascinated.

'Don't they do it up your way?'

'Not that I've come across.'

'Round here they say it sorts out the men from the boys.'

'Or the disgusting from the gross,' I add, 'the real aim being to see who spews up first.'

A podgy yuppy, the kind of over-eager bod who'll do anything to be thought a big man by his mates, has started the match off. He's a third down and has gone too fast. The trick is to take it at a steady gentle speed, swigging rhythmically so you've plenty of breath for the worst part, which is at the end when you have to lean back far enough to raise the tube nearly upright in order to empty the last of the beer out of the bulb. By then your arms are tired, you're just about gasping, and leaning back makes it very hard to swallow.

'Easy . . . easy . . . easy!' the yuppies chant, neo-soccer. The students whoop derisively. Both have the effect of over-exciting the already over-excited dolt. He raises the yard too fast. Beer floods out of his mouth, down his front, onto the floor, and puddles round his feet. As he gulps for breath someone rescues the yard. His clothes are soaked. The reek of body-warmed beer fills the room. His supporters mockingly commiserate; the students cheer. The yard is refilled as an undergrad is prepared by his seconds who camp up the boxing image

– extracting the piss out of the whole business in general and of the yuppies in particular.

Our sandwiches arrive.

'I'm eating mine outside,' I say.

'Got to see this,' Adam says.

'Suit yourself.'

Tess says, 'I think I'll go outside too.'

'I'll come in a minute,' Adam says, not taking his eyes from the arena.

❖ 5 ❖

The tables in the garden were occupied so we sat dangling our feet over the stone-paved edge of the river bank where, in summer, holiday boats moor for visits to the pub.

'For God's sake, don't encourage him,' I said while we ate.

'Why not? I like him.'

'I told you – he wants to stay.'

'He'd be fun. No one would mind.'

'I'd mind. There's something odd about him.'

'Odd?'

'The way he looks sometimes.'

'You just don't want any competition.'

'Rubbish! Anyway, it doesn't matter what you think, the toll bridge is my place, I'll decide who stays there, thanks.'

She laughed. 'I'm going to call you Janus.'

'Who's he when he's at home?'

'The Roman god? Well, pre-Roman actually.'

'Don't know any gods, I'm glad to say.'

'You ought to know Janus, though. For one thing he's the god of bridges.'

'Terrific.'

'As well as doors and passages and archways. And he has two faces. So he can see what's coming both ways, I suppose.'

'Or going, depending on how you look at it.'

'You keep the bridge and you're also two-faced, so I'll call you Jan, son of Janus.'

'Compliments now.'

'Well, you are. In the nicest possible way of course.'

'And what way is that?'

'Take Adam.'

'You take him, you're the one who's after him.'

25

'Are you sure about that?'

'What?'

'You say he's odd but really you're jealous because he's more good-looking than you and because I fancy him.'

'I get it – it's the truth game.'

'And you're being two-faced about Gill, who you're keeping on a string while making eyes at me.'

'I like that! You don't mince words once you start.'

'I've been kind to you till now because you weren't very well.'

'But not any more?'

'I reckon you're about as normal now as you'll ever be, don't you, Jan dear?'

'Prefer my proper name, if you don't mind.'

'You call me Tess. Just because I'm big-hearted enough to fetch your groceries from Tesco's sometimes. Why shouldn't I call you Jan? What's sauce for the goose.'

'Jan's a girl's name.'

'It's both, as a matter of fact. It means John in some languages. But when I use it it means a junior Janus who looks both ways at once and can't make up his mind which way to go because he doesn't know whether he's coming or going.'

There was a roaring cheer from the pub.

'Sounds like a winner,' Tess said.

'I suppose that means we'll be graced with the presence of the adorable Adam again just when we're having such a deliriously cosy chat.'

Another prolonged roar.

Tess said, 'You know it can only be friends between us? I mean, I like you a lot. But in the sort of way sex would spoil somehow.'

'Spoil!'

'Honest . . . Janus!'

'D'you have to call me that?'

'Yes, let me, go on, I like it!' She leaned over and kissed me on the cheek.

I was supposed to smile. 'All right, have it your own way.'

'Good. I win.'

'Was it a competition?'

Another, more drunken roar.

'There's a lot of it about.'

Followed by screams and shouts and then a sudden silence.

I recited,
> 'Almighty Mammon, make me rich!
> Make me rich quickly, with never a hitch
> in my fine prosperity! Kick all those in the ditch
> who hinder me, Mammon, great son of a bitch!'

'One of yours?'

'D.H. Lawrence.'

'How do you do it?'

'What?'

'Remember all that stuff.'

'Don't know. Always have. A gift, I suppose.'

'What teachers call clever, you mean.'

'Having a good memory?'

'For facts and figures and quotations and stuff like that. Not for people. Not for things that matter. No wonder they put you a year ahead. But get back to money.'

'Doesn't everything always.'

'There's nothing wrong with filthy lucre. Depends how you use it.'

'And how you get it maybe? Just think – they were like us once, that lot in there. Ordinary, normal, sane, poverty-stricken schoolkids.'

'Is that how you feel, like an et cetera schoolkid?'

'Yes and no. Yes up to the last few weeks, and no, not since The Glums started to clear. Don't know what I feel, to be honest, except empty. Haven't a clue what I want, either. Not whatever is supposed to come next though. Grown up or adult or whatever. Do you?'

She was feeding snips from her sandwiches to a family of mallards cadging on the water at our feet, who gobbled, cackled, and paddled off, as if they knew there was nothing more to be had from us.

'Don't think about it too much.'

'You're all now, you! Do you want to be, though? Adult and all that.'

'Don't you?'

'Not if it means being lumbered with some endless job and a family and a mortgage and a house to do odd jobs on every weekend or any of that sort of garbage.'

'All that responsibility is what you mean.'

'Yes, OK, all that responsibility. I don't want it, thanks. But I don't want to go on being a schoolkid, either. Had enough of that.'

'Stuck in limboland, then, aren't you? Don't know whether you're coming or going. Like I said – facing both ways again.'

27

The barman who'd served us came across the grass with the forced nonchalance of someone on an urgent mission who at the same time is trying not to frighten the paying customers and, crouching down between us, said, 'Weren't you with the young guy in the grotty blue sweater?'

We nodded, sensing trouble.

'Well, he's stirred up a bit of aggro in the bar.'

'What's happened?' Tess asked.

'Wanted to have a go with the yard-of-ale but the others wouldn't let him – they were having a competition, you see. Your friend insisted, and there was a bit of a row. Someone grabbed the yard, but it broke and, well – your friend cut himself. There's blood spilt and beer and not a happy reaction from the others. Could you come and help sort him out?'

'The idiot,' I said.

'Come on,' Tess said. 'We can't just leave him.'

'Yes, we can. We're not responsible.'

'We brought him.'

'So? We don't have to take him back, do we? He's a sponger. He'll just upset everything. Let him take care of himself.'

But I followed her into the pub.

❖ 6 ❖

Inside there is the kind of unnatural quiet with dark mutterings, and resentful glances, and one or two people determinedly ignoring what's going on that you only get in the aftermath of an unpleasant scene in a public place where people are supposed to be enjoying themselves.

The yuppies and undergrads have separated to either side of the disaster area, their undisguised belligerence directed at Adam, who is slumped in a chair in the middle of the deserted arena, wild-eyed and sullen. A brisk middle-aged woman, whom I take to be the landlady, is bandaging his left hand while a young barmaid mops the floor round their feet.

Tess and I edge our way through the throng, me trying to pretend we're nothing to do with this and are invisible anyhow, and take up stations on either side of the wounded public enemy.

'You all right?' Tess mutters.

'Yeah, I'm OK,' he says and suddenly turns on that surprising vulpine grin. It's as though he's a character in a play whose reactions are remotely controlled by a mischievous dramatist.

28

'Look,' says the landlady, 'it would be a good idea if you got him out of here.'

'Haven't had my go yet,' Adam says and stares nuke-eyed at the yard boys.

Tess says, 'We'll take you home.'

'Home?' I mutter.

'Shut up and help,' she mutters back, and, taking Adam by his good arm, says firmly, 'Come on, we're leaving.'

Irresistible Tess. Adam allows her to lead him away without another word, me following, a reluctant rearguard.

❖ 7 ❖

How easily circumstances change people, their moods, their feelings, their attitudes to themselves and the world around them. An hour earlier as we rowed upriver, relaxed, happy in the sun, I'd felt part of the landscape – at one with the world. Now, everything is reversed, Adam broodily nursing his hand, sitting where I had sat, in the stern cosied up to Tess, me tense as I row us downstream, sweating in what now seems an unfriendly sun, and feeling awkward, like an alien.

For a while I take out my simmering anger on the river, sculling through the water with as much force as I can. But soon my strength weakens; then only words will do.

I say, glaring at Adam, 'You're a pain in the arse, you know that, don't you!'

He refuses to look, his head turned away.

'Leave him alone,' Tess says. 'I'd have thought you'd be on his side, not on theirs.'

'I'm not on their side and I'm not on his, I'm on my own.'

'Selfish prig! You don't deserve any friends.'

'He's nothing but trouble.'

'And you're a jerk.'

'Oh, get stuffed!'

❖ 8 ❖

For the rest of the trip we all have lockjaw. At the bridge Tess coddles Adam into the house while I remain sitting in the boat tethered to the bank and sulk.

Quarter of an hour later Tess came out.

'I'm sorry,' she said. 'Didn't mean it.'

I won't speak.

29

'Are you really going to turn him out?'

Glowering silence.

'Seems to me people are always turning him out of somewhere. Can't he stay the night?'

'No.'

I felt a heel, which is exactly what she wanted me to feel.

'He's gone very quiet. I think he's a bit shocked. I've given him some sweet tea and made him lie down.'

'It's all an act. There's nothing the matter, really. He made a fool of himself and cut his hand, that's all.' I felt invaded, taken over. And jealous of all this pampering.

Tess said, 'Let him stay, just for tonight.'

'No.'

'Listen, I'll make us a meal. Mum'll give us some extra stuff. I'll say you've got a guest, unexpected. Which is true anyway. And I'll cadge some cans of lager off Dad. We'll have a nice time. It'll be a party. A house warming! You haven't had one yet. How about it? You'll enjoy it, honest . . . Come on, let yourself go for once, it won't hurt!'

Never able to resist Tess when she's determined, then or now, I gave in. 'All right,' I said, feigning unwilling agreement, the art of the spoilt boy (he who'd sworn he'd never pretend any more). I was on a loser, I knew. And that desire in me to be liked took over, a failing I hate but have never quite been able to shake off. 'But no passes at him while I'm around.'

'Cheek! I'll treat you both the same.'

'Great, a threesome. Now that could be fun.'

'You've got sex on the brain.'

'Not to mention other parts, and who hasn't?' I was brightening up again. Another of the virtues of Tess — something about her that dispels The Glums. One of life's natural healers, just as some people are natural destroyers.

Depression, of which a gloomy mood is a miniature version, is like being filled with iron filings all zinging about inside you, going every which way, pricking and stinging. And Tess is like the magnet that magics all the filings into a beautiful pattern, a force field, in which they act as one, harmoniously.

'I'll tell you what,' I said, 'while Prince Charming lies on my bed of his pain, let's you and me go blackberrying. Then we'll make a pud.'

'It's after Michaelmas.'

30

'Eh?'

'Ignorant yob. September twenty ninth. It's well known in these here parts that you shouldn't eat blackberries after Michaelmas because the Devil pees on them that night.'

'You're full of odd info today. Roman gods. Urinating devils.'

'I get it from Dad. He loves that sort of thing – country customs, folklore.'

'I'll chance it if you will. We can sweeten them with honey.'

We found a plastic bag and set off, Tess knowing the best bushes in the hedges between the bridge and the village. Blackberries big as the balls of my thumb. Not really. Long past their best, but we weren't to be put off. Doing together was what mattered.

As we picked, our fingers soon violet-red from juice and itchy-smarting from the pin-sharp thorns, Tess said, 'Why do you go on so much about responsibility?'

'I don't.'

'*Mon dieu*, you should hear yourself.'

'I don't like people expecting things of me.'

'Do they?'

'Parents. Teachers. Relatives. Don't yours?'

'Never bother to think about it. Wouldn't pay much attention anyway.'

'You're more easy-going than me. You just accept things. I envy that.'

'You are a bit heavy, that's for sure. I thought it was The Glums.'

'No, I was born that way. In most of the photos of me as a kid I'm frowning, like I'm worried to death.'

We stood back from the bushes and looked at each other. A new understanding.

'Mum calls you old-fashioned. I suppose that's what she means.'

'What?'

'That you take such a serious view of life.'

'Does it matter? To you, I mean.'

'It's how you are. I like you as you are.'

'Stodgy? Prematurely middle-aged?'

'I didn't say that! You do have your lighter side. Now and then!'

'Which is what you like.'

'If you really *must* know, Jan dear . . .'

'God, not *that* again!'

'. . . what I like most about you is your mind.'

'Not my lovely body?'

31

'No, not your lovely body. You make me think in a way nobody else has. I enjoy that, surprise surprise. And,' she added quickly, 'don't say another word about it now because you'll only go and spoil things by saying too much.'

'Can you?'

'*Sacré bleu!*' she said, but she was laughing. 'Haven't you learned *nothing* yet!'

'No,' I said.

'Oh – I dunno – how can anybody who's read so much be so – *naïve*!'

There was a sharpening of the air as the autumn sun went down. Our breath steamed. Tess's lips were purple. We started picking berries again.

'Look,' I said, 'if we're going to live off the land instead of out of your mum's freezer, what about us making cauliflower cheese for a main course? We can pinch a cauliflower out of your garden, there's about fifty more than your family will ever eat. I've plenty of cheese and milk. You just brought some butter. We'll have to cadge some flour though, I haven't any of that.'

'Haven't cooked it before.'

'I have. I'll show you. What you do is wash the cauliflower and divide it into florets. Cook in salted boiling water for ten minutes. Make a sauce by melting an ounce of butter in a pan. Blend in a couple of tablespoons of flour. Cook for about a minute, stirring all the time because it burns easily.'

'Do I want to know all this?'

'Take off the heat. Slowly stir in half a pint of milk. Put on the heat again. Keep stirring. Bring to the boil. Add about three ounces of cheese, and salt and pepper to taste. Put the cauliflower into a casserole dish, pour on the sauce, sprinkle a couple of ounces of grated cheese on top, put the casserole into the oven and bake for fifteen to twenty minutes. *Olay! Bon appétit*, et cetera.'

'Lawks a-mercy, *mon ami*, hidden talents! Where'd you learn that?'

'Haven't wasted all my time the last few weeks. What else do we housebound men have to do all day but learn to cook?'

'You've such a hard life. How about some spuds?'

'We'll bake them in the fire.'

'Great!'

On our way back from the garden, where we'd endured much teasing from the Norris tribe (father, mother, two sons, plus Tess, the youngest), Tess said, 'Don't you think this is a lovely chuckle? And we wouldn't have done it if it hadn't been for Adam.'

'Careful. Proof of the pud. Might turn out like Christmas.'

'How?'

'Better in the anticipation than the event.'

'Pessimist.'

'Romantic.'

'Cynic.'

'Estragonist.'

'Eh?'

'Sewer-rat, curate, cretin, crrritic.'

'What are you on about now?'

'Samuel Beckett . . . *Waiting for Godot* . . . the play?'

'I make a point of never knowing anything other people quote at me. It lets them feel superior.'

'*Touché!* Will you have it in a basket or on a plate?'

'This is all too heady for me.'

'Must be the Devil's pee on those blackberries you ate. I expect his piddle is pretty intoxicating.'

'Intoxicating perhaps, pretty not. Glad you're feeling perky again.'

❖ 9 ❖

When we arrived back at the house Adam had gone. Again. Along with some food – all my bread, a bag of fruit Tess had brought that day, and half the cake my mother had sent in her weekly parcel.

'This is getting to be a habit,' I said.

'I suppose you're pleased,' Tess said, not hiding her disappointment.

'Yes,' I said to irritate her. 'But he'll be back. He knows when he's on to a good thing.'

Not until later, when we took our blackberry pud out into the night frost to eat by the river, did we discover that the boat had gone as well.

Letters

. . . but, sweetheart, there was no need to be bad-tempered. Your father says boys of your age don't like to be questioned about their doings and having their parents interfere, he says he was like that himself. Well, *he* might have been but that doesn't mean *you* have to be, does it, and I wasn't interfering but only wanting to be helpful. After all, as I have to keep reminding him, you're on your own for the first time in your life, with no one to look out for your wellbeing, and I am your mother, darling, aren't I, it's only natural, isn't it, that I should want to know how you are and how you spend your time. You've never been secretive before. And I don't think your father is right anyhow. Your Uncle Bill was always full of himself when he was your age and told us about everything he did, and Mrs Fletcher's Brian doesn't hold back either, I know because she tells me in great detail all his news when we have our Friday coffee, he seems to be doing very well at college, just as you will next year, I'm sure, and probably a lot better because you were always much cleverer than Brian Fletcher, that I do know.

I can only think you're so reserved about your doings because you aren't really happy and don't want to say so in case it upsets your father and me. I know you, when you go quiet that means trouble. I expect something's going on that doesn't suit. You were always like that. But when you were a child you were a sweet-natured good little boy who always tried to please, and I could soon make you smile again, I knew the trick, as I still could if you were here. Well, it won't be long before Christmas when you'll be home again and we can have a good old heart-to-heart. Would you like us to drive down and pick you up? Your father says the car could do with a good long run, and there's no need for you to take the bus, even if it is supposed to be express, the car would be far more comfortable, and save on expense, and we'd be together for that bit longer. Your father and I do think it admirable of you to want to survive without taking money from us or depending on us at all, but things can go too far in this respect and fetching you home would give us great pleasure. So just let's take this as settled, shall we?

Gill is looking forward to seeing you then too. She was here on Sunday after you phoned as usual and told us funny but awful stories about the dreadful behaviour of customers at the bookshop. I must say I thank goodness your father and I never had to deal with members of the public in the service industries, there do seem to be some very strange people about and courtesy has gone out of the window, which I notice myself when shopping, as I said to Mrs Fletcher only last Friday after an embarrassing altercation at the cosmetics counter in Binns. Though it is bad enough for Gill it can't be any fun at all for you taking money in all weathers from people in cars, which, as I've said to your father many a time, seem to bring out the worst in people. They certainly do in him. He almost ran down a man in a Vauxhall the other day, you know how prejudiced he is against Vauxhalls. At least Gill is in the warm and dry, and working in a bookshop is quite respectable, if you have to work in a shop at all, besides being, as Mrs Fletcher remarked after we'd given Gill a wave on our way past, probably educational as well. She brought your father a very nice book on pruning roses which, as she admitted, she got cheap being an employee, but never mind, it was thoughtful of her.

Your father, being your father, said she was just trying to curry favour with him, but at least he went for his jab today. I told you he would if you had a word with him. You see how much we miss you and how much we need you. But as I say, my darling, Christmas soon, and we'll be together again . . .

❖ 2 ❖

. . . but I can't wait till then, can you? I'm desperate! Worse every day. Like thirst. I see Carole and Felicity with Daniel and Rod and can't stand it. I want you want you want you want you want you.

Besides, beloved, there's an important anniversary coming up. December 14th. One year. Twelve months. 365 days (and nights).

Remember the first time? I do, every second of it. Couldn't I come to you for our anniversary? I know it's near Christmas and you'll be home then. But we could celebrate all on our own, a whole weekend together with no one to worry about, no one to interrupt or spoil things or to have to think about at all. Just you and me. Us.

I could come down on the Friday evening. There's a train would get me to you about 9.0. And I could stay till late Monday afternoon. I could skip school that day. There wouldn't be too much fuss. Worth it however much. Three whole blissful days together. Three whole even more blissful nights together. It would be like never before, wouldn't it. Say yes. On a postcard. Just the one word. Or phone. We won't talk if you don't want to. Just say yes. That's enough. All I want. We can talk when we're together. And make love. Oh how I want to make love. I want you. Now. *This second*.

I love you love you love you.

❖ 3 ❖

. . . but I've tried to, honest. None of them was right.

It's all so complicated. How I feel, I mean, what I'm thinking. The depression isn't as bad, which is one good thing. I feel better most of the time. But sometimes it all comes flooding back. Not so often though. Like a wound healing. Some days it hurts, some days it just aches, some days, more and more often, I feel OK. Maybe depression is a kind of wound. A psychic wound, a ghostly wound that haunts you till somehow it's laid. (And not the sort of laid you mean.) Still, though, I need more time to get things sorted out in my mind.

I like it here. It's good for me. I like being on my own. That's something I've learned about myself. Actually physically enjoy it. It gives me pleasure. I don't know, maybe I'm one of those people who are best left to themselves, the sort who prefer their own company.

Not that this place is anything to write home about. Hardly even basic, in fact. Which is another reason I like it. It's stripped down to the essentials. Maybe I like it like this because I'm trying to strip myself down to my own essentials. To get to know the real me. Who is the real me? I don't know. There's so much garbage inside me already, so much *clutter*. And most of it dumped there by other people – parents, teachers, friends, neighbours, the telly, I don't know. Everybody. But not a lot of it put there by me.

Anyhow, what I'm really trying to say is please don't come here. I don't mean to be nasty or anything. But it's hard to explain. It's just – I'm not ready yet. Mother wants me home for Christmas. I suppose I'll have to. We can talk about it then.

OK? What I mean is, you said letters get misunderstood. Which is true.

And the same is true about memories. I remember our first time, of course I do. But memories don't help. They can even get in the way. It seems to me that most of the time people use their memories to make their past life seem better than it was, or happier. Or just the opposite. They only remember the worst. Either way, memories aren't real. They're a kind of fiction, if you ask me. Anyhow, people make them into what they want them to be, and then believe their life was like that. But I want to know what my life really was, really *is* now not then.

And yes, I enjoyed screwing you. You know that. But that's another of the reasons why I don't want you to come here. We'd screw all the time and I'd like it but it would only confuse things again. Confuse me anyway, about me and about you, and about me-and-you. Just when I'm beginning to sort myself out.

OK, so I'm crazy and mixed up. That's what people are saying, I expect. Well, I don't care what they're saying. I don't have to listen to them. Not here. Which is another reason why I like this place, and being on my own, and out of range of home and everybody who knows me. Or think they do! Maybe the truth is I'm not like they think I am. Maybe I'm quite different. When I find out, you'll be the first to know.

So let's leave it like that for now, yes? Till Christmas anyway.

I think about you.

He, Hi, Hippertihop

❖ 1 ❖

'"I think about you"! Honestly!'

'But I do!'

'Not the way it means when you write it, though. You're being deceitful.'

'I'm only trying to be kind.'

'Kind! *Très drôle!* It's not kindness she wants. If you can't see that . . .'

Exasperated, Tess slapped the letter down between us.

Two Sundays after Adam disappeared for the second time, and again sitting either side of the table, but a cold, windy, grey, leaf-swirling day, this one, the river rippling with irritated gun-metal waves, and the fire blazing for the bright comfort of it as much as for warmth.

'It's better than the last one, but honestly!'

'I'm not wasting any more time on it.'

'Suit yourself.'

'All the time I was writing, my hand kept cramping like someone was gripping it hard to try and stop me.'

She laughed. 'The toll-bridge ghost.'

'Superstitious crap.'

'There's supposed to be one. Dad says he's seen her. He says she kind of floats about between this room and the bridge. She was murdered by her lover in a fit of jealous rage. He chucked her body into the river. He was never caught, but she came back to haunt him and did such a good job he went mad and drowned himself. Serve him right too.'

'You're making this up.'

'No I'm not. Dad says only men see her, and only those she likes. Perhaps she's taken a fancy to you and will turn up one night all of a quiver, wanting a bit of spooky nooky.'

'It's the only hope of getting laid around here, that's for sure.'

'Whose fault is that? You could have Gill any time. You still haven't said whether you want her or not.'

'I've told you, I don't know.'

'Janus.'

'Shut it with that, will you!'

'So you'll send this one?'

'Yes.'

Tess stood up. 'Got to go. Sorry. We've company. Mum wants some help.'

Another spoilt Sunday.

'Look at me and smile.'

I said nothing.

'Please yourself. I'll come back after tea, if they go early. They probably will. OK?'

I stood up, went to the fire, stirred a log with my foot. 'Sure.'

At the door Tess turned back. 'Nearly forgot. Dad said to tell you he'll be here tomorrow about ten thirty with Major Finn and an estate agent.'

Major Finn was the landowner and therefore my employer. I'd never seen him.

'What's this, then, a regimental inspection?'

'There's talk of selling bits of the estate. Now he's not getting a lot in tolls the major needs the money.'

'But he'd never sell the house or the bridge, would he? He can't.'

'Dunno. Dad said will you make sure to tidy up and mind your manners while they're here.'

I knuckled my forelock. 'Yes, mum,' and bowing, 'know me place, mum.'

When she'd gone I kicked the grotty armchair, then tore up my letter to Gill and chucked the pieces into the fire.

❖ 2 ❖

They turned up next morning three-quarters of an hour late, the major, once he had struggled out of the estate agent's red BMW, refusing help from Bob Norris with a growl, and supporting a geriatric hip with a swarthy stick. An aged hangover from the Second World War, like a museum exhibit on a day out. His beetroot face with hawk nose and bristly grey moustache was topped off with a fraying panama hat. A crumpled tweed shooting jacket hung from his body as if he had shrunk inside it, which in a way, I suppose, he had. His baggy heavy-duty light brown corduroy trousers were stained an unappetizing yellow at the crotch. His feet clumped in robust ox-blood brogues. A mobile fossil he might be but he still talked in words clipped sharp enough to slice across a parade ground. There was about him an assumption of authority you just knew he'd been born with. Somehow I couldn't help liking him, even though I didn't want to.

Which is more than I can say for the estate agent, a thirtyish, blue-pinstriped oleaginous creep. Podgy and suntan-brown as well as greasy, he'd just been holidaying, he had to tell us, somewhere in the Caribbean, Dominica I think he said, and kept finding opportunities to slip offhand references to the place into the chat. He sleazed around the major, whom he treated, beneath his unctuous surface, with a condescension betrayed in his eyes and in his sneering answers to the major's questions. 'No, no, sir, that sort of thing went out years ago! . . . You've rather let the property decline, not a wise tactic, major, if I may say so. You'll be well advised to give it a good going over with a paintbrush, if nothing else . . . We'll do the best we can for you, major – there's always a dumb punter around who'll buy anything, if you know how to sell it.' 'Your job, your job,' commanded the major as to a parade (he was hard of hearing as well as regimental). 'And we'll do it, sir, we'll do it, leave it to me!' mimicked Brown-and-Greasy.

I watched him, and thought of them at school, with their careers advice. 'Banking is safe. Or you might like to follow in your father's footsteps and become a solicitor, or a barrister even. There's the stock market of course, but it's very competitive, which is hardly you, is it? Accountancy might suit you, that's fairly solid, though your maths isn't up to much, but it's a nicely paid profession. Or computing, what about that? Or business management? Or you could do worse than property and estate agenting. Pays well and you could combine it with the law and do well in both areas.'

Watching him, I heard them banging on about earning power and status and career prospects and security, and knew that oleaginous prat was what they meant, what they wanted me to become, and rejected it there and then, that very moment, finally, for ever.

I don't mean there's anything intrinsically wrong with the law or accountancy or business management or even handling property. What's wrong is why Brown-and-Greasy and his kind do it. As a means to something else. To money for money's sake, and living off the fat at other people's expense, usually the people who actually produce things that make the money the B-and-G brigade are after. They're bloodsuckers. And they have the cheek to parade about as if they are the ones who matter, the ones who are superior, the ones who make the world turn. When what they really are is a drain on the rest of us. Parasites. We'd be better off without them.

An hour after they'd gone, Bob Norris returned. I was reading by the fire.

'No more easy life for you, sonny boy,' he said, in no mood for jokes. 'The major's in a huff.'

'How come?'

'That flaming agent stirred him up. I knew he'd cause trouble. The major wants the place renovated and completely repainted, inside and out. I'll bring in a builder for the renovation work but you'll have to do the painting. And a proper job, mind, not just to make it look a bit better.'

'On my own?'

'He'll do another inspection in three weeks.'

'I'll never finish by then.'

'Do the best you can. He'll probably forget. Can't remember when yesterday was most of the time.'

'What about some help?'

'Think yourself lucky you're still here. He's laying off more men. We're down to three. Three! Used to be fifteen only two years ago.'

'But if I can't get it done?'

'Don't cross your bridges . . .'

'I'm not a professional decorator, you know that.'

'You'll manage. Learn as you go. Any problems, ask. I'll keep an eye when I can.'

'And I have to take the tolls as well, remember.'

'Look, son, stop moaning. There aren't many most of the day now. Hardly worth collecting at all.'

'I'm not happy about this, Mr Norris.'

'No, well, who is. Life's like that, you'll find. Just get on with it or do the other thing. And I've no more time to waste chewing the rag with you. The builder will be in tomorrow. There'll be a van out this afternoon with the gear you'll need. Get started as soon as it's been. Do the outside first while the weather's as good as it's going to be.'

'He's in a really filthy mood,' Tess said two days later when she stopped off on her way from school. I was stripping down the window frames at the front. 'He's upset with what's happening. He's even talking of looking for another job. He's too young to retire, but he's probably too old to find anything else. He's worked on the estate all his life. And Grandad before him. Mum says it would kill him if he had to leave.'

'He was pretty ratty with me this afternoon, that's for sure. Not enough done, and what was done not done right. He's never been like this before. It's hopeless on my own, but he won't listen. And besides that, the bloody builder expects me to be his labourer.'

'I'll give you a hand at the weekend.'

'You've got your own job on Saturdays. You need the money. And I don't care what your dad says, I'm taking Sundays off.'

'A couple of Saturdays won't matter that much. It's hellish boring anyway.'

'It's not exactly a laugh a minute decorating this place.'

'More fun than Tesco's though. I couldn't stand it at all if it wasn't for the other girls.'

'Wouldn't mind if I was doing it for a good reason. But so they can sell the place! You know what Brown-and-Greasy said? "Make a nice little bijou residence, major, for a London weekender."'

'What's a bijou residence?'

'I didn't know either.'

'But you looked it up.'

'Something small and elegant and tasteful, and then in italics: *often ironic*.'

'Piss-taking, you mean?'

'It'd be a crime. I know it needs doing up, but not like that. I mean, there's a whole history here. I hadn't thought about it till this happened. Hundreds of years of people crossing the river, millions of them, probably, by now. Talk about ghosts! I mean, think of it, all those feet tramping across the bridge. And people living in this house watching them coming and going and taking the tolls, hundreds of thousands of pounds, and hearing the gossip and the news and keeping the bridge in good shape and watching the river and the boats going up and down, and the river flooding and even freezing sometimes, and being part of all that. So now what do they want to do? Turn it into a tarted-up Wendy house for some part-time prat with money to burn who couldn't care less about what it's been, what it *stands for*. Something to be bought and sold and pulled down or chucked away or made into whatever the owner wants. This house and your dad, they're no different really. They've both been here all their lives. But that doesn't matter any more. Because what it all comes down to in the end is money and who has it and who doesn't, and how you get more of it, and if you can't or you don't want to, hard cheese, get stuffed.'

Tess was staring at me, all surprised eyes.

'Haven't seen you so worked up before.'

'No, well, haven't felt so strongly about anything for a bit.'

'Almost like you're enjoying it. I didn't think this place meant that much to you.'

'Neither did I till this week and having to stand there and watch Brown-and-Greasy poking about. It was obscene. I wanted to hit him.'

'He got on Dad's nerves as well.'

'I could see he was seething inside. But he couldn't do anything about it either.'

'Look, I've got to go. Bags of homework.'

I went with her to her bike.

'What're you going to do?' she asked through her helmet when she was ready to go.

'What can I do? What your dad tells me, that's all. I sure as hell don't want to pack up and go home.'

'Dad says it might all cool off in a week or two. The major's old, he forgets.'

'Brown-and-Greasy won't let him. Not while there's a nice fat commission in it.'

'You never know.'

'Optimist.'

'Pessimist.'

'Biker.'

'Janus.'

Brown-and-Greasy had arrived like a blight. 'Few responsibilities,' the ad for my job had promised. 'A cushy little number,' Bob Norris had said at my interview. Both were true until B-and-G came poking around. Then, suddenly, I could do as I liked no longer but from morning till night had to scrape at walls, and Polyfill damaged plaster, and glass-paper woodwork, and for a week act as cursed-at labourer for a sour-faced chippy ('You can't tell an awl from your arse, lad') while he replaced rotten skirting and floorboards and rehung doors and refurbished window frames, and, when he'd finished, I fetched and carried for a grumpy bricky while he repaired the living-room fireplace and chimney ('It's a wonder the frigging place hasn't burned down').

From cleaned-up neglect in which I could do as I liked, the house was transformed into a swirl of throat-clogging decorator's dust, a derangement of tools and gear, a rubbish tip of builder's waste, an echo-chamber of banging and sawing and the manic thump of Radio 1 without which apparently neither the chippy nor the bricky could function. As neither could they without mugs of coffee and cans of beer it was my job to serve up at regular intervals, like every hour, during the day.

By the Wednesday of the second week ABG (After Brown-and-Greasy) I was on my own again, left to paint the entire building inside and out, two undercoats and one gloss, ceilings and all. (Have you ever painted a ceiling? Even with non-drip it's murder.) It would take, I reckoned, four weeks' solid slog. Certainly till well after Christmas.

❖ 4 ❖

Mid afternoon, Thursday of the second week ABG. A clouded glowering day but dry, and warm enough to work outside, painting the roadside living-room window frames. There'd been very few tolls since early morning, even fewer than usual; and no movement on the river, the holiday boats being all laid up by this time of year. Even Bob Norris hadn't called.

Feeling lonely, abandoned, hard-done-by, I was brooding in the flat-headed way you get into (well I do anyway) while doing a monotonous physical job all by yourself when I spotted a movement in the house. I had to press my face close to the glass to see clearly, for the room was gloomy. The toll-bridge ghost, I thought, stupidly. But no, and yes, there he is, Adam, large as life, standing at the table, scoffing bread and chicken bits left over from my midday meal.

'Hoi!' I shout and bang on the window. He turns, sees me, waves, turns back to his – my! – food.

I rush inside, and confront him from the living-room doorway. 'What the hell d'you think you're doing?'

He flashes The Grin. 'How d'you mean?'

'Don't start that again.'

44

'What?'

I point the paintbrush I've forgotten is in my hand. 'Eating that!'

He drops the food as if he's suddenly been told it's poisoned. 'Sorry! Thought it was leftovers.'

'It is. Oh, never mind. Finish it now. What've you done with the boat?'

'Boat? What boat?'

'*The* boat. *Our* boat.'

Mouth stuffed full again, he shakes his head, frowning.

'Christ! The boat you took.'

He swallows, which somehow at that moment seems the most insulting thing he could do. 'Me? Don't know nothing about a boat. Walked here along the river from the pub. A bloke bought me a drink. Wanted me to go with him. Do him a little favour. Offered fifty quid. But I'm not that desperate.'

'But you took it.'

'Would you turn down a free drink?'

'The boat. Three weeks ago.'

'What? No, not me, sorry.'

'Course you did! When Tess and I got back, after you'd caused the trouble at the Pike, you'd gone. Disappeared. With our boat. With other stuff as well, you might remember. Including my clothes. The ones you're still wearing, I think. God, what a mess they're in. Where the hell have you been?'

He's staring at me blank-faced. Not even The Grin.

'What're you on about?'

'The boat, dammit!'

'Somebody else, mate, not me.'

'Jesus, I don't believe this!'

'Well, they could have. You don't know, do you?' He's suddenly very agitated, distressed, as if he's just woken up and doesn't like what he's found. 'You weren't here, were you? You've just said you were out. You didn't see me go, did you? So how d'you know I took the boat? Anybody could've done it. So I took some stuff. What's a bit of food? And these clothes, well . . . Anyway, I don't know nothing about no boat. All right?'

'Tell that to Tess. See if she believes you. It's her dad's boat as it happens. She'll be here in a minute.'

As suddenly as he'd turned sour he's his usual self again – or what I thought then was his usual self: laid back, smiling that annoyingly handsome smile.

'You're dripping,' he says.

Jackson Pollock squiggles cover the floor at my feet, expressionist doodle of my feelings while I've been standing there.

'Shit!' I scrub up the mess with the cloth I keep ready for the purpose, not yet having learned the trick of painting without dribbling.

'Want a hand?' Adam says when I'm upright again.

My instinct is to say no, just get out of here. But his incorrigibility, what my mother calls bare-faced cheek, makes me sigh and even smile, and in that short pause it suddenly occurs to me that he might be useful. So instead of chucking him out I say, 'Why not. I'm taking any help that's going. You owe me anyway.'

'Great!' He might just have been given a present he's wanted for years. 'Where do I start?'

'Finish the window I'm working on. It'll soon be too dark to see properly. While you're doing that, I'll get some more wood for the fire. And listen —' He's taking the brush from me. Pongs like a hedge-bottom. Can't have washed for days. 'Do me a favour —'

'Sure.'

'If you decide to disappear again, leave the brush behind, will you? I can't afford to pay for a replacement.'

'I'm not going nowhere,' he says. 'Not me. It'll be nice and toasty in here tonight.'

I don't reply, didn't say, 'Who says you're staying here tonight?' or 'You've got another think coming, mate' or any of the things my guts want me to say. Instead, I smile to myself and go down to the woodstore for logs. If this mutt likes painting so much, I think to myself, then let him. The more he does the sooner the job is finished. Then I'll chuck him out and get back to normal again. Tess calls me Janus so Janus I'll be. To guard bridges maybe you have to be. To guard yourself, come to that.

But I didn't know what I'd let myself in for.

❖ 5 ❖

When you keep a bridge you develop a third ear tuned to listening for approaching vehicles. I knew the sound of Tess's bike as well as I knew her voice; heard her coming over the bridge while I was splitting logs in the woodstore. (This was the half-basement under the house formed by the bank falling steeply down from the road to the garden-river level. The loo was in there too, and brass-monkey cold it could be in winter, as well as tools and other gear and the tin bath that's used in a page or two.)

By the time I'd lugged the laden log basket up the stairs into the house, she's talking to Adam. I see them through the window. She's taken her helmet off, which she never bothers to do unless she plans to stay a while, and is flirting her hair at him, and laughing, and giving him the eye.

Adam is replying at full throttle with The Grin, The Hand Run Through the Hair, and The Pelvic Thrust. And they're performing a slow-motion ring-a-ring-a-roses; the courting dance of Homo sapiens.

I dump the logs and go out.

'Have you asked him?' I say.

She doesn't take her eyes off him. 'He didn't do it.'

'You believe him!'

Adam is preening. I'm sure The Grin has stretched round to the back of his head. The Teeth flash white semaphore in the dusk.

'I remember now.' She looks at me at last. She's fizzing. 'You were in the boat. I came out and talked to you. We decided to pick blackberries. You climbed out and off we went, but you didn't tie up. I expect it just floated away.'

'So it's my fault now!'

'No, I didn't mean that. I should have noticed.'

'Oh, thanks! Maybe you should have noticed that I'd already tied up before you came out.'

'You had?'

'Yes.'

'Oh, well, I don't remember. And what's it matter. Listen, I was just saying to Adam –' She turns, they do a Grin-Giggle-Hands-Through-Hair-Eyeballing-Pelvicthrusting exchange, and then she looks at me again. 'I'll nip home, have tea and come back about seven, OK? We can talk then.'

But does not stay for an answer.

'Good thinking,' Adam says.

'See you,' Tess says, and winks at me as she passes.

[– I know you've got to tell this story the way you remember it, but this last scene just isn't right. I wasn't the way you describe me at all. I was never that flirty. I know you'll tell all the embarrassing details when the time comes, but at this point I don't recognize myself. And if you get me wrong here, aren't you likely to get me even more wrong later when more important things are happening?

I know people remember the same events quite differently. And I know you're trying to tell what happened to Adam and Gill and me and yourself the way you saw it then, rather than the way you think about it now, but still you can't tell it *only* like that, can you? Well, yes, you can but that will give a very distorted view of us.

You're always going on about how one person's understanding of anything is only part of the truth – how no one ever really knows everything, or ever knows enough. So how are you going to get more than your own partial understanding of what went on between all four of us into your version of our story?

What I know is, in case you go on getting me as wrong as you just have, I reserve the right to tell my bit of the story in my own way at some point.]

❖ 6 ❖

As we watch Tess putter away, the stink of hedge-bottom twitches my nose.

'Look,' I say, 'you're not ponging the place out again. Before we eat you're having a bath.'

'Yes, Dad,' Adam says. 'Lead me to the water.'

There was no bathroom complete with all mod cons, only one of those galvanized tin tubs, wider at one end than the other, like a man-sized sardine can without a lid. Or a coffin, depending on your mood. You see them in old photos of working-class houses, where they're usually hanging on the wall outside the back door. *The Road to Wigan Pier* through D.H. Lawrence country. The toll-house tub was kept in the basement, had to be carried up to the living room when needed, where it had to be filled by using a length of hosepipe from the only hot tap in the place, which was at the kitchen sink.

There was an immersion heater in a tank in the roof above the sink, but as I had to pay for the electricity out of my piffling wage, I used it as little as possible. An electric kettle was enough for ordinary purposes, or, better still because it cost nothing if the fire was in, an old iron cauldron Bob Norris had given me, which I kept simmering on the hearth.

Two or three times during my pre-Adam weeks Mrs Norris took pity and persuaded me to have a bath in their house. 'I'm sure it's easier than all that palaver, and you can give yourself a good soak,' she said and, laughing, 'You must look like a man half drowned in his coffin sat in that affair.' I've always liked Mrs Norris. She has the knack of being kind without making you feel obligated or done good to.

If I hoped all the palaver of bathing would put Adam off staying more than a night I was wrong. He revels in it like a kid in his play pool. And makes about as much mess.

While I clear up the painting gear from where he's dumped it (labourer now even to my own labourer, I grumble to myself), he prepares a place in front of the fire, lugs the tub up from the basement, strips, then ponces about with the length of hosepipe, obscenely camping up a weird song which he's learned from God knows where.

'Old Roger is dead and gone to his grave,
He, Hi, gone to his grave.
They planted an apple-tree over his head.
The apples grew ripe and ready to drop,
He, Hi, ready to drop.
There came an old woman of Hippertihop,
He, Hi, Hippertihop,
She began a-picking them up,
He, Hi, Hippertihop.
Old Roger up and gave her a knock,
He, Hi, gave her a knock.
Which made the old woman go hippertihop.
He, Hi, Hippertihop.
He . . . Hi . . . Hip . . . hip . . . hippertee . . . hop!'

Funny, raunchy, lightly done – I can't help watching and I can't help laughing. Even though a part of me wants to stop him – for I didn't like the way he was taking my place over, turning it into a kind of theatre for himself.

Of himself would be more accurate. What fixed me was, yes, his energy and the comedy of his randy send-up of this silly song (which I only discovered afterwards is a nursery rhyme – God, the things we stuff into children's heads!). He'd make an amazing actor, the kind who compels attention all the time, not just because of his talent, but because of his unpredictable personality, the game he plays of pretending to act a part which is actually a disguise for revealing a truth about himself.

Yet at the same time he's so crafty in displaying the disguise that the audience are never quite sure whether they're seeing the character who belongs in the play or the actor himself.

It was then, that evening, that I was won over by Adam. Won over *to* him I mean. Yes, sure, for a while I kept up a pretence of not wanting him around, but it was only pretence. Another pretending, this time as self-protection. From that evening on he fascinated me. As I watched him perform I felt he was ruled by some deeply hidden, risky secret. And I wanted to know what it was.

❖ 7 ❖

When he's done, and we've cleared up the mess he's made and I've cooked beans on toast, we sit either side of the table, Adam's skin still glowing.

'Look,' I say, 'there's some things we better sort out.'

'Like what?'

'Like I don't know anything about you.'

A suspicious look while he shovels beans, his fork in a fist-grip.

'Does it matter?'

'Yes, if you're staying. No promises though.'

'Cautious bugger.'

'Cautious maybe, anal screwer never. For a start, what's your name?'

'. . . Adam!'

'But Adam what?'

'Adam in the back seat. Adam in the hay. Adam on the kitchen table.'

'Groan. I meant your last name.'

'Haven't made my mind up yet.'

'Oh, come on! Stop messing about.'

'It's true. Never knew my parents. Brought up in a children's home. They made me leave when I was sixteen. So I reckon I can have whatever name I like. Nobody else cares a toss so what's the odds.'

'Well, how old are you now?'

'Seventeen. Just.'

'And what have you done since they chucked you out?'

'Odd jobs and that. But I wanted to travel a bit so I come down here. Haven't had much luck with a job though.'

I gave him a long stare.

'That's not what you said before.'

He didn't look at me. Went on shovelling beans.

'When?'

'In the boat, going to the Pike.'

'What did I say?'

'That you'd been chucked out of home by your father because you were always having rows and he was unemployed and you had two sisters still at school.'

Now The Grin. The Teeth. The Eyes. The Unblinking Gaze.

I gaze back, unblinking, unsmiling, daring him. 'Not that I believed you.'

'No? . . . Yes, well, I made it up, didn't I.'

'Why?'

'Don't want everybody knowing your personal details. Never know who you're talking to. People take advantage.'

'Have I?'

The Grin vanishes, leaving a blank-faced cold look, and suddenly occupying the eyes the other Adam, the one I'd always sensed behind The Grin – wary, troubled, a little frightened, the one who made me curious.

'Not yet,' the other Adam said.

Then The Grin banishes him again.

I say, trying to keep my own eyes steady, 'Why should I believe the orphan story?'

He shrugs, lifts his plate and, his eyes still on me, licks it clean.

'Good, that,' he says, putting the plate down.

I scowl.

He brazens it out. 'Want me to wash up?'

I don't respond.

'All right,' he says after a long pause, 'I'll tell you. But you have to promise to keep it to yourself. I don't want other people knowing. Not Tess, neither.'

'Why?'

'I just don't, that's all.'

'Depends what it is.'

'Nothing bad. I just don't want people knowing.'

'Why me, then?'

'Well, like you said, you've been OK.'

'And you want to stay.'

'Yes, well, that as well.'

'So?'

'Promise.'

51

'Cross my heart.'

He huffs and toys with his fork for a while, then sighs and says, 'I was adopted. When I was little. A baby. They told me when I was eight. All this stuff about how it was better for me than for other kids because they chose me. Other kids – their parents just had to take whatever they got. They were all right, my parents. The people I called my parents. They were nice and everything. But I just couldn't accept it. I hated being adopted. It felt like a disease. I wanted to know who my real parents were but they wouldn't tell me. Said they didn't know. When I was grown up, they said, I could try and find out for myself, if I still wanted to know. I hated them for that. I thought they ought to find out for me. I thought they ought to want to know for themselves. I mean, wouldn't you – wouldn't you want to know? Where you come from? Why they, why they got rid of you? Had to. Or wanted to. Or were made to. Sometimes that happens, doesn't it, young girls, they make them give their kids away. Don't they? Anyway, I kept asking, kept on and on, wanting to know, and them saying they couldn't find out, weren't *allowed* to find out. I didn't believe them. This went on till I was thirteen, fourteen, and we started having fights about it. I'd shout, call them all the names I could think of, break the place up, do anything to upset them. I was only trying to make them find out. I ran away once, tried to, but the police caught me before I got far. I hadn't planned it, just did it on the spur of the minute, so I bungled it. But that decided me. I planned the next time, every detail. Day, time, what to take, where to go, how to get there, how to cover my tracks, not leave clues, even disguised myself – dyed my hair, wore glasses, changed my clothes as soon as I was out of town. I reckoned they'd find out what clothes were missing and describe them to the police, thinking that's what I was wearing. So I'd bought some things specially and stashed them in a hut and changed into them. I saved money for months. Read about living rough. Did everything I could think of to make sure I'd get away and not be picked up again. Just wanted to vanish. And then, when they'd forgotten about me, or given up, and I could move around openly again, then I'd find out about my real parents. And when I know that, then I'll decide who I belong to. What my last name is. Who I am.'

He pushed his plate away, took a drink from his mug of coffee, wiped his mouth with the back of his other hand.

'That was six months ago. I ran out of money pretty soon. And it wasn't that easy keeping out of sight. Tried Birmingham for a bit but that was pretty foul. Tried London and that was worse. Everybody's out to get what they can from you. Some of the other kids were OK. But the guys around. Geez! Want everything, from your head to your arse. It's bad news there, I tell you. I wasn't having it, not me, might as well be dead. So I went on the tramp. Hedges are better than streets. Don't reckon much to people neither. Mostly out for what they can get, what they can do you for. In the country you can usually scrounge something. Anyhow, I survived, didn't I.'

He laughs, but humourlessly.

'Thing is, you get tired, you get really tired. You just ache for a place to stay, for somewhere you don't have to get out of in the morning, somewhere you can crawl back into at night, somewhere that's dry and warm, somewhere safe. They don't tell you about that in the survival books. Don't tell you what it's like to feel you're just a bag of rubbish, kicked around, useless, ugly, smelly, in everybody's road. Don't tell you nothing about that in books because you can't know what it's like, how bad it is, till you're there, till it's happened to you. And they don't tell you about it, I suppose, because nobody can describe hell.'

In the silence that followed I could neither speak nor move. The fire crackled in the hearth. The river surged under the bridge. Adam toyed with his mug, not looking at me. His skin shone, clean and fresh from his bath, his wet black hair hugging his round head.

His physical presence was almost overpowering. I sat looking at him and knew that this time I couldn't turn him out. Whatever his being here meant, its meaning included me. For better or worse and whether I liked it or not, there was no escape. Adam had come to stay.

Letters

. . . writing from the office, as there is news of your mother which I must give you without letting on to her. She doesn't want you to know, but in my judgement it is best that you should so that you are prepared when you come home for Christmas.

The fact is, your mother is going through a rough patch. Nothing you need be seriously worried about – she's not suffering from a life-threatening disease. The problem is more emotional and psychological. But she's going to need a great deal of support and understanding till she is out of the rough and back on the fairway again.

The best way of explaining the problem is to give you the background, which means telling you something your mother and I have kept from you, believing there was no point in your being burdened with it. However, as it is partly the cause of your mother's current difficulty, it is best that you know.

I might add that this is not an easy letter to write. Please forgive any infelicities.

You are of course our only son, but you are not our only child. Two years before you were born we had a daughter. We called her Amy. Sadly, she lived only five weeks. She died a cot death. Your mother blamed herself at the time, and has gone on blaming herself ever since, saying that if she had been more attentive we would not have suffered such a dreadful loss.

Nothing anyone has said – the doctors, close friends, or myself – has ever relieved your mother of the guilt she feels: I needn't tell you that there was absolutely no question of your mother being in the slightest neglectful. She doted on Amy, as she always has on you, and gave her all the attention anyone could expect. Cot deaths are far from rare and the cause not at all understood. It was just another of those unfair accidents of life.

The weeks after Amy's death were not easy for either of us, but slowly we helped each other back to something like normal, though your mother was never again the carefree lass she was when we were first married. Your mother and I were completely in love when we married. We were at our happiest in each other's company and never liked being apart. We shared the same interests and even liked the same friends – which I know you have already noticed isn't at all usual! After Amy's death it wasn't quite the same, I'm sorry to say. We remained, and still are, as devoted to each other as before. But it was as though some part of us, something of our completeness, had been taken away and it was impossible to fill the gap.

We did gain something, though, and I think this is also worth telling you while I am about it, as it is not the kind of subject you and I tend to talk about but which might be useful to you in your own life. What we gained was a different sense of the love that first brought us together. As I look back on it now, I realize that we might not have been *in love* at all but only have liked each other very much. From my experience as a lawyer I can tell you that many couples mistake liking each other for being in love. The divorce courts are full of those who discovered the difference too late.

In the months after Amy died we learned that we needed each other because we loved each other, and not the other way around. For whatever it was that helped us through those awful weeks was more than only liking each other could have made possible.

But your mother never recovered from the loss of her baby. Once we were on an even keel again, we both hoped that having another child would help heal the wound. And for a long time after you were born she did seem more like her old self. You were, as your mother has often told you, a wonderful little chap. Amy, in her short life, had been difficult. Her birth was difficult, she often cried for hours at night and was exhausting during the day. You were just the opposite. Your birth was quick and easy, you were always good-natured, quiet, a sound sleeper, and you continued like that as the years passed and you started school.

Of course your mother gave you every waking moment of her life, never leaving you alone for an instant. Even at night she wanted you beside her. I remember it was only with the greatest difficulty that I finally persuaded her to put you to bed in a room of your own. You were more than three by then, long past the age when most children sleep by themselves.

55

You see, the truth is that your mother invested everything in you, all of herself and her hopes for the future. We did try to have more children – I thought it would be a good idea from all points of view and your mother wanted it – but without success. And I suppose the disappointment of knowing there could be no more in the family strengthened her attachment to you.

I have to confess that I often worried about your mother being so wrapped up in you but I hesitated to say anything, for how could I know that my worries were anything but jealousy – there were times when I was very jealous of the attention she gave you. However, in your later childhood, I did try to make sure you had some time away from your mother to prepare you and her for the break when it came. Not all of my efforts were appreciated! You'll remember the Scouts was a great failure. As was my attempt to turn you into a golfing fan. But the school trips to France and Greece were useful, and you did enjoy our boating holiday on our own together when we taught ourselves to sail on the river not far from where you are now. In fact we sailed under your toll bridge more than once – well, not 'sailed' exactly, but dismasted and motored through, the arch being so low.

Your mother was aware of what I was doing. I didn't hide it from her. And one thing she never let on to you was how much she dreaded the day when you left home for good. She even found those times you and I were away very difficult to bear. She knew they were trial runs for the time when you left home permanently.

Nevertheless, she wasn't prepared for your departure this summer. She thought you would be at home for a year or two yet. And for some illogical reason, she doesn't think of being at university as leaving home. But your decision to go for the toll-bridge job took her by surprise and the way you stripped your room and stowed away all your gear – your boyhood things and your books – before you left upset her further. It seemed so definite, so final. Almost like a rejection of us and of your home.

I'm sure that is not how you meant it. And honestly, I'm not laying blame or saying what has happened since you left is in any way your fault at all. Please believe that. How hard it is to explain all this and not sound as if one *is* laying blame. (It has often struck me, as I sit in this office every day helping people sort out their problems, how bad I am at sorting out my own. Perhaps the truth is that none of us is much good at helping ourselves.)

But all that is water under the bridge, if you'll pardon the cliché.

The bare facts of the current situation are these. Soon after you left your mother began to behave oddly. At first it was nothing more worrying than sudden outbursts of tears for no apparent reason. At these times she would weep uncontrollably in the way she did in the days after Amy died, a weeping that seemed full of rage as well as sorrow. Then she began having terrifying nightmares in which she quite literally tried to climb the wall in her efforts to escape apparently nameless fears. These woke us both with the violence of her movements and the sound of her screams.

Then one day two weeks ago I was telephoned at the office by the manager of Binns. He had your mother with him. She had been apprehended shoplifting. As a result of that I discovered she had been stealing things for days previously from a number of shops. She had the stuff hidden away in your room – all baby things like talcum and clothes and toys.

Binns didn't prosecute, thank goodness. They are as familiar in their trade as I am in mine with this syndrome. Middle-aged women are sometimes afflicted with it. It goes with the menopause. I don't know whether you know anything about the female menopause. I doubt if they taught you about it at school. Though I can't think why not when you consider that my medical reference book begins its entry on the subject with the words: 'Sometimes called the change of life, the menopause is the middle-aged counterpart of adolescence, and its effects are comparable, and as natural.' No wonder a lot of middle-aged parents have trouble with their teenage children, if they are all suffering from their own versions of adolescence at the same time! Not excluding you and me and your mother. I suppose it is happening more than it used to because these days so many women don't have children until they are into their thirties.

Normally, or at least as far as I understand it, I'm not a professional expert, the menopause goes along with having hot flushes, when the woman blushes for no identifiable reason and often in a way that embarrasses her, and breaks out into very heavy sweats. This is often followed by bouts of cold shivers brought on, apparently, by a terrible nervousness, an anxiety that your mother says makes her feel breathless with panic. At these times she gets quite worked up about small things that actually don't matter, like forgetting to put the money out for the milkman or mislaying her reading glasses, and she worries about the house burning down while she's out shopping or burglars getting in when she's on her own.

Then there are other symptoms: headaches and bouts of feeling dizzy, and she sometimes finds it hard to concentrate on anything – even on TV, which is saying something. She can also be grumpy and easily offended, which, as you know, is quite uncharacteristic of her. For example, she saw me brush a cobweb out of a corner of the living room yesterday and became quite agitated, saying I was criticizing her housekeeping. Her appetite swings about as well; one day she'll vastly over-eat and another day she'll hardly eat anything at all. She says she doesn't decide these things, they simply happen.

As I say, all this is entirely normal, according to the doc, and is suffered by thousands of middle-aged women. The shoplifting isn't exactly normal, of course, but isn't unusual either, and not intentional. Your mother didn't plan it or do it for gain. The truth is the whole unhappy event seems to have nothing whatever to do with what anyone wants, least of all your mother, but is simply a matter of biology.

I say *simply*. Of course there is nothing simple about it. Knowing the background helps a little, I hope, but certainly doesn't explain anything. All I want to do in writing to you like this is to prepare you for when you come home and to ask that you try just to accept it, and help your mother by letting her behave in whatever way she feels she must, without making life worse for her or making her feel guilty or a failure because of what is happening.

It is something we should all three talk about together. Your mother and I have been learning to do this since the incident at Binns and I think it would help us all if you could talk about it too. But that must come from your mother to begin with, and at the moment she fears what your reaction will be if you know what has happened. More than anything, she fears the loss of your love and respect. That is why this letter must be only between the two of us. I'm sure in my own mind, dear lad, that you're mature enough now to cope with this kind of crisis.

If you'd like to talk, phone me at the office about five one evening, or write to me here if that suits you better, marking the envelope 'Private and Confidential'.

Your mother will give you the everyday news when you ring as usual on Sunday . . .

❖ 2 ❖

. . . that you'll let us come and pick you up. But you sounded a touch fed up, darling, I know that tone in your voice, are you sure you are all right? Are they working you too hard, I expect they are from what you said about decorating. It is such a silly business when you could be doing so much better here but I have promised your father I won't go on about it so will say no more now.

Your father also says I should tell you that I haven't been too well lately, nothing serious, don't worry, a temporary blip due to my age, which comes to us all, sweetheart, I'm afraid. I've been just a little off colour, that's all, and not feeling myself. By the time you come home I expect it will all be over and I'll be fit as a lop again. We can't expect to be on top of things all the time can we, everyone has their lows, as you know only too well, my darling, but you are getting over it, that's the great thing, so maybe the toll-bridge job hasn't been all a waste of time.

Now, my dear, you must let me know what you'd like for Christmas, or give me a hint at least, it's so silly to give unwanted gifts to someone of your advanced age, being, as your father insists on telling me every day, no longer a child, just so they'll come as a surprise. Much better give something that's wanted, so do say and I'll get it. I saw a very nice calfskin wallet that might be useful in Dressers this week when Mrs Fletcher was hunting for a Parker ballpoint for her Brian, who, by the by, has upset the applecart by announcing that he doesn't think teaching is his cup of tea after all and wants to leave college and go into computer software, which he says would pay better and have better prospects and suit him more. It seems his first taste of the classroom put him right off children, but then he never did have much patience which you certainly need with children, so perhaps it will be better for the children in the end if he does something else, though at the moment his mother doesn't agree and is very down about it.

I have always thought I would have liked teaching and even been good at it for I love children, as you know, and do have patience I think I can say without being immodest, but all I wanted at 16 was to get a job and have a lively social life and went into secretarial work instead, where anyway I met your father so some good came of it. Though this last few weeks since you left I have been thinking how nice it would have been to have a profession to take up again in my middle years. Your father suggests I should find a job of some kind anyway, as I have so much time to spare, not having you to look after, though my office skills are pretty rusty now, but I expect I could soon buff them up with a bit of effort and perhaps a refresher course. I quite fancy becoming proficient with a word processor, which these days is a requirement, and office life can be enjoyable if the place is well run and the other staff amenable. One thing for sure is that I wouldn't want to work in your father's office again, he's far too relaxed with the juniors if you ask me.

Well, we can talk about all this at Christmas and you can advise me. After all, new horizons might buck me up, don't you think . . .

A Kind of
Talisman

❖ 1 ❖

Next morning I woke regretting that I'd given in the night before. And to such a sob story, even if it were true. In the cold grey grainy fog of a late November dawn, when your clothes are clammy and the house smells of tacky new paint laced with the heavy sweaty tang of decorator's dust, then reigniting the living-room fire from the remains of last night's cinders and getting washed in tepid water at the kitchen sink and making breakfast are tedious enough. Having to attend to someone else as well – the space he occupies, somehow making the place seem smaller than it is, too small now, his coming and going, his noises and smells, his grunts and sighs and coughs and sniffs and belches and farts, his behaviour at the sink, splashing water onto the bench where I'm trying to cut bread and make toast for HIM, dammit, as well as myself – having to *think* instead of zombie your way into the day was enough to make me wish I hadn't been such a soft touch.

To make things worse, while Adam scoffed bread and honey as if stoking up for a winter famine, I got to reckoning the financial cost of letting him stay. Two can live as cheaply as one? Tell it to the birds. Two can live as cheaply as two. Or three, if one of them eats like Adam did that morning.

I soon learned that he usually ate very little, it was just that he liked snacky bits at times when I didn't – I'm a regular meal, no snacks eater, due to strict training as a child. In fact, I was the problem. I'd make plenty for two, serve him as much as myself and he'd leave half, which I threw away, till I realized after two or three days what was happening and gradually cut his share down. Not that Adam noticed. And eventually I learned how much to give him in order to satisfy his appetite with just enough left over that could safely be kept cold for him to snack on when he wanted. I even got to the point of enjoying this secret game. The pleasure came from the skill of judging exactly

61

how much food to make, how much to serve up at the meal and which things in the meal would do for snacks or keep till next day, when I could use them as part of another meal. He liked potatoes, for example, and he liked them done in their jackets in the fire, and he liked them mashed and fried. So I'd do more in their jackets than I knew we'd need, keep the leftovers till next day, when I'd mash them up and fry them as potato pancakes. I don't think he ever noticed that the pancakes were the old potatoes done that way. Which was another part of the game and the pleasure: his not noticing what I'd done. Of course, the weather being cold, stews were good, and keeping a stew pot of cheap scrap-ends going on the fire was easy. I simply chucked in any leftovers so that over a few days it went from being a meaty stew to being a thick vegetable soup. It was cheap and Adam could snack on it whenever he liked.

But this developed over the next few days. That first morning all I could think of was how I wouldn't have enough money to feed us both, even with the stuff Tess gave me and my mother's weekly parcel. But I was too morose to mention it. Just glowered into my tea.

And another thing niggled me.

'We'll have to get you a bed,' I say when we've finished eating.

'I'm not bothered.'

'But I am. The place looks like a dosshouse with you on the floor.'

He doesn't respond.

'And more bedclothes.'

'There's plenty.'

'No, there isn't. I was cold last night. It'll get worse as well, winter coming on.'

And that was the moment when the postman arrived, delivering Dad's letter about Mother.

❖ 2 ❖

'She'll be OK,' Adam says.

'I ought to go home.'

'Why? Your dad says don't.'

'He's just saying that so I won't feel pressured. He's always like that. Do nothing till you have to, that's his motto.'

'I like it! He's right.'

'What do you know about it?'

'OK, don't believe me, ask Tess.'

'No, no! I don't want her to know.'

62

'Why not? She could help.'

'No, leave it.'

'Why . . .?'

'Because I don't. I don't know why. I just don't, that's all. You said yourself, you don't want everybody knowing your personal details.'

'But Tess is supposed to be a friend.'

'Just shut up about it, will you! You say one word, and that's it, all right?'

'OK, OK, I'm not saying a word.'

'Well, just think on!'

'Calm down, will you. No sweat. I'll be tight as a duck's arse, honest. But at least talk to your dad before you go. Ring him. He says you can.'

'I'm not sure.'

'Yes, you are. Do it.'

'It's too early, he won't be at the office yet.'

'But as soon as he is.'

'There's the tolls.'

'Remember me? I'm here. I'll hold the fort. You'll not be gone for long.'

I dither.

'Told you I'd be useful, didn't I,' Adam says.

'Let's get on with it, then,' I say, clearing the table. 'Bloody painting. We'll never be done in time.'

Adam stands up, stretching in his loose-limbed animal way. 'You worry too much. Relax. Leave it to me. I like painting. You can see where you've been and it passes the time. Everything'll be OK, honest.'

'That a promise?'

'You betcha, squire.'

Suddenly I really am glad he's here. Everyone needs somebody to break the closed circle of his mind. Adam used a blunt instrument and banged his way straight in, no subtlety, no fash about wounded feelings. The quickest form of ventilation. If you can stand the blows. A month before, I couldn't have survived them.

❖ 3 ❖

Dad was adamant. Stay away. Mother would feel worse if I suddenly turned up for whatever excuse and she had to explain. Christmas was the right time. She was expecting me then, was preparing herself for it.

I told him about Adam. Or, at least, that I'd made friends with this out-of-work boy who was good at decorating so he was staying for a while to help me get finished.

'You'll need a bit of extra cash then,' Dad said. 'I'll send you something.' I suppose I knew he would and had subconsciously hoped he would. So didn't refuse, but felt a twinge of failure as well as guilt for exploiting him while talking about Mother's trouble.

❖ 4 ❖

Half past ten, Bob Norris appeared. We were busy clearing stuff out of the living room to get it ready for painting.

'Come outside,' he said to me while giving Adam a close inspection. 'Want a word with you.'

He took me to the middle of the bridge and leaned on the parapet, looking down at the water.

'What's this I hear about a friend staying with you? Is that him?'

'He's a good help. I need it if we're to get done in time.'

'How good a friend?'

'He's all right.'

'Known him long?'

'Long enough.'

'In other words, not long enough. You should have asked.'

'I only decided last night. There hasn't been time.'

'Look, son, you've done all right so far. Don't go and spoil it.'

I didn't reply.

'It's a position of trust, you know, yours. There's money involved.'

'We're hardly taking ten quid most days!'

'Ten quid is ten quid, and I've only your word about how much you take.'

'Are you saying I fiddle the books, Mr Norris?'

'No, no! Just the opposite. I trust you. It's this other lad. You're sure he's all right? It's not just money. There's property as well, and the bridge to keep an eye on. And with all this other business, these sackings and plans to sell, it's getting difficult, that's all. I'm having to be extra careful. There's a lot at stake.'

I recognized his tone of voice. The breathiness of anxiety. I'd heard it in my own voice only a couple of hours ago.

I said, 'I'm sorry. I didn't think. Is it OK?'

He stared down at the water and thought for a while before

saying, 'All right. But you'll have to answer if anything goes wrong. So remember, he's your responsibility.'

That word again! Another cold grey regretful realization. But I'd talked myself into it and pride wouldn't let me back out. At least I had enough wit left to say, 'While we're at it, Mr Norris, is there any chance there might be a camp bed or anything going spare somewhere? He's sleeping on the floor.'

It was the only time he smiled. 'I'll see. Might be something in the scout hut.'

'Thanks.'

His smiled faded. A few days before he'd have been joshing me now, but since B-and-G he'd become solemn, bad-tempered even.

'Sure you can manage, two of you, on your pay?'

I shrugged. 'We'll get by.'

He glanced at the toll house, his brows furrowed, lips pursed.

'Everything has its day,' he said.

'Sorry?'

He shook his head. 'Nothing. Just get on as fast as you can. The agent says there's a lot of interest. Wants to start showing the place as soon as things have settled down after New Year.'

He turned away and walked back to his van.

'There might be a sleeping bag as well,' he said as he climbed in.

❖ 5 ❖

'What did he want?' Adam asks.

'To know if I could trust you.'

'What did you say?'

'Yes.'

He smirks. 'And do you?'

'No.'

'Lied, then!'

'Yes.'

'Why?' He's serious now.

'Because I'm an idiot.'

He says nothing for a moment. Then he undoes a silver chain from round his neck and holds it out to me. 'Here, take this.'

'No. What for?'

'Because I want you to. Go on. It's worth a few quid. Real silver, nothing fake.'

'No. Why should I?'

'It's OK. It's mine. Didn't nick it, if that's what you're thinking.'

'I don't want it.'

'Wear it. Insurance.'

'Don't be stupid.'

'I mean it.'

'No.'

He moves towards me. I step back.

'Take it, craphead!'

'No!'

He lunges at me, grabs my shirt. I try to push him away but he pulls me to him and tries to get the chain round my neck. I knock his hand away, sending the chain flying across the room. We struggle, saying nothing, wrestling, not half-hearted, not playful, but using all our strength, meaning it. A contest. I am heavier, but he is stronger. The first time I feel his strength. It takes me by surprise. And he is so much tougher than I, harder muscled, and practised, knows what he's doing, where to hold, how to shift balance, when to move. And whereas I am tense, his body stays relaxed, supple all the time.

I feel trapped, become desperate, flay with my hands, swing and punch and strain against him and push. He easily dodges and absorbs and deflects and uses my movements to his own advantage, which makes me feel even more trapped, more a victim.

Soon I'm breathless. And Adam begins applying a painful force, a frightening violence that I don't know how to deal with except in the end by giving in, going limp, allowing him to put me down and sit astride my waist, his knees on my upper arms, like kids do in playground fights.

I stare up at his flushed face, on which a sheen of sweat has broken out, smiling, his eyes full of the pleasure of the fight.

The chain lies within reach. He leans over, causing me to cry out as his knee digs into my bicep, picks up the chain, slips it round my neck, and sits back again, regarding me now with that absent stare which turns his face into a mask.

For two, perhaps even three whole minutes we remain there, silent, unmoving, staring at each other, until able to bear it no longer I say:

'Have you done?'

The Grin then. Adam again. Pushes himself up. I too, dusting myself off. My arms ache from the bony pressure of his knees, and other bruises burn on my body.

A car horn tooted. I went out and took the toll. When I got back Adam was busy Polyfilling cracks round the fireplace. Neither of us said anything, not then nor later, about the silver chain. I went on wearing it simply to prevent another bout of wrestling. Or at least that's what I told myself. Every morning as we passed each other on the way to and from washing at the sink, he'd make a show of checking it was still there, and grin and nod, until this daily inspection became a routine, a ritual we would only have noticed had it not been performed.

I still wear his chain, never take it off, now as a kind of talisman, a memento, a charm against the evil comfort of forgetting. Insurance after all, though not of the sort Adam had in mind. Not that it was Adam who gave it to me, as I should have known from that mask-faced absent stare.

Toll-Bridge
Tales

❖ 1 ❖

One day we were painting the bedroom when we heard a noise like the sound of drunken children echoing up the approach road. We dropped our brushes and rushed outside, janitors ready to do a Horatius.

But there was no need of defence. Along the road came a party of about twenty Down's people. Four of them were in wheelchairs. One, a young man who was singing loudly in a strange tuneless falsetto, had no legs.

They weren't drunk on anything but happiness because they were having a trip out on a sharp, frosty, sunny December day. Five or six caretaking adults were sprinkled among them, shepherding them along and tending to the chairborne.

This patter of humanity strode, wobbled, limped, danced, skipped, hopped, rolled in well-behaved disarray towards the two of us, as we stood by habit in the middle of the road outside the toll-house door.

'Hello! Hello!' unembarrassed voices called as they approached. 'It's Timmy's birthday. Happy birthday, dear Timmy, happy birthday to you!'

Timmy was the legless young man.

'This is a toll bridge,' one of the minders said. 'It's very old.'

'As old as Timmy?'

'What's a toll bridge?'

'Dong, dong, dong.'

'You have to pay to cross.'

'Do we have to pay?'

'I haven't no money.'

'Timmy doesn't have to pay, does he, not on his birthday, do you, Timmy?'

We were surrounded, our hands taken and caressed, our arms

stroked. Faces beamed at us, some dribbling, others open, all glad to see us as if coming upon friends.

'You've been painting,' a girl said to me.

'There's a notice that tells who has to pay.'

'Where, what does it say?'

'I've no money today.'

'I like painting. I like the smell. Painting smells like you.'

'Well, it says "Four wheels twenty pence. Lorries and trucks fifty pence. Two wheels and pedestrians free."'

'What are pedestrians?'

'We are pedestrians.'

'Where are you painting? I'd help but it's Timmy's birthday and we're taking him out. He's eighteen.'

'Pedestrians are people walking.'

'Eighteen means you're grown up. I'm fifteen.'

'Four wheels pay,' Adam said, finding his voice and giving in kind. 'Two legs go free.'

'We've two legs.'

'We go free.'

'Timmy's on four wheels though.'

'So is Janice and Rachel and Jason.'

'Oh, Jason, you have to pay. Twenty pence!'

'Do I?'

'And Janice and Rachel.'

'Not Timmy though, eh, it's his birthday.'

'But he's on four wheels. We had to pay to cross the Severn and it was my birthday that day. They didn't make allowances.'

'Allowances.'

'It doesn't mean wheelchairs, does it?'

Adam said, 'No, no. I'll tell you the rule. It's like this. Four wheels pay. Two legs go free. No legs get paid.'

'Get paid!'

'Where does it say that?'

'What – you pay Timmy?'

'And Rachel and Janice and Jason,' Adam said, 'because they can't go on two legs.'

'They can sometimes.'

'But not today,' Adam said.

'Not that far.'

'There you are, Timmy,' Adam said, pulling coins out of his

pocket. 'That's your fare for crossing the bridge. And are you Rachel? OK, that's for you. And Janice. And Jason.'

There was an alarming cheer from the pedestrians.

'I needn't have legs if you don't want me to.'

'We'd better be getting on,' called one of the minders.

'We have to be getting on,' several voices ordered.

'What are you painting?'

'How much did he give you, Rachel?'

'We could come back this way and get some more.'

'What'll you spend it on?'

'I'll save it.'

'Bye.'

'You smell lovely. You could come with me if you like.'

'Come on, Sarah. The man's busy.'

'Kissy kissy.'

'Dong, dong, dong.'

Back inside, Adam grabbed his brush and slashed and slashed at the wall. Paint flew.

'Hey, steady, man, steady!' I shouted, guarding my eyes with an arm. 'What's up, what's the matter?'

He waved his brush towards the bridge and the dying sound of the Down's party. 'That's the matter! That!' A different Adam. The other Adam: the one only in the eyes before, now in this angry, violent moment all of him. 'The sodding rotten unfairness of it.'

'Being born like that?'

'Not their frigging fault. Didn't ask to be born. Life! Bloody life!'

He hurled the brush down and left the room. There was brittle silence for a few minutes before I heard him filling a glass at the sink. I got on with the painting. When he came back he was Adam again and calm.

I said, 'At least they seemed happy.'

'Happy? Yes, sure, really happy. A laugh a minute.'

'Life *is* unfair. You knew that already.'

'Just let's get on, OK?'

❖ 2 ❖

Like the early morning, when we were on our own together the evenings were a problem for a while. Reading: I liked it, Adam didn't. He could settle to nothing for very long, except TV. Obsessed

70

'And while we're on the subject,' I said, 'we'll have to do something about you and the telly and me and reading, unless you want to go into exile in the basement every night.'

'Why?' Tess said. 'What's the matter?'

That explained, she said, 'Easy. I've a set of headphones I used when I wanted to watch the telly at home and nobody else did. Now I've one in my room I never use them. Adam can borrow them, so he can watch while you read.'

'Brilliant,' Adam said.

'Only takes feminine lateral thinking.'

'You can go lateral for me any time.'

'I said *thinking*.'

❖ 3 ❖

One evening towards the end of the decorating there was nothing on TV that Adam wanted to watch and Tess dropped in bringing some beer she'd filched from the fridge and we were talking about sleep because when Tess arrived Adam was slumped in one of his sleep-snacks and I was reading a story about a dream, which comes into this story soon.

Adam perked up, of course, the second Tess came through the door and they joshed around, which they always did, flirting, that evening cracking suspect puns on being laid out and having a lie down and being wide to the world and heavy breathing and how thrilling a good zizz was, and when they'd got through with that Tess said they'd done something on sleep in biology the year before. They'd had to record their dreams as soon as they woke up in the morning (most of the time, of course, they hadn't dared tell the truth so they made them up) and they'd done experiments with REM (rapid eye movement – the wobbling of the eyes under the lids which happens when people are dreaming), and we nattered on about all that and the meaning of dreams and why they are so weird, till Adam suddenly said,

'What I want to know is why I wake up just about every morning with a whacking great hard on.'

'You do?' Tess said, leaning forward, agog.

'Like a broom handle.'

'Because of sexy dreams?'

'Not always. Happens quite a lot when I haven't been dreaming about anything.'

'Or not that you remember when you wake up.'

73

'Me too,' I said, no less than the truth, but rather so as not to be left out. 'Didn't they tell you anything about that in biol?'

'Grief, no! They only talk about sex in Human Relations and they didn't say anything about early morning erections then, only about Aids and not having babies.'

'What about your brothers,' I said, 'don't you know about it from them?'

'We're not the kind of family where the men lie around with their dingers on show, if that's what you mean. And you know my mum, she's pretty open but she wouldn't go much on talking about erections.'

'Well, all I know is I wake up stiff as a bat,' Adam said.

'Ready for a good innings,' I said.

'A big score, you're telling me.'

'Boys!' Tess said with mock scorn. 'Sex mad.'

'Unlike girls,' Adam said, 'who aren't, eh? They don't have nothing like that, I suppose.'

'What, like early morning blooming of the nips or clutching of the clit, that kind of thing?'

'Very elegantly put,' I said.

'To be honest, yes.'

'You do?' Adam said, himself agog now. 'There you are, then, it isn't just us.'

'Another of the uncontrollable pleasures of growing up, you mean. Like acne.'

'I enjoy it more than acne,' Adam said. 'All you can do with acne is pick it.'

'Easier to get rid of as well,' I said.

'Oo – you don't, do you!' Tess said, this time demonstrating shocked innocence. 'Not that I know what you're talking about, of course.' And we all laughed.

'But here, listen,' Adam said. 'I've been having a funny dream lately.'

'Funny ha-ha or funny disgusting?' Tess asked.

'Funny how it makes me sweat. I'm coming along this road, not walking or running or in a car or anything, just sort of floating along, and there's a bridge up ahead, not this bridge, just a bridge, a flat straight bridge, and as I come nearer I get more and more scared, I'm not sure why, because there's something dangerous on the other side I think, that's how it feels anyway, and I go slower and slower and all I can see is the bridge, nothing neither side, which is just a

74

blur, and there's nobody with me, I'm all alone, I feel lonely, and when I reach the bridge where the road becomes the bridge, there's a yellow line painted across the road and I stop just before it and I can't make myself go no further, just can't move at all, can't make myself cross the bridge, I'm stuck because of whatever it is I'm scared of, and I can't turn round and go back because there's something behind that I'm trying to get away from, I'm right stuck, and near freaking out, I'm breathing hard, and sweating, and . . . well . . . and, well, that's the end of it really, that's it, I'm stuck and I'm alone and I'm scared of something and I can't cross the bridge.'

He'd even broken out in a sweat as he spoke. Tess and I said nothing, seeing how disturbed he was and not knowing what to say. The Ancient Mariner. It was as if the whole evening had been working up to this point, when Adam would tell his dream.

He fell silent, his eyes grasping us, expecting, wanting us to say something that would release him from his nightmare.

'That's it,' he said after a while. 'That's all.'

Taking a deep breath, Tess said, 'I wonder what it is on the other side that scares you?'

I said, 'Maybe it's nothing to do with what's on the other side.'

'What then?'

'Dunno. Doesn't have to be something on the other side, though, does it? Could be the bridge itself he's afraid of. Or what he's running away from. Or the yellow line. What does that mean?'

Tess said, 'Does it have to mean anything? You're always trying to find a meaning in everything. Sometimes things don't mean anything, you know, they don't *have to*, do they? They might just be *there*.'

Adam watching us like a spectator at a tennis match, closely assessing every stroke.

I said, 'I don't believe that. Everything means something. Everything is there for a reason. Nothing just happens.'

'You're an appalling intellectual, you know that, don't you.'

'Why do people use "intellectual" as an insult? What's so bad about thinking? I enjoy thinking.'

'All right, don't let's go into that now. What we're talking about is Adam's dream,' Tess said. 'Dreams have their own kind of logic, don't they. They're not like . . . I don't know . . . like this happens, then that happens as a result, and then the next thing happens, and so on. They're weird. Everything is jumbled. Things don't seem to connect.'

'Exactly. They have their own logic. And all logic has a meaning. So things do connect. What you have to do is puzzle out the logic by finding some sort of pattern to it, don't you. Then the meaning becomes clear. Like poetry. Some poetry doesn't seem to make any sense when you first read it, so you just keep on reading it and rereading it while you puzzle out what the logic is, the ideas, the images, the words, all the rest of it, till you find the pattern – how everything connects in a way you hadn't noticed at first. I mean, that's one of the things that's so interesting about poetry, isn't it, you know that.'

'*Sacré dieu!*'

'I'm only trying to explain how I think about dreams, that's all. Look, I'll give you an example.'

'He's off, Adam, here he goes.'

'No, listen,' Adam said, 'I want to know.'

I went on, 'As it happens, I was just reading a story about a bridge. I'm interested in bridges at the moment, not surprisingly.' I fetched the book. 'It's a story called "The Bridge". It's by Franz Kafka.'

'The guy who wrote the one about the boy who wakes up and he's turned into a beetle?' Tess said.

'The very same,' I said, finding the place.

'Well then it's bound to be weird.'

'Want to hear it or not? It's very short, won't strain your powers of concentration.'

'Cheek!'

'Sure,' Adam said.

'OK, here goes:'

I was stiff and cold, I was a bridge, I lay over an abyss; my toes buried deep on one side, my hands on the other, I had fastened my teeth in crumbling clay. The tails of my coat fluttered at my sides. Far below brawled the icy trout stream. No tourist strayed to this impassable height, the bridge was not yet marked on the maps. Thus I lay and waited; I had to wait; without falling no bridge, once erected, can cease to be a bridge. One day towards evening, whether it was the first, whether it was the thousandth, I cannot tell – my thoughts were always in confusion, and always, always moving in a circle – towards evening in summer, the roar of the stream grown deeper, I heard the footsteps of a man! Towards me, towards me. Stretch yourself, bridge, make yourself ready, beam without rail, hold up the one who is entrusted to you. If his steps are uncertain steady them unobtrusively, but if he staggers then make yourself known and like a mountain god hurl him to the bank. He came, he tapped me with the iron spike of his stick, then with it he lifted my coat-tails and folded them upon me; he plunged his spike into my bushy hair, and for a good while he let it rest there, no doubt as he gazed far round him into the distance. But then – I was just following him in thought over mountain and valley – he leapt with both feet on to the middle of my body. I shuddered with wild pain, quite uncomprehending. Who was it? A child? A gymnast? A daredevil? A suicide? A tempter? A destroyer? And I turned over to look at him. A bridge turns over! And before I fully turned I was already falling, I fell, and in a moment I was ripped apart and impaled on the sharp stones that had always gazed up at me so peacefully out of the rushing waters.

Silence. The fire burned our faces.

Adam stirred, flexing himself as he did sometimes after a film he'd specially liked.

'Great!'

'You liked it?' Tess said, surprised.

'Is that all of it?'

I nodded.

'Let's have a look.'

Tess and I watched as, like a boy with a new toy, Adam pawed the open page and pored over the words, too.

'I'll have a read of this later on.' He looked up, smiling. 'I'm too slow for it now with you two watching.'

'But what does it mean?' Tess said.

He shrugged.

'But you like it?'

'Sure. You can kind of feel what it means.'

'There you are,' I said to Tess, 'he's a natural. He really knows how to read. Don't struggle with it. Just let it happen. Right? And don't snort at me. What do *you* think it means?'

'Oh no, you're not getting out of it that easy!' she said, laughing. 'I know you. You'll get me to say something stupid off the top of my head, having just heard the thing for the first time, and then you'll come up with something clever, because you've read it half a dozen times and been thinking about it for days! You're like Bishop at school, he does that, and it's not fair. It's easy to be clever about something when you've had plenty of time to work it out and the other person hasn't.'

'I've only read it once, just before you arrived, and I haven't a clue what it means.'

'Then why did you read it to us? Not just because we were talking about dreams and Adam told us his. That's too simple for you.'

'I really do want to know what you think. I'm not playing games, honest.'

'All right, I'll believe you though there's many who wouldn't. All I can say is that it seems to me to be a typical male fantasy about sex and failure.'

Adam said, 'How d'you work that out?'

'Let's have a look.'

Now it was Tess who pored over the pages. Adam watched as you watch someone who knows how to do something and hope by watching to learn the trick.

'I mean,' Tess said after a while, 'all this about being stiff and lying over an abyss! He even uses the word "erected". You don't erect bridges, do you? You build them, surely? Then there's the river. That's always got to do with sex, hasn't it. Water, flowing, channels. The image of the female. *And* it's a trout stream! We all know what fishes swimming in a river are supposed to mean.'

'What?' Adam asked, not batting an eye.

Tess shot a glance at me. Did he really not know?

'Well . . .' she said, 'penises, sperm, the male in the female . . . And then there's this dark stranger with the stick – I suppose you'll say that's another penis – which he plunges into the man's hair and then jumps onto the middle of his body. And after that the storyteller falls and smashes onto stones in the river and is ripped apart. All that is sex, and the failure is that he's supposed to be a bridge but he can't bear the first person who comes along without cracking up. So he's a failed bridge. Sex and failure.'

'So all you think it means is he can't get it up?' I said.

'But the figure who comes along is a man,' Adam said.

'Yes, well, I'd rather not go into *that*, thank you,' Tess said, making her mock-shock face. 'The whole thing seems pretty dubious to me. Unless the figure is his father, which would be bad enough. Which reminds me – it's time I left you two to it.'

'Now *there's* an Oedipal connection,' I said, laughing.

'Left us to what?' Adam said, beginning the banter of departure that matched the banter of arrival.

'Whatever you do when I'm not here.'

'Nothing near as exciting as we could do if you stayed.'

'This place is becoming a den of vice,' Tess said, making for the door. 'In your minds, anyway. Night all. May flights of angels sing you to your rest.'

When she had gone, the sound of her bike echoing down the road, Adam picked up the book again and sat reading for long minutes. After a while he started humming (was he conscious of doing so or not?) a tune I couldn't at first remember; then it came back: '. . . like a bridge over troubled waters I will lay me down . . .'

When at last he looked up, his expression serious, his eyes the other Adam's eyes, he said, as if making the meaning plain, 'It's the stones, the stones in the rushing water.'

I nodded, pretending I understood. But I didn't.

[– You and me, being so so clever, did we sense that talking about bridges and what *bridges* might mean wasn't a good idea that night? It's funny, but I can't remember. I can remember the evening and saying the things you say we said – or most of them; I don't remember any of those twittish puns! I do remember what we did and what we said and I even remember how I felt, but I don't remember what I *thought*.

But I'm off the point, which is that it didn't seem to occur to us that Adam's dream was about a bridge and Kafka's story was about a bridge and that there we all were sitting by a bridge, and that bridges are always about connecting two separated things, about joining things together that can't meet otherwise, and about crossing from one side to the other. In either direction. That bridges are borders and boundaries. And are walls with holes in them. That things (rivers, roads, cars, boats) and people go through and under them as well as on and over. That they are places where people meet, where they hide, where they go to look down on what goes under. From where they fish, play Pooh-sticks, and sometimes have to pay to cross. And even throw themselves off.

We hadn't found wonderful Calvino then, more's the pity, or we might have also known about Marco Polo in *Invisible Cities*, and you might have read that to us, which would have made a lot of difference to the way we thought about Adam's dream. I'm thinking of this bit:

Marco Polo describes a bridge, stone by stone.

'But which is the stone that supports the bridge?' Kublai Khan asks.

'The bridge is not supported by one stone or another,' Marco answers, *'but by the line of the arch that they form.'*

Kublai Khan remains silent, reflecting. Then he adds: 'Why do you speak of the stones? It is only the arch that matters to me.'

Polo answers: 'Without stones there is no arch.'

I think the thing we didn't really understand was what Polo says to Kublai Khan. We didn't understand yet that, yes, we are each individual stones, but that together we can make an arch. We hadn't made that connection. We hadn't bridged that gap.

By the way, you really were painfully jealous of Adam and me, weren't you! Perhaps you were so jealous that even now you find it hard to admit? Or is writing it a kind of confession? Come to that, isn't this whole story a kind of confession? Or do I read it like that because I'm a lapsed Catholic from a family of lapsed Catholics? That's what you'll say, I suppose, never having been anything yourself but a lapsed atheist.]

❖ 4 ❖

One day a raven came to the bridge, perching on the peak of the toll-house roof, and returned day after day. Adam took a fancy to it.

The raven would stand on the roof and peer around with its reptilian eyes, spying for food I expect, as it was winter.

They are so impressively big are ravens, bigger bodied than a carrion crow, and armed with a long heavy beak set off by shaggy throat feathers that give them an evil predatory appearance. You can see why they get such a bad press. But Adam admired our visitor and would stand in the road and speak to it. Not the billing-and-cooing of sentimental animal lovers, as if animals were human babies of low intelligence, but in something that sounded like a foreign language, with its own rhythm and music and vocabulary. I can't capture it in writing, it would look like gobbledegook. He didn't speak loudly, either. There was the raven up on the roof, and there was Adam down on the road, and he would look up at the raven and mutter his animalian no louder than he would speak to someone standing right in front of him. You wouldn't have thought the bird could hear. But it would turn to face him and stretch its cruel head down and fix him with its cold eyes and twist and cock its head as if listening hard to every nuance.

Adam did this for four or five days in a row whenever he heard the raven's coarse deep-throated croaking from the roof. I began to wonder if it was actually calling for him. He would go out and talk for two or three minutes and then come back inside. Nothing else.

But on the sixth or seventh day he was there so long that I went to the window to see what was happening. He was standing in the middle of the road as usual, but this time holding his right arm up, gently beckoning with his fingers and murmuring his animalian so quietly I could hardly hear him from inside. He's never, I thought, at once feeling fearful, he's never trying to tice it down!

But that is exactly what he did do. I'd only been watching for a few seconds when the raven swooped shockingly into view, the great black metre-wide fans of its wings throbbing the air, powering the bird round Adam's head, once, twice, three times, while it let out a high-pitched metallic cry as it circled, Adam standing statuesquely still, until it came gliding in, claws extended, and clutched Adam's wrist, where it settled, after a dodgy wobble back and forth till they both found the right balance. Then the two of them stood still, gazing into each other's unblinking eyes.

By now I had broken into a cold sweat. And the sight of that scimitar beak only a fist away from Adam's eyes completely unnerved me. My knees buckled and I sat down on the windowsill, grasping the edge to keep me from falling. But I couldn't stop looking.

Adam waited for a while that seemed an age, murmuring murmuring, the tension so great I desperately wanted to pee.

The pair of them remained there, the one talking, the other listening, for endless minutes. Then Adam began to move slowly, slowly, careful step by careful step, first in a wide circle, then in a straight line up the middle of the road onto the bridge for a few metres before turning and coming back again. All the time he talked his quiet animal talk. And all the time the raven stared at him, only occasionally looking away with a sharp twist of its head as if to assess the view.

When they were near the house again, where I hoped he would launch the bird into the air and be done with his circus act, Adam paused for a moment. But then set off again, slowly, slowly, this time towards the front door.

Dear God, I thought, he's never going to bring it in!

But he did. Step by step, and pausing every two or three steps, allowing the raven to take in what was happening, and talking his lingo all the time, calmly, lightly, soothingly, gradually edging his way through the door, and on into the living room, right past me, where I sat pressed against the window utterly speechless, every muscle paralysed though I could hear my heart thumping in terror and feel an effusion of sweat soaking my clothes.

At last, reaching the centre of the room Adam gently turned so that he faced me and the door, and stopped, the bird twisting its head and stabbing its beak nervously in this direction and that, and Adam's monologue the only sound.

Could he have got away with it? Might he have kept the bird quiet until he had taken it outside again? We never found out because a car arrived just then. I was so spelled that I wasn't aware of it coming. The first I heard was the noise of an engine outside the house. There was a moment when we all – Adam, the raven, myself – cocked our ears in its direction, Adam like me thinking, What now?, and the raven gathering itself for flight.

At which second the car's horn blew and the raven took off, seeming in one spread of its wings to fill the room. Instinctively, I threw myself onto the floor and lay there, curled up as tightly as I could and shielding my head with my arms while the bird blundered and buffeted around the room, squawking loud angry croaking cries and banging into walls and ceiling light and furniture, such a confined space being far too small for it to achieve proper flight. Adam ducked and dodged as it flayed about his head, its wings raising a draught that swirled up clouds of dust and caused the chimney to backfire, sending wood smoke billowing into the room. In seconds the place looked and smelt like a dungeon in the bowels of hell during an attack from an avenging angel.

In the middle of this confusion the car must have driven off, at any rate it wasn't there a few minutes later when everything was under control again. Probably the driver took fright at the noise, which must have sounded like ritual murder, and decided he was better off out of it.

After beating about for I don't know how long, time being now a commodity I'd completely lost sense of, the raven careered headfirst into a wall, fell onto the back of the armchair, clutched at it wildly, dug its claws into the upholstery, and found itself perched there, ruffled, agitated, defensive (that cruel beak stab-stab-stabbing) and the room suddenly silent again.

Slowly the swirls of dust and smoke settled to a haze. And as if to mark the time a lone black feather floated lazily down from the ceiling, coming finally to rest at Adam's feet.

He by now was hunkered half under the table watching with a satisfied smirk as if this were the very scene he had hoped to create.

From my exposed position flat on the floor I muttered, 'What the hell do we do now?'

'Hush,' Adam said. 'Keep still.'

And he started talking his beastspiel again. I thought, This time it won't work. But it did. Slowly, oh so slowly! His patience was impeccable. I remember thinking, How can he be so calm and patient at a time like this when normally he's such an unpredictable volatile fidget? Which only goes to show how little I understood Adam or myself or human nature in general.

With delicate care he approached the nervous bird, coaxed it after repeated attempts onto his arm, and then half-step by half-step eased his way across the room and through the living-room door and at long last through the outside door and into the road, where for a moment he stood still, the pair of them again like a sculpture, 'Boy with Bird', before he raised his arm, and the raven launched itself cleanly into the air and flapped off, soaring into the sky, repeating as it went its deep-throated cry in farewell.

Once the bird was out of sight the tension broke. The relief was almost as unbearable.

I stormed outside yelling, 'What in hell's teeth d'you think you're playing at! You must be crazy! You could have lost an eye! That was just about the stupidest thing I've ever seen anybody do! You're mad! Never do anything like that again, d'you hear! Never!! *Jesus!!!*'

Adam grinned at me as I frothed.

'And don't stand there grinning!' I blathered on.

'It was fun.'

'Fun! You call that fun!'

'Sure. Gave you a thrill as well.'

'Me!'

'You loved every minute.'

'I did not!'

'Yes, you did. Look at you, you're shaking with excitement.'

'I'm shaking from anger, you great steaming ape, that's why I'm shaking.'

He raised his hand to run it through his hair, that irritating tic whenever he was excited. It was then that I saw blood soaking through the arm of his sweater.

'What's this?' I said, catching hold of his hand.

'Nothing.' He tried to tug his hand away, but half-heartedly.

I eased the sweater back. Blood was oozing from torn flesh just above his wrist.

'Christ, its claws must have dug into you! Thank God it missed the vein. We'd better see to that.'

He allowed me to lead him to the sink where I cleaned the wound and dressed it as best I could with strips of cloth torn from a T-shirt. Doing that calmed me, maybe for the same reason that the raven calmed Adam.

'Why the hell did you do that?' I said quietly as I worked.

'Just to see if I could.'

'Well, I hope that's all the proof you want.'

'Till I think of something better.'

'Not while I'm around, if you don't mind. The beak on that bird! You could easily have lost an eye. One peck – And look at your arm. It's a mess.'

'Worth it though,' he said.

❖ 5 ❖

'Hey!' Tess called out.

We turned from our work. Her camera clicked.

'Not again!' I said. 'How many more?'

She was taking photos for an optional course on photography at school. She'd chosen the toll bridge as a topic, photographing it regularly for six months. At the beginning she thought it would just make an interesting subject, a study of stones and water and people and the effect on them of weather and the changing seasons. She called the finished portfolio 'Tolling the Bridge'.

Adam enjoyed being snapped enormously, camping up the poses if he got the chance, which Tess liked for a while, but when she'd had enough of it, would creep up on us and take us unawares. Early on, she persuaded Adam to perform his Tarzan act for her (not that he needed much persuading of course), which she shot in black and white from various angles – on and under the bridge, from the garden, from the back-door steps, from the river (she had to get into the water for these shots and nearly died of the cold), even from above in the tree itself. It took three sessions during which I was required to act as general runabout and slave to the pair of them. Of course I pretended to be sniffy about this at the time but I have to admit the resulting pictures are my favourites, beautifully capturing the sense of movement and energy. (The school made Tess cut the sequence out of the portfolio before putting it on show with the work of the rest of the group because Adam was in the nude and Tess refused to crop away or cover with airbrushed shadows the full frontal naughty bits. Another example of how prissy puritanism still rides shotgun in certain sectors of the British social system. [– Compare and contrast in two hundred words the 'page three' popsies in the tabloid dailies and then write three hundred words in their defence, imagining yourself to be one of the dishy dolls.])

❖ 6 ❖

One drizzly morning a Range Rover stopped at the door. I went out to take the toll but already the driver, a young guy, incipient version of B-and-G, dressed in a cheap grey junior businessman suit and sporting one of those fluffy moustaches that grow on the faces of insecure post-adolescents who want you to think they're older than they are, was hauling out of the back a large notice on a pole. FOR SALE, the notice said, and the usual details of agent's name and phone number. Plus the inevitable emblem – not head of Greek god, nor flourishing oak tree, nor prancing black stallion but blue swallow in full flight. Why never anything nearer the truth, like a brace of money bags or a vulture picking on a corpse or a shark with a bloodstained mortgage in its teeth? Stupid question, really.

What does puzzle me, though, is why we put up with such pollution of the mind. We go on and on about dodgy food and acid rain and nuclear radiation and other threats to our bodies but we don't bat an eye at abuse of symbols or poison pumped into our minds by advertisers and other con artists, or foul emissions spewed out every day by, for example, so-called 'news' papers and politicians and TV's self-appointed public opinionaters. What's the point of a living body without a living mind to go with it? *Nichts*. All the evidence I need is here.

The driver, studiously ignoring me, was carrying the sign to the corner of the house.

'Has Mister Norris OK'd this?' I asked.

'And who might you be, squire?'

'The toll keeper.'

Sizing up the stonework for a place to fix the pole, he said, 'I'm impressed.'

He leaned the hoarding against the house, returned to the back of his Rover from where he was taking a claw hammer and a handful of round-head spike nails when he caught sight, as I did from following the line of his surprised gawp, of Adam, who must have come outside while our backs were turned, quietly taken possession of the hoarding, and was now casually bearing it, raised like a banner, towards the bridge.

Speechless, the agent's agent watched as Adam, reaching the middle of the bridge, lifted the hoarding over the parapet, hoyed it into the river, ran to the other side, watched it float through and swirl away downstream, after which, without casting a glance in our direction, he walked calmly back to the house and disappeared inside.

Only then did the agent's agent find his voice.

'Who the hell was that?'

'Him? Just my assistant.'

'Your *assistant*!'

'Now you're impressed.'

'What the shit does he think he's playing at?'

'Pooh-sticks.'

'Eh?'

'Do return when you have obtained written permission to molest the building,' I said with all the hauteur I could assume, and stalked into the house, quietly closing the door behind me.

Adam was standing in the middle of the living room, clenched fist raised and pulling victory faces. We wanted to burst out but stifled ourselves in order to hear what went on outside for, there being no curtains, we didn't want to spoil the effect by being seen looking out. Not that there was long to wait before a cruel slamming of car doors, over-revved engine and squealing tyres told us all we needed to know.

A futile gesture but spine-tinglingly satisfying. Naturally, fluffy lip was back by noon, flapping an officious piece of paper in our faces and braying his FOR SALE sign to the wall with all the crucifying passion of a minion with a score to settle. Another episode in the comedy of rage.

❖ 7 ❖

After three weeks of painting and decorating I began to feel ill. Irritated lungs, runny nose and eyes, heavy aching head, dizziness sometimes, queasy stomach, wanting to puke. This went on for a day or two, me thinking I was coming down with the flu, when one night I woke up and made it to the back door just in time. Soaked in fever sweat, freezing in the night frost and dark December air, I threw up till there was nothing left to throw and retching was itself a pain. When it was over I stumbled back inside, washed, drank a glass of water, stirred up the slumbering logs on the fire, and hunkered as close to the warmth as I could, shivering, sniffling, and miserable.

Adam didn't move. I resented that for a while, all my only-son reflexes, I suppose, conditioned to expect coddling and consolation. But as the spasm wore off I was pleased he'd stayed where he was. This was the first time since I came to the bridge that I'd been physically ill. It had never occurred to me that I would be. Now it had happened I felt suddenly vulnerable and was glad there was someone else in the house, but I certainly didn't want him fussing over me, and suggesting remedies.

Once I was warm again and the spasm was properly over, I felt so washed out and weary all I wanted was to crawl back into bed. Which I did, and slept so soundly that I didn't wake next morning till I heard Tess's voice saying my name. She was standing by my bed dressed in her biking leathers, Adam at her side.

'Hello. Are you all right?'

'What time is it?'

'Eight thirty. Is anything wrong?'

'Just a bit queasy.'

'You don't look too terrific.'

Adam said, 'He was spewing half the night.'

'I'll get up.'

Tess said, 'You might be better in bed. Was it something you ate?'

Adam said, 'We both had the same.'

He was, as ever, the epitome of health, being one of those people who look tanned even in the dead of winter.

'I'm all right.'

They looked at me like mourners surveying a corpse.

'Shove off. I want to get dressed.'

'If you're sure,' Tess said.

'I'm sure, I'm sure. Go!'

They went, closing the door behind them. There was mumbling from outside before Tess's bike started and drove off, not over the bridge, as it should have done if she were on her way to school, but towards the village. So I wasn't surprised when Bob Norris turned up twenty minutes later in his van, Tess puttering along behind. By then I was sitting by the fire, feeling like Lazarus, nibbling half-heartedly on a piece of dry bread, which was the only food I could face.

'Traitor,' I muttered at Tess when she and her father came in with that apprehensive look people wear when visiting the uncertain sick. Adam, who had been outside taking tolls, tagged along behind.

'What's this?' Bob Norris said in his foreman's bantering style, which he hadn't been using much lately. 'Skiving, is it? Day off? General strike? Go slow? What?'

'Inquisition followed by public burning, by the looks,' I said trying to respond in kind, but it sounded more like accusation than joke. While I sat quiet I seemed fairly normal; as soon as I spoke, or worse, moved, I knew I wasn't.

'Haven't lost your appetite, I see.'

'Favourite breakfast, dry bread.'

'Stomach is it? Bad chest, snotty nose, dizzy head?'

'Flu, I expect. Nothing to bother about.'

'Sick in the night though.'

I glared at Tess.

'Painter's colic,' Bob Norris went on. 'Breathing those fumes for too long. Not enough fresh air. Not enough ventilation. Windows shut at night to keep out the cold.'

'I'll take a walk.'

'You'll do nothing of the sort. You'll come home with me in the van. The wife'll see to you. You need some time out of here and a day or two recuperating before things get worse.' He turned to Adam, who was leaning in the doorway. 'Can you cope without him?'

'Sure.'

Tess said, 'I could stay and help. We're not doing much at school.'

Her father gave her a wry glance. 'You've done your bit for today, girl. Best get going, you're late already.'

'Girl indeed!' Tess stretched up, pecked a kiss on his unshaven cheek and said, 'I do not bite my thumb at you, sir, but I bite my thumb, sir.'

'Eh?'

And bending down, pecked a kiss on my cheek too. 'O, flesh, flesh, how art thou fishified!' I was too addled to remember what she was quoting. 'Get well soon, dear Jan.' And she clumped away in her biking boots. 'See you, Adam. 'Bye all.'

Mrs Norris fed me bread and milk, a potion for sickly children I'd only ever read about in books, hustled me into the spare bedroom, and left me luxuriating between fresh-smelling pink flannelette sheets, a radio playing quietly, curtains drawn against the light, and firm instructions that I must sleep. A brisk good-humoured spoiling quite different from my mother's all-consuming full-time attention.

For the rest of that day I drifted pleasantly, cosily, in and out of sleep. In the waking times my mind played with memories of the past year and thoughts about my time at the bridge and about Mother and Dad and everything Dad had told me in his letter, and about Gill and me and my confusion about what I really wanted, and about Adam and Tess and the strangeness of everything, the unlikeliness of all life, the unrealness of its reality. For it wasn't only because I was mildly ill that other people and life in general seemed such a puzzle, so surprising and beyond understanding, so *unknowable*, and yet so fascinating. So beautiful and yet so ugly too. In a less fevered way, that is how it was for me always and still is: the surprise and fascination, the otherness, the not-me of it all.

Lying there in the Norrises' spare bedroom, gazing dozily at the wallpaper covered in big-patterned dark green vine leaves entwined with huge bunches of ripe red grapes, and at the family knick-knacks neatly grouped on every flat surface, and at the furniture – heavy dark-wood dressing table and matching wardrobe, cane bedside table, wooden milking stool, ancient Windsor rocking chair with bright red cushion – most of which must have come down from generations before, solid and brightly polished as a freshly opened conker, my own deep confusions about myself became all the more disturbing, and I wished that somehow I could belong to the settled, ages-old certainties that the Norrises lived by. But knew I never could, and maybe only wanted to now in a fit of sentimentality brought on by painter's (melan)colic.

Among the knick-knacks one especially caught my eye, an object so strange, so unlike any of the others, that I had to get out of bed to pick it up. The size of a small mug, it was crudely hand-made of mud-red clay with a stubby almost straight handle across the top so that the thing was like a small pottery bucket. But for carrying what? Raised from the surface of the mug, to each side of the handle, was a plump face, one solemn and stern and clean-shaven with pursed lips, the other moustached and goatee-bearded and smiling mischievously.

The faces were framed by ringlets of hair falling like twined snakes behind the ears – large ears on the stern man – and were circled by a crown, as if both faces belonged to one head.

I knew as soon as I picked it up that this weird antique must have something to do with the god Janus. And as I caressed its pitted cracked sandy surface, and with a delicious shock found that the pad of my thumb and the tip of my index finger fitted exactly into the hollows where the potter had pressed the ends of the handle into the rim of the vessel, I felt a kind of awe, as if some magnetic power emanated from this ancient piece of crudely shaped clay and took me into its possession. I was suddenly afraid the holy pot might break or even crumble to pieces in my hand, yet did not want to put it down, wanted to keep it with me, hold it to me, hide it on me. I actually had to suppress a strong desire to steal it.

Ever since that moment I have been able to understand the magic power of sacred objects. I cannot explain how the magic works but I no longer scoff at anyone who believes in it.

At midday Bob Norris came to see me, bearing a bowl of Mrs Norris's vegetable soup and a chunk of brown bread. He spotted that I'd placed the Janus on the bedside table where I could look closely at it while I lay in bed.

'Like it?' he said.

'Very much. How old is it?'

'Roman-Egyptian, circa first century BC – about two thousand two hundred years old. Know what it is?'

'Something to do with Janus?'

'One face is Dionysus, the Greek god of wine and fruitfulness and all vegetation. He bestows ecstasy and is also the god of drama. They used to worship him with very sexy goings-on. The other is Satyr, a goat-like man who drank a lot and danced in the procession behind Dionysus and chased the nymphs. Bit of a randy devil.'

'Quite a pair.'

'And they make Janus, the god of gates and doorways and bridges and of beginnings in general because when you go through a door or cross a bridge you enter something new, a different place. That's why the Romans made January the first month of the year. For them he was the god of gods, coming even before Jupiter. He's very very ancient, one of the true gods who was worshipped long before Roman times. They took him over and made him into their own, the way they took over Christianity and turned it into an Imperial religion.'

'Doesn't sound as if you like the Romans much.'

'I don't. Totalitarian fascist bunch of thugs.'

'But what was the mug for? Not for drinking out of, surely? You can't get your nose in.'

'It's not a mug, it was used for carrying a prayer. When you went to the temple, you bought one, probably from a stall outside, along with a small strip of lead. You etched your prayer into the metal, bent the strip in two so that no one else could read it, put the prayer into the pot, then took the pot into the temple and stood it on the altar as a kind of supplication to the god.'

'Looks like a pretty down-market example, this one.'

'Does, doesn't it. Made in two halves, each pressed into a mould then joined together, I should think, wouldn't you? Quickly done. Their equivalent of cheap mass-production probably. You can see the join where the two halves were stuck together, the potter hasn't even bothered to smooth it off, and there's pitting on the surface of the faces where the clay wasn't pressed into the mould firmly enough.'

'And the handle! It looks like the sort of thing we used to roll out with modelling clay in infant school.'

'Have you put your finger inside?'

'Mine fits exactly!'

'It does? My goodness! Mine's too big.'

'Weird sensation.'

'Wonderful.'

'Fingers abolishing time.'

'Aye, and space. One thing's for sure – the man who made this doesn't have a headache any more.'

We smiled and nodded at each other, acknowledging the kinship of understanding.

At four thirty, full of fizz, Tess brought up tea and buttered scones along with news that Adam was slogging away at the house and enjoying it all so much he hadn't stopped to eat anything so she was going back to cook something for them both. They were having a ball, I could tell just from the grin on her face.

I said, 'I'll come.'

'No you won't, Mum won't let you. The place reeks of paint, you'd be ill again straightaway.'

'I'm still coming.'

91

Tess went to the door and called out, 'Mum, he says he's going back to the bridge.'

Which brought Mrs Norris pounding up the stairs. 'Oh no he isn't. You're staying where you are, young man, you're staying here tonight, so compose yourself to it.'

Tess was ushered away, bedclothes were efficiently tidied, Janus returned to his place among the other knick-knacks, the whole room given a critical survey and the door firmly closed. Leaving me to my unwilling isolation and the torture chamber of my imagination, which for the next few hours was filled with gradually more agonizing fantasies in which Tess and Adam performed with enthusiastic gusto all of the sexiest Dionysian dramas in my then, I must admit, not very extensive repertoire.

I sizzled with desire, sweated with jealousy, prayed to Janus to set me free, groaned with frustration and pique. I was like a lone spectator who, locked in an empty cinema, is forced to watch a film specially made to reduce him to a state of lust-racked blither. And the really ridiculous thing about times like that, the thing I always laugh about later, is that you do it to yourself. You are your own jailer, your own film-maker, your own torturer. The fantasies are your own. It's your own imagination that invents them and your own will that lets it happen and your own mind that puts the show on. You could stop it at once if you wanted to but you don't because it gives you some sort of twisted satisfaction. And it's my belief that there's a side to the human race that loves plodging around in this kind of clart. Sometimes we like to be right up to our necks in it. Sometimes people even drown in their own psychic shit.

A film fantasy can't go on forever but the fantasies inside your head can and then other people call you mad. Maybe my feverish fantasies drove me a little mad that night. In the end I could bear them no longer. I had to know what Tess and Adam really were up to. And in my place, my sanctuary, dammit! I had to be there with them. So I got up, dressed as quietly as I could, mumbled a prayer to Janus to protect me, and stole down the stairs, feeling like a burglar in reverse. The noise of the TV, which the Norrises were watching in their living room, covered any give-away sounds.

Outside, I ran all the way to the bridge. Arrived panting so hard I stopped to recover my breath when I came in sight of the house. My inclination had been to burst in before they had a chance to stop whatever it was they were doing. But while I caught my breath, a deeper, stranger desire took hold of me. I wanted to see them as they were, on their own, without me. As a kid I was always wondering what other people did when I wasn't there. Maybe because I knew I had a secret life of my own which I only ever let show when no one else was around, I supposed that other people were like that too. And I felt a consuming desire to know what those private selves were that parents and relatives and teachers and friends hid from me. So I would sometimes steal around, peeking in at windows or snooping at doors in the hope of discovering those hidden selves revealed.

I had not done this for years, however. Had even forgotten that I used ever to do it. Now, as I recovered my breath, that childhood desire overwhelmed me again. The fun of observing people when they are completely unaware of being watched, the nervous excitement of it – the same excitement that experimental scientists must feel, and Peeping Toms as well, I guess.

I checked that no vehicles were approaching before padding quietly up to the house. The bedroom was dark but the living room was softly lit by low table lamps that hadn't been there before, one each side of the fireplace.

It was not the lamps, however, that immediately caught my eye but Tess and Adam tangled naked on the floor in front of the fire. Hollywood TV soft corn. Much pawing going on and sucking and kissing and licking. More complete in range than in my fantasies. More surprising. More tantalizing. More fleshed out would be true to say. Fantasies depend, like everything else, on information. My experience of life so far hadn't informed me all that well; and obviously I hadn't read the right books. They were doing things to each other with fingers and mouths that were stunning news to me.

For a while I watched with the amazement of an initiate secretly learning the mysteries of his trade. Till another kind of amazement grew beside it: amazement at my own reaction to the scene before me. For deep inside I was watching myself with just as great intensity as I was watching them. Observer observing himself. And what amazed me was that instead of anger or jealousy or resentment or envy or hard-on lust there came over me a calm – or maybe I ought to say a calming – satisfaction. I can only compare it to watching a close friend doing something he's good at and doing it very well. You might wish you could do it well too while knowing that you couldn't. But mainly you feel pleased for him, happy that he's achieved the reward, the recognition, the satisfaction, the pleasure he wanted and deserved.

Naturally I felt a little sad for myself too because this was the moment when I properly knew – when I accepted – that Tess was not, would not be, for me nor me for her. Not in the way she was being for Adam right there before me. I even wondered, as he entered her with a shudder of pleasure, whether she knew I was watching, whether she had expected I would find her doing this now, here in my room in my house, whether even by some trick she had planned it. Her way of forcing me to accept what she had told me about us was true. Ridiculous, of course. Another fantasy.

I had not seen 'sex' happening between two people before. I don't mean pretended sex between actors, nor played at by gropers at parties or in public places, nor the clinical demonstrations in sex-education videos at school, but the all-out sweatlathed juicegreasing bodysquirming limbtangled skingreedy gutmelting mindlost neoviolent reality. So I didn't know by first-hand observation, much less direct experience, about its animalness. The exclusive bodiliness of it. The utterly absorbed uninhibited unselfconsciousness of those involved in it as they writhe self-absorbed, lost to the world around them, lost, in fact, just like the cliché says, in each other.

As I watched I realized that I'd never achieved that state with Gill, never been mind-less, never been totally unselfconsciously absorbed, but had always been thinking about it, always been aware of what was going on, always observing myself do it, even as I now observed them and observed myself observing them. An observer by nature, that's me. Did this explain my confusion over Gill? But if it did, *what* did it explain?

I also saw why there is so much talk about sex, why there are so many scenes about it in books and plays and films. Why it causes so much trouble, too. And why those who get it and those who don't make such a fuss. And why there's so much pretending about it – people pretending that they get it when they don't, or pretending that they perform exotic contortions when actually they are as straight as a pencil. And why people who are born with sexy good looks get things easily.

Not that I'm any exception. Adam breaks into my bedroom, scaring the wits out of me, but as soon as I see him stripped, with his foxy good looks and lithe neatly built body and his exceptional dick, I let him stay and sponge off me instead of kicking him out. Not just because the sight of him turned me on but because I'm human, and everybody's like that. I didn't think about it at the time. Animal biology made the decision for me. As I reckon it does countless times a day between people everywhere. The fact is we're all succoured by sex, and some of us are finally suckered by it too.

So I'm standing there for ten, maybe fifteen minutes, watching them, and watching myself watching them, and with a hard-on by then to be honest, making no effort by now to hide myself, when my bridge-keeper's third ear alerts me to the sound of a vehicle I know approaching along the road from the village. Bob Norris's van.

He's bound to stop, even if he's on his way to somewhere else. Bound to see his daughter *in flagrante delicto* with a footloose horny yob he doesn't trust enough to keep the bridge never mind screw his daughter, and me, who he counts responsible, standing outside doing a convincing impersonation of a dirty old man.

I suppose I could – ought to? – have rushed inside, yelling a warning, and hustled the coupled pair out of the back door before Bob arrived. But I doubt if there'd have been time, for at that moment the final act wasn't far from its climax, her on the floor under him, legs over his shoulders, locked together and going like the clappers, in such a state of pleasure that had I burst in they would probably have been beyond recall anyway.

No, that's just an excuse. The truth is more shaming. I was curious to know what would happen when Bob arrived.

Not that any of this was thought out. The second I heard Bob's van approaching, I slipped across the road and vaulted over the bridge onto the bank just where it dropped steeply down to the river. Hidden there I could squint between the urn-shaped balusters.

The van drew up. Bob got out. Tried the house door. Locked. Stepped, without knocking, to the lighted window of the living room, raising his hand to rap on the glass, but, seeing in, never did, his hand arrested in a clenched-fist salute.

I could only see his back silhouetted against the window. For a moment he was a statue spelled by what he saw. Then, as if punched in the stomach, he slumped forward and turned away. I heard a groan as he paused a brief moment then came stumbling across the road directly towards me, reached the parapet, the edge of which he grasped, arms spread for support, right above me, where he struggled to control what were not groans, after all, but angry grieving sobs.

I had not seen a grown man weep before. Not like this – so unrestrained, so racked. A second first in basic emotions within moments of each other: I had wanted life stripped to the essentials and I was getting it. And again I was observing myself as I observed the other. The sight of Bob Norris possessed by such naked tears came as a shock, entangling my embarrassment with a sense of double betrayal. I cowered in my inadequate hiding place, head down, terrified that Bob would see me – yet, oh, if only he would see me! – and torn as well by an impulse somehow – but how? – to comfort him. Besides, his sobbing made me want to weep too, for suddenly I saw the scene in the house not with my own eyes but with his, and felt a confusing mix of shame, regret, anger, and worst of all of loss.

Just as I had never seen a grown man weeping, I do not think I had ever really known till that moment what compassion felt like. A third first.

Eventually Bob gained control of himself. Snuffled back his tears. Swore. Spat over the parapet, a gob that landed like a rebuke on my bowed head. Breathed in and out deeply a few times. Returned to his van. But did not start the engine. Instead, letting off the brake, allowed the slight incline to carry the vehicle backwards down the road until a safe enough distance away to drive off without causing alarm in the house.

As soon as his tail lights were out of sight I climbed from my hiding place and set off after him, dregs of guilt stifling an impulse to steal a last glimpse through the toll-house window.

Walking through the village fifteen minutes later I spotted Bob's van parked outside The Plough. Knowing he wasn't a pub man, and even at home not much of a boozer, 'drowning his sorrows' came to mind.

He was sitting on a stool, slumped on his elbows against the bar nursing a large whisky, obviously not his first.

'Saw your van,' I said, half-perching on a stool beside him.

He gave me a sideways look through reddened eyes. 'Had enough of mouldering in bed?' And downed his whisky in one go.

'Something like that.'

'Want a drink?'

He ordered a glass of cider and another large Scotch.

When they had arrived he said, 'The wife was telling me about your mother.' He downed half his drink. 'Sounds badly, poor woman.'

I said nothing, unwilling to talk about that subject.

He turned away, sat square to the bar, not looking at me, thinking, and after a moment said, 'Hard job, being a parent.'

Attempting relief with a smile, I said, 'Wouldn't know.'

'No.' He downed the second half. 'Just as well. If we knew the worst beforehand, maybe we'd never take it on.'

'Is it that bad?'

He ordered another large Scotch.

'If you ever have any –' his words were slurring a little, 'don't have daughters.'

'Didn't know you could choose.'

He huffed ruefully. 'Too true.' Another half glass went down.

I said, chancing my arm, 'Tess doesn't seem so bad.'

'Tess!' he said, swivelling to me, 'Tess! What d'you call her that for? Not her name. Katharine. Her name's Katharine. You know that. Katey, if you like. Not Kathy, though, don't like Kathy. But *Tess*! Dear God!'

'Sorry. Private joke.'

'Wonderful girl. Always was. Right from birth. Beautiful little thing. Nice-tempered. Lovely. Always loved her. Moment I saw her at the hospital.'

'Well then?'

'Another,' he said to the barman.

'Are you sure, Bob?' the barman said. 'Not like you.'

'One more. That'll be it.'

'One more. But leave your van. Walk home, OK?'

He waited till the replenished glass was in front of him before looking at me with that close, slightly unfocused watery gaze of the not-quite-drunk intent on making a point too difficult to get words around. 'What you think then? Of our . . . Tess?'

'What do I think of her?'

'What do you think of her?'

'I like her.'

'Come on, you can do better than that. How much?'

'Dunno. A lot.'

'Fancy her?'

'Well –'

'Go on. Don't be shy. Man to man.'

'Yes, but –'

97

'But? Can't be buts about fancying.'

'She's a friend, that's all.'

'Never done it. That what you mean?'

'With her? No!'

He slurped from his glass.

'Listen. Tell you something. It hurts. Know that, do you? Hurts like hell. Know what I'm talking about? Children – daughters – specially daughters – most specially . . . Tess. Katey . . . Lovely beautiful Katharine. Daddy's girl. What her mother calls her. Daddy's girl.' He chuckled. 'But they grow up, see? Love them. Want the best for them. Worry.' He shot a glance at me. 'Get jealous. Know that? Know what I'm talking about? Bet never thought that, eh? Fathers get jealous. Eh? Thought that? . . . *I* get jealous. Put it that way. Understand?'

Gripping the bar to steady himself, he slid uncertainly to his feet. Sweat glazed his face.

'Let's go. Too bloody hot here.'

He staggered. I caught his arm and guided him to the door. Outside, the cold December night slapped us. He braced himself against me, took two deep breaths, pulled his arm from my grip, and set off uncertainly towards his van. I skipped ahead, placing myself between him and the door.

'Mr Norris, I don't think you should drive. Let's walk home.'

He stood scowling at me, swaying slightly. 'Tess! Thought about her name careful, wife and me. Important – names. Yes? Important. You know – mean things. Don't they? . . . Tell something else. Sometimes I feel – sometimes I want . . . Better not. Can't hurt then. Member that.'

'I will, Mr Norris, I will, but I think we ought to walk home now.'

I didn't wake until after nine next morning. By the time I'd pacified Mrs Norris for going out the night before and returning with her husband drunk (a calamity she somehow seemed to blame on me) and argued her into letting me go back to the bridge it was ten thirty. When I arrived Adam was lolling by the blazing fire, supping coffee and looking smug, the room bright with fresh paint. Tess, it turned out, had been busy with Adam all day yesterday while I lay brooding between her mother's flannelette sheets. She had skipped school and she and Adam had finished off glossing the woodwork and then titivated the entire place – living room, bedroom, kitchen area, even the basement lavatorywoodstore.

No longer was the house like the tidy squat Adam first took it to be. Now it was a newly decorated home. Not an especially well-off home, but still, a place where people lived. On the mantelpiece and windowsills winter berries and sprigs of evergreen sprouted from make-shift vases – bottles, old jugs. Stoneware cider flagons had been converted into table lamps to match the one I'd made for a bedside light, only these were topped with wickerwork shades like Chinese hats instead of naked bulbs. Tess had even managed to find an old rust-red rug for the floor. My books had been divided into collections of similar kinds, each collection shelved on its own: poetry on a newly fitted shelf in the living-room alcove to one side of the fireplace, nonfiction books on a shelf on the other side, fiction on the mantelpiece in the bedroom. Posters Sellotaped to the walls (Hockney's 'Bigger Splash', Tom Phillips's 'Samuel Beckett', Jimmy Dean walking in the rain at night). The television set stood on a crudely cobbled table. Even the lumpy old armchair looked revived, a bright red cushion nestling in its seat.

'Like it?' Adam asked.

'You mean, Tess was here all day?'

'Wanted to make the place nice for you. I made the table for the telly though.'

'Where did all the stuff come from?'

'Dunno. Very resourceful is Tess. Knows a lot.' He chuckled, double-meaning. 'All finished. No more painting.'

'Terrific,' I said flatly. Was the place mine any longer?

'Aren't you pleased?'

'Delirious. Had a good time, then?'

'Great.'

'I'm glad. Worked hard, eh?'

'Want some coffee? There's some letters by the telly.'

Letters

❖ 1 ❖

. . . unless you say no I'll come on the Friday and leave on the Monday . . .

❖ 2 ❖

. . . NO NO NO NO NO NO NO NO NO NO NO NO NO . . .

❖ 3 ❖

. . . a friend of his. My dad is his boss. I expect he's told you that he's decorating the toll house because the owner is thinking of selling it (which we're all against, I'm thinking of starting a Save The Toll House protest group). At first he was working on his own – well, I do help a bit when I can – but for the last couple of weeks another boy has been helping and they reckon they'll be finished by the end of next week, which is great because it means they'll be all done just in time for Christmas.

I thought it might be a good idea if we had a surprise party on Friday 13th (nothing like tempting fate!) to celebrate the end of the decorating. And I wondered if you'd like to come. He's talked about you a lot, that's how I know about you. I sneaked your address from a letter I saw lying on his table. I hope you don't mind, but it was the only way of finding out where you live without him knowing.

It would be great if you could come, the best surprise of all. It would do him good after everything he's been through and working so hard, and anyway I'm dying to meet you . . .

100

Surprise Party

❖ 1 ❖

Maybe the trouble is thinking of days as clock time, regular mechanical measure, when, maybe, time isn't like that at all. We just like to pretend it is because then we feel in control of it. When probably there is nothing to control. What we're doing is confusing different kinds of words. You can measure length. You can't really measure time. How do you measure the past or the future? And the present doesn't have any length, being simply Now. If we try to measure 'now' we find it's always gone, has become part of the past. We shouldn't use measuring words about it, then we wouldn't get so confused about what Time is.

Besides, it seems to me that everything we know of in the universe, everything from clocks to supernovas, every*thing* is both a physical object *and* a shape of energy. Nothing exists, nothing happens without energy. Energy *is* things; things *are* energy. Life is energy. People are energy made flesh. Maybe Time is a form of energy as well?

Is that true? If it is, then it is also true that energy can be compressed into concentrated, powerful units (50 watt bulbs, 100 watt, 2000 watt: energy packaged as light). We know this. We experience it every day around us. So why not the same for human beings and for Time? Surely our lives – our lives as we live them during one day, and our lives as we live them during another day – are also packets of energy? And on some days we somehow concentrate more energy into the day and get more done in the same period of clock time than we did another day when our energy was on low wattage.

So time is not really like clockwork at all, but is a variable resulting from the interaction between energy and thought expressed as event. Energy + Thought = TimeEvent.

Which explains why sometimes we talk of *filling time* (meaning: being easy on ourselves by living our lives at low wattage). And of

101

making time (meaning: not that we make more of it in quantity, but that we make more of it in quality – living life with as high wattage as we can). And of there being *not enough time* to do all we want to do (meaning: our ambitions for our lives can't be satisfied and all our flooding energy can't be used up). And of *killing time* (meaning: we wilfully squander the present moment). And of *passing time*, and *wasting time*, and *saving time*.

When I was a baby my mother hung a plaque above my bed, a sliver of varnished wood with these words literally burned into it:

Think big and your deed will grow,
Think small and you'll fall behind,
Think that you can and you will,
It's all in your state of mind.

When I was fourteen I took the plaque down and secretly burned it because I thought it embarrassingly corny. I mean, who wants to bring friends to his room and have them see that kind of kiddy kitsch hanging over the bed? Anyway, it was asking for ribald jokes. But the trouble with clichés is that they stick. I haven't forgotten it because in its trite and twitchy way it is also true. Even time, and how much we can do in a set time, depends as much on our state of mind as it does on anything else. Because of my time at the toll bridge, and because of my time with Adam I know I want to be a user of time, not a filler of it, a maker of time not a killer of it, a compressor of energy not a so-whatter. Adam did not teach me this, but I learned it from being with him at the bridge.

But this part of the story is about a twenty-four-hour stretch into which we all crammed enough watts, gave each other enough surprises, and suffered enough shocks to last a lifetime.

Do we ever know our friends? Do we ever know ourselves?

❖ 2 ❖

Earlier that afternoon, Adam said, 'Don't half fancy a movie.'

'Go!' Tess said. 'Both of you. I'll guard the bridge. Go on! Don't dither! Shop on the way back. Go!'

A stratagem, of course. Betrayal. Returning that evening the house is sardined, pulsing.

'Surprise, surprise!'

Wild cheers.

'What the hell's going on?'

Shopping bag grabbed from my hand.

'Who are all these people?'

Replaced by slopping glass.

More wild cheers.

Tess, beside me, blows one of those referee's searing whistles.

'Listen, everybody,' she yells.

Hushings. Exaggerated party laughter.

'This is a surprise party for Jan, my friend.'

'Who certainly looks surprised.' (Isn't he one of the university cohort we saw that day with Adam at the Pike?)

Laughter.

'With a bigger surprise still to come,' Tess goes on.

'Ooo – naughty, naughty!'

Cheers. Obscene fingers and fists.

'Also, this is the first meeting of PATHS.'

'Hear, hear!'

'Which, for Jan's benefit, as he doesn't know yet, means Protest Against the Toll House Sale.'

'Bravo!'

'Encore!'

'He doesn't know yet because we've just decided it while he was out.'

'Right on!'

'Let's hear it for the toll house. Hip, hip . . .'

'Hooray.'

'Henry.'

Laughter.

'What we're going to do for a start is collect names on a petition to stop the sale.'

'Right on!'

'Where do I put my cross?'

'We'll decide other things later. Now, everybody enjoy yourselves.'

Someone – Adam – sets taped rock rolling. The sardines writhe.

The noise is blinding. Anger withers my mouth. I gulp from the drink. Tastes multicultural.

'What is this?'

'House warming. Come on, let your hair down.'

Tess makes me dance with her. Or what passes for dancing in a sardine tin. Mass squirming.

'Who are they all?' I have to shout, mouth to ear.

'Friends from school,' she replies, her lips tickling my lobes. 'A few from the village. One or two of the girls from Tesco's. Don't know the others. You know how it is. Word gets round.'

'Could've warned me.'

'Wouldn't have been a surprise then, would it, idiot!' The house throbs. If I go outside, will I see the river rippling in harmony, the bridge undulating in rhythm? My mind gives up. There's no competing with a noise that pulsates your teeth.

❖ 3 ❖

Before long Adam has cast himself as a one-man repertory theatre: MC, sergeant major, DJ, mein host, pack leader, party clown, games master. That is, he becomes one of those people who get a kick out of powertooling everybody else. Embryo dictator.

He insists we play some games.

Game One. The Balloon Burst, otherwise known as the Pelvic Bang.

The boy holds a blown-up balloon in front of his crotch. Or stuffs it up his shirt or sweater, as preferred. The girl has to burst the balloon by thrusting her pelvis at it, front on. Close encounters of the pudic kind. Which end in giggles and, on the occasions when the balloon goes off, in exaggerated shrieks. Some cheat by using finger nails or other penetrants.

I opt out, not needing to pretend needing a leak.

On my way back I'm groped at the bottom of the steps by a cruising figure dressed entirely in black.

'Sorry, not my line,' I mutter.

'Could give you a nice surprise. It is a surprise party after all, and you're the party boy.'

'Thanks for the offer.'

'Don't know what you're missing.'

'No, well, another time maybe.'

'Name the day. I do house calls.'

'Don't call me, I'll call you.'

'You've no heart.'

'Nothing against you or anything.'

'Forget it, chuck. Not my lucky night is all.'

He pecks me on the cheek, the rough male kiss of blankets, allows his hands to linger before saying, 'No hard feelings!' and fades away.

It's all happening. You can't say I lack for excitement or that I don't see life stuck out here in the middle of nowhere. Would I have had better luck on the grand tour?

Back inside, Adam is starting yet another game, the remaining participants behaving like nine-year-olds going on seven. Those who have dropped out are mostly draped around the edges of the floor engaged in whatever other party games have taken their fancy. Playing at experimental physiology being the popular choice.

Tess grabs my hand. 'Come on, you can partner me for this one.'

Game two. The Ping-pong Ball.

The boy stands. The girl kneels down in front of him, puts a table-tennis ball inside one of the boy's trouser legs and works it up with her fingers from the outside until she reaches the crotch over which she manoeuvres the ball and then lets it fall down the other trouser leg. The winner does it the fastest. Naturally, everybody goes as slow as she can.

Like mere pastime stories, this game creates a lot of excited anticipation at the beginning, has an extended middle with plenty of sexy high drama that climaxes in sometimes unexpected thrills, after which it ends with a quick denouement.

This evening there are predictable actions, reactions and dubious dialogue, especially during the crotch scenes.

Tess and I went third. She is busy crossing my crotch and making a meal of it to considerable encouragement and applause, coming at me from front and back at the same time, when Gill appears in the front row of the stalls, sober and ominous and travel-weary.

I don't see her straightaway because I have my eyes screwed shut. I am thinking of a butcher's slaughterhouse, as a matter of fact, in an effort to control my privates by taking my mind off what is happening to them. So Tess at last finishes with my crotch and the ping-pong ball is dribbling down my other leg when I open my eyes with relief only to find Gill glaring at me. Even then I don't react immediately. My first thought is that she is an hallucination brought on by the multicult punch while having my bat and balls played with by someone other than myself for the first time since Gill and I were last together months ago. Only when it dawns on me that she is not gazing at me with the sloe-eyed Mona Lisa smile her face usually assumed during such activities, do I accept that she really is there, touchable flesh, spillable blood, and distinctly unhappy.

❖ 4 ❖

Outside in the road, where I hustled Gill, Tess following as it dawns on her who this is, I said:

'What the hell are you doing here?'

'I was invited.'

'Invited?'

'Me,' Tess butted in, 'I invited her.'

'You? What for?'

'Seemed like a good idea at the time.'

'When?'

'What?'

'Didn't think,' Gill said, stunned, 'it would be such a big party.'

'Wasn't meant to be,' Tess said, 'just a bit of fun.'

'So I saw.' Gill looked at me then Tess then me again.

'Nothing like that,' Tess said.

'Could have fooled me.'

'Come on, you know what parties are like.'

'Look,' I said. 'What are you doing here? What are you two up to?'

'Us two up to!' Gill said. 'Don't you mean you two?'

'I told you,' Tess said, 'it isn't like that. Just a game.'

'You planned this just to humiliate me.'

'What the hell are you going on about?' I said.

'Shut up, you,' Tess said. 'This is between me and her.'

'I've never seen you like this.'

'I've never seen you like that.'

'Look, Gill –' Tess said.

Heavy metal started pumping out of the house.

'– I thought it would help him to see you –'

'Help me?'

'– I thought you wanted to see him.'

'How would you know what I want?'

'Your letters were –'

'You've read my letters?'

'Oh, *merde!*'

'You showed her my letters!'

'Look, piss off, will you, I didn't ask you to come here.'

'Thank you! Thank you very much! It's only me you're talking to – your girlfriend.' Looking at Tess. 'At least I thought I was!'

'Typical male,' Tess said.

'Eh –?'

'Yes,' Gill echoed, 'typical male. In the wrong so turn violent. At least you could say sorry.'

'Hang on a minute, I wasn't the one who started this.'

'All everybody else's fault, I suppose,' Gill said.

My head is exploding.

'If you'd answered Gill's letters –'

'Instead of ignoring them –'

'I tried.'

'Excuses.'

'Excuses.'

'Oh for Christ's sake! Get lost, will you! Both of you. Just leave me alone.'

'You said that before. And what do I find?' Gill shouted – the music is *very* loud by now. 'But all right, if that's the way you want it. Two can play that game.'

She turned and stalked into the house.

'Now you've done it!' Tess said. 'Couldn't you just have been nice to her, nothing strenuous, nothing too extreme, just ordinary everyday glad to see you stuff, I mean she is your bloody girlfriend after all . . . oh, Christ! . . . *Merde!*' and after uttering a few home truths in my direction she sloped off into the house.

I felt deeply furious and miserable and wanted to hit them both, hard. The old Adam. Or Cain, more accurately: mark of. Loud echoes of the old Glum enemy rumbled in my guts.

I couldn't believe all this was happening. Stared at the house. The FOR SALE sign crucified to the wall was defaced with luminous spray paint into PATHS FOR ALE. Heavy metal pulsed from the house. Sex-teased squeals and hyena laughter punctured the beat.

They'd completely taken it over, polluted it, the place where I was recovering, stripping myself down, remaking myself, had been invaded, desecrated, defiled, raped.

Suddenly I hated them.

Yes, Gill, Adam, Tess as well.

All of them.

Paradigm of humanity.

I hated their noise,

their occupation of my space,

hated their sprawl and splurge and clutter and mess.

The splat of their lives.

107

Hated most of all the pretended individuality of their slavish conformity.

They were not me, nothing I wanted or wanted to be, everything I did not want. Defined by negatives. There was no way I was going back inside while any of them were still there. Trespassers. But there was no way I could get shot of them either, not in the state they were in by now. Worse still, the state I was in myself.

I stood there trembling with impotent rage.

What to do?

Where to go?

Nothing.

Nowhere.

Not with people.

To hell with people.

Nowhere where they'd find me.

I crossed the road and leaned on the bridge and glared downstream, my mind a match for the pummelling noise behind me and the surging swirl beneath my feet.

Just then a thin moon splintered from a bank of clouds, its mist-smeared light revealing the shrouded shape of a wintering cabin cruiser snugly tethered to the bank a couple of fields away downstream.

Because he wasn't there, Jan doesn't know what happened next so I'll tell it, but I'd better say at the start that I'm not a writer, not like Jan is, he really loves it, anyone would have to, to work all day then come home and write most of the evenings, not to mention weekends. I have to prise him from his room if I want him to go out, and God knows when he gets to bed most nights. I'm bad enough, being addicted to watching videos in bed, I can still be at it, eyes glued at two in the morning, but if I go to the bathroom to try and break the spell he's still there scribbling away. I think he's only ever really truly happy when he's writing, it's the only time when he's in focus – when he's doing what he says he lives for.

I envy him, because there's nothing that's like that for me. Well, sex of course, but that's different, that's because I'm human, it's nothing extra, nothing special. What makes me happiest, as a matter of fact, is just life. I mean eating and sleeping and having sex and lying in the sun and playing tennis, and reading a really gripping book curled up on my bed, and being with friends, and wearing just the right clothes, and looking, just looking, at other people doing ordinary things, 'watching the passing' my grandmother used to call it. I completely lack ambition, I suppose, I'm just happy to be here and to enjoy what comes along.

Some of my friends ask why I let Jan stay with me, he can't be much fun they say, but they don't see the best of him because he's so private. Writing Adam's story has something to do with his hiddenness. I think it's a story about himself, maybe a declaration. I'm not sure. But what I am sure of is that he needs me to be here, or rather he needs to be here with me. Not that I do much for him. I don't do his laundry, for instance, and he feeds himself (and me as well) most of the time, and being an inveterate tidier he tends to do most of the house cleaning. In fact, he doesn't make any demands, I wish he would sometimes because it's nice to be asked to do things for a friend, but he never does, I have to suss out what he wants and then offer or just get on and do it. I've talked to him about it, of course, we talk about *everything*, which is another reason why I like him so much (love him, I suppose), and he goes on about imposing on people, hating to feel that someone is doing something for him only because they have to, or worse, because they've been manipulated into doing it, emotionally blackmailed.

[– Aren't you supposed to be telling what happened after I left the party?
　– I'm going to, be quiet, please.
　– And you're the one who says she doesn't like writing!
　– It's just the way it's coming out.
　– You never could tell a story.
　– Rubbish, there's more than one way to tell a story.]

The first day I saw him, standing in the toll-house living room, he looked like the ghost of a ghost. Bony-thin to the point of wispy, blenched, miserable, those big, gripping, hard, grey-green eyes red-rimmed and bleary and staring at me with a mixture of fright and defiance. So first it was the eyes that got me and then later, as he picked through the stuff I'd brought and the eyes were busy elsewhere, it was the hands – long-fingered, thin-boned, talking hands. (I have a thing about hands, I love them, I think they're one of the most beautiful parts of the body, but I can't stand people with ugly hands, especially short stubby fingers and fat palms.)

I thought he was just weary after a bad night and nervous in a new place. But I soon realized he was ill. I don't think he remembers how bad he was. He'd go for a whole day without eating and say he wasn't hungry. Then in the middle of the night he'd scoff all he could find and next day he'd sit around staring at the blank walls refusing to say anything.

He'd also do weird things like spend ages standing on the bridge staring down at the river. I even found him there one day in the rain soaked to the skin. There was a kind of dottiness about his behaviour that sometimes made me want to shake him hard and tell him to snap out of it. Mum said he was like somebody grieving, but who for or what for?

One way and another, what with Dad keeping him steadily busy and Mum coddling him a bit and me being with him, after a month or so he was sleeping and eating properly, and looked much better, less wispy, more *there*. And he always read a lot, even when The Glums came over him again, crushing him down, which happened every few days. He could be awful then, saying bitter destructive things if you made him talk to try and lift him out of The Pit. I soon learned not to try and cheer him up but just to sit with him, letting him read or stare into space. Being there was all the help he needed, I think, but he never said so, though afterwards, when he was properly recovered, he did.

I suppose that's when our friendship really began, which has always seemed kind of odd to me – that a friendship should begin with the bad times and not with the good ones. While he sat there suffering, it was then we felt we recognized each other, knew each other, without explaining or talking about it, and knew that whatever happened we would always be a pair. Complementary. Life companions. Regardless of who else in the future we loved or lived with or kept as friends. We're still like that, and though it always looks to other people as if it's Jan who needs me, I need him too, only what he does for me doesn't show so much. He sustains me in the way I need just as much as I sustain him in the way he needs, and we both know it, so what does it matter what other people think?

By the time Adam turned up Jan was much better. The wraithiness had vanished, he'd filled out nicely, his skin was clear, his eyes not crazed any more. His hands, roughened from the work he'd done, were even more beautiful. He'd persuaded me to chop his hair very short because he said it would be easier to keep right that way, and though it was ragged it suited him, adding a slightly dishevelled severity to his lean looks. Mum said he reminded her of a novice monk, and it is true, he is a bit monkish. And innocent unworldly too – he doesn't quite understand what makes the world go round, though he likes to think he does.

That business with the estate agent, for instance. What got up his nose as much as anything is that B-and-G was so obviously a turd, and what's worse a not very clever turd, and Jan can't understand why people were taken in by him. Jan can't see that people admire the B-and-Gs because the B-and-Gs of the world are clever in a way Jan isn't – they're clever with cunning and self-confidence and at knowing how to manipulate people's whims and fancies. They appeal to people's weaknesses. They know that most people are impressed by flash cars and designer clothes and exotic holidays and the extravagant signs of money and power.

Neither does he understand the way sex works, doesn't see that the B-and-Gs play that game too. Most people's brains aren't in their heads, they're in their crotches. So the B-and-Gs aren't oddities, they're typical. Jan is the oddity, that's the fact, and he gets upset and angry because he doesn't want the world to be the way it is and can't understand that most people don't mind, they actually like it the way it is. People revel in their weaknesses, it seems to me, and admire those who become successful by exploiting weaknesses. Their own and other people's.

Jan wants people to live up to something better than they are. Mostly, they never will so he's bound to suffer for the rest of his life. He's like someone who lacks a protective layer of skin. Every brush against the world hurts. Life will never be what he wants it to be, he'll never quite understand why, other people will always think him a little odd, so he'll never quite be accepted. And, if you want to know, I think his depressions started when this began to dawn on him. Which is why, in my opinion, he came to the toll bridge, to be on his own while he sorted it out. And he was running away too, of course, which was obvious to everybody except himself.

Jan ran to the toll bridge and Adam ran into him there. Two runaways colliding, and the story gets more complicated to tell now because I come into it, like a third particle colliding with the other two.

Yes, it's true, I did have a thing about Adam. From first sight I fancied him. His earthiness, his utterly relaxed, unbothered attitude to life. He wasn't very tall but was supple and beautifully built. I mean, he just oozed sex. But from the very first sight of him I felt that inside him there was a vulnerable, almost frightened boy. Don't know how I knew this. Intuition, I suppose. And perhaps something in his eyes. Didn't think about it. But the mix was irresistible.

Something else made the situation even more sensational, something Jan didn't know because he couldn't see it, being part of it. I mean the two of them together.

Like sea against cliffs, hills against sky, each heightened the quality of the other. Emphasized the other's being and beauty. And each was beautiful, I don't know how to describe it, when you see it you know it, and it has as much to do with personality as it has to do with body.

Anyhow, I admit I let myself be carried away. There I was with these two males, one who made me think and talk like I'd never

112

thought and talked before, and one who I fancied like crazy. And both of them needed me. How could I resist? Why should I? That day Jan was sick from painter's colic arrived like a gift and I grabbed it.

Adam was playful and full of jokes and bursting with energy. I was lusty and insatiable and I didn't care. I never now smell new paint in a room without remembering that day, feeling it in my skin, in my flesh, in my nerves and on my tongue again, and the rough texture of the blanket spread on the bare boards of the floor and the tang of woodsmoke in my nose and the tingle of heat from the fire as we lay beside it and the slip of sweat between us and its salt taste and the sound of the river outside and our blood surging inside as though both might engulf us at any moment and sweep us away, and best and most remembered, the feel and touch of his hands and his kissing and biting and the excruciating pleasure of it.

And then the bittersweet after-taste of melancholy, with Adam beside me dead to the world though I longed for him to hold me and give me his eyes and his mind as he had given me his body and not to drift away and drown in sleep.

In a while I covered him with a blanket and stole away home along the river bank through the empty dark, glad to be alone, glad to be myself in the dank winter night.

But I learned something from what happened later: Never to be taken but ever give. Never to be one but ever two. Never to be possessed by another but ever possess myself.

Jan didn't tell me till long afterwards about Dad seeing us. Thank God for that. Dad's never mentioned it but I realize now that it was about then that his attitude to me changed. For one thing, he became less physically affectionate. Before, he'd always been a hugger, liked to sit with his arm around me while watching telly. After, he became more distant, wasn't so spontaneous in showing his feelings. At the time I put it down to the strain he was under at work, but the real cause must have been seeing me with Adam that night.

The next day was the surprise party and that can't have helped either. Dad has always said I have a wicked streak. 'My little devil,' he used to call me when I was small. When I got older, in my teens and not so cute any more, it irritated him, but by then it was too late, the mould had set. Parents should be careful which traits they coddle in their children. Cute can easily turn into crass. No one can ever escape all her-history. (A Jan-type joke and a truth he finds it hard to live with.)

Not that having a surprise party and inviting Gill was only devilment. I really did think Jan needed to see her if he was to make up his mind about her. There were all sorts of things that made me think this.

For example, there were a lot more letters from her than he's mentioned. For a few weeks one came every day. At the beginning he read them all. But they upset him. He's said nothing about that. I got to know about it because one day after he'd been at the bridge about three weeks I arrived on foot after my bike had conked out, so he didn't hear me coming. I saw him through the living-room window, sitting at the table with a letter in his hands, tears streaming down his face. I rushed in of course and comforted him and eventually got out of him that the letters kept him feeling tied to everything he was trying to cut free of – his parents, his home, the school, the town. And what he felt were the demands Gill made – her wanting him so much, her clinging to him, which he said felt like being suffocated.

Anyhow, after that he stopped reading the letters. Now and then he'd try one just to see if he felt any different about them, but he never did. Instead he pinned them, mostly unopened, to the back of the living-room door where they accumulated, always with the name and address right way up, Gill's neat round schoolgirlish handwriting repeating Jan's name and address again and again as if for a school punishment. Then one day I decided the joke had gone far enough and started taking them down. Jan flew into a rage, yelling at me to stop meddling and treating him like a kid, I wasn't his mother, etc. etc. Very vicious and emotionally violent.

After that we didn't speak for two days.

But I've side-tracked. Back to the day of the party.

That morning I felt terrible. As soon as I woke it came over me what I'd done. For the rest of the day during school I reassessed my values in life, as only the self-condemned know how. I didn't exactly pray that if God didn't strike me down with everything from herpes to Aids I'd never do anything so foolish again, but nearly. Then, after school there was shopping for the party and the business of getting Jan out of the house and making everything ready, which took my mind off my worries. In fact, typical me, I went to the other extreme and over-compensated by throwing myself body and soul into the party.

Which party, I admit, went over the top, as usual once word

114

gets round, especially in an area like ours with a university in range. By the time Gill turned up the house resembled a scene in Caligula's palace during one of his more ingenious periods.

At any rate, Gill flipped into a kind of catatonic shock. After all those weeks of writing all those letters and not getting a kind word never mind a letter in return, and all the time being patient and understanding and making allowances, she arrives to find him apparently having his balls massaged by a black-haired hussy in the middle of a crowd of zonked spectators lolling about in various states of *déshabillé* and at various stages preparatory to coition, if not already at it.

[– Laying it on a bit, aren't you?
 – Enjoying it.
 – Wasn't quite that colourful, though, was it?
 – Moderately hectic. Anyway, that's how it's come out, so however it was *then*, that's how it is *now*.
 – So much for history.
 – History is only accepted fiction.
 – Hey-up! That's not you!
 – You mean, you don't think I'm clever enough.
 – Come on, be honest.
 – Caught you out for once! Read it somewhere. Can't remember.
 – So much for memory.
 – While memory holds a seat
   In this distracted globe, remember thee!
   Yea, from the table of my memory
   I'll wipe away all trivial fond records.
 – Oo, climb every mountain, chuck!]

The row outside the house sets my nerves jangling and jogs my worries and brings me back to my senses. This isn't my day, I think, wishing I'd never suggested the wretched party in the first place. Blame Jan, I tell myself, it's his fault for dithering. (When in doubt, transfer the guilt.)

I follow Gill inside after exchanging a few more ill-chosen words with Jan. But can't find her. The party has reached the slow-(e)motion phase already. Heaven knows what's been going the rounds. Adam isn't there either.

I begin not to care, nudge myself a space on the living-room floor near the fire beside a friend from school who is sitting alone staring at the glowing embers (no one has enough wits left to put a fresh log on) while morosely brooding. She immediately starts to tell me about the loss of her boyfriend and bursts into tears and says she'd better slope off home because she doesn't want people seeing her like this, which she does, leaving *moi* on my *sola* again, not a happy girl, my turn to stare regretfully at the embers.

What happened next happened very quickly and at the time was very confused, anyway confusing.

After the row outside Gill had stomped back into the house, intending to grab her bag which she had dropped on the floor of the living room, and set off for home, or anywhere – she just wanted to get away. But her bag wasn't there (somebody had shoved it into a corner). That's when she saw her letters pinned up on the living-room door, and she flipped.

She ran out through the back door, where the outside light showed her the steps down to the lawn. Dashing down them, she slipped on their frosty surface and grazed her knee (she didn't even feel it at the time, we found out later). She then blundered onto the path that led her along the river bank and under the bridge.

There she stopped, breathless from distress and sensing she had come the wrong way and should go back. But she didn't want to go anywhere near the house again in case she met Jan or me. 'I felt I'd be sick if I did,' she told me later, 'I was so weary and angry at what had happened.'

So she paused while she caught her breath and tried to decide what to do. But after a while, as she stood there in the dank cold with the arch of the bridge curving low over her head like the roof of a dungeon, and echoing the full-spated river swirling at her feet 'as if,' she said, 'it wanted to sweep me away,' she felt so abandoned, humiliated, and churned up with rage that she burst into tears. 'How could they!' she kept spluttering. 'How *dare* they!' No one had ever treated her like that before. 'It was the first time I'd ever really felt betrayed.'

By this time she was in such a state that she wasn't aware of anyone approaching until she heard a male voice right behind her asking, 'Are you Gill?', which so startled her that she screamed, swung round, slipped on the muddy path, and fell, slithering into the river up to her waist before she was grabbed and lifted upright, instinctively grasping at her rescuer, who clung onto her, holding her tightly against him.

Relief turned to panic. She didn't know who this man was. Now she was trapped in his arms. He kept saying, 'It's OK, it's all right, it's only me, Adam, it's OK.' But she didn't know any Adam and it wasn't OK. She struggled against him, screaming loudly again. 'It's all right,' Adam shouted as she struggled and kicked.

'I'd always wondered what I'd do,' Gill said later, 'if someone tried to attack me, you know how you do, but when it starts happening, you just panic so much, you can't think, you just don't want to get hurt and you're scared of doing anything that might make him more violent.'

Her screams must have panicked Adam. At any rate, Gill said, he suddenly let go of one of her arms to squash a hand over her mouth while shouting, 'Shut it, will you! Shut it!' And that, she said, is when anger took over from everything else. She had an arm free so she grabbed him by the hair and yanked his head back as hard as she could. At the same time, bracing herself against the wall, she brought her right knee up into his groin as hard as she could.

The result was that Adam let go and did a kind of whiplash – back and then forward – as the pain in his groin doubled him up. Gill dodged to one side. Adam's head smashed into the wall and he fell to the ground, where he lay curled up, squirming and moaning, with his hands clasping his crotch.

Gill didn't stay to watch after that but fled back towards the house, desperate for help. She and I collided with each other at the top of the back steps.

'God, what's happened?' I said, taking her inside.

'A man attacked me,' she managed to get out. 'A man. Under the bridge. It was awful.'

She started shaking so violently she could hardly speak at all. The others crowded round, asking questions.

'Look, shut up,' I said to them. 'She needs some calm.'

'Shouldn't we see if he's still there?' someone said.

'Some of the boys should go.'

'Get the police,' someone said.

'God, no – the police in here! Have some sense!'

Gill was completely distraught.

'I'll make her a hot drink,' someone said.

*

The search party returned, unable to find anyone. They'd looked under the bridge, along the river path, around the house, on the bridge itself, and had even made a sortie to the other side just in case. But no one, except for people deserting the party double-quick. Jan wasn't anywhere to be found, either. Nor Adam. Several of my friends offered to stay in case the guy was a psycho and might try again, but I'd had enough of everything to be honest, and just wanted to be on my own and sort things out with Gill and Jan (who I thought was probably sulking nearby and would come back once everybody had gone).

So I made people clear off and went round picking up the mess while Gill huddled by the fire looking shattered. Jan's little alarm clock said twelve forty-five. Less than an hour since Gill's arrival! I'd thought it must be ages later.

When I'd done as much clearing up as I could bear, I sat with Gill by the fire. I'd been putting off this moment.

We stared at each other, strangers and not strangers, having to make a fresh start. I knew what had to be done but being me it took a big struggle inside myself before I could force myself to say, 'Sorry – sorry, sorry, sorry – this is all my fault.'

Gill looked away and shrugged.

There was a long silence before she said, 'I wish I knew what was going on.'

She was near to tears again.

'Look,' I said. 'Let's start at the beginning – what else have we got to do?' And I tried to tell her what had happened since Jan arrived at the bridge. She hardly interrupted at all, just a question here and there, until Adam came into the story, when, for the first time, she suddenly startled.

'Adam?!' she said.

'The boy who's helping Jan. I mentioned him in my letter.'

'Not his name. You didn't mention his name.'

'I didn't? Thought I had. Why, though? What's the matter?'

'The man who attacked me. I remember now. He said his name was Adam. "It's only me," he said, "Adam – it's OK".'

I stared at her. 'Christ! – are you sure?'

'Certain. I'd forgotten till you said his name.' She shivered. 'It was so awful,' she added bleakly, no tears, just cold fear.

'But it couldn't have been – Just a bit taller than me. Well built. Black hair –'

'I couldn't see! How could I see, it was so dark and we were under the bridge, and I was so upset and so scared –'

'Sorry, yes, sorry, 'course, wasn't thinking –'

Which wasn't true at all, just one of those things we say at times like that. I was thinking hard. I was thinking that if it were Adam, where was he now? Why hadn't he come back? Or was it obvious why he hadn't? If he'd been trying to help, and Gill had misunderstood, not knowing him when he thought she did, and he'd hurt his head and had his goolies crushed, wouldn't the natural thing be to come back inside and get help? Unless he hadn't been trying to help at all. But I didn't want to think about that. The night before came flooding back, exactly the night before: twenty-four hours ago in front of this same fire on this same floor in this same house with someone who might be – That didn't bear thinking about either.

Perhaps there'd been another Adam at the party? But if there were and he was the attacker, why would he say 'it's only me'? Only one Adam would have said that – our Adam. *Our* Adam! Dear God!

And if it were 'our' Adam and he had attacked Gill, what did that mean about 'our' Adam? And might he even be a psycho and be hiding somewhere nearby, waiting his chance to come back to try again – I started to feel scared myself.

Where the hell was Jan? Why didn't he come back?

It was nearly one thirty. Mum and Dad knew we were having a party – though they didn't know it was the kind it had turned into or Dad would have been down sharpish and put a stop to it. They'd have gone to bed, but I knew Dad would be lying awake, waiting for me. And I desperately wanted to go home now. Wanted to feel safe and in my own room and out of all this mess. But I couldn't leave Gill on her own. Apart from the toll-bridge psycho, there was the prospect of her having to face her beloved again: she wouldn't want to do that on her own. And as I'd brought all this about, I did feel it was my fault, my responsibility, and I couldn't just leave her to it.

The only thing I could think of was to get Gill and myself out of there. In the morning things might look different. So I said,

'Look, Gill, we can't stay here all night. I mean, we're both knocked out, and I doubt if you'd feel comfortable trying to sleep here. I've a motorbike. D'you think you could stand to ride pillion, just for ten minutes? I could take you home. My parents won't mind, they're OK, they're used to me having friends overnight.

We could get some sleep and think about what to do in the morning.'

We looked each other straight in the eyes for a moment, neither of us needing to say anything more. And then the natural thing seemed to be to take her hands in mine. She gripped me tight, and nodded, and we hugged each other and had to swallow the tears.

Gill's jeans were still damp, but she pulled them on. I found her bag and tamped the fire down, switched off all but one of the lights, and we left, locking the door behind us and hiding the key in the usual place so Jan could get in, and drove off, me hoping there were no late-night bobbies cruising round the village on the hunt for teenage L-plate delinquents. L for life as well as driving, I thought.

Coming To

❖ 1 ❖

Inside, the boat was perishing cold. Trimmed for winter lay-up, no food, very little of anything pinchable left behind and what there was stowed away and locked. Had to force the cabin door. Guiltily. But desperation overrides everyday honesty. There was a Gaz lamp, found when feeling my way round the cabin in the glim of moonlight filtering through the little head-high windows. Matches in a drawer by the galley stove. I used the lamp for long enough to find a blanket in an unlocked locker under one of the bunks and lie down fully clothed, then doused it, fearing detection or attracting a curious boozer from the bridge. Party noises drifted to me, brittle on the frosty air, among them at one moment not long after I'd lain down a girl's screams that didn't sound like party pretence or genuine delight, but I paid no attention, not wanting to know.

Everything a violation. The Glums threatened.

Maybe because of the drink, maybe because of the colic, or of Peeping Tom the night before, or of having had so little to eat all day, or the combination of cold damp in the cabin and warm damp in the wrap of the blanket – whatever it was, and against the odds, I somehow contrived to fall asleep. For how long I couldn't tell when I was woken by the boat lurching as someone clambered aboard. Adrenalin pumped. I sat up and listened.

Hands fumbled with the fasteners that secured the cockpit awning.

I called out, 'Who is it?'

The fumbling stopped.

Silence.

'Hello?'

Nothing.

I pressed my face to a window but, the moon now hidden again, could see nothing except the darker darkness of the river bank. But as

121

I peered into the dark an object suddenly fell onto the narrow walkway of deck that ran at window level immediately outside. It took a moment for me to realize that the object was a human head. And only after I'd scrambled off the bunk and lit the lamp and held it close to the window did I see that it was covered in blood, which was oozing from a gash in the forehead, that the eyes were closed with the sucked-in dead look of the unconscious, and that the head was Adam's.

What is it about the sight of unconsciousness that makes you desperate? Is it because unconsciousness is halfway to death, and your natural impulse is to save the victim from going all the way? Or maybe that instinct I so much hate in humanity – the instinct to try and keep everybody else in the same state as you're in yourself, even when you know your own state is dangerous or hasn't much to recommend it – as when druggies tice others to shoot up, just to take an obvious example. Deadly conformity, dire conservatism. I'm what's called alive, so you must stay alive as well, even if your life is rotten and worse is likely to beset you, because life is always believed to be better than any kind of death (though how does anyone know, as no one has come back to tell us what it's like?). So taking your own life goes by offensive names – suicide, self-slaughter, sin, crime, self-destruction – and people are pitied who attempt it, as are those who by accident are associated with anyone who succeeds in doing it. What fools these mortals be.

And being no different my mortal self, I'd unlatched the window before I'd thought about it, and was reaching a hand through to touch Adam's face, as if by laying on my hand I would bring him back to consciousness and know he was really there, unquestionably alive.

He groaned at my touch, which was reassuring.

'Adam,' I cried, 'Adam – what's happened? Adam? Adam! Are you OK? Are you all right?'

He groaned again, stirred, turning his face away.

A new imperative possessed me at once. To get him inside, out of the cold.

'Wait! Don't move! I'm coming.'

Blood on my hand. And then standing at his feet on the side deck, holding the lamp over him. How difficult to lift him from that awkward space and down into the cabin. Help from the house? No lights. No noise. What time? Two thirty by my wristwatch. Could it be over already, an all-night glug like that? But anyway, there and back – He needed help now. Freezing. Blood.

122

He stirred again, trying to struggle to his feet, all his athletic animal ease gone. Awkward stiff angles, yet floppy, a puppet with its strings cut. He wouldn't make it. Might tumble overboard. He slumped to the deck again. I scrambled across the cabin roof to the side deck at his head, stood the lamp on the roof so as to free both my hands, and, taking him by the shoulders, lifted him into a sitting position, his head lolling against my shoulder, his cheek pressing against my cheek, the oily wetness of cold blood lubricating our skins.

❖ 2 ❖

Why am I doing this? I asked myself again and again. Only because I knew him? What if he were a stranger, would I have left him to it? Who could, except some kind of psycho? Another of those human instincts? The law of the irrational. I hate doing something I haven't thought out and decided for myself I want to do. But how often is it truly by thought that we come to do things? I remembered the moment of *déjà-vu* when Adam first came to me. The assurance of the inevitable.

Whatever, there I was stuck with him. Again. There were also moments in the next ten minutes, which is what it took to manhandle him into the cabin and onto a bunk, and retrieve the lamp so that I could see what to do next, that I felt like a one-man Laurel and Hardy (a Laurelandhardy) in the scene where they try to deliver a piano up a long flight of steps. And remembering that saved me from losing heart or even my temper; only it also reduced me to laughter at the thought of how bizarre was my present predicament – another fine mess you've gotten us into – that I had to sit for a while till I recovered myself. I think I was near hysterical from exhaustion after the last forty-eight hours.

When I finally got Adam inside and could give him a close inspection I saw just how bad he was. His skin was putty-coloured and clammy, as if he were sweating chilled water. His breathing was shallow and quick. I tried his pulse, because people always seemed to do that when dealing with sickness; it seemed weak and fast, not a steady confident throb but more like a racing echo of a pulse. The gash in his forehead was neither long nor deep but blood oozed from it in alarming quantity quite out of proportion to its size, and was smudged all over his face so that he looked as if he'd been badly battered. Of course he was covered in muck. And he smelt awful. He'd vomited onto his clothes which were smeared with a rancid porridge of mud and blood and sweat and puke that filled the air in the confined space of the cabin with such a sour stench that I gagged and had to retreat outside till I could catch my breath and prepare myself for the onslaught again.

This was one of the times when I wondered why I was doing what I was doing. And this time, I then thought, I'm not going to be defeated, it's only a putrid pong, after all, not a case of chemical warfare.

Back inside, I watched him closely for a few minutes, trying to assess the state he was in. He seemed to be drifting somewhere between unconscious and semi-conscious – groaning, moving a little but erratically, and not much aware of what was happening, as far as I could tell. When he wasn't trying to move, his body was a floppy dead weight. I said his name into his ear two or three times but got no reaction.

I guessed that somehow or other he'd taken a bang on the head and was suffering from concussion, not that I knew what concussion actually meant, only that anybody suffering from it had to rest and take it easy for a while. I knew from times when I'd banged my own head that it could make me feel sick, so I supposed a very bad knock might actually make you vomit. Also, Adam had been drinking the multicult punch pretty freely so that wouldn't have helped matters either. Maybe he was suffering from a hangover as much as from anything else. But what if he was really ill from something I didn't know about, like a heart attack or . . . or what? That was the problem. If I didn't know about it, I wouldn't recognize it! I suddenly felt utterly ignorant about everything to do with the body. Why didn't I know more, why hadn't anybody told me?

What I knew for sure was that I couldn't leave him lying there in that filthy condition. Somehow I had to clean him up and make him more comfortable. But how? There was no water on board so it would have to be river water. Somewhere, though, there ought to be a First Aid kit; at least that might provide a bandage and some sort of antiseptic for his wound.

Finding a First Aid box in a locker by the cabin door raised my spirits no end. And in a locker by the transom was a plastic bucket. So I opened the First Aid kit and put it on the table in the cabin, and then half-filled the bucket.

At which point, ready to start, it suddenly came over me in a wave of weakening fastidiousness that I'd never cleaned up anybody before. I didn't at all relish the idea of messing with another person's gunged-up body.

I stared at Adam, seeing him in a different light. Not as 'Adam', but as a physical being made up of legs and feet and arms and various parts – fingers, toes – and organs with holes in them, and private nooks and crannies I'd never even seen before, let alone handled and washed and dried and closely inspected.

I began to shake and for a moment wondered if after all the best thing wouldn't be to fetch help. If there was no one in a fit state at the house, then I could run to the phone box in the village and call an ambulance. How long would that take? Half an hour? An hour? Would he be safe alone for that long? What if he came to enough to get up, and then stumbled into the river? And if I called an ambulance, think of the fuss there'd be afterwards. The hospital would want to know how he got into such a mess. The police. Bob Norris. Questions about the party. Trouble for Tess. Mayhem for me. I was supposed to be in charge. They'd hold me responsible, dammit! Maybe if I cleaned him up and brought him round, I could find out what had happened and if he really was in a bad way I could do something about getting him to hospital then.

Nothing else for it, whether I liked it or not, but to swallow my revulsion and clean him up and tend his wound as best I could. So where to start? With his face and head and the wound? Staunch the flow of blood? The First Aid kit included a packet of cotton wool. With a wad dipped in water I dabbed at the outer edges of his face, gingerly at first but with growing what-the-hell, I'll-never-finish-it-like-this confidence, wiping away the blood and muck. The First Aid kit also included a small bottle of antiseptic. I used some of that on a wad of cotton wool to clean round the edge of the cut, which really was quite small in fact. Then, with wincing delicacy, as if it might hurt me too, gently sponged the wound itself, at which Adam did stir and groan and flinch and try to push my hand away so at least I knew he was feeling something.

The antiseptic had the added advantage of scenting the air with something that smelt clean and healthy. But by then I'd grown used to the stink and was feeling quite proud of myself. I'd have fainted just at the thought of doing this only a few days before.

What next? Bind the wound. I readied the bandage, made a pad of cotton wool which I placed over the cut, then wrapped the bandage round his head a few times till there seemed to be enough to keep the dressing in place. To do that I had to keep lifting Adam's head. How heavy an unconscious head is, like a leaden stone! Alas, poor Yorick!

125

Heads I win, tails you lose. With his head tucked underneath his arm he walked the bloody tower. If you can keep your head when all about you are losing theirs and blaming it on you. Lay your sleeping head, my love, human on my faithless arm.

What stupid things come into your mind at such times. Yet not stupid, if you think about it. Pertinent and true in odd unthought ways. Is anything that comes into your mind ever arbitrary, ever meaningless?

That done, I was going to clean up his hands but realized he'd only mucky them again every time he touched his clothes, and besides, they would carry the muck to his face. Take off at least his outer clothing.

I sat him up and managed by a combination of rolling it up from the waist and easing it over his head to slip his putrid pullover off. My pullover, in fact – the best blue one he took with him when he first disappeared and he'd used ever since so that now it was stretched and sloppy which at least made it easier to get off. Next his boots. Then his pungent jeans. Leaving him in grubby white T-shirt and none too attractive blue Y-fronts. My T-shirt, my Y-fronts.

Covered with the only blanket, that was the best I could do. After which, the confined space looking a mess, my conditioned reflexes took over and I tidied up. The bundle of clothing chucked into a corner of the cockpit. The bucket emptied and stowed away. The First Aid box ready on the table in case of need. The wads of soiled cotton wool stuffed into the empty waste bin under the galley stove. I'd clean up properly when daylight came.

What now? Nothing, except watch and wait.

Very soon Adam seemed no longer to be drifting between unconscious and semi-conscious but to be sleeping. He was more 'there' and also, strangely, more relaxed. Before, he'd been floppy but somehow struggling inside himself; now he wasn't floppy any more but together and at ease. His breathing was better, his skin less waxy, less pale and clammy. I tried his pulse: the beat was stronger and steady. I don't think I'd realized before that relaxation is a form of action, of *being*; that when you're relaxing you're *doing something* just as much as when you're walking or eating or reading or running the marathon. It's a particular use of energy.

❖ 3 ❖

Adam was also pleasantly warm under the blanket, which is more

126

than I could say for myself. The exertion of getting him into the cabin and tending him had kept me warm – in fact I'd been so busy that I hadn't been aware of the cold. Now that he was settled and all I had to do was sit there and keep watch, I quickly cooled till I was shivering and had time to notice how I felt. Which was bone weary and miserable. The muscles in my arms and legs didn't just feel weak, to say which implies they still had some strength, but were in an anti-energy crisis. I was sure that if I stood up my legs would flobble under me like a couple of sausage balloons losing air. And if there'd been anything to drink, which I dearly craved, I couldn't have picked up the glass because my arms would have lolloped around as they do when you've lain on them too long.

Sleep was also something I longed for but couldn't achieve. Sitting up, I'd nod off and startle awake again at once. Lying down, the bitter cold seemed worse and woke me up. And so sitting up and lying down by turns a dreary hour passed.

I didn't get far, wondering what to do next, either. The only thought that occupied my mind with any tenacity was a dreary sequence of variations on the theme of unfairness. Which went something like this:

How in hell has all this happened to me? Just because I've been fool enough to give houseroom to a down-and-out would-be squatter, a half-drowned burglar with a big cock and the smile of a dog on heat? Just because of an accident, a quirk, a happenstance – unplanned, unintended, unwanted, unwilled, unprovoked (after all, I'd only been minding my own business stuck out in the middle of nowhere), uninvited, unannounced, undeserved, unforeseen, unforetold, unforgivable, unimagined, unfair.

Unfair, that's what it is, unfair, unfair, unfair.

Et cetera. On and on.

Unfair is such a playground word. The kids' game complaint. The blub of the impotent. The rail of the naïve against the wily. The howl of the baby-innocent against the street-wise. The battle cry of those who desire that no one in the world shall be better off than they are themselves. The pule of the weak benighted temporary deluded mistaken human race against the unthinkable unplumbed unmoved eternal infinity of the vast unregarding forever. What fools these mortals be.

I sat there, lay there, huddled against the frosted night, and whinged.

I'd come to this place, this wilderness, to escape imposition, to strip myself down in order to gain control of myself and build myself up in my own image, and what had happened? Taken over and buggered up, sod it!

Oh, lusty satisfaction of the sexual curse!
    Curse of the inarticulate.
    Sentence of Cain on the able.
    Rape of the word.
    The body's stiff big finger erected against the mind.

❖ 4 ❖

The Gaz lamp stuttered; fuel running out and no spare can. I took a close look at Adam before the light died. Sound asleep, lying on his back, one bare arm curled loosely round his head, a patch of dried blood staining the bandage that circled his brow. The failing light softened the features of his face, deepened the blackness of his dishevelled hair, lent the patina of stone to the folds of grey blanket that cloaked his body like a shroud – disturbing image of a sculpted memorial to a fallen soldier. Not one of those hero-lies, no no, but a boy cut down before the truth of life had woken him from the sleep of innocence.

Soon the cabin would be as dark as the grave. Already it was cold enough for a tomb and I cold enough to be a ghost. Certainly, I felt like one, standing over Adam, as if waiting to welcome him to the afterlife, a prince of death beside a sleeping beauty.

Smiling to myself at that thought, I bent down and kissed him lightly on the cheek. But he flinched at the touch of my chilly lips, shifted his head away, caught at his breath, drew his exposed arm under the blanket, turned onto his side, and slipped into deep quiet slumber again.

For sure, being no prince of any kind I lacked the magic touch.

At that moment, as if on cue, the light went out with a final flare and an expiring hiss.

❖ 5 ❖

Sailors say the dogwatch is the worst. Four till six in the morning. Sitting in the deep before-dawn dark with only my own thoughts for company, this dogwatch was the hardest time of my time at the

128

bridge. A time of reckoning. Of recognition. A slithery time of fractured memories bobbing up from buried passages of my life, and only intuition for guide – the ancient way of knowledge that bridges old Adam to new.

> *when he woke to consciousness*
> *he wondered if it was really him lying there*
>
> *never one*
> *ever two.*
>
> *every I is a You*
> *every You is an I*
>
> *I think therefore I am*
> *I am therefore I am observed*
>
> *which one is you now?*
> *which one would you prefer?*
> *can't I have both?*
> *I've never tried being both at once*
>
> *all one in making*
> *the kiss of two cones*
>
> *constant ambivalence*
> *happy ambiguity*
>
> *wish you were here?*

❖ 6 ❖

The minutes flicked, the hours passed, the smudge of dawn finally arrived. Seven thirty-five. Time to make a move.

We settled down for the night, Gill in the spare room next to me in mine. But after half an hour, when I was warm and cosy and might have drifted off, I heard Gill's door open and the bathroom door close, followed by the pitiful sound of retching.

I went to the bathroom door and said as softly as I could, 'Gill, are you OK?' No answer, just more retching. Mum poked her head out from her room, the very thing I was hoping wouldn't happen. I waved her back inside, whispering, 'I'll look after her,' and luckily she didn't insist.

After a few minutes Gill came out looking sheepish (why do people feel guilty when they've been sick?), I asked her if there was anything that would help, she said that it sounded silly but what she wanted more than anything was a bowl of cornflakes and warm milk, so downstairs we went to the kitchen, which was at least toasty warm from the Aga, where I sat her at the table, heated some milk, and let her make her own cornflake mix, which ended up a soggy stodge that she gobbled up as if she were starving.

After that we sat back and looked at each other. Neither of us said anything for quite a while, the house breathed around us, the coal in the Aga shifted in its belly, the kitchen clock click-clacked.

Now I could look at her properly, not fashed by goings-on at the bridge, and she'd had a wash and tidied herself up, I could see that she was actually rather pretty, sexy even, blonde straight hair, triangular face, wide apart large blue eyes, a straight firm slim nose, long mouth with full lips, good and attractively irregular teeth, chin a little too sharp-pointed perhaps, and a slim figure. Not good hands, though – too plump, thumbs a bit stubby – no match for her boyfriend's.

Out of genuine curiosity and not just for something to say, I asked her how she and Jan got together. 'Piers,' she said, 'I can't think of him as Jan, sorry!' 'Piers,' I said. It always seemed such a naff name to me, Piers Plowman at one end (not Jan at all!) and Piers out-of-the-top-drawer at the other (not Jan either), but nor was he a Pierre or a Peer or a Pedro or a Pietro or a Pyotr or a Cephas or any kind of Peter, which was too stone-age man to suit him, no rock he, and no no no not a Pete or a Pet, none of those, and yet they say what's in a name – everything, it seems to me. People should be careful with their names and the names they give their children. In fact in my opinion there ought to be a custom whereby everyone has a chance to pick the name they want for themselves when they are, say, sixteen or eighteen or whatever age we're supposed to become adult. After all, actors change their names to fit the image they want (Marion Michael Morrison became John Wayne, 'nuff said), writers often have pen names (George Eliot = Mary Ann Evans, George Orwell = Eric Blair), nuns and monks take different names (Sister Mary Joseph could once have been Ms Cheryl Smith, God help her) and of course women are always changing part of their name when they get married and thereby become the nominal possession of their husband and *his*tory, a slave collar that won't be hung round my neck by anyone, let me give notice.

I didn't say any of that to Gill just then of course, and anyway she launched into the story of their romance as if she'd been waiting to be asked.

She'd had the hots for Jan-Piers for a few weeks before she got him to pay her any attention. Something about his eyes and (oddly to my taste) his ears, but mostly it seemed his legs, which she'd been able to view during compulsory games, when he played a bad scrum half at rugby, and to better effect when he was playing tennis, and to best effect of all during swimming sessions in the school baths. She was in the same year as Jan but not in the same class so she couldn't get to him that way. There was gossip about him, isn't there always, which said he didn't have a girlfriend, steady or unsteady, and there were some in whose opinion he was a closet gay. This mix of information and guessery made Gill all the keener. Everybody agreed that Piers was quite bright if not outstandingly so – some said he had been accelerated too early by his pushy dad and that he was now running out of steam – but that he didn't flaunt it and was in general OK if not particularly exciting and sometimes a bit standoffish and secretive. On this assessment Gill decided that the way to this man's heart, probably to his penis as well, and for sure to his legs was via his head. So she started sending him intellectual morsels rather as in a different case she might have sent him love notes. Via the gossip line she researched his current fads, and sent him photocopies of poems, passages of prose, obscure footnotes from obscurer books, postcard pics of the appropriate personages (pin-ups for the mind), etc. etc., all accompanied by little offhand personal messages such as 'I hear you like Dumpty Dum too. Have you come across this? Isn't it great!' (the *appeal confrère*) or 'I can't get the hang of these lines from *XYZ*. A mutual friend says you're the expert around here on this kind of thing. Can you help?' (the *appeal supplicans*). *Mon dieu!* But it cheered me to hear that Jan didn't rise to this ploy, replying only with such putoffs as 'I prefer page 86, it's funnier' or 'Ask Fairbairn [one of the teachers], he'll explain.'

Nothing daunted, Gill decided to take the bull by the horns (what a vivid cliché in this context, Jan would have muttered) and make the approach direct. Having carefully prepared herself for every hoped-for eventuality (i.e. like us all, living for her fantasies) she called at his house one evening about eight, Eng. Lit. set book in hand, and shot a nice line about having an essay crisis, and could Piers please rescue her (the approach *damsel distrait*) and give her a bit of help with lines twenty-five to eighty, Act Three Scene Two.

This time she made an impression even though that evening she got no further than Act Three Scene Two examined in close proximity with the desired as they sat side by side at the dining-room table while desired's mother bobbed in and out every now and then, bearing first some fruit then some coffee and bickies and finally an offer (refused) of ice cream, all actually in aid of keeping an eye on sonnyboy and temptress.

Just before making her grateful what-a-relief thankyous and goodnights, Gill played an inspired unprepared gambit: Would Piers like to accompany her to the play at the Civic Theatre next Thursday, she had a couple of tickets, having intended to take a girlfriend, but the friend couldn't go after all, the ticket was going begging, her dad had paid for both so if Piers would like to . . . well, she'd just love it. Why not? said Mum, by now won over, and Piers fell for it. (Oh Jan-Piers, I'd hoped you were made of sterner stuff!) Of course in truth she didn't have a spare ticket at all, her friend had one of her own, and tomorrow Gill would have to persuade said friend to hand over said ticket as a matter of life or death, which said friend did, what else are friends for, though only after being let in on the reason and after promising a blow by blow (pardon, that one was accidental) account of the evening and to keep said friend informed of advances thereafter, which Gill did until things between her and Piers became serious, after which she naturally kept her mouth shut about the personal details. And she must have done pretty well with him that night (she said it was one of those times when everything goes just right) because only three days later, on the following Sunday afternoon, they were in her bed together while the rest of her family – parents, younger brother and sister – visited relatives for tea, she crying off because she had urgent homework to finish. From the faraway smile on her face when she described this moment in her story I could tell she had enjoyed her homework *très bien*.

I didn't say anything, letting her savour the memory, but she suddenly came to with a jolt, her face clouded, and she looked at me with eyes pained with suspicion and an unasked question.

'No, I haven't,' I said.

'When I saw you at the party –'

'Only a game. Didn't mean a thing.'

She nodded but I could tell she didn't believe me. Why should she? In her place I wouldn't.

'Why didn't he ever write?' she said. 'Or even phone.'

'Not because of anything between him and me.'

'And pinning my letters to the back of the door –'

'Honestly, Gill, I think you ought to ask him about that.'

'Does he still have The Glums?'

'Not lately. He's a lot better than when he first arrived. Pretty normal, in fact, I'd say. Well – his normal anyway!' Gill didn't smile. 'Not that I know what he was like before, so it's hard for me to tell.'

'Has he talked about me much?'

'A bit. Now and then.'

'You mean, he hasn't.'

'To be honest, no, not much. But he hasn't wanted to talk about himself much, either – I mean, his home and everything.'

'So what has he talked about?'

'What he's reading –'

'Might have guessed.'

'Movies, music, his work. People he's talked to while taking tolls. Stuff in the news. What he's thinking – you know how he likes to argue.'

133

'Do I know!' She managed a trace of a smile. 'Sounds like his old self again. He'd lost that by the time he left home. Wasn't reading anything except what he had to for school, wouldn't go out, wasn't even arguing, at least not about the things that interested him. All he did was row or bitch or groan on and on about being depressed and how stupid he was and how pointless life was. Or he'd pick fights with me over nothing – that was the worst. Wouldn't have been so bad if the times between had been OK, like at the beginning, but they weren't, we weren't even having any sex by the time he left home. And what a change that was! Our first few weeks, he was all over me, couldn't get enough, it was the only thing he seemed to want. I think he was catching up with what he'd missed. From Christmas to Easter we had a pretty good time, with only a patch of The Glums now and then, but during the Easter holidays the depression seemed to take him over and after that he got worse and worse. Funny when I think about it now – we had seven months together before he came here, only two months were the really bad times, but they seem like the longest part.'

'Twenty-eight point five per cent.'

'Sorry?'

'Can't help it, do maths at school. Two months is twenty-eight point five per cent of your seven months together. Not far off being a third. Probably more than a third if you add in the times when he had The Glums before he got really bad. And worst at the end. It must have been pretty awful, trying to cope with him and to help and getting nowhere.'

'I kept trying to remind him of the good times in my letters, hoping it would help, because it's always easier to remember the rotten times than it is to remember the good times, isn't it, all the details, I mean, don't you think?'

'That's why I like taking photos. Why most people take photos, in my opinion.'

'To remind them of the good times?'

'Well, people don't take photos of unhappy times, do they, not usually. Some professionals do, but not ordinary people. Nobody wants photos of themselves being ill or being angry or crying or things like that. They want pictures of having fun on holiday or of getting married and having parties and stuff like that. Nobody takes pictures of funerals or of themselves being divorced or having an operation or when they're in the huff. They just don't.'

'And isn't it funny how everybody has to smile, no matter what they feel like, nobody's allowed to look sad, are they. And as soon as people realize they're being taken, they start fixing their hair and tidying themselves up and pose and put on an act!'

'Vanity, vanity, all is vanity, my dad says, but if I try to snap him he slinks away.'

'Got to look your best, my mum says.'

We were laughing now and I saw how likeable Gill could be, what fun, if she were given a chance.

'Do you take a lot of pictures?' she asked.

'Quite a few. I do Practical Photography as an optional at school.'

'Have you taken any of Piers?'

'Would you like to see them?'

'Could I?'

'They're in my room.'

We viewed the pictures slouched on my bed. Fifteen or sixteen, starting with one taken the first week Jan was at the bridge and finishing with one taken a couple of weeks ago. Having gone through them once, Gill asked me to put them in chronological order. They hadn't been taken at regular intervals, and Jan wasn't in the same pose each time – they were snaps really, catching him off guard doing different things, I don't like posed shots – but still, between the first and the last you could see how much he'd changed, how much better he looked, his face had filled out, his hair of course was very different – long and twerpishly tidy when he arrived, short and natural after he cut it. His body seemed more developed, not so skinny-willowy any more. He was a lot sexier, to be honest. In the early pics, whatever he was doing he looked crushed, dead-eyed, hang dog, an unsmiling withdrawn wimp. In the later ones, he was on the *qui vive*, sparkier, the difference between a plant drooping from lack of water and the same plant revived after a good drink.

Gill noticed, stared at the pictures one after the other, inspecting each closely, another plant slaking a thirst, but she said nothing. Two or three of the later pics included Adam and there were some of him on his own that I'd put to one side after sorting out the ones of Jan.

'Who's that?' Gill asked as she went through the pictures for the third time.

'You don't know?'

'No, who?'

'Adam,' I said as offhand as I could, not only because I expected

Gill to react but also because the sight of him frightened me suddenly.

Gill stiffened, peered at the best shot of him, nose almost touching, then sat up cross-legged on the bed, holding the picture between her knees by thumb and first finger.

'Good-looking,' she said, trying to sound calm.

'Too good –'

'Not as tall as I thought, though.'

'And stronger than he looks.'

'Oh?' She glanced at me to make sure she'd guessed right.

'Told you you didn't have to worry about Jan and me.'

'Like that?'

'Once. The night before last.'

I told her everything, trying to be offhand about that too but couldn't help crying a bit by the end of course, it was all still so near the nerve and such a relief to tell someone. My turn to pass on the hurt.

Gill sat and listened, didn't react, didn't interrupt, didn't cry along with me, just sat there, cross-legged, her eyes never leaving me, the picture of Adam held between her knees, till I'd finished the story and had scrambled off the bed for a tissue. Then she said, 'You'll be OK. You know how it is.' Very matter-of-fact. So there's a cold side to her, I thought as I mopped my eyes, and said,

'Till one day it really is what you dread.'

'But he was all right with you? I mean, he wasn't violent or anything.'

'No no. Well, a bit. But –'

'If it was him.'

'There weren't any other Adams around, not that I know of.'

Gill stacked the photos like a pack of cards, the one of Adam and Jan on top, which she sat staring at, face in hands, elbows on knees, broody.

This is no good, I thought. At this rate we'll end up clinically depressed ourselves.

'Let's get some sleep,' I said. 'And tomorrow, I mean this morning, let's go and face those two. They've both got some explaining to do.'

Gill reacted like a startled rabbit. 'I couldn't, I can't.'

'I know how you must feel, but honestly, it's the only thing to do. We'll go together, I'm used to Adam, I know how to handle him, you needn't worry about him, if that's what bothers you. You know what boys are like, they'll pretend nothing's happened if we let them, they'll just go on as if everything's all right. Well, something *has* happened and it *isn't* all right, and we've got to sort it out for our own sakes, never mind theirs.'

'Only . . . I feel so confused, so humiliated.'

'I know. Me too. And we'll go on feeling like that unless we do something about it.'

I don't remember any more of what we said, not accurately enough to write it down. Nothing of any importance I don't think, but we burbled at each other about the usual things, this time seen through the fog of the night's events. If the earlier talk had been about passing on the pain, now it was about calming each other down, jollying each other along, edging ourselves towards doing what we both knew had to be done.

It was four o'clock before Gill's eyes began to close – I was telling her about them putting the toll house up for sale and why we didn't want them to – till finally she dropped off completely, half curled across the diagonal of the bed, head to foot. I slipped a pillow under her head, lay down beside her, covered us with the duvet, and was soon asleep myself.

Morning After

Adam was still dead to the world. But he couldn't stay where he was much longer. He needed what the house offered: fresh water, food, clothes, warmth. How to get him there? Carry him? Too far. Float him in the boat? Current against us. Nothing else for it: tow.

Hauling a boat the size of a four-berth cabin cruiser upriver on your own isn't easy at the best of times. This was not the best of times. Doing it without anyone to steer is murder. The bow keeps nudging into the bank and sticking. After a couple of bodged goes that got me all of ten metres nearer destination in as many minutes, I managed to secure the tiller with just the right amount of turn to edge the boat out and counter the tendency of the tow rope to drag it into the bank. After that things went well if you allow for a few minor impediments along the way, like slipping every few paces on the muddy path and twice being dragged backwards by the pull of the current when my stamina ran out, requiring me to dig in and hold everything at a stop while I caught my breath and untwisted my muscles.

Tug-of-war donkey work for the four hundred metres to the bridge. The world a collision of contraries: The boat wanting to glide away from the bank and slip downstream, me pulling it into the bank and forcing it upriver against the current. The morning air biting from overnight frost, me sweating from the effort but feeling frozen. Dawn of a new day, me unslept from the old, a refugee from the night. Adam flat out and sleeping in the boat, unaware of anything, me puffing and panting and struggling and aware of every straining cell in my body and of the impelling world around.

> *all things counter, original, spare, strange;*
> *whatever is fickle, freckled (who knows how?)*

138

with swift, slow; sweet, sour; adazzle, dim . . .

Gerard Manley Hopkins lifted my spirits, helping me find in the tug and swing, dig of heels, cut of rope, pain of breath, stretch of muscle, the Force of dotty Dylan T.'s breath

> *that through the green fuse drives the flower*
> *Drives my green age; that blasts the roots of trees*
> *Is my destroyer,*
> *And I am dumb to tell the crooked rose*
> *My youth is bent by the same wintry fever.*

Helping me know again that

> *The force that drives the water through the rocks*
> *Drives my red blood; that dries the mouthing streams*
> *Turns mine to wax.*

Poetry is useless, it never changes anything? Tugging the boat upstream, four hundred metres metered by metre. By life lines changed. It changes me. Useful to have something that enables you to be useful.

❖ 2 ❖

Inside, the house was a tidy mess. My guts said, Go now, never come back. My mind said, There is only one thing for it, knuckle down.

Leaving Adam in the boat, tethered where I could keep an eye from the living-room back window, I set to work.

First, blankets and pillows and a drink of water into the boat for Adam. Still out. Fixed him up as comfortably as I could, left the glass of water on the table where he'd see it if he woke, and went back to the house. I wanted everything ready before taking him inside.

Next, the fire resurrected.

Then, every scrap left from the party stuffed into rubbish bags:

> a shoal of plastic glasses,
> a contagion of empty cans and bottles,
> an epidemic of crunched and squashed, trodden and
>   half-eaten scraps of food,
> a gallimaufry of discarded clothes:

139

a sicked-on sweater,
a crotch-stained pair of women's tights,
a pungent jock-strap,
a once-white sock,
an almost shredded T-shirt,
a pair of brand-new ultra-maxi-brief frilly knickers,
half an A-cup bra,
two used condoms,
a rash of joint and cigarette butts,
two slippery empty bottles of sunflower oil,
various pat-cakes of unrecognizable
   coagulated gunge limpeting on furniture,
   floor, walls, and ceiling,
a black close-toothed blonde-hair-clogged comb,
a necklace of lurid plastic beads,
a muddy right-foot Reebok,
a blood-stained handkerchief with hand-stitched
   marigolds decorating its scalloped edge,
a scrunched packet of weary jelly-babies,
an empty tube of KY,
the joker from a pack of cards.

(That's all I can remember.)

From among these icons of a fun-filled evening, I rescued my books, radio, own clothes (those still in a state worth rescuing), bedclothes, kitchen and toilet gear, etc. After that, sweeping, washing, mopping, dusting, polishing, reorganizing. Returning the place to myself.

Then returning myself to myself. Wash, shave, change of clothes, breakfast.

By nine o'clock tolls were interrupting progress as the Saturday early shoppers went through.

Checks on Adam every fifteen minutes monitored no change. Deep heavy-duty sleep.

All this achieved by keeping my mind in neutral.

Nine thirty, at the table, breakfast just finished, coffee mug in hand as I took five minutes off before making an attempt at getting Adam inside, Tess walked in.

[– Let's tell the next bit together, then we can get in everything we both knew.

– You just want an excuse not to have to write anything!

– Hard *fromage!* He's guessed! But it would be better that way, admit it.

– Wouldn't work.

– Yes it will, you just want to give up all that I-ing all the time. You're such a bloody narcissist!

– Rubbish.

– Yes you are. You like nothing better than staring at your navel all the time. And you're possessive.

– Stop bossing. Just for you, I'll give it a go.

– Good. But we keep it simple, none of your male-order stuff like those titles and numbered sections and everything all very ordered and in charge, and literary crossword puzzles and quoting from poets nobody reads and stuff like that. You're not writing a novel, for God's sake. This is going to be right to the point, OK?

– Conditions already! Keep it simple! Dear God, it'll be only words of one syllable next. Afraid of the dictionary, are we? Afraid we might come across a word we don't know? Afraid we might have to think a bit?

– Go!]

Tess and Gill walked to the bridge together. The two girls had arranged beforehand how they would behave. While Gill waited outside, Tess would discover whether Jan and Adam were there.

When Tess came into the living room Jan was facing her across the table, his hands wrapped round a mug of coffee. Image of so many Saturday mornings. Except this morning he looked desperately exhausted.

But as soon as he saw Tess, all Jan's weariness and the anger he felt for what she had done during the last three days evaporated. The very sight of her was enough to revive his spirits.

Stopped in her tracks by the sight of Jan, Tess suddenly felt confused, all her determination draining away, surprised by the strength of her feelings at seeing him again, as if they had been parted for years.

They gazed at each other for a long moment, neither saying anything, both aware of the moment's significance, knowing beyond a doubt for the first time that each was irreplaceable to the other no matter what, each satisfying in the other some essential need, and each unable therefore to do anything but pay the eternal toll of friendship: forgiveness of the other's failings. It was a sweet moment that could have lasted for ever, neither would have minded, a sublime kind of knowledge that was a strange new pleasure.

But the spell was broken by a car approaching the bridge.

'I'll get it,' Tess said and went.

When she returned a mug of coffee was waiting. Tess sat and avoided Jan's eyes by looking round the room.

'Quite a clean-up.'

'Needed it.' Intending to be genial, Jan heard himself sounding accusatory. Tiredness talking. He cleared his throat and braced himself in his seat. 'Back to normal.'

142

Tess smiled warily. 'Your normal.'

Jan returned her smile. 'My normal.'

Both were baffled. Having thought so much during the night about this meeting – how it would be, what would be said – it was not as either had imagined. Both also felt an intrusive urgency, Jan for Adam, Tess for Gill. But that intense moment of mutual recognition had come between what had been and what was, changing everything, and leaving each at a loss for words, tongue-tied, waiting on the other to bridge the gulf.

Jan spoke first.

'I need some help.'

'Is it – can it wait a minute?'

'What for?'

'Gill. She's outside.'

'Gill! She's still here? What's she want?'

'To talk to you of course.'

'Not now. I need some help with Adam.'

'Adam!'

'He's in a boat, it's a long story, I'll explain later, he's had some kind of accident, his head was bleeding, it's a cut, he was unconscious but he's sleeping now. I'm not sure what to do, he seems OK, but would you have a look at him and see if you think we ought to fetch a doctor?'

'Christ!'

'I also need some help to get him into the house, it's cold out there and there's nothing in the boat – no heating or water or anything.'

'God! But what about Gill?'

'Can't she wait?'

'You don't understand. She was attacked last night, during the party, under the bridge. It might have been Adam.'

'Adam! Is she sure? I mean, she didn't know him.'

'He said his name.'

'Jesus!'

'Exactly!'

'Can't have been! What did he do? Was she hurt?'

'Not physically. She doesn't know what he was up to. She's not sure. She was confused. It was dark and she was so upset already.'

They stared at each other, appalled.

'What now?' Jan said.

'I'd better get Gill. We can't leave her hanging about out there. Anyway, she's involved. She has a right to know what's happened.'

While Tess went for Gill, Jan visited Adam again, who was still flat out, hardly having moved for the last two hours.

As Jan returned to the living room by the back door Tess and Gill came in by the front. There was an awkward pause as Jan and Gill scowled across the room at each other.

'Hi,' they said in inevitable comic unison.

'I've explained,' Tess said quickly.

'He's still sleeping,' Jan said.

'I'll take a look,' Tess said, and hurried off, glad to escape.

Jan and Gill stood in silence contemplating each other, figures posed in a domestic still life.

When the silence became unbearable Gill said, 'We should talk.'

'Tess won't be long.'

'But we must.'

'Coffee or something?'

'No! Thanks.'

Unable to help herself, Gill closed the living-room door. Her letters were gone. She let out a gasp.

Jan, knowing, said nothing but went to the fire, stirred it with a foot and laid on another log.

Gill wandered round the room, inspecting it distractedly. Before, she had always poked about among the things in Jan's room and he hadn't minded, had rather liked it, in fact, as he had liked her caressing him while they sat and talked – playing with his hair, fiddling with his ears, stroking his legs. He was one of those for whom physical contact, the language of the fingers, was a needed way of communication. But it was also a privilege of friendship. Handling his possessions was an extension of this tactile pleasure. Now he found Gill's assumption of the privilege irritating. He wanted to tell her to leave things alone as he would have told a stranger. He knew that this was unreasonable: Gill was only continuing their relationship from where they had left off. It was he who had changed.

'Why didn't you answer my letters?' Gill said with the sudden brusqueness of someone forcing herself, through clenched teeth as it were, to speak. Having got it out, she turned to face him.

'What's this about Adam?' Jan said.

'Nothing.'

'Nothing!'

'Yes! No, not nothing. I don't want to talk about that, I want to talk about us. You're hurting me, you know that, do you?'

'I don't mean to. It's just the way things are. Don't know what to say.'

'That's a change!'

'Is all this just because I stuck your letters on the door?'

'No, all this is not *just* because you stuck my letters on the door, though that's bad enough. It's not even *just* because you didn't answer them, either. It's about what those things mean. Can't you see that? It's about you and me and about you paying me some *attention*. Don't you know how important that is to people?' Tears welled in her eyes. She brushed them angrily away. 'No one has ever hurt me the way you have. Never! It hurts so much I don't know what to do!'

Tears flowed again. Again she wiped them away. Took deep breaths.

She turned impatiently from him, went to the front window pretending to look out at the bridge. Jan remained unmoving by the fire.

After a while she said, 'Didn't mean to say that. Kept telling myself not to say things like that. It's so *boring* saying things like that!' She gave a little rueful laugh and slapped her thigh in frustration. 'And I was determined not to cry. I don't want to. I'm not trying to use it against you.'

Jan, struggling with his own feelings, managed to say, 'You know me well enough to know I don't think like that.'

She turned to face him again. 'But I don't seem to know you well enough to know why you're hurting me the way you are.'

Jan couldn't look at her. 'I'm not sure I know myself. That's why I'm here, to find out things like that.'

'Can't we at least talk about it? Don't I deserve that? Don't you owe me that much?'

Jan heard himself take in and let out the long slow breath of resignation.

He nodded, unable to speak.

His silence was broken by Tess shouting his name.

For Tess, climbing apprehensively down the two narrow steps that led from the cockpit into the cold clammy gloom of the cabin, entering the boat felt like descending into a tomb.

She clasped her hand over her mouth as she looked down at Adam's unconscious pasty face and the blood-stained bandage wrapped like a

145

sweatband round his head. He was breathing heavily through a gaping mouth, each breath rasping in his throat.

There are moments that change people. No, wrong; try again. There are moments when people change. These moments are not isolated, not separate, not removed from the rest of life. They are not independent atoms of existence that suddenly break into your life for no reason. They are made, are created by the alphabet of your life – the ever-shifting phonemes of existence, which sometimes gather into concentrated patterns of such intensity, such unmistakable clarity and significance, that suddenly you know something about yourself, your own *self*, for the first time. Some hidden part of you enters your consciousness. Recognized, acknowledged, accepted, it becomes part of the you you know.

This is how Jan thought later.

Tess, overcome in the cabin at the sight of Adam, knew only the impact of the moment as the narrowing cone of the past few weeks, past few days, past few hours, past few minutes reached a concentration sharp enough to penetrate her soul.

What phonemes spoke to her as she stood in the waist of the boat?

Regret: limb-weakening, stomach-sickening
Fright: bowel-loosening, nerve-jangling, sweat-making
Pity: tear-inducing
Disgust: fist-clenching, mouth-twisting
Anger: breath-catching, heart-gripping

And, counterpoint to these negatives, a positive that held them in play as the pulsing rhythm of a harmonic holds discords, the beat of the heart driving the flow of blood, she was also possessed by (God, how words fail us now!)

Joy
Gladness
Exhilaration
Zest

As she endured this, Tess felt as if she were split in two: one part of her suffering regret and guilt and sorrow; the other dispassionate, detached, cool, observing the self who suffered and taking pleasure in it.

How can I be like this? she wondered. Am I mad? Or sick? Or am I wicked? Evil?

Tess did not know whether she believed in Evil – in an entity, an out-there presence or force. The Devil. Her mother did. But Tess regarded that as a hangover from her mother's Catholic convent-school upbringing. Her father never used the word. She didn't know whether he believed in Evil or not. He always avoided talking of such things. Right and wrong, yes, he talked about that. But never about Evil. She herself had never thought it mattered enough to think about. Yet here she was, using the word about herself! Was it her mother speaking in her?

Tess had sometimes caught herself thinking and saying things that came straight out of her parents' mouths. Just as she sometimes caught herself walking like her mother or using her hands like her father. Or, most disturbing, she'd look in the mirror and suddenly see not her eyes but her father's, not her nose but her mother's, and always her father's wide mouth – his lips, their shape and length and thickness, and the odd little upward curve at the left-hand corner that made her look even when blank-faced as if she were smirking slightly, a feature that sometimes landed her in trouble with touchy teachers. How weird, she thought, to be such a mix-and-match product of your parents. And not only your parents but of all your ancestors back to Adam and Eve!

Eve and evil! Dear God! No, not evil, whether Evil existed or not. A stupid idiotic muttonheaded cretinous moronic crapbrained grade-A fool perhaps, but not evil. And not sick. Just a doltbungler. Not mad. Just a pukefaceturdtwit. And enjoying it!

She went on bludgeoning herself with words till the tears ran; and observed herself crying with pleasure. She was glad that all this could happen to her, she wouldn't deny it, which was not mad nor sick nor evil but life, human life – being alive. Pleasure not at *what* she had done or what she was, but *that* she had done and that she was. The tears were merely an outward and visible sign that she wished for better *than* she had done and than she was.

Perhaps it is in this attitude to herself that Tess differs most from Jan: she glorying in what she is, what life is, happy or sad, and, yes, bad or good, a born optimist; he suspicious of himself, sceptical of life, a born pessimist. Tess feels at home in the world, at home with it; Jan feels a stranger, a visitor only, uncomfortable with the world, alien even, someone waiting, bags packed, ready to leave.

Foraging such thoughts, chastened in her soul, she wiped the tears away, before bending over Adam to give him a critical look.

As her face came close to his, Adam's eyes opened and he saw her.

Tess stepped back, letting out a little gasp. Adam sat up, mouth gaping as if to shout, but no sound came.

'It's all right, it's only me!' Tess spluttered.

Adam's mouth moved as if talking fast but again no sound came. His eyes were wide and wild. He sprang to his feet, the blanket tumbling from him, but sat down again on the edge of the bunk as if felled by a blow, his face wincing with pain. He put a hand to his head, found the bandage, felt it with both hands, panic now adding to the look of pain.

'Don't move!' Tess said. 'You've hurt your head.' And instinctively took a step towards him, but Adam scrambled away along the bunk until he was wedged against the bulkhead, glaring at her like a wounded cornered animal.

Tess retreated to the cabin door, at a loss to know what do, jabbering, 'It's only me, Tess, you've had an accident or something, I'm not sure, but anyway calm down, it's OK, I'm not going to hurt you.' She heard herself laugh in the hysterical way people do when they're frightened. 'Should I get Jan? You'd probably prefer to talk to him.'

She began to back out of the cabin. 'Stay quiet. Put a blanket round you, you're only in your – you'll get cold, it's freezing in here, you probably have concussion or something, I'll just fetch Jan, hang on –'

As soon as she was on the bank she started yelling Jan's name.

Jan came running. Gill followed as far as the steps outside the back door.

'Something's up,' Tess said, meeting Jan halfway across the lawn. She was trembling. 'He woke up and went crazy. I thought he was going to attack me.'

'Bloody hell!'

'It might be just because it's me. You know – he might be scared of what will happen after last night. He might be all right with you, he knows you best –'

In the cockpit Jan bent down to look into the cabin. Adam was hunched up in the far corner of the bunk, a blanket gathered round him.

'Hey, Adam,' Jan said quietly, cheerily, 'it's me. You OK?'

No answer. Adam's eyes, ringed with dark circles, blazed at him.

Jan straightened up, looked at Tess watching from the bank, shrugged at her, bent to look at Adam again.

'How'd you like to come into the house where it's warm?'

No reply. Jan stepped down one step into the cabin, Adam stiffened, Jan stopped.

'Look, it's all right, what're you worried about?'

He took another step.

'I'm on my own.'

Another step brought him to the cabin floor.

Adam was shaking his head and making pushing-away movements with a hand. His mouth was working too but all that came out were gasping breaths.

Jan said quickly, 'I'm coming no further, it's OK, I'll just sit here, all right? Just want to talk to you.'

Adam waited. Jan perched on the edge of the bunk, ready to flit, his eyes never leaving Adam as he tried to weigh up his odd behaviour. By instinct he kept up a flow of soothing placatory talk.

'What's up? Is it your head? Does it hurt? I think you banged it somehow, anyway there's a cut just above your forehead, not a big one, but it was bleeding and I bandaged it, I think it'll be OK, nothing serious, it'll heal in a couple of days, but you might be suffering from a bit of concussion, what d'you think?' He paused. No reply. 'I don't know what happened, probably an accident. D'you remember?' No reply. 'Well, you really were soaking it up last night, you have to admit.' He tried a smile. Nothing in return, only the puzzled frightened watchful stare. 'Probably suffering from a hangover as well.' Still nothing. 'Damn near blotto, I expect.' He returned his face to its concerned serious look. 'You don't remember anything about last night?'

A pause. Then Adam shook his head, just once, but enough. A small triumph.

'No, well, I'm not surprised, to be honest. You'll be fine by tomorrow. Need to sleep it off, I guess. How about coming into the house? It's warm in there. The old fire blazing. I'll make you something to eat if you like. Some breakfast maybe, eh? Then if you want you can go to bed. Sleep better in your own bed. How about it?'

He felt like an over-tolerant dad wheedling a pesky infant.

Adam shifted, easing forward from his position huddled in the corner. His mouth started working but again made no sound. He jabbed a finger at his face followed by a frustrated gesture that signalled, 'I can't, I can't!'

Jan said, appalled, 'You can't talk?'

Adam shook his head, eyes pleading.

'Grief!' Jan heard himself say before he could prevent it. A new panic flushed through him. He'd heard of concussion causing temporary loss of memory but never of it causing loss of voice. What if Adam was really badly hurt? Brain-damaged even?

'Look, Adam,' he said, man-to-man serious now, 'we'd better get a doctor, there might be —'

The effect was alarming. Adam sprang to his feet, wild and hunted again, and frantically waving both hands, *no no no*. Jan jumped up too, thinking he was about to be attacked, his own hands raised as a man at gunpoint. 'Right, OK, no doctor, no doctor —'

The pair of them were square to each other now, an arm's length apart, Adam poised for flight, the blanket thrown aside.

There was a pause. Adam began to shiver. Folded his arms round his chest. But the shivering grew worse till he was shaking all over.

'Come on,' Jan said, picking up the blanket. 'Let's go into the house. You can't stay here.' He held the blanket as one holds a coat for another to put on. 'I don't know what's happened, but we can't do anything about it till you're feeling better. You've got to come inside and get warm or you'll be really ill.'

He waited. Adam stared at him for a moment before abruptly, as if acting on a decision before he could change his mind, he grabbed the blanket out of Jan's hands and clutched it round himself.

Jan nodded and smiled and led the way out.

Adam wrote, *Who are you?*

'Jan,' Jan said. 'Well, Piers really.'

Why Jan?

'It's what Tess calls me.'

Adam raised questioning eyebrows.

'The girl in the boat.'

Why Adam?

'That's what you said your name was.'

They were sitting at the table in the toll house. When they came in from the boat an hour ago Tess and Gill had gone.

Jan had coddled Adam through the process of washing, having his bandage changed, dressing in warm clean clothes (Jan's yet again), going to the lavatory, and eating the usual breakfast, which Adam gobbled up having by then calmed down, though he was still jumpy.

Breakfast over, Jan placed a pad of paper and a ballpoint in front of Adam, sat down beside him and, saying nothing, waited. After considering Jan and the paper hesitantly Adam took up the pen and started writing.

Now Jan said, 'Don't you remember anything?'

Where is this?

Jan told him.

When did I come?

Jan began recounting their history together. When he reached the fight over the necklace he pulled it from under his shirt and held it for Adam to see. From his reaction Jan knew at once that Adam recognized it. About the raven, however, Adam's reaction was quite different. As Jan told about the wound, he took hold of Adam's hand and pushed back the sleeve of his sweater, revealing the scabby marks of the raven's talons on Adam's forearm. At the sight of them

151

Adam braced in astonishment, as if the marks had suddenly appeared by magic. He snatched his hand from Jan's grasp and inspected the wound closely. When he looked up again he was frowning. He thought for a moment then wrote:

Could have pinched necklace. Seen mark.

'Why would I make up a story like that? Why would I say you've been living here if you haven't?'

Adam shrugged.

'You don't believe me?'

Adam shook his head.

After a moment's thought, Jan said, 'Hang on a sec,' and brought from the bedroom two of Tess's photos which he laid side by side on the table. One was of Adam and Jan painting outside the toll house. The other was of Adam taking a toll from a car.

Adam studied them intently.

'You don't remember any of this?'

Adam shook his head.

'Nothing? Nothing at all? Do you remember anything before you came here or where you came from?'

This time there was a pause before Adam looked away.

'But you know who you are?'

Eyes averted, another shake of the head.

'Don't even know your name?'

Another denial.

It was Jan's turn not to believe.

'Look,' he said, undoing the chain, 'you'd better have this back.'

Adam hesitated a moment before taking it.

From the second he heard Tess yelling his name Jan had been, as he put it later, flying by radar. He had no experience, the basis of all thought, to go on, for he had never been faced with anything like this before. But now as he sat watching Adam, stubborn but discomforted beside him, he felt an echo of the irritation he used to feel when Adam first invaded the house, and the same desire as then to chuck him out. He wanted to say, 'Oh, come on, don't give me that! You can remember all right, why are you lying?' But he knew that if he did it would be the end, Adam would go, and though Jan could not fully understand why, he wanted him to stay. To let him go, to send him away, would be a loss to himself and a dereliction.

Kafka's strange story came to his mind and vividly the memory

152

of the three of them talking about it as they toasted themselves by the fire. Now the story seemed oddly appropriate to this moment in his life. He and Adam and Tess: each other's bridges, as Kafka's young man had become a bridge for someone else. But was the story prophecy or nightmare — what would be or what could be?

As Jan thought of this, he remembered too the morning after Adam's first arrival, when, coming back into the house from talking to Tess, he had the weird sensation of *déjà-vu*.

Could these be mere accidents, unconnected coincidences? A deep nerve of intuition prickled in his spine, telling him they were part of a larger pattern that made a kind of sense he had yet to puzzle out. Till he could discern the pattern he would have to accept that irrational intuition, take it on trust.

Never before in his life had Jan consciously taken such a risk. Just the opposite, in fact. Ever since he stopped being a child — a change in his consciousness he dated from an early summer afternoon when he was thirteen and an older friend took him into a garden shed and taught him how to masturbate — Jan had only trusted thought. Feelings, he had decided as his adolescence progressed, were often misleading. They came and went with distressing fickleness and speed: likes became dislikes, strong desires turned into revulsions. They seemed to be uncontrollable and to come from somewhere outside himself. He did not feel responsible for them (feelings about feelings!) yet was required by others — parents, neighbours, teachers, friends — to behave as if he were. Of his thoughts, however, he felt more in charge. Unlike his feelings, his thoughts did not immediately shape his behaviour before he could prevent it. And only when he wanted and was ready need he reveal his thoughts to others. He possessed them rather than being possessed by them.

So in all things Jan had come to prefer the life of the mind. Thinking gave him physical pleasure. He wanted never to stop thinking, not even when he was asleep. He had learned to regard his dreams as raw material for thought — mind teasers, puzzles with special peculiar secret codes of their own, which he enjoyed trying to crack. That's why he liked Kafka's story so much. It was a dream full of possible meanings, some of them contradictory, yet all existing in the one story. Their very complexity and coexistent difference pleased and satisfied him.

And now there was this unaccustomed intuition about Adam, about losing him, about their staying together, about being one another's bridge to something else. Another kind of code. Not a code in a story he had read, but a code in the story of his own life as it was being lived there and then, here and now, moment to moment.

Stirred by this revelation, unable to sit still, he got up from the table, and went to tend the fire, thinking as he did so that Adam must stay, must be humoured, must be looked after until he could tell the secret Jan was sure he was hiding.

Be Janus, Jan said to himself as he laid a fresh log on the glowing embers and swept away the ash that had fallen onto the hearth. He smiled as he thought of Janus as his renewing defining all-containing name. There and then he accepted it. Never again did he willingly call himself Piers. December fourteenth was ever after his own, his chosen birthday, the day he became a janus, called Jan.

The effect upon him at that moment was like a lens bringing an image into focus. He recognized himself clearly for the first time, knew who he was, felt the urge of his own life, the pulse of the will to be.

He turned from the fire to face Adam, who was slumped at the table, dejected, crushed, staring at the photos in a brown study.

'Listen,' Jan said gently, 'aren't you worried about not being able to talk and not remembering anything?'

Coming to, Adam lifted his head, looked weary-eyed at Jan, and nodded.

'Me too. If you aren't back to normal soon, a day or two at most, we'll have to do something about it. See a doctor. Maybe all you've got is concussion and it's only temporary. If it is concussion, I think you're supposed to take it easy. Go to bed, I mean, and try and sleep. I don't know what else to suggest. What do you think?'

Adam, listening anxiously, didn't move.

Jan went on, 'There'll be people here soon. Tess. A girl called Gill who's a friend of mine. They'll want to talk to me. And my boss, Tess's father, could come in any time. They know you, they've seen you before, they know you're living here for a bit. If you're in bed, I'll say you're not feeling too great after the party. They'll believe me and leave you alone. And tomorrow being Sunday there won't be much doing, no tolls, you could get up then, see how you feel. What about it? . . . You'll be safe. I'll be here to look after you . . . Promise . . . OK?'

There was a silence while Adam studied Jan's face, weighing up whether he could trust this person he said he did not know. Then with the resignation of one who realizes he has no option, he eased himself up from his chair, holding onto the table for support, obviously groggy, a wince of pain creasing his face as he stood up straight, and now a frightened, confused, pleading look in his eyes.

Jan went to him, put a supporting arm round his waist, and led him to the bedroom.

In town, where they had gone to be out of the way, Tess and Gill mooched from shop to shop saying little.

It was while they were poking aimlessly about in Marks and Spencer's, more to keep warm than anything, that Gill suddenly stopped in her tracks and said, 'I can't stay. I'm going home. It's stupid to stay.'

Tess said, 'But don't you want to see him, don't you want to talk to him?'

'No, it's no use, I've got to go.'

Outside, Gill stopped, confused. 'Which way to the station?'

'You want to go this minute?'

'Yes. Is that the way?'

'No, this.' They set off at a brisk pace. 'But why? What about your things?'

'Don't matter. Got my ticket and some money with me.'

They were almost running.

At the station Tess said, 'What shall I do about your stuff?'

Gill shrugged. 'Leave it with Piers. There's nothing I need. Just overnight things. He can post them or bring them when he comes home. And thanks for last night. You've been great. And look – don't feel bad about inviting me to the party. You were only trying to do the right thing. I'm grateful. No – I am. If you hadn't done it, I'd have gone on and on not knowing, thinking about him all the time, worrying – you know how it is. I've been a fool. I shouldn't have let it drag on. Shouldn't have thought it was all up to him. It wasn't, it was up to me. Everything is, in the end, isn't it, up to yourself? I shouldn't have put up with it and shouldn't have kept on letting him know how much I wanted him. I should have kept quiet. If he'd wanted me, he'd have done something about it, wouldn't he? If people really want something, they go for it, don't they? And, you know, I was thinking this morning on the bus, when people know you want

155

something from them very much, they don't let you have it. So maybe the worst thing you can do is let someone know how much you want them. And especially how much you want them to love you. Perhaps it puts them off. D'you think so?'

Tess sighed. 'Don't know. Could be.'

As they stopped to say goodbye, each searched the other's face before spontaneously they hugged and held on with genuine emotion.

It was Gill who let go first and, turning away, walked onto the platform without looking back.

By the time Tess arrived back at the bridge about midday Jan too was in an emotional slump. She found him sprawled full length in the armchair, his feet in the hearth, his face collapsed, eyes drooping. Adam was asleep in the bedroom.

Tess herself felt much better. Gill's departure meant a considerable complication was out of the way.

Jan had been gloomily considering the prospect of a heart-to-heart with Gill. He couldn't think what he wanted to say and was still suffering bouts of resentment that she was there at all. So when Tess arrived on her own and told him that Gill had gone back home he perked up and chuckled with relief.

Suddenly they were both desperately hungry, and while Jan told Tess what had happened during the night she made Welsh rabbit, double helpings of which they consumed with gusto, both feeling the meal was a celebration, a recovery of their own treasured private rituals, though neither said so.

When Jan had finished his story, Tess told hers: the attack on Gill, their overnight talks, the events of the morning. That done, the meal finished, a quietness settled on them. They sat back, the unadmitted euphoria having evaporated, leaving in its place the awkward unresolved problem of Adam, whose slumbering presence seemed to hang heavily around them.

Their mood was changed again by Jan hiccupping. 'Ate too fast,' he said, standing up and clearing the dirty plates into the sink. He began washing up and tidying away the mess Tess had made. (She was [is] a disorderly cook, never putting anything she used [uses] away and managing to spread her jumbled leavings over all available surfaces. Jan regarded[s] this as bad work[wo]manship; Tess regarded[s] his tidiness as obsessively fussy, a sign of a dangerously neurotic closet-authoritarian personality.)

Later, having looked in on Adam (sleeping still) and at the boat, they sat by the fire and discussed what to do next.

The easiest decision was that the boat must be cleaned up and returned to its mooring before anyone noticed it had gone. They agreed that Jan would clean it while Tess took tolls and kept an eye on Adam. Then they'd shift it downstream together under cover of dusk.

The problem of Adam was not so easy to deal with. They agreed it was unlikely he was any worse than badly concussed. But Tess wanted to call a doctor, saying they shouldn't chance it, and being anyway secretly keen to get Adam off their hands. Jan refused, they started arguing, Jan became stubborn, irrational, almost belligerent, and they ended up having a row.

'Why?' Tess demanded. 'First you didn't want him anywhere near the place, now you won't let him go, even when he might be very sick.'

'You can talk! You're the one who wanted him to stay, and now you want to get rid of him. I wonder why! And he's not very sick. Not *physically* sick.'

'How do you know?'

'I just do, that's all.'

'*Doctor* Jan now is it?'

'Oh, shut it!'

'I won't. I can't see why you're going on like this. Why are you protecting him? What is there between you two?'

'Don't want to talk about it.'

'No, I'll bet you don't! I'm fetching Dad. See what he thinks.'

Tess sprang up and made for the front door. But Jan was there before her, arms spread.

'No!'

'Yes!'

'Wait!'

'Get out of the way.'

They were nose to nose.

'I promised him.'

'Don't care.'

'For me, then, just for me.'

'Why?'

'Because — we've got to give him a chance to explain. Oh, I don't know – I keep thinking . . . It's as if he were me. No, not me. I mean – the other me. Christ; I don't know! It's too hard to explain.'

'But you do know? You can make some sense of what's going on, can you?'

'Not in a way I can say it. Not yet. And I told you – there's something terrible he's afraid of. I don't know what it is but I've never seen anybody so scared. Till I know, I have to help him. I don't know why. I'm responsible . . . Anyway, he's ill, for God's sake, you can see that for yourself.'

'So you admit it, after all, he is ill! And if he's ill, you're not being very responsible keeping him here, are you?'

'Tomorrow. Wait till tomorrow. If he isn't any better then, we'll tell your dad and get a doctor. Promise.'

'Another promise.'

'Yes.'

'One cancels the other out, so what are they worth?'

Jan took a deep breath, dropped his arms, stared at Tess and said in a quiet placatory tone, 'Don't.'

'Don't what?'

'Make it a game. Let's be honest, you and me. That's what makes us possible. It's what I care about, the best thing we have together.'

'So?'

'I want him here . . . I need him here . . . Don't ask why yet.'

Tess took that in before giving a scornful self-protective hoot. But she turned away and went back to her seat by the fire.

Afraid that their noise might have woken Adam, Jan quietly opened the bedroom door and peeped in. Adam was lying on his side, back to the door. Impossible to see if he was awake, but he was very still so Jan closed the door and went back to Tess.

After that they took care of the practical jobs: cleaning up the boat, returning it to its moorings, cashing up the week's toll money so that Tess could take it home and give it to her father in the hope that this might forestall a visit tomorrow.

Tess went off home at teatime, returning later with an extract about concussion jotted down from her mother's home doctoring book.

Identification: Pale clammy skin, shallow breathing, fast weak pulse; may vomit or pass water. Disturbance of consciousness may be so slight as to be momentary dizziness or so severe that unconsciousness continues for weeks.

Treatment: Quiet, dark room, head low until consciousness returns, then raised on two pillows. No stimulants. In severe cases, bed for two weeks at least.

After effects: Usually none, except that memory is absent, and sometimes greater memory loss. Headache may persist, and occasion irritability, and lack of concentration, for some weeks.

This so matched Adam's condition that they were reassured. And Jan was quite cocky that, partly by accident, he'd administered the right treatment. They agreed Adam was suffering from a moderately bad concussion and that if they went on treating it properly there should be no serious after effects. Only the loss of voice continued to worry them but they decided it was probably safe to do nothing about it till next day.

In the afternoon they had talked of spending the evening together huddled by the fire. Snow had begun to fall, big white feathery flakes that sidled lazily down from a leaden sky. But when the time came to settle themselves they both felt so drained, so weary, that the prospect of sitting by the fire talking to each other had lost its attraction. They wanted to be together, wanted to repair the damage, wanted comfort from each other, wanted to be encouraged and reassured, wanted in fact to be coddled, but neither yet possessed the knowing confidence, in themselves or in each other, to say so. And anyway, mistaking tiredness for signs of irritation – he had never seen her so exhausted before – Jan suspected Tess was fed up with him for leaving the party and, worse, for opposing her over Adam. Tess, for her part, mistook Jan's silences for sullen resentment at what she had done in the house and at her springing Gill on him, when all his silences actually meant was that he was too beat to talk.

So nothing of their real desires was uttered. Instead Tess said, 'I'm dog tired,' and Jan said, 'Me too,' and Tess added, 'Perhaps I'll just slope off home and flop out early,' and Jan sighed and said, 'Sure. See you tomorrow about twelve, OK? Give me time to work on Adam a bit,' and Tess trudged off, torn between relief and disappointment and feeling deeply discomfited inside herself at the way the day was ending.

Jan, when she had gone, sat staring into the fire. When he eventually came to, he damped the fire down for the night, used the loo, cleaned his teeth, locked the doors, put out the lights and undressed in the dark before slipping quietly into the bedroom. There he had left a candle burning for Adam should he wake and wonder where he was. He was still lying curled up on his side, but facing the door now. Jan bent over him to check he was all right and saw frightened wide-awake eyes gazing back at him, unblinking, large – hypnotic at that moment in their effect.

What then happened seemed, even at the time, like an inevitable natural culmination of all that had gone before. Suddenly sitting up, Adam flung his arms round Jan, clinging like a child frightened by a nightmare. Jan's immediate impulse was to push him away, but before he could recover from his surprise enough to do this, a deeper instinct took control and he was hugging Adam as resolutely as Adam was clinging to him, one hand stroking the feverish skin of Adam's back, the other holding Adam's head firmly against his own, and he was murmuring a kind of litany, 'It's all right, it's OK, I'm here, I'm with you, you're safe, we're alone, there's no one else, don't worry, it's all right.'

They remained like this for a long time, until the tension in Adam's body was soothed away and he relaxed the urgent fierceness of his embrace. But still he held on, and when at last Jan tried to ease his position Adam gripped tightly again to prevent him letting go. Not that Jan wanted to. The satisfaction he felt was so complete and, he acknowledged to himself, so long desired, that he wanted it never to end.

After a while he became aware of the icy cold of the room chilling the exposed parts of their bodies. Reaching out with a hand, he fumbled for the duvet which he pulled over them as he and Adam shuffled down into the bed, rearranging the mesh of legs and arms till they lay comfortably wrapped together.

Soon afterwards Adam began breathing the heavy rhythms of deep settled sleep, and Jan heard through his bones the slow primeval pulse of Adam's heart. For a few more minutes he revelled in the press of Adam's body against his own, the warm moist fusion of skin on skin, the touch of his fingers caressing the firm contours of Adam's limbs, and he thought: Now I am myself, will never want more for myself than this. Then he too drifted into his first dreamless, peaceful, surrendered, reviving sleep since the start of his headaches and the onset of The Glums.

Jan was woken by the cawing of the raven. For a moment he drifted in that blissful limbo before consciousness fully returns. Then the raven croaked again and everything came instantly back. He was suddenly aware of being alone, and not in his own bed either, but Adam's, and of the duvet irritatingly tangled, and of the dim grey miserly early morning light, and the chilly, slightly fetid, damp-fingered air in the room, but also of a warm glow inside himself as from embers hidden at the heart of a night-banked fire.

Anxious about Adam, he struggled to his feet, groaning at the stiffness of his body, the ache in his muscles, and pulled his clothes on fast, gritting his teeth against their icy shock. He thought fleetingly of his centrally heated room at home (home?) and was pleased with himself for not regretting it even at that moment. He wanted to be where he was, was glad of it. Of course he knew this surety was for Adam; and knew in his bones it could not last long and that its end might be painful. But in the longing of the moment he didn't care. Nor did he yet know the reality of such a pain, never having suffered it before. Knowledge of consequences, after all, depends on at least a little experience of them. Sensing the possibility isn't enough, which is why it is so hard to learn anything that matters without living at least a sliver of it.

Adam was standing stock-still in the middle of the road gazing up at the toll-house roof where, Jan knew, the raven must be perched. He was holding out his right arm and making clucking noises with his tongue and saying, as he might to a child, 'Come on, come on down, *cluck cluck cluck*, come on then.'

Thank God, Jan thought, he's talking!

But there was something pathetic about the sight. And when Jan appeared the raven took off, flapping away over the bridge.

161

Adam turned on the spot, arm still raised, following the bird's flight. Dressed only in his (Jan's) tattered sweater and distressed jeans, no socks or shoes, he paid no attention to Jan but went on staring after the raven, even when it dipped out of sight behind a parcel of trees a field away on the other side of the river. The previous day's snow had vanished. The trees were bare black bones.

Jan waited a moment before saying as lightly as he could, 'Talking to the birds!'

There was a long pause before Adam said, 'It wouldn't come.'

'No . . . Maybe, you didn't speak the right language.'

'Maybe,' Adam said, an edge of mimicry in his voice, 'and maybe it never happened.'

'It happened. And your voice has come back. That's the main thing. Come inside. You'll freeze to death out here.'

'Good,' Adam said, but turned and went into the house. Leaving Adam to brood, less anxious about him now he was talking again, Jan revived the fire, prepared breakfast, which he made more substantial than usual, boiling the last of the eggs because he thought Adam would be hungry and anyway needed nourishment. While he was busy Adam stalked about, the restlesss, angry, desperate, defeated, slow, irritating tread of a caged animal.

They ate, Adam wolfing his food, hardly noticing, saying nothing, eyes avoiding Jan, who, eating very little in small bites, struggled to keep more than his thoughts to himself, for what he wanted most was to reach across the table and take Adam's hands in his own. But intuition – his newly trusted guide – warned him that Adam would shy away from such intimacy.

He thought: I've never been faced with anything like this before – somebody of my own age who is so unhappy. But I recognize the look. I've felt like that. He's badly hurt and I can help. What matters is that I treat him decently. As far as I'm concerned – me myself and what he does to me, what he means to me – I need to work that out on my own for myself and honestly face the truth of it.

Wondering what to do, he remembered Tess sitting with him when he was in the pit of The Glums those few weeks ago that seemed at this moment like so many months ago. Her sitting with him, knowing that all she could do and what he most needed was that she be there with him – enough just by being there, physically *there* and not fussing, not harassing him with busy helpfulness, but simply waiting with him till

162

he was ready for more and then providing the energy, the willpower, the impetus he needed to live eagerly again.

How wise she had been, how truly loving, how truly a friend. And why? Why had she given herself to him in that way? Had she been utterly unselfish? Was there such a state as utter selflessness? He doubted it.

What he did know was that he was not so unselfish in wanting to help Adam. There was, if nothing else, a physical reward. Till last night he had never known the power of physicality. Not cock-pleasure, but satisfaction of the body. Flesh and bone on flesh and bone. And the gut-felt, beyond-thought need of it. His argument with Adam about gifts came to mind.

He cleared away the breakfast things, brought a book, allowed himself to move his chair to Adam's side of the table so that he was in reach should Adam want him, and there settled down to read with whatever patience he could muster. I am Janus, he thought, guarding the bridge, biding my time. Dually watchful. Of the other, of myself. Of outer, of inner. Of my him, of my her. Constant ambivalence, happy ambiguity.

Ten, fifteen minutes went by.

Then Adam said in a sudden rush, 'Last night . . .'

'Yes?'

'I'm not gay.'

'No.'

'Don't mind, just, I'm not.'

'Didn't think you were.'

'Didn't want you jumping to wrong ideas, that's all. Didn't want to disappoint you.' He attempted a smile.

'I wasn't. It's OK.'

'Don't know why I did it. Never done nothing like that before.'

'What's wrong with having a cuddle?'

'Well – it just happened, that's all.'

'You've had a rough time. Wanted some comfort. I was the only one around. What's wrong with that?'

'Didn't seem too surprised.'

'Maybe I needed a cuddle as well.'

Adam said nothing.

Jan said, 'And I'm here if you want any more.'

*

They sat in silence again. The fire crackling, an occasional vehicle crossing the bridge, the constant muffled surge of the river, never as loud inside the house during the day as it seemed during the night. Listening with pin-drop extra sharpness, Jan realized how much he had come to love the river and its ever-present noise, its slip and slide, its shifty moods, its always-the-same never-the-sameness, the hidden mystery of its opaque uncertain depths, its changing colours, the vein of it flowing through the countryside, and he remembered the holiday he and his father spent along this very reach, when he was twelve, the last wonderful week of his childhood, when each evening after their day's boating, his father read aloud from *The Wind in the Willows*, the book that had been the favourite of *his* childhood, and still Jan vividly recalled the passage that came at the end of their first exciting day, when Mole asks Rat whether he really lives by the river and Rat replies, *By it and with it and on it and in it. It's brother and sister to me, and aunts, and company, and food and drink, and (naturally) washing. It's my world and I don't want any other. What it hasn't got is not worth having, and what it doesn't know is not worth knowing. Lord! the times we've had together! Whether in winter or summer, spring or autumn, it's always got its fun and its excitements*, and he had thought how glorious that was, and in his father's face was the look of a boy the age of Jan himself, and for a strange moment he felt as if he and his father were the same age, boys together sharing this riverborne holiday without any adults to harbour them, and the next day they rowed their dinghy and Jan caught a crab just as Mole does in the episode his father read out that evening, while they giggled till tears ran and hugged each other and said what a day they'd had, and next day, his father, still in his boyhood mood, tied a rope to a tree overhanging the river and showed Jan how to play Tarzan just as Adam had his first morning at the bridge and Jan had said he had never played it for fear of what he might have to admit if he said yes and told all.

'Tell me again what you told me yesterday,' Adam said.

'About you being here?'

'Yes.'

Jan retold the story, more shaped this time after yesterday's rehearsal.

'Don't remember any of that,' Adam said afterwards, 'none of it. Doesn't even sound like me.'

'Want to see the photos again?'

'If you like.'

He pored over them, pursing his lips and shaking his head.

'I've never decorated nowhere, don't know a song like the one you say I camped up.'

'How'd you know if you don't remember anything even from before you came here?'

Adam eyed him warily. 'Just do, that's all.'

'Have you remembered something?'

Adam lowered his head to the photos and withdrew into silence.

Unable to sit still any longer Jan left Adam to his brooding and set about the housekeeping chores. Made the beds, tidied the bedroom, washed up the breakfast things, fetched wood for the fire, swept up ashes from the hearth. It was then he remembered Gill's bag left by Tess behind the armchair. He took it into the bedroom, intending to stow it there till he was ready to return it.

But in the bedroom curiosity got the better of him. And more: a desire to handle Gill's belongings, to touch things that had intimately touched her.

As he unzipped the bag and spread it open the familiar smell of Gill's body breathed out, a mix of talcum powder, her soap (Cusson's Imperial Leather), her favourite perfume ('Penelope' by Lauren, which she wore because Jan had given her a small bottle as a birthday present), and the faint musky tang of her sweat. His nose twitched and his mouth watered, and he felt an echo of her hand caressing him between the thighs, which made him feel suddenly very lonely.

He eased the crotch of his jeans and began unpacking. Conscious of his illicit behaviour, he treated each item with delicate fingertip care, laying them out neatly on the bed.

Aubergine jumper.

Breton-sailor-style T-shirt, one of his that Gill had 'borrowed' because she wanted something of his to wear.

Two large sloppy T-shirts, one white with Shakespeare's head on the front in black (bought on a visit they'd made together to Stratford) and a plain red one.

Pair of washed-out pale blue cuff-frayed jeans.

Three pairs of flimsy pink cotton panties.

Flimsy halter bra to match (memories of the pleasure of removing it).

Two pairs of socks: one pair pink; one pair white-and-red stripes.

Traveller's electric hair drier trailing the twisted snake of its umbilical cord.

Orange and yellow polka-dotted hand towel.

Mauve toilet bag with pattern of blue and yellow Matisse flowers containing:

> pink small-handled toothbrush,
> small tube of peppermint 'Sensodyne' toothpaste,
> Body Shop lipstick, mascara, lip balm, face
>   powder, powder brush, little case of make-up like a child's
>   paint box, eye-shadow pencil,
> small bottle of Johnson's Baby Oil,
> roll-on odourless deodorant,
> small bottle of Balsam shampoo,
> packet of six 'Extra-safe, Extra-sensitive,
>   Featherlite' condoms – 'gossamer thin for that intimate
>   touch'.

He held the packet of condoms in the palm of his hand, thinking of the message it bore of a time that might have been and Gill must have hoped would be; and remembering their times together before. Collision of past and present, of sight and smell and touch.

He sat on the edge of the bed surveying Gill's possessions, acutely aware as never before of the difference, the *otherness* of the female from the male: different other smell and texture, difference of *weight*, difference – he searched for a word, for a phrase that named the deepest, most different difference and found: *density of being*.

He fingered Gill's things, his imagination busy. Images of images, he thought now – now in this my now, now in your now, me now not me then. Marks on paper. Bridge between subject and object. Outside over there from inside under here. Janus in this hand, these eyes, this mouth, this head.

Everything was there, what was true of him and why. All there in Gill's possessions neatly laid on the bed and Adam next door and Tess soon to be on her way to them. All there at the bridge. But bridges freeze before roads. So cross with care. But cross you must. And the time when he must cross, he sensed, had come.

He was about to repack the bag when he saw there was something else inside. At first he thought it was a picture postcard. But no: it was a photograph Tess had taken of himself and Adam, arms round each other and laughing. Had Tess given it to her? She had told him about Gill looking at her pictures but had said nothing about giving one to Gill. Had Gill taken it without Tess knowing? Stolen it? Why had she wanted it anyway?

Suddenly, as if a blockage had been cleared, a membrane breached, there rose from the pit of his belly a sickening sense of remorse at his treatment of Gill. He suddenly saw all the past few months from her vantage, saw how he and everything at the house must have looked to her. He could not believe that he had been so unthinking, so unfeeling, so unknowing. Battering himself with self-reproach, breaking into a sweat, too weak to stand, he could not bear the sensation of being imprisoned in himself, unable to escape his self-accusations. Again and again he sighed and thumped his thighs with his fists and rubbed his hands back and forth, back and forth.

He suffered like this for some while before the bout subsided. When at last it did he felt a refreshing sense of relief – the relief of knowing at last something you have not even recognized before. And knowing what to do about it.

He stood and stretched himself, reaching for the ceiling with his fingertips, like a man after a long sleep. Then he carefully repacked Gill's bag, carefully stowed it under his bed, and returned to the living room to attend to Adam.

Time to dress the wound. There had been no more bleeding; the cotton-wool pad had left the skin chicken-skin wrinkled and white. Jan sponged the area with a damp disinfected cloth. Adam flinched as he dabbed at the cut.

'You'll live,' Jan said, 'but best leave it uncovered. Probably heal quicker if the air can get at it. What about the headache?'

'Gone.'

Adam turned away and inspected his wound in the shaving mirror above the sink then, without another word, began making two mugs of coffee. Maybe now he would start talking.

But he didn't. Instead he sat in the armchair and gazed unseeing at the blank TV screen, as shut-in and unwelcoming as before.

When he'd finished his coffee Jan said, trying another strategy, 'Feel like a walk? I phone home on a Sunday morning.'

Adam shook his head.

Maybe some time on his own would be good for him.

Jan stood up. 'You'll be OK?'

Adam nodded.

'Not be long. Half an hour or so.'

As he reached the door Adam said, 'Jan –'

Jan turned.

'Thanks.'

'No problem.'

'I mean for everything.'

Nonplussed by this unAdam-like declaration, Jan could only smile and nod.

Snow began falling again as he left the bridge, thick feathery flakes slowly descending as in the aftermath of an astronomic pillow fight. On the phone, he had the usual conversation with his mother: everything was fine, his father had been doing this and that, Mrs Fletcher had had a nasty attack of angina but her son was doing wonderfully in his new computer software job, they hadn't seen Gill yet this weekend but perhaps she'd call later, had this week's parcel (a fruit cake) arrived safely? (yes), had he decided about school next term? (yes, he was staying in his job), she was longing to see him at Christmas, etc. His father followed, talking for five minutes about the garden and painting the inside of the tool shed, telling a lawyer joke heard in court, and working in a coded message – 'Your mother's been in good fettle', meaning she was getting along well after the recent crisis.

Duty done, he took a deep breath before punching Gill's number, the call he really wanted to make. On the way there he had composed a short speech on the lines of how sorry he was about the weekend and everything else, that he hadn't meant to hurt her, that he'd be writing a letter trying to explain and would talk to her at Christmas, but he was ringing to find out that she had got home safely and was all right.

Gill's mother answered. 'Oh, it's you, Piers.'

'Hello, Mrs Redmond. Could I speak to Gill, please.'

There was a muffled pause before Mrs Redmond said, 'Yes, well now, Gill's not here, I'm afraid, well, no, she is here –'

'Could I –'

'– but the fact is, Piers, she'd rather not speak to you today –'

'But if –'

'– and to be honest, we're rather cross with you, her father and I, for the way you've treated her –'

'Would you please ask –'

'She arrived home in a terrible state. I don't know quite what went on between you, she wouldn't tell us, but one thing I do know she's very upset –'

'I'll explain if –'

'So we think it would be best if you left her alone and didn't try and contact her for a while –'

'But –'

'She'll get in touch when she feels up to it –'

'Couldn't I –'

'And frankly, Piers, I'm surprised you've called now after being so silent all the time you've been away, which wasn't very friendly, you must admit, especially when you consider how much Gill did for you before you went away, how much we all did. So I'll say goodbye for the present.'

The dialling tone burred in his ear. He slammed the receiver down and cursed. And remained where he was for some minutes, blank of mind, until Tess's voice brought him to his senses again.

'Making your Sunday call?'

He nodded and they set off together towards the bridge, hunched against the snow, hands in pockets, heads down.

'You all right?' Tess asked as they stomped along. 'Seem a bit down.'

'Tried Gill.'

'But she didn't want to talk.'

'Right.'

'I know, I phoned her as well.'

'She talked to you?'

'Sure.'

'Bloody hell! So why won't she talk to me?'

'Oh, come on! Why didn't you answer her letters?'

'Just wanted to know she got home OK and tell her I'd be writing this week.'

'Promises, promises.'

'I will, I've been thinking.'

'Try doing.'

'Been doing as well, looking after Adam.'

'And how's he this morning?'

'Talking.'

'Thank God! So what's the story?'

'Still can't remember.'

'D'you believe him?'

'About the time he's been here. But I've a feeling he can remember before.'

The snow was brisker now, blown by a gusty breeze the flakes having turned to spelks of ice stung the face.

Jan said, 'The raven came back. He tried charming it, but it wasn't having any, which set things back a bit.'

Tess stopped abruptly.

Jan had taken eight or nine paces before he realized she was not beside him.

'What's up?' he called.

She shrugged, head down, huddled into herself.

He went back. 'Something wrong?'

'Can't face it.'

'Face what?'

'Him.'

The unTess-like pitifulness of her voice anguished him. They were on the outskirts of the village, nowhere to get out of the snow. But a few metres ahead was a bus shelter. Jan put an arm round Tess's shoulder and guided her into it. Doing so, he felt a decisiveness that was new; Tess too, and in the calm part of herself she thought: He's changed, grown. More certain of himself. How much I like him.

In the shelter Jan turned Tess to him and held her loosely, his arms round her neck.

'Come on, this isn't my Tess.'

She tried to smile but was close to tears.

'What's up?'

'Everything.'

'What's everything?'

'The last few days, Adam, Gill, me – everything.'

Jan said nothing. Brushed wet hair from her eyes.

Tess sniffled, wiped her nose on the back of her hand. 'Hardly slept since Wednesday.'

Snow swirled round their feet. They nestled closer, Tess resting her brow on Jan's chest, his chin on her head.

'And I'll have to see the doctor,' she mumbled.

Jan tried to take a step back to look her in the face but she prevented him.

'What's matter? Are you ill?'

'He'll give me a heavy lecture, I expect. You'll laugh.'

170

'Why? What about?'

'Taking stupid risks, not being responsible.'

'What sort of risks?'

'Wasn't going to tell you, but –' She sniffled and raised her head and wiped her nose again and could look him in the eyes now. 'Thursday night, while you were at my place –' She paused, the words clogging in her throat.

Jan said, 'I know.'

'He told you?'

'No.'

'Guessed?'

'Saw.'

Now it was Tess who tried to step back and Jan who held her still. He told her of his jealousy and his lust and about stealing out of the house and running to the bridge and peeking into the living room and watching her and Adam at it in front of the fire, and how happy he'd been for them. But he left Bob out of the story.

Tess squinted at him, tears staunched by an astringent douche of embarrassment.

'You never!'

He nodded, grinning.

'Pervert!'

'Sexpot!'

'Voyeur!'

'Crrritic!'

They cuddled against the cold and hung on for a while before Tess said,

'I will, though, have to see the doc I mean, and I'm worried sick.'

'You'll be OK.'

'How can you say that! How can you know! I was stupid. I've always told myself I'd never be that stupid, but I was, and now I'll have to have awful embarrassing tests and wait till the results come through, and even then, if I'm HIV, nobody can tell for months, longer – years –!' She was crying now.

'Hey, hey! Steady!'

'It's all right for you to say that! Steady! What does *steady* mean? Doesn't change anything, does it!' She stamped her foot in desperation.

'I know, I know, but I don't know what else to say. I don't blame you or anything. And I'm not going to desert you whatever happens . . . I'm here . . . OK?'

'I'm sorry, I'm sorry, I know, I'm being hysterical, but I *feel* hysterical, dammit!'

'Now listen, you! Don't you desert me now. You go twitchy, who've I got to keep me right?'

'I need to be kept right sometimes as well, you know.'

'Now she tells me! And I've always thought of you as confident, knowing who you are, what you want.'

'Well, I'm not!'

'You're not! Dear God, another shock! Well, it's enough for me that I believe you are, so don't go letting me down.'

He wiped her tears away and they clung to each other again, weaving gently back and forth, till Tess said,

'Hello, friend.'

'Hi, pal.'

'I'm feeling the cold a bit.'

'Me too. Want to go?'

'Dunno whether I can face it.'

'I'm hardly the one to say so, but maybe that's the very thing you should do.'

'On the falling off a horse principle?'

'Something like that.'

'You know, when it comes down to it, you're a terrible moralist.'

'There you go, insulting me again.'

'Well, somebody has to tell you the truth about yourself.'

'And what else are friends for?'

'Something like that.'

Tess released herself, glowered at the snowbound scene around them. The breeze had dropped, the snow had eased. She said, 'Come on then. Mount up.'

'Joy at last.'

She laughed and turned to go, but before setting off, her back to him, said in a small voice, 'Jan, seriously – do I matter that much?'

Jan took a deep breath. 'Nobody more.'

Tess left a pause before saying, 'Why?'

'When I understand that myself, you'll be the first to know.'

She turned to face him again, smiling. 'I was right to call you Janus.'

'I know.'

'Now you do, then you didn't.'

'Maybe that's the reason.'

As we came round the bend into the straight stretch of road leading to the bridge, Tess said, 'Do you see what I see?'

An unmistakable figure in the middle of the bridge by the downstream parapet.

'Now what's he up to?'

There was something about his posture that made the pit of the belly lurch.

'He's fiddling with something round his ankles.'

'Doing up his laces?'

It was hard to be sure through the curtain of snow.

Before we could see clearly, Adam stood up straight, leaned on the parapet, peered down into the river as if checking he was in the right place, shuffled round, hitched his bottom up onto the parapet, swung his legs up and then pushed himself to his feet.

By this time we were close enough to see clearly.

'Rope!' Tess exclaimed. 'Round his ankles!'

'Christ, no!'

We started to run. A car appeared, driving slowly over the bridge from the other side.

'Adam!' Jan shouted. 'Adam! No!'

Adam's head snapped round in our direction. He yelled, 'Go away!' and shuffled, trying to twist himself towards the river. The car, almost to him now, blew its horn. Adam swung in its direction, his hobbled feet slipped and he fell backward just as the car went by, hitting its roof, bouncing off, and falling to the road. The car swerved, braked, and, its wheels locking, skidded across the bridge, turning back to front as it went and ending up with an almost delicate bump against the corner of the house.

We reached Adam seconds later. He lay on his side, growling and groaning and cursing and holding his leg at the knee.

As we bent down to take hold of him a man's voice shouted from the car, 'Don't touch him! Lie still!'

We both straightened up like children yelled at in school. The car was a black Ford Granada. We could see the driver through the windscreen, the wiper still going: short-cropped silver-grey hair, large round florid face; he was using a car phone.

But Adam went on howling in pain and anger. He tried to get up but instantly collapsed with an excruciating scream that shook us out of our schoolkid obedience. Jan pulled off his anorak, rolled it into a bundle and placed it under Adam's head before holding him by the shoulders, all the time saying, 'Steady, steady, take it easy, you mustn't move, looks like you've broken your leg.' Adam's face was pallid, a sickly yellow against the snow, except for the wound on his brow which shone a hot raw red.

While Jan tended Adam, Tess was examining the rope tied round his ankles, tracking its length over the parapet and down and looping back up again before it reached the water, the other end tied to the neck of one of the urn-shaped balusters. Her heart thumped with horror, for she realized what it meant; had sensed what Adam was doing from the moment she saw him.

'We've got to fetch help,' she said and set off, only to be stopped by the man getting out of his car, holding out an arm and saying, 'Hang on, where are you going?'

'For help.'

'Done. Phoned for an ambulance and the police. You'll be needed as a witness.'

Tess didn't like the sound of him: officious, overbearing. She said, 'And I should fetch my dad.'

'Why, what's he got to do with it?'

'He's in charge of the bridge.'

The man hesitated, giving her a suspicious look before saying, 'On the phone?'

Tess nodded.

'Use mine. You shouldn't leave before the police get here.'

Tess got into the car. The driver walked over to Adam and surveyed the scene with a detachment that made Jan wonder whether he had any feelings.

'What the hell was he up to?' the man said, but seeing the rope added, 'Oh, yes, like that, is it.'

'We can't leave him here,' Jan said, 'he'll freeze to death.'

The man crouched down and inspected Adam's leg, feeling it as if prodding a marrow for ripeness. Adam let out a yelp. 'Fractured, I'd say.'

'The ambulance could take ages. Has to come from the hospital in town, and with this weather –'

The man straightened up. 'Doesn't matter. Could be injuries to his back, his head, anything. Dangerous to shift him. And you know how bloody touchy the insurance is these days.'

Adam went suddenly silent. He stared at the man with wild panicked eyes.

Jan felt trapped, all the old home-school constrictions clamped over him again. He wanted to pick Adam up and run.

'At least we should try and keep him warm,' he said, hearing the desperation in his voice. 'I'll get some blankets.'

'Where from?'

It struck Jan that the man didn't know who he and Adam were. 'The toll house. We live here.'

His eyes swam. He glanced down at Adam, beautiful lost desperate frightened Adam-that-was-not-Adam, in whose eyes glaring back at him he read the same understanding: that this was the beginning of an end. He bent down, kissed him on the forehead, said quietly, 'I'll be back. I'm going for some blankets.'

[– The rest of that day was horrible.

– One of the worst of my life. *The* worst.

– Do we have to write it all?

– Do I, you mean. The police, the ambulance, your father, that bull-headed Granada lout, all of them wanting to know who Adam was and what had happened and how and why and the lout yammering on about his precious car and his insurance and how innocent he was and how obvious it was what Adam had been 'up to', and Adam being taken away and them not letting us go with him. It was awful.

– So do we have to write it all? Just thinking about it makes me feel sick.

– The thing I shan't ever forget, even if I forget all the rest of it, is them lifting Adam into the ambulance, strapped down, and him pleading for me to help him, and not being able to do *anything*, not a thing, and the doors closing and the ambulance driving off across the bridge and disappearing through the snow like a sarcophagus on wheels. I dream about it.

– I know, I know.

– And do you know that 'sarcophagus' comes from a Greek word meaning 'stone that devours flesh'?

– No, I didn't know that and I think I wish you hadn't mentioned it.

– Appropriate though, don't you think? Poetic. Remember how spelled he was by the stones in the Kafka story?

– I told you this part would get you all upset.

– Upset! What's wrong with being upset? Should I just dam it all up, keep it in, wear a good old English stiff upper lip?

– Don't.]

175

Of course, as soon as they discovered we didn't know who Adam really was, consternation collided with the vent. What on earth did we think we were doing? Didn't we know what a risk we'd taken? What if he were a violent nutcase? Didn't Jan realize how irresponsible he'd been? Et cetera, *ad infinitum*. They demanded the whole story. We gave them an edited version with the ultra-private bits left out.

The mills of officialdom ground small. Telecommunications bleeped all day. One of Tess's photos of Adam was sent for matching against mugshots in the missing persons / wanted files. A policeman with a Dutch-uncle manner and a cool smile hinted about the possibility of charges against us for aiding and abetting and being accessories after the fact should Adam turn out to be 'a naughty sort of laddie'. Statements were culled and written and signed.

Could I [Jan] see Adam?

Breath sucked between clamped teeth: No, no, not till everything was properly sorted out.

How was he?

In good hands, a bad break but he'd mend.

Had he said anything?

Nothing to report on that one, 'old son'.

At least they agreed there was no need to contact Jan's parents 'unless and until anything untoward comes to light'.

All this at the toll house: a couple of policemen, Bob Norris, Tess and Jan, the Granada driver having been dealt with first and sent on his way.

A bizarre moment in the middle of the questioning: They decided to break for coffee. Because they were in Jan's place, he was asked to make it. Mind-split from shock, observing himself performing the chore. The bobbies and Bob Norris warming their backsides at the fire as if they'd just dropped in for a friendly visit, discussing the weather and the prospects for the local soccer team. Jan glanced at Tess who was sitting forlornly at the table. She got up and joined him.

'I'm going on ten,' she murmured. 'What about you?'

'Old enough to be sent to bed without any supper.'

'That's what comes of being caught wanking in public.'

'How crude.'

'In training for life in the slammer.'

'Is there anything we can do?'

176

'Weep?'

'Not in front of the children.'

'I'm sorry, Jan.'

'If I'd been here – if I hadn't left him –'

'It's not your fault, don't blame yourself.'

One of the policemen returned to the table saying, 'Now, you two, how about that coffee?'

And the questioning began again and went on till they'd had enough or got what they wanted and went, leaving us 'in your tender care, Mr Norris. You'll see they behave themselves, won't you, and that they remain in the locality in case we need to question them further.'

Throughout the ordeal Bob Norris bridged the gap between us and everybody else. Jan's admiration and liking for him deepened. Not that Bob wasn't upset, furious even, but typical of him, in front of us at least, he was calm, amenable, unruffled.

After the police left he held his own interrogation, guessing there was more to the story than we had let on. We told him about the party, about Gill, about Adam being unconscious all night, about his desperation after he came to, and we explained what we had planned to do. Bob pursed his lips now and then, shook his head, huffed, smiled at our various panics, but took everything in without comment. As for us, we were glad to talk to someone older who we could trust. We both felt a great weight lifted from us and – though we would not have admitted it – relief that it was over.

Tess and Jan spent the rest of that Sunday huddled together by the fire, and went over everything again and again. They snacked but ate little. Two or three times they walked through the still falling snow to the village phone and called the hospital, always to be told that Adam was 'comfortable but not allowed visitors'.

They parted reluctantly late that evening, Tess not wanting to face the family's questions, Jan not wanting to be alone. But they had no choice and they ended the day in an empty exhausted silence before Tess plodded off, her feet crunching and squeaking on the crisp snow while Jan watched the beam of her flashlight to the bend in the road, from where she shone it back at him and blinked it off/on, off/on in a final farewell.

Monday. Snow thick on the ground, reflecting the dawn light up into the bedroom and filling the room with an unfamiliar glow.

Jan was up early, unable to lie still. The river was oiled metal edged with frayed lace. Bird and animal tracks criss-crossed the white blanket of the garden, surprising in number, a crowd had they all visited at once.

The comfort of daily routines got him through. But he was heartsick for Adam.

In her room at home Tess was also awake, but she stayed where she was, curled up in bed, horrified by what she had seen at the bridge and wishing and wondering and regretting and berating herself. She got up and left for school at the last possible moment. Because of the snow she took the bus, so didn't see Jan that morning. She passed a dreary abstracted day, only half aware of the excitements caused by the snow and taking nothing in during lessons. Her friends, dying to talk about the party, quickly learned not to try. During the dinner hour her period started, relieving her mind of at least one worry.

Bob Norris turned up at the bridge early that afternoon. Jan could tell from his face there was bad news.

'Adam?'

'Haven't phoned this morning. You?'

'No.'

Bob sat at the table, refused coffee, asked how Jan was, talked about the weather, the state of the roads. Then silence.

Jan waited; Bob always took his time. When he was ready he said with strained quietness,

'There's something I have to tell you.'

'Yes?'

'To do with the estate.'

178

'They've found a buyer for the house.'

'Worse than that.'

'Worse?'

'The whole estate.'

'All of it?'

'The lot – lock, stock and toll bridge.'

'Dear God! When?'

'Last week. Huge multinational. Plan to build their new European headquarters here.'

'But that means . . .' Jan tried to grasp the implications.

'The whole area will be affected. Lot of new building. New jobs as well of course.'

Jan took a deep breath. 'So what happens now?'

'I've instructions to tell you that your job will officially end on the last day of this month. You'll be sent a letter in the next couple of days.'

Jan could think of nothing to say. Like anyone who's been sacked, he felt like chattel, a powerless object to be discarded at will, that his time at the bridge had been wasted.

Bob went on, 'Traditionally, if you'll pardon me for using a rude word, *traditionally* no tolls are taken from Christmas Eve till the second of January. You were going home for that week anyway so you might as well pack up and leave for good on Friday. Sooner, if you like. The extra few days won't matter. And the new manager says he won't object.'

It took a moment for this to sink in. When it did, Jan said, 'The new manager?'

'Arrived this morning.'

'But you're –'

'Redundant.'

'But they can't!'

'They can and they have. All very proper and legal, redundancy settlement and all that. And they've been generous enough to give me three months to find somewhere else to live. Our house belongs to the estate of course.'

'The bastards!'

'Welcome to the real world, son.'

'Is it?'

'You'll see.'

'No. There has to be a better real than that.'

179

'Oh? Let me know when you've found it. In the meantime, the new boss has a job or two for me so I'd better stir me stumps.'

Neither moved. They stared across the table at each other.

'You must be devastated,' Jan said.

'It's not unexpected. I thought something like this might happen as soon as the major brought in the estate agent. And there've been men in Jags and expensive suits up at the house quite a lot lately. So it isn't the shock it might have been. The major's come up trumps as well, I'll give him that. He'll cover us for a new house wherever we decide to live.'

'So he bloody should after the years your family's given him. Cheap at the price!'

Bob smiled. 'Bolshie.'

'Well, it's true. He'll come off all right, I'll bet.'

'Won't be short of a penny, that's for sure. But at least I'll not be as badly hit as a lot of men in my position.'

'What'll you do, though? Retire?'

'Lord, no! Not ready for the geriatric ward yet. The wife says I should use some of the redundancy to set up on my own – jobbing work. She says people are always complaining they can't find reliable men for small jobs – repairs, maintenance, a bit of building and decorating. But I don't know. Running your own business isn't all it's cracked up to be. And anyway, the paperwork would get me down. Don't mind hard work, but writing letters and filling forms and keeping the accounts. No no, not for me.'

They were silent again before Bob said, 'And what about you? What'll you do?'

'Go home, I suppose, what else? Don't want to, not to stay. Made the break, don't want to go back.'

'Take a tip from me. Finish school, get yourself to university. A good education is the best start you can give yourself. That's what I didn't have. Wouldn't be in this predicament now if I'd had an education. And don't give me that sour look.'

Jan managed a smile.

Bob stood up. 'I'd best be off,' he said and made for the door. 'Let's know which day you decide you'll go. The wife says come for dinner before you leave. We've liked having you around. Oh, and by the way,' he added as if an afterthought, 'brought you this.'

He took a small brown-paper parcel from his pocket and put it on the table.

'What is it?'

'Memento. Christmas present. Something of that sort. See you later.'

Inside, wrapped in bubble pack and layers of tissue, was the prayer mug with its two-faced Janus.

Tess heard the news from her mother when she came home from school. She arrived at the bridge blazing. Jan had never seen her in such a megaton rage before. It both frightened and exhilarated him.

When her anger had vented itself they turned their minds to thinking what to do next. Jan's main concern was Adam. All day long he had been nagged by worry about him.

'I can't decide what to do myself till I know what's happening to him.'

'You've rung the hospital?'

'This afternoon. Same story: comfortable but no visitors. I rang the police as well. Nothing. They'll let me know, et cetera. Can't reveal any details, the case still under investigation.'

'You want to see him, is that it?'

'Course I do. Want to know how he is and want him to tell me who he is and what's been going on. Don't you?'

'Don't just *want* to know. *Need* to know. That's right, isn't it?'

'Yes.'

'So we'll find out.'

'How?'

'Go to the hospital. There's bound to be a visiting time in the evening.'

'But he isn't allowed visitors.'

'Oh dear oh dear, we didn't know, what a pity, and we've come all this way just to see him, we're close friends of his, he was staying with us when he had his ... accident, couldn't we just wave to him through the window or something? ... What d'you think?'

'Won't work.'

'Wimp!'

'Bully!'

'Defeatist!'

'Who said there'd be no wars if women were in charge?'

'Sexist. We can at least *try*. And it'll be better than hanging round in this condemned cell all night, I'd just go *mad*!'

The reception area was busy.

'Hang on,' Tess said. 'Let's weigh things up before we take the plunge.'

'Must be the strain.'

'What?'

'Makes you talk in clichés.'

'Don't start, *please*!'

They stood against a wall opposite the reception desk, to one side of which was a notice board listing the wards.

'Know which ward he's in?'

'Seven.'

'Fifth floor.'

Some visitors went to the reception desk, others, knowing their way, went straight to the lifts. Almost everyone was carrying hospitalish gifts.

'Ought to have some flowers or something,' Tess said. 'We'd look more convincing.'

'Maybe if I limped they'd think I was a patient.'

'Maybe if I gave you a tweak you'd shut up and follow me.'

They made their way to the lifts and took the next one to the fifth floor.

'Look confident,' Tess said as they approached the ward. 'That's the secret.'

'Not good at acting.'

'Leave the talking to me.'

'You're enjoying this! I'll never understand women.'

'Not women. Me.'

At the nurses' desk they waited behind a family of four – anxious parents, two bored children of about seven – while the ward sister chatted about their relative. A nursing aide was filing papers and eavesdropping; she glanced at Tess and Jan but did not speak.

The family disposed of, Sister turned her professional smile on Tess.

'We're here to see –' Tess began and dried, suddenly realizing she didn't know what to call Adam.

'Adam,' Jan said quickly, anticipating the dilemma and knowing fom his phone calls that this name worked.

But Sister looked from one to the other, puzzled. 'Adam?'

'The boy in C2,' the aide said.

'Oh, him. Poor lad! Yes. You're too late, I'm afraid. They took him away about an hour ago.'

'Took him away?' Jan said.

'Where?' Tess said.

'Who took him?'

Sister was wary. 'Are you family?'

'Yes,' Tess said.

'No,' Jan said. 'No, not exactly. We were with him when he had his accident. He was staying with us.'

'I'm sorry,' Sister said. 'I can't tell you anything. Not allowed. It's a police matter, you see. Nothing I can do.'

Jan said, 'Was it the police who took him?'

'And a doctor. Now, that's all I can tell you. You really will have to ask the police.'

They retreated into the corridor.

Jan said, 'I don't believe this. They can't just cart him off and not tell us. What the hell's going on?'

They made for the lift.

'I'm going to the police station,' Jan said, pressing the button.

As they waited, too bewildered to speak, the nursing aide came hurrying up to them and said, 'Can I have a word with you?'

She led them through swing doors marked EXIT: STAIRS.

'You're Jan and Tess?'

They nodded. The nurse produced an envelope from the side pocket of her uniform. 'He asked me to post this to you. I shouldn't. There'll be trouble if you tell. I was going to bring it, to make sure.'

'We won't,' Jan said.

'No, we won't,' Tess said.

'He was such a nice kid. His name was Aston Davies, by the way.'

'But where've they taken him?' Jan said.

'Norton Psychiatric Unit. It's near Leeds, a special detention unit for disturbed young offenders. Look, I've got to get back.'

She was gone before either of them could even thank her.

They made themselves wait till they were on the bus home before opening the envelope.

As Jan pulled out a folded A4 page Adam's silver chain slithered onto his lap.

Have to be quick, coming for me soon. Wish you had not stopped me, it is my life, I should be let do what I want with it, I am not fit to live. You were good to me though Jan you tried to help me and I want to thank you and the nurse who gives you this who is nice says I should explain if I really mean it. I do not know how to start, so many things to tell and the main thing that happened is not the only thing.

The main thing is I killed another boy. Did not mean to, it just happened. That is what all we murderers say I expect. 14 then, 17 now, was playing with a gang of other boys, seven of us, larking about with a tennis ball, playing a game, I do not remember what but it had winners and losers and the losers had to give a penalty. I lost and would not give the penalty, I was fed up of losing, I was always losing. The boy who was the leader, he was called Tony, he was older, about 16, was always making snide remarks about me and this time I would not pay the penalty, I was fed up of him. But the others said I had to and I said no it was stupid and the others said Tony had to make me pay, it was the rule. He said Come on you have to do it and I said get stuffed, who are you anyway, you are just a loser yourself or why are you playing with us. I was up against a wall, and when I said that Tony started tossing the tennis ball at me aiming so it would just miss and bounce back, but I kept saying no and then he started calling me names and tossed the ball harder and harder and closer and closer and then the ball hit me in the face. It didn't really hurt, I started swearing at him and crying and I picked up a pebble, threw it at him and he said Come on cry baby you aren't hurt, and threw a stone and the other kids started throwing them as well and after that it all got out of hand. They started throwing bigger and bigger stones, anything they could find. I do not remember much about the rest except I chucked the stones harder and harder back at them and they came closer and closer so I ducked to the side where one of the smaller kids was standing and grabbed him and held him in front of me to protect myself, I thought they would stop then, but they didn't, they just kept on, and I don't know what happened then, I must have flipped or something, I was not seeing anything, it was just a red blur, but in the end the boy I grabbed was on the ground and I was beating him in the head with a big rock in both hands which I only know because it is what the other boys said in court.

Will not tell you all the stuff about the doctors, they said I was not to blame, it was a one-off, but could not promise it would not happen again so they put me away and give me treatment which I will not tell you about either, it makes no difference what they say or what they do, they do not have the dreams, they do not have the headaches which I have because of what I did.

I am sorry I killed the boy, I am to blame aren't I or who is? I know that even though I do not understand what happened to me or why it happened and am afraid about it happening again. I was so scared when I come to on the boat the other night, I was afraid I might of done it again you see, and you helped a lot, you really did, you are a good bloke, Jan, I wish I was as well, we could be friends I know that and wish I could stay with you at the bridge where I think I could be happy if it was not for what might happen. But they are taking me back where I ran away from which I do remember but I do not remember any of the time you told me about at the bridge, I was telling you the truth, it was just a story to me, I wish it was me, I think I would have liked to be me if I was Adam, you had a lot of fun.

I want you to keep the chain, I have nothing else to give you and I want you to remember me and to wish you all the very best of luck in the world which you deserve.

Daffodils in great swaying clumps all the way up the drive to the main building. I never see daffodils now without remembering that day. They have always been my favourite flower, such brave bright beauty, fresh yellow clown-collared heads nodding to the world on their straight-limbed stalks.

The unit was a complex of buildings clustering round an old Victorian mansion. The approach looked ordinary, nothing like a prison, but beyond the main house were ugly modern functional buildings behind high security fences and walls.

The reception area in the entrance hall had that hard echoey emptiness of public institutions that occupy old family houses. I had to wait for half an hour, sitting in a plastic-covered armchair that was sticky to the touch, before Doctor Pelham arrived: flapping white coat, jeans and Adidas trainers, bony face, grey eyes, fleshy lips, thinning salt-and-pepper hair, balding at the front, wispy long at the back, big heavy hairy hands that were labourer-rough and gripped hard. He wasted no time on pleasantries, just said, 'Hi, you ready for this?'

'Nervous, a bit.'

'Just take what you see, be neutral. If it upsets you, come back here, don't display in front of Aston, OK?'

A visitor's identity pass was clipped to my sweater, I signed some kind of permission form, after which the doctor led me through a maze of corridors, and outside, through a security gate in a high fence, along a path by the side of what looked like living quarters with bars over the windows, through another security gate in a high ancient brick wall, which let us into a large walled area that I guessed must have been the nursery garden in the old days. There were oblongs of ground cultivated as flower beds or vegetable patches with grass paths between. A couple of warders were on duty, watching five or six young men in regulation trousers and jackets who were hoeing, digging, planting. The doctor spoke to them as we went by, the matey professional, everyday cheery stuff about their gardening. One of the men called out, 'A new chicken for the coop, doc?' Pelham laughed and waved and called back, 'Never know your luck, Freddy.'

The far corner of the garden, away from the flowers and vegetables, an area about forty metres square bordered by paths on two sides and the angle of the high brick wall on the other two, had been allowed to grow wild. A tall Norway maple dominated the area, already thickly dressed in spring-green leaves. A rope ladder dangled down through the branches. Under the tree was a makeshift tent made of an old patched tarpaulin draped over rough-cut wooden poles tied down by improvised guy ropes. In its entrance stood a rickety-looking table and chair each cobbled together out of oddments. There was a book on the table on top of what I thought was a magazine. Cluttering round the tent were wooden orange boxes and packing cases and a barrel. Nearby was a pile of wooden palings about three metres long, also rough-cut. From one wall to the other, curving around in front of the tent and tree, marking it off like an enclosure, was a length of rope held up by stakes stuck into the ground at two- or three-metre intervals, with no gap for a way in. The whole place had the look of an adventure playground in the early stages of construction, yet everything was tidy and neat and carefully arranged as if for some serious adult purpose.

The doctor brought me to a stop at the rope barrier facing the entrance to the tent.

'Hello, there,' he called. 'Aston?'

'Hi, doc.' The voice came from high in the tree, Adam's voice but lighter than I remembered, boyish, a child's voice.

'Would you like to come down for a minute?'

'OK.'

Branches shook, the rope ladder danced, bare feet appeared, legs in tattered jeans chopped off just below the knee, a body in a loose garment, half shirt, half jacket, cackhandedly home-made of pieces of thick brown cloth (curtain material?) stitched together with red gardener's twine, and the unmistakable head with its jet black hair long now and rumpled.

He reached the ground and turned to approach us, smiling broadly at the doctor – that wide anguishing grin, white teeth showing, eyes wrinkling. I wanted to run and grab him and hold him to me. Pelham must have sensed this because he took hold of my arm as if ready to restrain me. What held me back, though, was the complete lack of any sign of recognition in Adam's face. And he moved, not as the Adam I knew, but as a child would, a little less coordinated, uninhibitedly unaware of himself, yet a hint of wariness too, not entirely trusting. His face was grubby, his hands and clothes smeared with moss and dirt from the tree. Already, as he came towards us, it was hard for me to see Adam, but instead a boy who had been made to break off from play.

He reached us and stood dutifully waiting to hear what the doctor wanted.

'So how are you today, Aston?'

'OK.'

'The leg holding up?'

'It's OK. Doesn't bother me.'

'No pain or anything?'

'It's all right. Hurts a bit if I jump on it, but it's OK.'

'Well, take it steady for a few more days.'

'OK.'

'This is Jan.'

The eyes turned on me: the other-Adam eyes. 'Hi.'

'Hi.'

'Jan's having a look round.'

'Is he a savage?'

'No, I don't think so. Would you like him to join you?'

I was inspected more closely. 'Was he sent by Providence?'

'Could be.'

Further scrutiny. I stood, smiling back, trying to be calm and unrevealing, though inside my stomach churned.

'Not Friday, though.'

'No?'

Pelham let go of my arm and took a step away, exaggeratedly viewing the enclosure. 'Looks like you're about ready to start your fence.'

'A wall for my habitation.'

'Finished your chair as well.'

'Robinson took five days. I only took two.'

'Great! Well done. Perhaps you'd like to show Jan your books?'

'Life and Strange Surprising Adventures.' He pronounced the words like a rune.

'Would you?'

'Well . . . OK.'

He went to the table and brought them back, handing them over with the anxious pride of a fan offering his most treasured souvenirs to someone who might not be properly respectful. The book was a modern edition of *The Life and Strange Surprising Adventures of Robinson Crusoe of York, Mariner*, with black and white illustrations. The magazine wasn't a magazine after all but a well-thumbed American comic-strip version of *Crusoe* in colour. I flipped through their pages, and, as Crusoe when he first saw Friday's footprint in the sand, stood like one thunder-struck.

'Good, eh?' Adam said.

'Amazing.'

Doctor Pelham took the books and handed them back, saying, 'Need anything?'

'I'll search for it myself.'

'I'll see you later today as usual, then.'

'Can I go now?'

'Sure.'

'So long, doc.'

'So long, Aston.'

I wasn't even given a glance. He turned, ran to the ladder, and climbed into the tree.

'He didn't remember me at all!'

'That's one way of putting it. Another way is to say you haven't entered his life yet.'

'Don't understand.'

'The person you just met is not the Adam you knew, nor is he the seventeen-year-old he is biologically. The person you met is Aston Davies, aged eleven.'

We were sitting on a bench by the wall at the other end of the garden five minutes later.

The doctor said, 'Aston was fourteen when he suffered his trauma. After that he went through a kind of hell of guilt and remorse. It was so bad he twice tried to kill himself. Part of the difficulty for anybody trying to help him is that no one can explain why he acted as he did – why the sudden switch from a childish game to uncontrollable violence that ended in horrific, brutal murder. He doesn't know how bad it was because he was quite literally mindless at the time. He doesn't remember

189

anything about the final moments, and the worst details have always been kept from him for fear of what the knowledge might do to him. But he does dream them. Terrible nightmares, which he believes are some kind of warning of what he might do one day rather than being records of what he once did.

'In August he escaped while on a routine outing. Psychologically speaking, he wasn't really running away from us, he was trying to run away from himself. When he was brought back in December he could vaguely remember making his escape but then nothing till he came to on the boat.'

'So what happened? When he broke into the toll house he wasn't desperate, anything but.'

'We don't know the details, of course, but we do know about his condition. The fugue state isn't very common but it's well documented. The patient goes on the run – becomes a fugitive, if you like, and completely loses his memory of his previous life. He invents a whole new personality, even down to the smallest details. We're not sure how this works. It might be a moment to moment thing, like making up a story as you're telling it. Or it might be that the new personality is made up of wishes and desires and aspects of the patient's personality that have been suppressed or have never found expression. So someone who has always been shy and fearful and meek turns into an open, outgoing, confident person who does all sorts of things that in his other life he never dared try. There are even cases where the patient has spoken a language he's never been taught, and others who have performed skilled tasks, like a medical operation, for which they've never had any training. The people they meet are usually completely convinced that they are who they say they are. One thing they all are, however, is restless. They usually keep moving. Physically or mentally, they're always in flight. In fact, the fugue state is a kind of suicide.'

'So when he broke into the house he wasn't Aston but his other invented person?'

'Right.'

'And when I said I didn't know him from Adam –'

'He accepted that as his name. Built it into his new personality.'

'But did he know what he was doing?'

'We don't think so but we don't really know. No one ever comes out of a fugue state remembering what happened while they were in it so they can't tell us. Just as they forget their previous life when they go into the fugue, they completely forget their fugue life when they return to their normal personality – whatever normal means.'

'That's incredible!'

'What is it we say up here? All the world's queer save thee and me, and even thee's a bit queer!'

'Thank God!'

He laughed.

I said, 'Sometimes there was something that bothered me. In his eyes.'

'The windows of the soul – the great betrayers of falsehood.'

'Was Adam false? Maybe he was the real person and Aston the false one?'

'Could be. Or both are the real him in different versions.'

'That as well, OK. But those times, it was like somebody else was looking at me. I used to call him the other-Adam. What changed him back from Adam to Aston?'

'Banging his head on the wall of the bridge during the struggle with Gill, I should think. Blows to the head often occur in fugue cases, seeming to switch the patient into the fugue or out of it.'

'And when he came to, he could remember his Aston life but not his Adam life?'

'Correct.'

'So why did he lie and say he couldn't remember anything at all?'

'Fear. He was afraid you'd turn him in once you knew about him. But worse than that, he was terrified he might kill someone again. He'd been told, you see, that this was possible. It's one reason why he's kept here.'

'And it was all so awful that he tried to commit suicide by jumping from the bridge?'

'The ultimate fugue.'

'And the rope? That seemed so weird.'

'Not so weird when you think about it. Logical and well planned, in fact. He wanted to make absolutely sure he drowned. Tethered by his feet he wouldn't be able to swim, and, if you work it out, you'll see he wouldn't be able to raise his head above water. Like a fish on a hook, except the hook was in the tail. The current rushing through the narrow arch of the bridge would be too strong for him to twist round or do anything to save himself. And what irony, don't you think, to tie himself by the feet – the very limbs on which one runs away.'

'He must have been utterly desperate. Poor, poor Adam.'

'Poor Aston, you mean. Adam was a happy-go-lucky uninhibited

191

guilt-free sexy young man. He'd never have tried to kill himself. The very opposite of Aston, the inhibited shy guilt-ridden inadequate boy who found it hard to make friends with anyone but especially with people his own age. Adam was everything that Aston wanted to be but couldn't be.'

Across the gardens I could see Aston-Adam working in his enclosure, standing on a crate, hammering a paling into the ground, the beginning of his fortification. Boy at play, young man at work.

I said, 'I don't understand what's happening to him now, though.'

'He came back in deep depression. His leg was in plaster of course. He couldn't be very active and needed quite a bit of nursing just to keep him physically healthy. For a few days he remained like that, a depressed immobile frightened angry patient. But then he began to withdraw completely into himself, would say nothing at all, and started behaving like a child.'

'A kind of regression?'

'Regression suggests something negative, or a going back, as if life were a linear journey, birth point A to death point Z. I don't see it like that.'

'How then?'

'We coexist as our *selves*. We are multiple beings. A mix of actualities and potentialities. One of the many things the so-called mentally ill have taught me is that we so-called healthy people are not very good at exploring our possible selves. Perhaps because we feel reasonably happy with the selves we are living. But perhaps we are the most imprisoned of all because of that. Whereas the mentally ill, being uncomfortable with their actual selves, sometimes explore their potentialities and find selves they like better and try them out.'

'But surely with Adam, I mean Aston, it's another flight, isn't it? He's become what he was once before.'

'Not quite. As a boy of eleven he couldn't have done what he's doing now as well as he's doing it. He's being eleven only as a seventeen-year-old young man can be eleven.'

'But why eleven?'

'Because that was the happiest time of his life, just before the onset of the bad feelings about himself, the feelings of powerlessness, of always being a loser, a failure, of never making it, and always being picked on, that ended with the murder. In that sense, the murder was a mistake he couldn't correct. What do you do when you've made a mistake you can't put right?'

'Start again?'

'But you don't just go back to the point before you got into difficulties, you also use what you've learned from the experience of getting it wrong to help you get it right next time. We do that in everyday life all the time. Aston is doing it rather more dramatically and obviously, that's all.'

'No matter. Try again. Fail again. Fail better.'

'Clever.'

'Beckett.'

'What?'

'Quoting. Irritating habit. Samuel Beckett.'

'Ah yes, well, he's right. The secret of a happy life.'

'And the Crusoe stuff? How did that start?'

'After he became eleven he was cheerful of course, and much more active. Instead of being withdrawn, he was quite a busy handful. He took no notice of his plastered-up leg. Paid it no attention. Just hobbled about regardless. So he'd have a plausible reason for it we told him he'd fallen out of a tree while climbing.'

'What did you tell him was the reason for being locked up?'

'He never asked. Perhaps the deep secret mind of his soul screened the question from his conscious everyday mind because it knew better than to let the question be asked.'

'You mean, we only ask what we need to know?'

'Something like that. Shall I go on?'

'Please.'

'In what we call the family room there are books and magazines. Among them was the comic-strip version of *Crusoe* that you saw. Aston became very attached to it. Acquired it as his own property, read it and read it, time and again. Not only that, he started talking about the story during his therapy sessions. When I realized this was more than a passing fancy, I bought him the copy he showed you of the original novel. He devoured it, every word. Began talking about Robinson, as he always calls Crusoe, all the time, as if he were alive and his best friend. He'd tell the story to anyone who'd listen.'

'So he started to identify with Crusoe.'

'No, no! You're missing the point. He doesn't believe himself to *be* Crusoe – that would be a kind of madness, and Aston isn't mad, not at all. As I say, Crusoe is his friend, a companion, someone he

193

admires and likes, who helps him through life, especially at a difficult time.'

'So why *Crusoe*? Why that book?'

'Now come on, don't leave all the work to me.'

'Well – whatever the reason, you'll let him play it out? Build the fence and live like Crusoe and all that?'

'We'll see, I expect so, if that's what he needs.'

'Even sleep in his tent and everything?'

'I doubt that he'll want to. You're quite right, it is a kind of play. A very serious game. You saw how he behaved. He knows what he's doing, takes it totally seriously, but knows he's playing, knows the boundary between the everyday real and the imaginary real. Both are real and he knows the rules that apply to each.'

'But how long will it go on?'

'Sometimes a phase like this doesn't last more than a few days, sometimes it can go on for years.'

'And how will it end? Will he become his proper age again?'

'I'm waiting to find out. It's like a story with an ending you can't quite predict. It might end the way you think it will from all the clues, or there might be a twist in the tail. Or there might be no conclusive ending at all, it might just stop, in the middle of a sentence even. It's my job to stay with the story and help him if I can while Aston works it out for himself. He'll devise his own ending when he's ready, which means when he's got everything out of the story – out of the act of telling it – that's useful to him. Then, perhaps, he'll move on to another story, try out another imagined real, another version of himself, become yet another Aston. Till eventually he may even become the person the deep secret mind of his soul wants him to be, and then we'll say he's cured, though all we'll mean is that he doesn't need me or anyone like me any more, because this story is enough to keep him going on his own. He'll be content with himself.'

One of the warders came up to us.

'Wanted inside, doc. Darren trouble again.'

'Be right there.' The doctor stood up and held out his hand. 'Got to go, sorry. Duty calls.'

I shook his hand. 'Is it OK for me to come again?'

'If you like. If you need to. And not too often. It won't mean anything to Aston of course. But if it would make you feel better –'

'It would. I mean, if he becomes the Adam who remembers me

again, I'd like to be there, if he wants — Well ... you understand?'

'I think so. You've also got a story to tell. Everybody has.'

Afterword

An author's books are rather like a family. There is, for instance, the quiet one that isn't often talked about, the popular one, the one that causes problems, and the one that's frequently misunderstood. In the family of six novels of which these two were the third and fourth to be published, *Now I Know* is the one that has the fewest close friends, but all of them passionately devoted, and *The Toll Bridge* is the one people like in a companionable way, feel comfortable with and enjoy having around.

As far as I can tell from letters and emails and what readers tell me, *Now I Know* gathers fewer close friends than my other novels because its main interest is the clash between rational thought and irrational belief, which is a topic that seems to make many people uneasy. To complicate matters, its story is told in three voices and in a time sequence that isn't chronological but is decided by the association between one scene and the next. It isn't a story about one thing – one event – happening after another, but one thought and memory and feeling leading to another. Some readers have told me it feels like the book has been made of pieces of the story that have been fitted together to make something that isn't straightforwardly representational, but is more like, say, a cubist painting or one of those colourful engineered sculptures by Anthony Caro. To some degree that is true: it is what I intended. Readers do have to work out for themselves the patterns of the plot and the voices telling the story. But for those who admire the book, that is part of the fun. They say it makes them think more deeply and differently from the way they do when a story is told in a simpler fashion. And besides, it is a way of telling the story that accords with its central theme: the relationship between rational thought and irrational belief and what each is at its core.

The Toll Bridge is quite the opposite. Its story flows along like the river that flows under the bridge where the story is set. Perhaps that's why so many readers feel comfortable with it. It's rather like being on holiday in a small boat with two or three friends, enjoying the journey and the scenery as you float along, and the talk and the personal secrets that are often revealed when you are away from home, and before you fall asleep on a balmy night after a good meal and you are soothed by the slap of water against the hull. Not that Jan and Tess and Adam's life together at the bridge, and the reader's with them, is without storms and upsets. Nor does their story, their journey, take place on the river but on the bridge by the river. It's a story full of paradoxes, about people who get somewhere by going nowhere.

That, at least, is how both books seemed to me when I was writing them and seem to many readers who like them. And curiously enough, each book came to me in similarly appropriate ways. *Now I Know* began as nothing more than the title. I was reading a scene in Milan Kundera's superb novel *The Book of Laughter and Forgetting*, in which the narrator's father points at a passage of music he is trying to play on the piano and says again and again, 'Now I know! Now I know!' It was one of those passages which seem, at the time you read them, to be glowing with significance of such profundity that you can't put it into words but know is important to you. I read the passage out to my wife, Nancy, who was quite unimpressed, but said, 'Now I know. What a good title that would make.' And suddenly the significance I couldn't 'see' for myself was crystal clear. At once I opened a notebook – something I always do when I start a novel – and began to play with the three words. For example: the initial letters of the words make the name Nik (there was a tv newsreader at the time who spelt his name like that). Spelt backwards it made 'kin'. Who were Nik's relatives? Ditto and Hal, of course, the central characters in *Breaktime* and *Dance on My Grave*. Nik is also an anagram for ink, and it was only of ink that Nik and his story would be made. Nik is short for Nicholas; Nicholas was St Nicholas; St Nicholas is Santa Claus. Obviously, there is a religious and Christ-mass element to the story. The two previous novels had concentrated on physical sensations –

the life of the five senses – and obsessive emotion. The natural next stop was to explore with Nik the nature of the intellect and belief. The rest, as they say, was simply a matter of writing his story.

The Toll Bridge had a beginning in everyday life. While I was writing *Now I Know* I had to drive once a week over Swinford toll bridge on the way to a college on the outskirts of Oxford. The money was always collected by the same man, standing in the middle of the road, always dressed exactly the same whatever the weather, in an old mucky woollen hat, a tired old macintosh, old woollen mittens, old grey trousers tucked into old boots, and with an old leather bag for the money slung over his shoulder. He never uttered a word, but every time he took the money I saw his Adam's apple go up and down. It was the Adam's apple that made me wonder about him. Why did it go up and down when he took the money, even though he never said anything? One day it occurred to me this happened because he used to say 'Thank you' each time he took the money, as English people tend to do, and that sometime or other he stopped actually saying the words but his Adam's apple still went through the motions. I mentioned this to a bookseller friend, who later gave me a little booklet published by the local history society to celebrate the two hundredth anniversary of the bridge. There were photographs in it, one of which was of a very young man dressed in a clean macintosh with a new leather bag over his shoulder and new-looking trousers and boots, but no hat or mittens, and quite certainly the same man who was still collecting the tolls more than twenty years later. It was then I wondered why anyone would do such a job for what indeed turned out to be the whole of his working life. That was how Jan's story began, though it ended quite differently from the story of the real man on the bridge.

Readers often ask writers where they get their ideas. For me, those two stories are my answer. Ideas come from anywhere, and I have many of them. So how do I know the ones that *must* be written? Because they won't go away. They nag and grow and finally take over until they inhabit me so completely that I have no choice but to write them down in order to get them out of my system. And I've learned with hindsight that I need to write them because in doing so they tell me as much, or more, about myself as they do about their characters. In the end, I write novels in order to make sense of myself and to help me to understand life itself.

The other novels, in companion editions and with their own Afterword, are:
Breaktime and *Dance on My Grave* in one volume,
and in separate volumes:
Postcards from No Man's Land (winner of the Carnegie Medal in the U.K., the Printz Award in the U.S.A., the Andersen youth fiction award in Italy) and
This Is All: The Pillow Book of Cordelia Kenn.
You can find out more about these books and all of his work from Aidan Chambers's website www.aidanchambers.co.uk

breaktime
Aidan Chambers
dance on my grave

Two fantastic novels in one volume

In *Breaktime* Morgan thinks literature is crap but Ditto doesn't agree and sets out to prove his cynical friend wrong by writing an account of what happens to him over half term – his father has a heart attack, he gets involved in a drunken brawl with a couple of burglars and has a life-changing encounter with the girl of his dreams . . . But is it true or is Ditto just playing a game with words? It's not for Morgan alone to decide . . .

Dance on My Grave is Hal Robinson's own story of love and obsession during one extraordinary summer in his seaside town. From Hal's first meeting with Barry to the relationship that follows and its devastating end, Hal tells of feelings so intense, experiences so bizarre and happenings so dramatic that they leave him changed forever.

The first and second books in *The Dance Sequence* – six ground-breaking and provocative novels that explore different aspects of teenage love and self-discovery.

ISBN 978 1 862 30288 4

postcards from no man's land
Aidan Chambers

WINNER OF THE CARNEGIE MEDAL

Jacob Todd, abroad on his own for the first time, arrives in Amsterdam for the commemoration of the Battle of Arnhem where his grandfather fought fifty years before. He meets Geertrui, a terminally ill old lady, who tells an extraordinary story of love and betrayal, which links Jacob with her own Dutch family in a way he never suspected and which leads him to question his place in the world.

This richly layered novel, spanning fifty years, powerfully evokes the atmosphere of war while brilliantly interweaving Jacob's exploration of new relationships in contemporary Amsterdam.

The fifth book in *The Dance Sequence* – six ground-breaking and provocative novels that explore different aspects of teenage love and self-discovery.

'A SUPERBLY CRAFTED, INTENSELY MOVING NOVEL'
Sunday Telegraph

'THE TYPE OF SERIOUS TEENAGE FICTION THAT SHOULD BE CHERISHED' *Independent*

ISBN 978 1 862 30284 6